THE ANONYMOUS SIGNAL

INTEL 1, BOOK 3

EREC STEBBINS

Only one thing is impossible for God: to find any sense in any copyright law on the planet.
—Mark Twain

This book is a work of fiction. Any references to historical events, real people, or real locales are used fictitiously. Other names, characters, places, and incidents are the product of the author's imagination, and any resemblance to actual events or locales or persons, living or dead, is entirely coincidental.

Published 2015 by Twice Pi Press, erecstebbinsbooks.com

Edited by Michael Matheson.

ePub ISBN-13: 978-1-942360-23-0

Kindle ISBN-13: 978-1-942360-08-7

Paperback ISBN-13: 978-1-942360-09-4

Hardcover ISBN-13: 978-1-942360-10-0

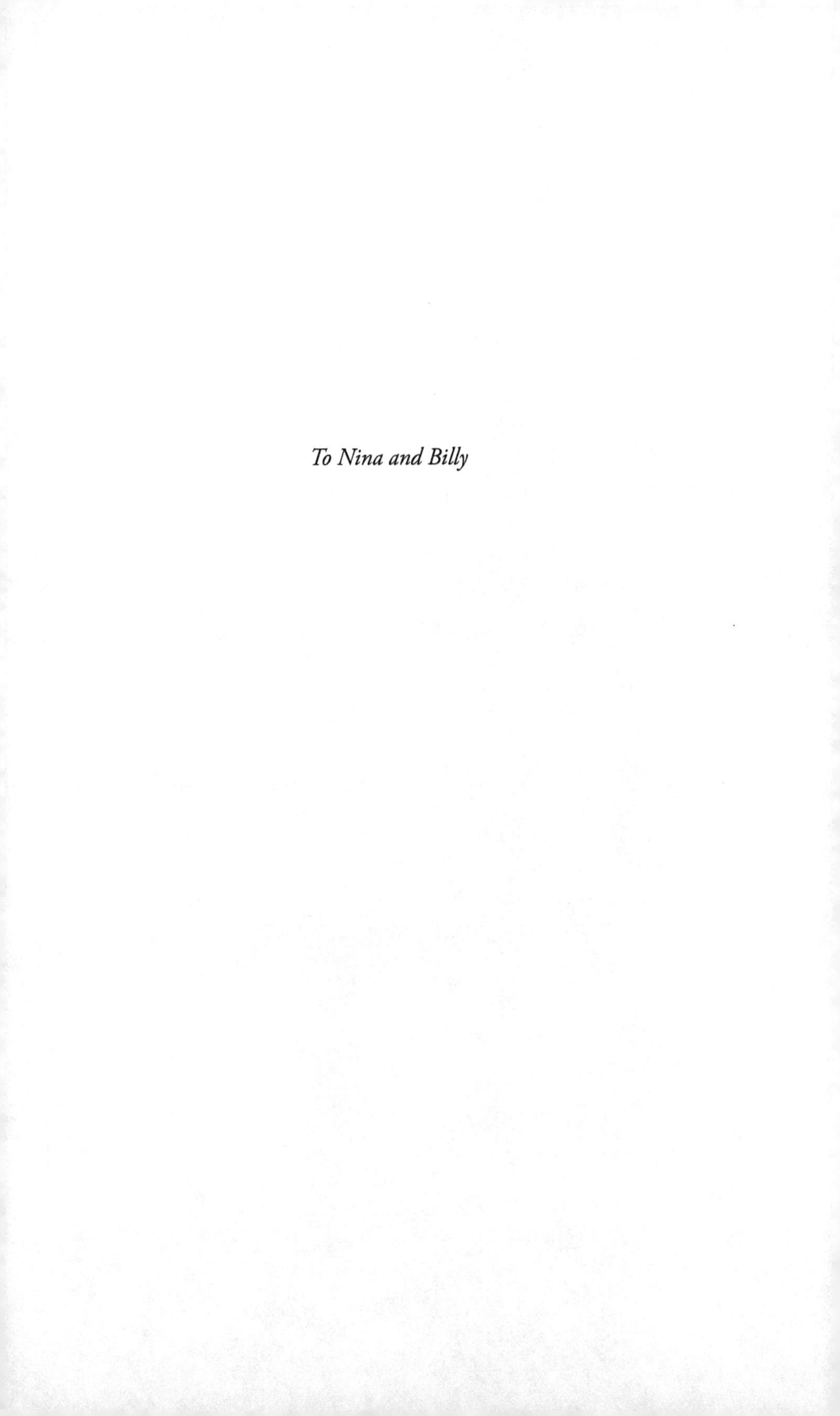

To Nina and Billy

A thousand years scarce serve to form a state;
An hour may lay it in the dust.

— Lord Byron Childe Harold's Pilgrimage, Canto II (1812), Stanza 84.

PROLOGUE

The baby pulled on a string and the toy's small disk chimed. A lion roared and birds tweeted. A dog barked, and the disk stopped spinning. The baby giggled and pulled again.

The room was dark except for multicolored stars projected onto the ceiling. A window was cracked open, letting in crisp spring air. Across the room, a tired-looking woman rested, eyes half-closed, in a rocking chair, watching the child.

The baby grew bored with his toy and turned to a mobile above. A panda-headed cord dangled there, and he could just reach it. Lights blinked and a tune played. The baby smiled.

He pulled himself up awkwardly, legs wobbly. With one hand the baby grasped the panda, with the other the thick string hanging from the disk. With jerky movements, he pulled back and forth on each, nearly stumbling as each mechanism activated in succession. A light shone on the child's face, an obsessive gleam in his eyes as they darted between the two chiming toys.

Jenny smiled and suppressed a laugh. Even so late at night, when really all she wanted to do was crawl back into bed with her husband, watching her son play was magical. She'd suffer tomorrow for another interrupted night, but it was worth it. He was so happy!

She rubbed her eyes and sat up stiffly in the chair, getting a better view into the crib. Her expression clouded as the toys continued to chime, her son now sitting again on the mattress, bouncing lightly as the racket continued.

Shivering, Jenny draped a shawl around her shoulders and stood up, stumbled to the window and closed it. She turned to the crib and yawned. "How you reaching them down there, pooh-bear?"

She stopped and stared as the baby pulled on the string to the animal disk again. The mechanism clicked and the heads began to rotate. At the same time, the mobile above lit up and played its little tune. The baby smiled and giggled.

"How did you do that?"

The string with the panda was wrapped around one of the animal heads of the disk, so as the disk advanced slightly with each pull, the tug on the mobile activated the second toy, the mechanisms now linked. There wasn't any slack left in the mobile string, and she detached it from the lion head the string had looped behind.

"There," she said. "You'll break it, silly boy."

The baby pulled on the animal disk string and it moved. He stared at the mobile expectantly. Nothing happened. He pulled on the string again. His lip quivered, and he began to cry.

"Shh. Sorry, pooh-bear, but you got it all tangled." She smiled and cooed at him. He didn't seem to notice her and continued to tug on the string in frustration. The woman sighed. "We got to get some sleep, sweetie. Mommy's tired."

She walked back to the rocking chair. "Mommy's just going to close her eyes for a few minutes."

She slumped down and exhaled deeply, the chair swallowing her whole like an ocean pulling her down into slumber.

And then the sounds again. Animal noises followed by the little tune. Dancing, dancing together in her mind one after the other. The patter of them landing on her like rain. Where had she heard them before? Oh, yes. But the string would break...

Jenny snapped awake and knuckled at her eyes. Sure enough, the baby had done it again. The string from the mobile was fixed to the other toy disk mounted on the side of the crib.

She got up slowly and walked to the bed, reaching in to untangle the devices again. The baby began to cry.

"Sweetie," she began and then stopped, staring quizzically at the child. She reached up and slowly detached the string, letting the panda head drop downward back under the mobile. She watched her son closely. His complaining slowed and then he toddled up, reaching deliberately over to the panda head to pull it to the side, and yanked the string clumsily to the disk.

After several failures, the string latched around one of the animal heads. The baby squealed and dropped back down. He pulled the string and the two toys danced in unison.

She repeated the process to the same effect.

Then she ran from the room.

~

"Look, Henry, just look!"

Jenny stood beside the crib, Henry, the boy's father, yawning. He watched his son.

"See? He's hooked them together. They both play when he pulls one string!"

"Okay, Jenny? So he tangled them up. We just undo it and it'll be fine."

"No. Don't you get it? It's on purpose."

His forehead creased. "On purpose?"

"Yes! He likes it when they both play. He figured out a way to link them together."

"At nine months? Jenny, come on. You need sleep."

"No, listen! I undid it like three times. He keeps putting them back together."

"Honey, how about I take over tonight and you get some rest?"

She pushed forward, the wild look in her eyes causing him to backpedal unconsciously. "Henry, do you know what this means? Do you?"

The man shook his head.

"It means he's a genius, Henry."

The father had reached the doorway, yet she pursued him, grasping the folds of his robe and pulling him toward her.

"Our baby is a genius!"

PART I

WORM

Remember remember the fifth of November! Gunpowder, Treason and Plot! I see no reason why Gunpowder Treason should ever be forgot!— English Folk Verse (c.1870)

BEFORE:
THE ANONYMOUS EVENT COMMISSION

DEPOSITION IN THE MATTER OF:
UNITED STATES ARMED FORCES SPECIAL TRIBUNAL, Plaintiff,
versus
JOHN SAVAS, Defendant
Case No. M120039E-007X

DEPOSITION OF:
Franklin Joeseph Miller
called for examination by Counsel for the Defendant, pursuant to Notice of Deposition, at the Independent Council Offices, located at [REDACTED] Washington, D.C.,
when were present on behalf of the respective parties: [REDACTED]

Counsel on Behalf of Defendant (CBD): Will you please identify yourself for the record?

MR. MILLER: Franklin J. Miller, Special Agent, Counterterrorism. Intel 1 division.

CBD: You have a service record?

MR. MILLER: Yes. Three tours in Afghanistan. Honorably discharged.

CBD: Honorably? I'd say that is an understatement. Medal of Honor, if I'm not mistaken? Second Battle of Fallujah, according to your records here.

MR. MILLER: That's correct.

CBD: Would you care to elaborate for the panel?

MR. MILLER: I would prefer not to.

CBD: Thank you, Mr. Miller. You understand that your testimony here is on the record, and your words might later be used to charge and try you as an enemy combatant of the United States?

MR. MILLER: No, I don't understand that.

[REDACTED]: Have you not been informed of your rights and requirements under the new Tribunal Act?

MR. MILLER: Yes, sir. But none of this makes any sense to me.

[REDACTED]: You have been informed of the law?

MR. Miller: Yes. Jesus.

CBD: Mr. Miller, how long have you worked with the defendant?

MR. MILLER: Nearly a decade.

CBD: And in what capacity?

MR. MILLER: First I was a special agent in the Intel 1 division under the umbrella of Larry Kanter's counter-terrorism branch. After the attacks on our division, I served under him in the restructured Intel 1.

CBD: And it was serving in this role during which the events in question occurred?

MR. MILLER: Yes.

CBD: And how did you and the Intel 1 division become involved?

MR. MILLER: John likely knows the chronology better. But-

CBD: You mean the defendant, former agent Savas?

MR. MILLER: Former?

CBD: Agent Savas.

MR. MILLER: Yes. Special agent in Charge, *John* Savas.

CBD: Continue.

MR. MILLER: I mean for the rest of us it was a relatively normal day, if you can ever consider counterterrorism a normal job. We had our usual reports, chatter, kidnappings by more extremists, talks of retaliation for the French raid in Algeria. It was also the ceremony for John's medal, and that morning we were all in front of the Mayor and Attorney General.

[REDACTED]: And the Anonymous case? Please focus your responses to material relevant to this inquiry.

MR. MILLER: Right. It started with the bombing, obviously. As far as I know, NYPD was the first on the scene but they called us in fairly quickly.

[REDACTED]: You know this because?

MR. MILLER: John told us.

CBD: Can we just back up and get the events from you one step at a time. Tell us from what you remember what happened.

MR. MILLER: I wasn't there for a lot of it, but we were all briefed.

CBD: That's fine. Just your words, please.

MR. MILLER: All right. Like I said, it started just like any other day.

OCTOBER 17

1

BIRD OF PREY

"Mr. Craig, sir."

A man in a chauffeur's uniform held a door open patiently. The CEO of Goldman Sachs stalked toward the car. Silver-haired, dressed in a tailored business suit with a golden watch that glinted in the sunlight, his thin-framed glasses gave his harsh features a predatory intelligence. The black leather handle of his briefcase contrasted sharply with his golden wedding ring. Two bodyguards left his side and walked to a second car parked immediately behind.

Jack Craig nodded to the chauffeur and stepped into the limo. He dropped his briefcase onto the leather seat, pulled out his cell phone, and dialed as his driver shut the door. The interior was spartan compared to the cars kept by many of his equals at the top echelons of corporate power. But Craig had never taken to the ostentatious bravado that infected so many of his peers. To his mind, there was no surer sign of dominance than the refusal to flaunt it.

The driver entered and started the engine. "World Financial Center, Miles." The driver nodded and pulled the car out into midday Manhattan traffic. Craig engaged the auditory dampening system, sealing him off from the driver. "*Yes*, Heidi. I understand that there are midterms coming, but this bill cannot come up for a vote. It's got Warren's dirty paw prints all over it and it's a step in the wrong direction." He paused, listening. "No, it doesn't matter. You won't lose your position on the committee.

Hell, given how much you lot have gerrymandered things I doubt I'll be alive the next time you lose the House. We've got you more than covered with the advertising, believe me. Kill this vote. You've got nothing to fear." He pulled the phone away from his head to mitigate the shouting on the other end of the line. "For fuck's sake, Heidi! Least of all the press! Not even the *Times* has anyone off the payroll now."

Craig nodded several times, satisfied. He ended the call and sighed. *No one in Congress has any balls except that damn bitch Warren!* And they hadn't been able to find a price for her. He doubted there was one, but they still had many years to find out. Especially if they could couple it with some dirty laundry and rattle her cage a little. He swiped across the phone and hit an entry, placing a call.

"Hi, sweetheart!" For the first time that day, Jack Craig smiled. "No, I can't make your show today, I'm sorry. Daddy's got a very important meeting with the *President.* Tell that to your friends!" He frowned as a whining pitch escaped from the speaker. "I know, I know, honey. I'll bring you something special tonight, from that new toy store they opened, what's it called? The one with the giant bear?" There was a sound on the other end. "Right. That one. A surprise, okay?"

The vehicle pulled out onto FDR Drive and sped south beneath the Hospital for Special Surgery, the sun glinting off the East River on his left. Craig cracked the window open a wedge, gazing toward the looming mass of the Queensboro Bridge and the white sailboats bobbing along the currents.

"Now, Daddy's got to go. You give him a kiss." A pop sounded on the speaker. "Thanks, honey. Talk to you later." He closed the connection.

Continuing to stare outside his window, Craig felt a weariness descend. Soon, he knew, they would reach their exit and the nasty courting ritual would begin at the hotel. A presidential speech on financial reform, dutiful agreements from the top managers, handshakes, TV moments, and reporters' questions. Too much money had changed hands for there to be any real concern. They owned the committees. The damn politicians had to trot them out every few years, give them a public tongue-lashing, and then it was back to business as usual.

A black spot in the sky in front of them caught his eye. *What the hell?* He disengaged the sound suppression.

"Miles, can you see that thing in front of us? I thought it was a plane, but it's something else."

While he was accustomed to the low-flying aircraft along this route—

helicopters heading to the Hamptons and tourist planes lumbering overhead—something was wrong. The craft, whatever it was, seemed way too low. *Too small.*

"Look at it—it's off the river and over the damned FDR."

He could see his driver straining upward and nodding. "Some kid's remote control helicopter or something, Mr. Craig."

Craig shook his head. "Maybe. Damn if it's not going to hit us."

The object careened straight for them, slowing its approach until it paced the car. He could see it better now: four helicopter-like blades spun equidistant from each other separated like the points on a square. A mass of spidery arms underneath held what looked like a cylinder, the bottom shining like a large metallic disk. Craig felt a strange unease. *It's like some giant insect from Mars.*

"Miles, take the next exit. There. The sign that says 53rd. Take that exit."

"But sir, we'll get snarled in the local traffic."

"Just do it!"

Craig wasn't sure what was happening, but his instincts were never wrong. He had lived too long as a predator and master of the games of power. When soldiers around him died in Vietnam, he made it out alive. It was a sixth sense, background processing, *something* that always alerted him to danger and opportunity. Right now, his alarms were ringing frantically.

The limo darted across lanes toward the exit to a chorus of horns. The small flying thing matched their motion and continued to close the distance.

Miles grumbled as the wheels hit the exit ramp. "This some new paparazzi thing?"

Then, the impossible! The small craft accelerated and slammed directly onto the roof of the car.

Craig jumped. *Shit!* "Pull us over, Miles. Now!"

But there wasn't a place to stop the car. Still exiting the off-ramp, the driver accelerated and hurtled toward a curbside ahead.

"Goddamn thing is stuck to the rooftop," yelled Craig, grabbing the handle of his door. He prepared to leap out of the vehicle.

A large explosion rocked the corner of 53rd and Sutton Place. Windows of surrounding buildings shattered, facade stone fractured and fell, and debris from a black limo blasted outward with a fireball that set nearby trees and garbage on fire. Smoke surged upward from the demolished vehicle, only a chassis and partial skeleton remaining. Alarms sounded from cars parked near to the blast radius, and voices screamed over the din. Bodies were strewn motionless around the inferno. Wounded screamed for help.

Above the growing chaos, unseen by anyone below, a frenetic buzzing purred. An apple-sized object hovered hundreds of feet above the fire, a propeller whirling above an octagonal hardware collection ending with a downward-pointing lens. The mechanical insect observed the scene with a cold stillness. As the first sounds of sirens began to spill toward the carnage, it climbed above the buildings and disappeared into the sky.

2

STORM FRONT

"So it is only fitting that today, five years after the events in New York and around the world that brought us to the brink of international conflict, we honor a man who was instrumental in bringing us back from that cliff."

Special agent John Savas squirmed in his metal fold-out chair and prayed that this horrific political pageantry would reach its inevitable and dreaded climax. His salt-and-pepper hair was trimmed similarly to that time five years back, a time when the home-grown terrorists of Mjolnir had aimed a nuclear warhead at the Muslim holy city of Mecca during the great Hajj pilgrimage. But no amount of self-delusion could hide the fact that it was considerably more *salty* now than it had been. While he still worked to keep himself in shape, at fifty-five, age was beginning to finally have the upper hand, and his increased desk time as the director of Intel 1 hadn't helped.

But it was more than simply age. As for the nightmares—Savas was too mired in a dying male culture to do much about them. PTSD was what psychologists talked about on cable news, not what men had or admitted to. Only his wife of three years, agent Rebecca Cohen, truly knew the extent of the damage. And that because she shared the trauma as well.

Savas watched the new Attorney General of the United States bring the speech to a point of tension and transition. The former prosecutor looked in his direction and nodded.

"And without further delay, here to receive the Award for Exceptional Heroism, please welcome a true American hero and pride of New York City, John Savas!"

Savas surged to his feet, flashbulbs exploding around him, applause drowning his thoughts like a churning waterfall. He moved as confidently as he could toward the stage, remembering to paste a reserved smile on his face for the evening news. A row of officers from the NYPD and local FBI branches greeted him with handshakes and pats on the back. Nearing the podium, reporters' cameras pummeling him like strobe lights, and he shook hands with the Attorney General with one hand while grasping the medallion case and plaque in the other.

As they paused for the photographers, Savas instinctively searched among the front row of FBI agents for a diminutive brunette. Her long hair would be secured formally behind her. For events like this she usually wore her blue pantsuit. He would see her radiant smile beaming toward him, his desire to impress her flooding him with energy.

But she wasn't there. He knew she wouldn't be there, but looked anyway. She was hundreds of miles away in a secret location only a handful of people knew, checking up on two charges that Savas had personally assumed responsibility for. Deep in a forest, high in the mountains, Rebecca Cohen was at this very moment in the company of the nation's most wanted fugitives.

Savas shifted his focus back to the Attorney General. He smiled for the cameras.

~

EXHAUSTED, Savas dropped into his office chair and stared forward blankly. The medal and certificate stared back at him from his desk. He didn't want them. He didn't join the FBI after his son's death on 9/11 for honors, and he hadn't risked everything, even Rebecca, to stop Mjolnir to get a damned medal. He could think of thousands of victims of terrorism who deserved much more than he did. Who would repay them and their families? He could think of one man, Husaam Jordan, who had stopped a nuclear holocaust by sacrificing his own life. But what good were medals to the dead?

He grasped the award materials and unlocked a key-coded drawer in his desk. He yanked it open and pulled out a thick file folder, dropped the medal into it, and closed the drawer. It clicked loudly as it locked. The label on the file, bold black ink on white, left an afterimage in his mind: *The Ragnarök Conspiracy.*

Savas loosened his tie and sighed deeply. Now for just five minutes of peace.

"Captain Overlord, sir, transitional paperwork is now one hundred percent completed."

He startled at a bald woman framed by his office door, her arms grasping the metal frame above her head. Savas tried not to gawk at her toned body, hammered and stretched by several years of intense combat training. Gone were the waist-length orange hair and the Amish dresses. Piercings ran up her ears, in her lips and eyebrows. Today she wore fatigues and a green tank revealing rippling muscles on a thin frame—some punk version of Sigourney Weaver in *Alien 3*, but with orange eyebrows, green eyes, and a more spaced-out glare.

Another casualty. The meek girl he had known was gone, murdered just as surely as many in the ground. In her place stood something far more potent.

"Morning, Angel. Here to ruin my day?"

"It's part of my mission statement," she said.

"You know, agent Lightfoote, I've spent every favor I had left to let you parade around here like GI Jane. A little protocol every now and then would be nice."

"Stopping a madman and saving the world buys some unique capital, Fearless Leader." Her face darkened. "Steals other things though."

Savas absorbed her words silently. The losses could never be measured. Talented people, good people who could never be replaced.

"John, it's not your fault they died. Not your fault that you're the best to run Intel 1. Trial by fire," she said, nodding to herself. "They cut the fat. Axed all those 9/11 counter-terrorism toys or put them under you. Larry couldn't have done a better job."

Visions of a house bomb rushed through his mind.

"I don't know about that. He was a genius."

"And things are different now. Larry didn't know shit about cyber-crimes. *You* set up the Operations Center under Manuel, not Larry. After what happened, you knew where crime and national security were headed: *digital.*"

Savas shook his head. "Big picture only, Angel. I still can't figure out my email sometimes."

"Boss Man is supposed to be big picture."

"At least making you head of cybercrimes means someone can call you Captain Overlord or whatever for a change. How is your command and control center coming along?"

Lightfoote pouted. "John, there's no budget! We cannibalized the Operations Center, but it's not nearly enough. It's outdated. We need server farms to handle the loads of searches and to fend off digital attacks. DNS floods are *daily*. Everyone wants to bring down FBI or get in our systems."

Savas nodded. "I know, Angel. But times are tight. Budgets are bleeding. You're going to have to be creative. If the criminals can do it, so can you." He smiled.

"So Mr. Big Picture is telling me to emulate cybercriminals? You know blowing things up is a lot easier than building them."

"Angel, don't twist—" An alert tone rang on his phone. He scanned the message. "It's Rebecca."

"Yeah? How's her *special assignment*?"

Savas frowned. "It's very *special*. Now I need to take this." Lightfoote beamed at him. "*In private*." She grinned more broadly and left the room, closing the door behind her.

Savas sighed and opened the connection. A woman's face appeared on his smartphone, brown hair and eyes, a smile on her lips. *God, it's good to see her.*

"Agent Cohen, it's been too long."

"Yes, I've been stuck with babysitting duty. *In the mountains*. Now, who was it that stuck me here?"

"A heartless boss."

"No doubt. If he hadn't, Agent Savas, I could be there now. Next to you. Much *closer*." Her eyes smoldered.

"Yeah, definitely way too long. I hope this call means you'll be coming home tonight?"

Her smile was mischievous. "Booked my flight. In by ten."

"*Good*. There's *a lot* to catch up on." His face darkened. "And how is Gabriel?"

Cohen looked to her side. "Gone now. Back to the cabin. They're adapting, but getting restless. They've made it a home. But the world has made it a prison."

There was a long pause as he considered her words. "No one said this would be easy for either of them. It's wrong, but the setup was too good. A fight we couldn't win."

"I think they need to continue to fight, even a guerrilla war."

"It's on the agenda. We've finally put things back together over here and I'm coordinating with Fred Simon at CIA. We won't leave them hanging. There's a lot to be done."

The landline on his desk buzzed. *Now what?*

"Hang on, Rebecca. This is from NYPD, on my red line." He pressed the button to go to speaker. "Hi, Will. Don't hear from you often."

"John, we need you and a crime unit up to the East Side, Sutton Place. *ASAP.*"

"You sound rattled. Boys in blue don't want this?"

"It's a car bomb. A big one with some collateral damage."

Car bomb? "Anyone killed?"

"Several bystanders and those in the car."

Savas furrowed his brows. "Your crews are about as good as ours. Why me?"

"This one's different."

"Might be a challenge to ID those in the car if the fire was bad."

"That's just it, John. We know who was in that car. Phone GPS confirms it."

Savas glanced to his smartphone. Cohen's face looked tense. He turned back to the speaker on his landline. "Well, who was it?"

"Jack Craig, CEO of Goldman Sachs."

"Ah, hell. Are you sure?"

"Unless someone else had his phone, it was him and the driver."

"Dammit. A car bomb?"

"So it looks. That's why we're calling you in. It's getting out already and it will stir all the hornets' nests. And a car bomb, Goldman CEO? Whatever it is, it's big. Mafia, some Unabomber type, or maybe one of these new terrorist groups. Too radioactive for us."

"Understood. Moving on it now. Where are we headed?"

"Sutton Place south, fifty-three. Or just follow the GPS coordinates on all the photos flooding the internet. There's no hiding this."

BEFORE:
THE ANONYMOUS EVENT COMMISSION

DEPOSITION IN THE MATTER OF:
UNITED STATES ARMED FORCES SPECIAL TRIBUNAL, Plaintiff,
versus
JOHN SAVAS, Defendant
Case No. M120039E-007X

CONTINUED DEPOSITION OF:
Franklin Joeseph Miller

MR. MILLER: We sent a crime unit. I was there, too. Jesus, what a mess. I hadn't seen anything like that up-close since Afghanistan. I think without the GPS data we'd have spent a while trying to figure out just who the hell was hit.

CBD: And the target was confirmed by location data and DNA analysis to be Jack Craig, CEO of Goldman Sachs?
MR. MILLER: That's right. There was no question.

CBD: And how did the defendant react to this event and information?
MR. MILLER: Well, sir, John Savas is a good as they come. Everyone was shocked. John, too, but he was professional. Got the division primed and assigned several agents to the case. They-

CBD: The agents assigned would be you and Agent Cohen?
MR. MILLER: Yes, that's right.

[REDACTED]: What about the other members of Intel 1?
MR. MILLER: They were on other duties.

[REDACTED]: Why didn't Savas treat the bombing with the full attention of the division?
MR. MILLER: Well, we didn't know then what it was all linked to. I mean, it was a car bombing in Manhattan. That's pretty fucking serious but still isolated. Still with more unknowns than knowns. There were a lot of serious things with unknowns going on in the world and we were

charged with keeping tabs on a lot of it. I mean, it wasn't long before the whole finance thing started to go FUBAR and that ate our cybercrimes subdivision.

CBD: We'll get to that. Let's focus on how this began and what you remember. So, how did Intel 1 respond at this point?

MR. MILLER: Well, John—Agent Savas—personally got involved with the footwork.

[REDACTED]: Why?

MR. MILLER: He's like that. I mean he can't do it in every case, but he's very hands on. Goldman CEO? This had PR nightmare all over it. John went personally.

CBD: Went where?

MR. MILLER: To talk to the employees at Goldman about our investigation. To try and find out if they could shed any light on the situation.

CBD: He went alone?

MR. MILLER: No, he and Agent Cohen.

[REDACTED]: For the record, let it be noted that Agent Rebecca Cohen is the defendant's spouse. Mr. Miller, can you comment on FBI policy with respect to employees and nepotism laws? Romantic associations?

MR. MILLER: I don't much read the regs, sir.

[REDACTED]: Can you or can you not tell us if you know that it is against Bureau policy to have superiors and those under their authority in personal relationships?

MR. MILLER: No. That stuff never mattered to me. Besides, we always did everything a little different at Intel 1.

[REDACTED]: Yes, that is becoming more and more clear.

CBD: Let's return to the events immediately after the bombing. You say Savas and Cohen went to Goldman.

MR. MILLER: Yes. The morning after. We had already pulled a late night and put together some interesting information we had to run by them.

OCTOBER 18

3

VAMPIRE SQUID

Savas and Cohen stepped out of the Crown Victoria in front of 200 West Street in Lower Manhattan. A towering glass skyscraper rose into the sky before them. Known as the Goldman Sachs Tower, the new forty-four story structure gleamed in the morning sun as it looked down from the northernmost end of Battery Park toward the World Financial Center. Savas could almost feel the power radiating from the monolith.

He closed the door and stared upward. "No logo. Not a letter or word on it. World's most influential financial institution, and it's basically anonymous."

Cohen stepped beside him. "It is kind of eerie, that's for sure. But I'll take it over yesterday's carnage, thank you. Forensics was picking things up with tweezers. I've had enough bombings for one lifetime."

"Hits too close to home." He turned to look behind them. "Look at those playing fields. Still brand new. This whole area was rubble and soot."

Cohen looped her hand under his arm. "It's hard to take, I know."

"Thanos died a few blocks from here. A lot of people did. Sometimes I think they should have left it like that. Broken. Raw." Kids squealed as they kicked a soccer ball across the field. "World moves on, and somehow we're all supposed to be okay with that."

"John, here they come."

Representatives from the bank rushed out to greet them. Two men and a woman, they wore appropriately moderate smiles for an occasion that consisted of their CEO having been blown up the day before, ushering them politely inside. Savas paused momentarily as they entered the lobby.

"That's impressive."

It was spectacularly cavernous, the ceiling higher than an opera house, works of modern art draped thirty feet in the air above them. It reminded him of standing in some of the newer airport terminals, only that everything was fashioned at several notches above the quality required for mass transportation hubs.

The woman nodded. "We're very proud of our new building and contributions to the revitalized financial center," she began, the delivery so perfect it seemed long rehearsed. "There are twenty-one million square feet and six trading floors, each larger than a football field. It's a very environmentally friendly building with floor ventilation, cooled by a hundred storage tanks containing nearly two million pounds of ice. Views of the Hudson River and New York Harbor are available for our most senior members."

"Like CEO Craig," said Savas.

The woman's faced paled. "Yes. Please, follow me."

The building spanned two city blocks, and to Savas it felt like the walk to the elevator took them across the length of it. No one followed them inside, and the three Goldman employees were silent as the elevator sped upwards and stopped on the eleventh floor. Stepping out, they found themselves in a second, less gargantuan lobby, which required yet another trek to a second bank of elevators. Windows covered the walls and portions of the ceiling, bathing their path in light.

They passed the second bank of elevators and stopped in front of a doorway. The woman swiped a card over a reader and then keyed in a passcode. The door opened, revealing a short corridor to a smaller, lone elevator door.

"For our top executives," she began as the elevator opened, "we have implemented enhanced privacy and security protocols. This elevator leads to the offices of the CEO and other top Goldman Sachs staff." Her eyes darted away. "Unfortunately, we do not control the security outside of Goldman."

Savas could see pain in the woman's face. "You seem to have known Jack Craig well, Ms.?"

"Greenwald. Susan Greenwald. Yes, I was his personal administrator. His right-hand woman, you might say. Geoffrey and Kendall here are my assistants." She nodded toward the two men. "As we discussed on the phone, you will be meeting with our interim CEO Donald Freiheit."

The elevator doors opened. Before them an expansive conference room ran across the floor, centered on an enormous table of cherry wood. A man at the end of a polished, wooden table rose and ambled over in their direction.

Susan Greenwald reached over and tugged on Savas' jacket, whispering to him. "I don't care what you hear about us in the press, but Jack was a good man. He's done more for this country, for this city than anyone I know. Find his killer." With that she turned on her sharp heels and entered the elevator, the doors closing quickly as she vanished from view.

"Agents Savas and Cohen," came the voice of Donald Freiheit. "Two names that need no introduction."

Freiheit shook their hands, an expression of genuine interest on his face. He was a short man, bordering on stout, with thick glasses and a mass of gray and black curls that gave him more the look of an elder artist at a poetry slam than a new CEO. He led them to the table and poured water for each, sitting next to them like a professor before two students at office hours.

"We've had several rounds with the NYPD and FBI since yesterday. All of Jack's scheduling data, emails, phone logs—they're now in your hands one way or the other, either from us or your national databases. I'm not sure what else I can tell you, but I'm honored by the visit."

Savas nodded to Cohen and she got immediately to the point, removing several photographs from her briefcase and placing them before Freiheit. "Surveillance footage from a handful of operating CCTV cameras identified some very unusual elements in the bombing."

Freiheit glanced at the images. They were grainy, the black limo blurred in the still shot, even the street signs hard to read at the resolution afforded. However, his eyes immediately gravitated to the anomalies she referred to.

"What is this black thing on the top of the car?"

"That's what we're trying to find out, Mr. Freiheit," she said. "Look at this image, taken from another camera closer to the exit ramp from FDR Drive."

"It looks like some giant bird or something. What's it doing?"

Cohen shook her head. "We don't know, and we were hoping that you might could shed some light on it."

The CEO adjusted his glasses. "Me? How?"

Savas bent forward motioning between the images. "Between the time when the vehicle containing Mr. Craig took the exit ramp and the time the bomb exploded, something descended onto the roof of the car. Our analysts are still conferring with the military, but our best hypothesis is that we're looking at some sort of remotely piloted aircraft, an unmanned aerial vehicle that was tracking the CEO's position and then moved to intercept the car immediately before the explosion."

"Unmanned aerial vehicle?" Freiheit seemed stunned. "You mean a drone?"

"Yes," said Cohen, "a drone."

"Doesn't look like a drone."

"Not like the military aircraft shown on TV," said Cohen, "but there are hundreds of other military and civilian models of more designs than you could imagine out there. We can't get enough information from these low-quality images to positively ID the model, or even establish that it is a drone, but it's our best working model right now."

Savas focused intently on the new CEO. "Is there any way this could have been Goldman surveillance? Your Ms. Greenwald was extremely protective of Mr. Craig. Does your company use drones to monitor or keep tabs on Goldman execs?"

Freiheit shook his head vigorously. "Absolutely not. I've never even heard it floated as an idea. I'm not sure it would even be legal."

"It wouldn't," said Savas. "Not yet anyway, but the laws on domestic drone use are in dramatic flux. Some honest mistakes could have been made."

"Not by us, I can assure you. We've never had such a security effort and currently have no plans for one. I find these images very disturbing."

"So do we, Mr. Freiheit. But before we went on any wild-drone chases, the obvious step would be to see if Goldman was in the business. The topic is sensitive, and, I hope I don't need to emphasize, confidential. So we did need your time today."

He nodded. "I understand."

Cohen placed the images back in a folder. "A final item. FBI analysis of phone logs indicates that Mr. Craig made a series of calls to Washington the morning he died. The numbers were resolved to those used by Heidi Moss, the Utah Senator. Since these calls were only minutes before he died, they are of special interest to us. Do you know his relationship with the Senator?"

Freiheit licked his lips quickly and shook his head. "No. I mean, Goldman has many supporters, as well as enemies, on Capitol Hill. It's not unusual for some of our most important lobbying efforts to come straight from the top, as it were. Business, you understand?" He smiled wanly. "Beyond that, I really have no idea what those conversations might be about."

THE INTERIM CEO walked the agents to the elevator. "Susan will meet you on the Sky Lobby, the eleventh-floor lobby. You should take some time there if you can. It's quite a view." Freiheit smiled as the doors closed.

Cohen smirked as the elevator descended. "Bad actor."

"Yeah, he's lying," said Savas. "Not about the drones—I think he was honest there. But there's something going on with the senator."

She began typing into her phone. "Next shuttle to DC?"

"Think so. Have the team give Moss the heads up that we'll need to speak with her today."

"You going to run it through the Washington branch?"

Savas grimaced. "I should. But that will delay everything. I'm so used to the autonomy at Intel 1. I can't stand the bureaucratic dances, anymore. It's likely a dead end, so no harm, no foul. Right?"

"Okay," said Cohen raising her eyebrows. "You know best."

Savas frowned at her.

BEFORE:
THE ANONYMOUS EVENT COMMISSION

DEPOSITION IN THE MATTER OF:
UNITED STATES ARMED FORCES SPECIAL TRIBUNAL, Plaintiff,
versus
JOHN SAVAS, Defendant
Case No. M120039E-007X

CONTINUED DEPOSITION OF:
Franklin Joeseph Miller

[REDACTED]: Why did Savas purposefully keep other FBI divisions in the dark?

MR. MILLER: I'm not sure. That was a judgment call, maybe the wrong one. But it would have cost time and John felt he was on the scent.

CBD: And that's why the two agents immediately flew to D.C.?

MR. MILLER: Yes. At that point we didn't know what was happening. Just got a text message that they were following up on a lead that led them there. Ring the senator's office and let them know.

CBD: That would be Senator Moss?

MR. MILLER: Yes.

CBD: What did the senator say?

MR. MILLER: I wasn't there, but we were briefed when they returned.

CBD: And what were you told in that briefing?

4

TERROR ON THE HILL

Dusk had arrived in Washington. Street lamps engaged, drivers switched their headlights on, and the buildings took on a checkerboard pattern of light and dark. The large window before the FBI agents looked down to the busy streets, the view blocked by the form of an older woman before them.

"This is highly irregular and very short notice, but I understand the circumstances are unusual," said Senator Moss.

Savas and Cohen had rushed to meet with the congresswoman as fast as possible, but extracting themselves from New York and navigating the D.C. rush-hour traffic had put them in much later than they would have preferred. They were lucky to catch Moss before she left for the day. High-level phone calls had helped constrain the situation—when the CEO of Goldman Sachs is blown up in Manhattan, normal etiquette is suspended.

"Indeed they are, Senator," said Savas as they took seats around her desk. Moss was nearing sixty, yet still carried the grace and self-assured mannerisms of the opera singer she had been a lifetime ago. Cohen had quickly filled out her resume for them on the way over. A fourth-term Republican from Utah, she had been a vocal critic of internet freedoms because of cyber-threats to national security and had worked to enact laws to bring the wild online world under increasing surveillance and regulation. As chair of the Subcommittee on Science, Technology, and Innovation, she now exercised enormous influence on national telecommunications.

Cohen leaned forward toward the senator. "Only minutes before he was killed, Goldman Sachs CEO Jack Craig made several phone calls to your office number, Senator. Can you tell us what these calls were about?"

"Those are privileged communications. Unless we want to get very messy with the lawyers, I can't divulge what was discussed. However, it was nothing out of the ordinary. Issues of business and telecom, with Mr. Craig arguing for certain approaches that he felt would be beneficial to the country and his business."

She smiled. For far too long. Savas picked up the thread.

"Could it perhaps have something to do with the highly unusual series of votes that have come from you the last month, Senator?" Moss' smiled faltered. "My colleague here has tallied not only a surprising reversal of several positions on the congressional floor, but also an increasing number of articles in the press trying to figure out just what exactly is going on."

"I'm not sure what you are talking about. The press is always looking for a critical angle, you know that. My positions have always been clear. Certainly, different pieces of legislation can embody my positions to different degrees of satisfaction, and voting for or against a bill is often complicated by the sausage-like production methods of these laws, where the good and bad can be mixed together."

Cohen didn't mask her annoyance. "I'm sure that's true. But there are bills that hardly changed where your votes have flipped. For example, Murdock-Holsen. A bill that would have denied the NSA certain access to internet communications. You initially opposed that bill, gave speeches against it, opposing the very nature of limited access by our surveillance branches." Cohen read from her tablet. "To quote from your speech, you called it 'A dangerous bill that would tie the hands of our law enforcement agencies and aid the work of criminals and terrorists.' Yet three weeks ago you stopped speaking against it and have voted twice to move the bill through committee to a vote."

"I believe that the concerns I had were adequately addressed in the revised version."

Savas could see the woman's lip trembling, the tightness in her hand grasping the side of her desk. Cohen seemed to notice as well. This topic had put Senator Moss under tremendous stress, and his instincts told him she was lying to them. *What are you so afraid of, Senator Moss?*

"Has the topic of domestic drones ever been part of your conversations with Goldman Sachs?" asked Cohen.

The terrified look intensified, and the senator glanced quickly toward photo frames on her desk. She seemed to half-whisper the next words. "No. Never. Why do you ask?" The false smile almost seemed macabre, now.

Cohen ignored her question. "You are on the record as supporting their use."

"Yes," she said distractedly, seeming not to see the FBI agents anymore and gazing behind them. "They are needed for homeland security. To make us safe. That's what I thought."

Savas furrowed his brows. "What you *thought?*"

She blinked quickly and regained focus. "What I *think*, yes, agent Savas. Law enforcement can make great use of drones to pursue criminals when vehicle chases would be impossible or dangerous, take surveillance without endangering officers, many things."

"And what of arming them?"

She cocked her head to the side. "That has been discussed in closed-door sessions, but I don't see that as necessary or likely in the near future."

Savas sensed her resolve returning and saw that they were losing the advantage. He spoke on a hunch. "Are those your daughters?"

Instantly, an anxiety seemed to spread over her features. She smiled stiffly. "Why, yes, yes. Margaret and Sophia. Twins. They're in college now, opposite sides of the country." Her fingers curled inward toward her palm, the nails digging slightly into the wood. "Identical twins and so different. Isn't that strange?"

"How are they doing?" he continued.

"Well!" she nearly shouted. Cohen leaned backward, and the senator adjusted her tone instantly. "Sophia's pre-med, 4.0. Margaret's still finding her way, but she's doing great. Absolutely great." That smile again.

"Well, try to appreciate every minute, senator," said Savas earnestly. "I can tell you, you never know what you have until it's gone."

Her face blanched. "Yes. You know all too well, agent Savas. I will. I promise you."

~

THEY STEPPED out of the Russell Senate Office Building into the brisk

October evening, a black town car before them, waiting by the curb. Savas pulled his collar up and turned to Cohen.

"Well, what do you make of *that?*"

She shook her head, a cool breeze tossing brown hair about her face. "She's been compromised, John. Did you see the terror in her eyes? You pushed a very bad button with her kids."

"But who? And what? And why with fear? Don't the players just buy their way to influence these days? Corporations are people, all that?"

She nodded. "This doesn't make sense, and it feels very dark. Moss is a believer, John. You can see it all over her record. I'm not saying she's above lobbying or influence, but nothing in her twenty years in the Senate compares with what's happened the last few weeks. She's either had a mental breakdown, a stroke or something, or what we saw means somebody has her in a very bad vice."

"Her kids?"

"We should look into them. Check on their whereabouts, status. Start tonight with social media, get some shoes on the ground at their schools."

"If they were snatched, we'd know."

"True. But maybe something will come out of it if there has been some kind of threat."

"Political? Dirty laundry?"

"Always in play with these folks."

They arrived at the vehicle, and Savas opened the back door for Cohen. They got in and he slammed it shut distractedly.

"Reagan National," he told the driver. He whispered to Cohen. "A CEO car bombed. A US senator looking blackmailed and changing her votes. What's going on?"

She stared out the window. "Nothing good, that's for sure."

5

WORM

Halfway around the world, off the tip of the Malay Peninsula, the city-state of Singapore was an engine churning into morning overdrive. Businesses hummed, planes were launched around the world, financial transactions from hundreds of nations sped through the computer systems of their exchanges.

In a gleaming new building of blue and gray, on a wide and open floor lit by a bank of windows facing toward the front of the structure, rows of digital detectives sat in front of their computers. Near the middle of the floor, a short, gray-haired man of European descent hunched arthritically beside the desk of a young Asian woman. He wore a stunned expression as he stared at her screen.

"Are you sure about this?"

Yi Ling nodded to her superior. The thin fingers of her right hand drummed nervously on her keyboard. She reflexively tugged at her chest-length hair with her left. She could not afford to be wrong about this.

It was only two months ago that she had landed this job at the newly opened INTERPOL Digital Crime Centre in Singapore. The DCC was a dream job, letting her use her computer skills in her home country under the auspices of one of the largest and most respected law enforcement agencies in the world. Her friends were all impressed. It paid very well. But now, everything was threatened by the discoveries she had made over the last two days. It had taken her all of yesterday to convince herself that should risk raising the issue with her superiors.

"Yes, Mr. Rosenfeld," her perfect English hardly accented by her native Mandarin. "It's always on the derivative bets. All off-market."

The older man coughed and adjusted his glasses. "Nothing from the exchanges?"

"No," she said, wetting her lips with her tongue. "See these modifications to the contracts? They occur after the parties have established the contract terms but before the instrument is finalized."

Rosenfeld nodded. "That's incredible. How are they not noticing the modifications?"

"I don't know, sir, except that few check the source code anymore. Everything is automated these days, everything comes out of code. Maybe that's why nothing was tried on the exchanges since there'd be too many eyes on the trades. There's a code injection into the contract scripts here." She indicated a row of text on one side of the display. "The siphoning is minimal and scaled to the return on the instrument. They'd have to dig through the layers of fees and clauses to root it out."

"God damned penny shaving. But these are pretty big pennies. How on earth are these modifications getting in there?"

"I'm not sure, but look at this. The losses don't show except for hundredths of a second because an equal amount of money comes into the account."

"From where?"

"It's random. Shell-accounts, investment banks, everywhere. And that's what happens in every instance. There is a loss and nearly immediate plug of the deficit." She didn't want to say more and hoped Rosenfeld would reach the conclusion she had.

"I'll be damned. It's some sort of light-speed Ponzi-scheme."

Yes. "I think so, sir. And I think it works because of the epic nature of the worm infection. There are so many compromised accounts, tens of thousands, that the code left on the systems can continuously shuffle money, even in these increased amounts, so that for no length of time does any one account report much of a loss. It's fantastically complicated, but there is so much unregulated and unmonitored in these dark markets. I think that explains how it's gotten away with this for so long and with so much money involved."

"Just how bad is the spread?"

"I don't know for sure, but unprecedented. I couldn't believe how systematic it is. I've been using the NSA share-data on the known financial OTC trading, and I haven't found any derivative contracts of significance in the last six months that haven't been modified. It's got to total in the trillions."

"Incredible."

"And as long as the contract is viable, it's funneling the money. Untraceable. The money trail disappears in one offshore account after another."

"Like some damn invisible parasite. Thank God we have access to the OTC bids. We'd never have known. Chalk up a success story to the NSA octopus."

The woman swallowed. "Well, that may be part of the problem, sir."

The old man looked at her face and pulled a chair over. He sighed, sitting down. "I'm not going to like this, am I? Go on."

"I'm not sure yet, but there seems to be an association with the NSA data hacks and the timing of the code penetration." God, she hoped she wasn't making a fool of herself. She was prodding a dragon. She knew that.

Rosenfeld removed his glasses. "Wait. You mean that whoever is behind this might be piggy-backing on the NSA worms and backdoors?"

"I think so, sir."

"*Oy vey.*" He put a hand to his head. "This is going to explode."

Yi Ling felt her stomach churn.

After a silent moment, the old man replaced his glasses and patted her on the back. "This is incredible work. I'm going straight to Richards with this, getting this off my plate as fast as possible. We'll see how the bigwigs are going to handle it. I need you to prepare a presentation. I'm going to put you as point. This is going to bring in all the agencies and spooks. Governments are going to freak out, especially the US. We're looking at a game-changer here."

The slight Asian woman trembled with excitement. "Yes, sir. Immediately."

The old man stared grimly forward. "You might just have uncovered the biggest financial cybercrime in history."

6

FORMATIVE YEARS

"Jen, what the hell is your son doing at my computer?"

The black hair of a young boy popped up from behind a monitor, his eyes wide behind oversized glasses. Several books were positioned around him on the desk, and his hand clutched a computer mouse in an iron grip.

A red-faced man stood in the doorway to the home office, his teeth bared, high-end casual clothing draping an athletic form. A woman rushed past him into the room, placing herself between the boy and the man, hands up as if to ward off a blow.

"Now, Richard, he just wanted to try some programming. It's for his class presentation." She smiled wildly. "His will be so much better than all the other children's! He's a genius, you know!"

"A genius. Am I hearing this right?" He stepped into the room deliberately. The woman's smile faded. "Your second-grade brat is fucking up my workstation for a goddamned school project? I have trades on that machine, client information, our taxes! Important documents! Where do you think all this comes from, lady?" He gestured dramatically around the room. "Your nice clothes? Your car? That bitch therapist? Or those ritzy lunches you have with your girlfriends?"

Her shoulders slumped and she backed away from him. 'Richard, it's only—"

"How many times have we talked about this? I don't know what his father

let him get away with, but the little prince has got to learn the rules around here! My desk and my things are off limits! They're not toys! Do you understand that, kid?"

"He is *doing serious work, Richard!" The wild smile returned. "See? He wants to be like you. He's got your books out and he's learning to write those programs like you do! I'm so proud of him!"*

"So you're defending him in spite of what I just said?"

"Yes?" she said, her face falling.

Richard lurched forward, left arm whipping across his body to backhand Jenny across the face. Her head snapped back with a crunch, and she dropped to the ground, catching herself on her palms.

"Mom!" The boy leapt up from the chair, then froze. Without turning his face away from his mother, his wide eyes darted toward the broad shape in the middle of the room. He began to shake.

Richard stared down at the crumpled form of the woman, drops of blood falling to the floor from the back of her hand, the overturned palm already filled like a bowl with a thick, crimson fluid. The anger drained from his face.

"Fuck!" he said, turning to the boy. "This is your fault, you know, you little brat. I don't want to see you touching anything of mine again without my permission, or I'll beat the shit out of you, too." He spun and stormed out of the room. "I won't be back till late. Try to clean that mess up."

There was a jangle of keys and then a door slam. The house fell silent.

"Mom," said the boy again, moving away from the desk. His hands reached out hesitantly toward her.

"No, no!" she said loudly, keeping her face angled away from him, her voice distorted, mouth full. "It's okay, pooh-bear. Don't come closer. Mommy's okay."

"Mom, your nose—"

The woman tried to stand, swayed and steadied herself on a chair nearby. Her face and shirt were stained red, her nose bent gruesomely.

"Can't get blood on his chairs," she mumbled, stumbling sideways with her hands cupped under her face. She reached the bathroom just off the office and closed the door behind her. The boy heard her retching.

For several moments he didn't move. Just faced the door of the bathroom, breathing labored, body shaking. He closed his eyes. Water ran behind the door and the sounds of muffled sobs leaked into the office space. His breathing slowed.

Exhaling, he opened his eyes. His upper lip twitched. He turned to the computer and sat down in the chair, pushing his glasses up the bridge of his nose.

Richard was too big. He knew that. He couldn't punch him the way Richard had hit his mother, not unless he wanted a worse beating. He couldn't hurt him that way. But if he didn't do something, he would hate himself forever. He knew that. He couldn't just let him get away with it. His mind raced.

His stepfather didn't like anyone to use his things. His stepfather's computer was important. *The things on the computer were* serious work. *Maybe it was true, maybe he didn't know how to code like a grown up yet. He wasn't sure. No one would teach him at school and his programs didn't always work like he wanted. He knew he needed to learn more.*

But he could delete files. He knew how to do that.

He could delete ALL his stepfather's files.

He opened a terminal window and began typing.

BEFORE:
THE ANONYMOUS EVENT COMMISSION

DEPOSITION IN THE MATTER OF:
UNITED STATES ARMED FORCES SPECIAL TRIBUNAL, Plaintiff,
versus
JOHN SAVAS, Defendant
Case No. M120039E-007X

DEPOSITION OF:
Rebecca Ruth Cohen
called for examination by Counsel for the Defendant, pursuant to Notice of Deposition, at the Independent Council Offices, located at [REDACTED] Washington, D.C., when were present on behalf of the respective parties: [REDACTED]

CBD: Will you please identify yourself for the record?
MS. COHEN: Rebecca Cohen, FBI special agent, Intel 1.

CBD: You understand that your testimony here is on the record, and your words might later be used to charge and try you as an enemy combatant of the United States?
MS. COHEN: I want to petition for a civilian lawyer and habeas corpus.

[REDACTED]: Your requests have already been noted and processed. Until such a time as they are ruled upon, please focus on the inquiry at hand. Do you understand the law as it applies to you?
MS. COHEN: I was told that this is a deposition. Isn't it a bit unusual to have [REDACTED] with my counsel? Cross-examination?
[REDACTED]: Please answer the question. Do you understand the law as it applies to you?
MS. COHEN: Oh, I understand, all right. This is a damned inquisition.

CBD: To the matter at hand, Ms. Cohen.
MS. COHEN: Do I have a choice?

CBD: There is some discrepancy about when and how the Washington FBI divisions were informed of your suspicions concerning Senator Heidi Moss.

MS. COHEN: Clarification. By "your" you mean Agent Savas and myself?

CBD: That is correct. Can you shed light on this?

[REDACTED]: Enough! Damn the protocol issues. Agent Cohen, it seems pretty clear that Intel 1 kept this information to itself for some time. Now, when you and Savas returned from D.C., what were his actions at Intel 1?

MS. COHEN: We didn't have any time to do much. All hell was starting to break loose. The virus was already eating through the world financial system, and the first big break on that, hell, the discovery of it, was made in Singapore.

CBD: You knew this then?

MS. COHEN: No. But that's the timeline.

CBD: Let's stick with what you knew at the time and how the defendant behaved.

MS. COHEN: How did he behave? We were both exhausted from racing around trying to piece together what the hell was happening with the car bombing, when bam! A VIP kidnapping spree and a fucking boat-bomb!

CBD: Wait, one thing at a-

MS. COHEN: We were hardly given a moment's rest and then I'm racing to midtown while John and Frank are landing back in D.C. to interface with the local FBI divisions on the snatches there. My work cell is firing like a receptionist's and our division is split across the city and between cities. Then, the next thing you know it's the NSA on the line and-

CBD: Ms. Cohen, please! One thing at a time. We need things to be clear.

MS. COHEN: You want clarity? You have us isolated and jailed under military law, asking all sorts of questions about our protocol during those days! Protocol! You want clarity? Try following protocol when VIPs are disappearing and blowing up in real time around you, when you get informed that a cyberworm is chewing through the modern monetary system!

CBD: We understand that this was a difficult time, Ms. Cohen, but-

MS. COHEN: You don't understand anything!

CBD: Please. I'm his counsel, I'm on your side, here.

MS. COHEN: Are you?

CBD: All right, let's calm this down and try again. After your return from D.C., what happened?

MS. COHEN: What happened? Everything happened.

OCTOBER 19

7

SNATCHED

Citigroup CEO Mitchell O'Kelly glared across his desk at his chief of security. He couldn't believe they were wasting his time on this, but the directors had insisted and there was one thing even the CEO couldn't ignore, and that was the Board.

He had known Jack Craig personally, of course. They'd been sparring frenemies for their entire careers across a slew of different corporate locations. O'Kelly had always found Craig an uptight puritan who couldn't help but judge everyone else around him. But he had respected Jack. The man was a fucking genius with the nose of a shark, and you were a fool to bet against him unless you were holding one hell of a hand.

What had happened last week was indeed disturbing. Certainly O'Kelly was worried for his own safety, but the odds that this was something corporate CEOs in general were going to have to be concerned about were very low. He still didn't have a working model for who could have committed such an act—nor had law enforcement as far as he could tell—but it was most likely related to specifics of Craig's business dealings, his personal life, or a random nut job like John Hinckley or Mark Chapman. Sure, beef up the security, scramble the schedules, and then get on with business.

If only.

"Mr. O'Kelly, we have contacted a private security firm that was active in Iraq for VIPs."

"Active in *Iraq*?" This was getting ridiculous!

"Yes, sir. They have a lot of experience dealing with threats of violence against vulnerable and important targets. They are mostly former military, highly trained, experienced with this sort of thing."

"This is *Manhattan*, gentlemen, not Kabul or Baghdad. We're not going to be driving around in bombproof Humvees. Let's get a grip."

"Sir, we've been personally contacted by the Chairman. He supports our recommendations. With threats of this nature—bombings, IEDs, whatever—we need people who have clocked hours with this sort of thing. The landscape changes."

Holy shit. "What does this mean? Armored vehicles? SWAT escorts? Can I go to my son's soccer games without a parent shakedown?"

The two security men glanced at each other anxiously. The older man spoke. "We don't know yet what they will recommend, but we have scheduled a meeting with them tomorrow, first thing in the morning. They're eager to find work in the States, sir."

"I'm sure they are."

"We'll get recommendations and then brief you and schedule a second meeting all together to iron out a course of action."

Ah, to hell with it. "Fine. Do what you need to do. Now, out. This nonsense has taken enough of my time today."

The two men excused themselves with apologies and quickly exited the CEO's office. O'Kelly swiveled his chair away from the closing door and glared up at the dim ceiling of the executive suite. The second floor design hadn't been renovated for years and still possessed the wood and metal, mirrors and leather sensibility of a previous era of financial power. He found the stately atmosphere helped clear his mind, focus his thoughts on the tasks at hand.

His cell phone rang. He scanned the caller ID.

Franklin?

His son had grown up with a special rule in the house: Dad isn't to be bothered during the work day unless it's an emergency. In sixteen years he had never called. Not once. Not during his parents divorce. Not even when he had smashed his first BMW on the Long Island Expressway. Why was he calling now?

"Franklin, what's going on?"

A harsh voice cut through the speaker. "We have your son, O'Kelly. Don't do anything rash, anything stupid, or we will not hesitate to kill him."

O'Kelly jerked upward and stood at attention, his gaze wild. "Who is this?"

"You know what we did to your partner in crime, Jack Craig. We blew him to bits. His bones litter the streets of this city, one of many he robbed for so many years. We will do much worse to your brat if you do not follow our instructions to the letter."

His pulse racing, sweat building on his brow, O'Kelly paced the plush floors of the executive suite in panic. "How do I know—"

"Dad?"

It was Franklin. O'Kelly closed his eyes.

"Dad, God, please. They're not kidding." He seemed to be choking up. "They *killed* Coach Larsen. Shot him. *Dead!* It's my fault, Dad! He was just trying to—"

Abruptly his son's voice was cut off.

"Convincing enough for you?"

"Yes," he whispered, his mind racing for solutions. He walked to his desk and the red panic button.

"You have two choices, O'Kelly. The first is that you kill you son by calling the cops, the Feds, your new military men," said the harsh voice.

"How do you know—"

"*Or*, you act normally, alert no one, and do exactly what we say. You have no guarantees from us except that we will kill him. I think you know we are willing. But we don't give a damn about your son. Only about *you*."

A voice cried from the background.

"Dad! No, don't—"

O'Kelly heard a slap, then silence.

"We are more than willing to let your spawn escape to gain increased cooperation from you. Because we have a special use for you. And you will be helpful to us because you know that your son will never be safe."

"What do you want?"

"There will be no ransom. There will be no stalling. There is a black SUV waiting below on Park Avenue. If you are not in that vehicle in five minutes, your son dies. You are to come down from your second-floor perch. Do not bring your armed muscle."

"They will follow me once they see I'm leaving."

"Make sure you get outside. Then whatever happens, do not pause, do not stop, do not seek to do anything except find your way to that vehicle. Do you understand?"

Thoughts and scenarios flew through his mind, options and risks and assessments that could not be made with any confidence without data, without time.

"This is not something the both of you are going to get out of, O'Kelly. Make your choice: your life or your son's. In four minutes, a decision will be made one way or the other."

The connection was broken.

Mitchell O'Kelly did not hesitate. He had been presented with an impossible choice, and he didn't need any more deliberation to make his decision.

Outwardly calm, he walked quickly out of his office and down the hall. Luckily the ground floor was only two flights down, otherwise there would be no chance to escape without being closely followed. Completely contrary to habit, he entered the stairway to the surprised expressions of the secretaries and leapt down the steps in painful bounds. His aging frame wasn't up to this sort of shock, but it seemed likely he would soon have more serious concerns.

The CEO of Citigroup burst out from the lobby stairwell and walked like a man possessed toward the main entrance. He was not spotted until he had crossed nearly two-thirds of the distance. Shouts came from the voices of his security team, and his peripheral vision sensed several shapes converging from behind. They would reach him in seconds.

He was through the doorway, the sunlight of the clear October day blinding him momentarily, his eyes squinting desperately to find the black SUV.

There. Blackened windows hid the occupants. O'Kelly surrendered all pretense of casualness and sprinted toward the truck.

"Mr. O'Kelly!"

His bodyguards cried behind him. The men were under the strictest orders. They would have him in their arms within seconds for this dangerous breach of protocol, especially after recent events. The black vehicle was still fifty yards away. He'd never make it.

Hornets buzzed past his head. There were screams. He heard bodies fall heavily to the ground. He didn't look back. He ran harder, the back door of the SUV opening, arms grabbing his, pulling him in violently. The vehicle lurched forward with screeching tires and he was thrown backward into a seat.

But he had seen. In a split second upon entering the truck and turning his head toward the plaza in front of the building, it was all too clear.

The fiends had shot and killed the men that had been charged to protect him. Their bodies were strewn across the cement and steps, people racing in panic away from the scene.

O'Kelly closed his eyes. God only knew what they were going to do to him.

8

VANISHED

Rebecca Cohen sat in the back of the FBI vehicle, nearly sick from the lurching dash through traffic. Staring at the choppy video feed on her phone was surely not helping the situation. They should have just called. But they needed to see each other.

"On the tarmac, Rebecca," said a pixelated Savas, his phrases peppered with staccato pauses. "This is getting a bit insane."

They had not been back a day before the next crisis had pulled them apart again. This time it was sudden disappearances of important people both in New York and in Washington. Congressman, aides, more CEOs, workers at the Federal Reserve Board. Whatever theories they had before were jettisoned. Whatever was going on, it was highly coordinated and professionally implemented.

"Feels like we're back under siege from Mjolnir," she said to the frozen face of Savas. "John?"

There was a pause, and then the connection reestablished. "Lost most of that except for Thor's Hammer. But I think I know what you were saying."

They had split their team at Intel 1. Savas had taken ex-Marine Frank Miller with him to DC. They would soon be on their way to the Capitol. Cohen had called another agent on their team, JP Rideout, and they were going to meet at the headquarters of Citigroup. The other cases were reported disappearances, no shows and quiet vanishings. But not at Citi. There were witnesses. There were bodies. There had been a failed pursuit by NYPD.

The sedan jerked to a stop and Cohen dropped the phone, the connection with Savas lost. She quickly texted him that she had arrived and would talk to him later. He would soon be busy as well.

The driver opened the door for her and she stepped out quickly, heading for the crowd of police and decorations of yellow tape in front of the building. The glass and steel structure towered above her. Horns blared like a strong wind from the snarled traffic of rubberneckers. *Here to see the bloodbath.* She counted four bodies. Two were near the exits, and two had moved toward Park Avenue before they were cut down. A black NYPD detective met her.

"Agent Cohen?" he asked. "I'm Tyrell Sacker. You're it for the Feds?"

"No, we have a crime group en route and another special agent from my division."

"Which is?"

"Intel 1."

The cops eyes opened wider. "Well, we need the best. Reports are coming in from all over the city. The radio's total chaos."

"I know. Look, we're going to go through this thoroughly, but can you tell me what you've put together? Is there enough for a summary?"

Sacker nodded. "A crowd of witnesses, and security cams to go back to and verify. But it still doesn't make sense, even if the testimony agrees so far. Their CEO literally comes sprinting out of the building, ignoring the calls of his security team, running straight for a van or SUV. He was scheduled for meetings all day and was already late for one in the building. It's like he went nuts. His team bolted after him, and, well, you can see what happened to them."

"Shots came from the vehicle?"

"Doesn't seem so. None of the witnesses reported seeing anything in the truck but some dark figures pulling O'Kelly inside. The shots were professional, agent Cohen," Sacker said, looking back toward the bodies. "No evidence of misses. I mean, how often does that happen? I'd bet there were gunman positioned and waiting."

"We'll have our ballistics teams here soon, and we'll need to get all the CCTV footage from all security cameras in the area."

"On that. I'm point for this scene, so you'll be talking to me."

Cohen smiled. She liked Sacker immediately. He was gritty yet polite, sharp with an underlying empathic feel. She hoped that she could trust him.

"All right, we'll work out the coordination of this investigation soon. For now, take me up to the crime scene. I want to get a look at the victims."

~

The Capitol Police officers glared at the hulking form of Frank Miller with suspicion. Savas stood with him before the grand entrance of the Russell Senate Office Building. The stately marble, lofted steps, and the presence of twenty to thirty uniformed officers in combat gear sporting military-grade automatic weapons made an undeniable impression. He was as polite as possible.

"Yes, special agents Savas and Miller. These are our IDs. We're en route from New York because of an apparent coordinated abduction connected to those here."

A nervous officer stood several steps above them. "We have explicit instructions not to allow anyone except approved law enforcement officers into the building."

"We *are* approved law enforcement officers!" growled Miller. "We're here *by request* of the agency acting on orders from the fucking president! The little headsets you're wearing with mics—try them out and contact your damn superiors."

Several weapons were pointed their way.

Miller was losing his temper, as he tended to do. A decorated former soldier, he had been shot twice saving Savas' life in the line of duty as an FBI agent. He didn't suffer fools well, and there wasn't much that scared the man. Which is what frightened Savas.

"Okay, Frank, let's just back off and wait for the red tape to unspool. There's a lot of tension right now. We're all on the same side."

They returned to their car and waited out the next half hour. Evening began to fall, and the streets were a ghost town. The Capitol had been completely locked down.

The wall of police opened and a figure in a suit shuffled down the steps. Savas immediately recognized him—Tim Cox, Assistant Director in Charge, a lanky, bespectacled man and former Secret Service agent. The local branch had brought in the big guns on this scene. People were shook up.

"Agent Savas," said Cox extending his hand with a surprisingly strong grip. "Your reputation precedes you of course, but you're a long way from home."

"Things are moving very fast, sir, and there hasn't been time to coordinate investigations. But the murder of Goldman CEO Jack Craig may be tied in some fashion to Senator Heidi Moss."

The Assistant Director squinted. "How so?"

"His last phone calls, minutes before his death, were to her. We paid her a visit and while nothing concrete came up, it was clear that she was under some sort of threat of some kind."

"And you did not bring this to the attention of my office, because?"

Great. Miller glanced at him and Savas tried hard to ignore it. "It was a hunch, sir. And if not for the kidnappings of other CEOs and members of Congress today, it would have remained a completely unsubstantiated hunch. We can't bother you with every possible idea."

"Still, Savas, this is our turf. Let us decide what is worthy of our attention."

"Point taken, Assistant Director." Savas hoped they would be cooperative. "As you know, we have multiple events in New York, some still coming in as people are reported missing. I'm back here to begin coordinating with you on this seemingly related set of disappearances."

Cox nodded. "It's unprecedented. We have three missing Congressman, a high-level official at the Securities and Exchange Commission, and just as of ten minutes ago, it seems that the head of the Federal Reserve did not get off her plane at Reagan National."

"Louise Lelann?"

Cox sighed. "So now you see the magnitude of this. Homeland Security is descending like a storm cloud, as if they didn't eat up enough of our departments already. We're on lockdown, the president's day has been scrambled. I'm not sure who knows where he is. It feels like a terrorist attack."

"I think it is," said Miller.

"Well, then you folks are the right ones for the job."

"There's no one claiming responsibility? No ransom demands? Anything?"

Cox shook his head. "Nothing. But the game is still early. It's certainly different than anything before. The murder of Craig—it could have been anything. But it was *murder*. A car bomb. A terrorist-y thing. Abductions of state officials? Corporate CEOs? What the hell is the play here?"

Savas looked at Miller and back to Cox, the cold night air bringing more of a chill than was warranted.

"I'm sorry to say, Assistant Director, I have no idea."

9

UNDER THE RADAR

"Senator, Mr. Avram's yacht is probably the *safest* place you can be today," said a gorgeous blonde hanging on the old man's arm. She turned toward him conspiratorially, whispering in his ear. "They say it even has a radar system to detect missiles." The senator reddened as her ruby lips brushed his earlobe.

The boat carved its way through New York harbor like a titan. Nebula was the world's most expensive privately owned yacht, three years in the making and boasting a pool studded with Havana bars, a helipad, five water jets, a cinema, and a four thousand square foot master suite. Nine decks, each with entry and exit points, rose from the waterline and gave the vessel more the appearance of an aerodynamic condo than a private cruise boat.

"Truly," came the deep voice of Robert Avram, "she's the safest boat in the waters today."

They stood on the upper deck, lower Manhattan a frozen collection of ten thousand Will-o'-the-wisps of skyscrapers, apartments, and bridge lights. A full moon rose into the night sky and painted the gleaming surfaces on the yacht in luminescent hues. The blonde escort smiled broadly at the CEO, her sequined dress a light show reflecting the moonlight, the plunge of her neckline scandalous. Soft jazz floated on the crisp air from below.

"I hope so," said the senator, vacillating between the seduction hanging on his arm and a set of internal worries that he could not completely dismiss. "I'm actually scared to go home tonight. People have disappeared from their own houses!"

The woman purred. "Maybe you don't have to go home tonight."

Avram smirked and left the pair to their courting dance. He had no doubts the woman would be in the old fool's bed this evening. He had hired the cream of the crop. And he had made sure that useful photos would be taken discretely at opportune moments. Robert Avram ran his business like an old Mafia boss, and he was proud of that fact.

Stepping down the stairway toward the floor below, he felt a buzz in his shirt pocket. He removed his phone and answered. Almost immediately his face turned ashen.

"You can't be serious?" He closed his mouth quickly, glancing around the harbor in panic. "Yes, I'm listening." His eyes widened as a man's voice spoke on the other end. "You want me to what? This is crazy! Why should I—"

At that moment, a light flashed above him. A second later the event repeated. "Yes, I see it. No, you're right. Our radar can't detect objects that small. Yes. I see. Yes, of course you are." He looked down to the guests mingling below. "Can I at least warn the others?"

His face grimaced as he placed the phone in his shirt pocket again. His hands gripped the railing tightly, and he breathed in and out slowly several times. *This is not happening.*

But it was. And he had been told he had little time. He rushed down the stairway. Several people approached him, but he ignored them, darting into the heart of the vessel. Forgoing the crowded stairways, he would avoid being seen this way. No one would bother him, ask questions. He would not have to think about what was happening. He pressed his thumb to the scanner by the elevator.

The doors opened immediately. He entered and hit the button to the sea-level floor. The elevator descended, the doors opened, and he dashed toward the back of the vessel.

The area was empty, all the guests and staff concentrated on decks above with better views of the harbor. Avram removed his jacket and tie, kicking off his shoes and socks as well. He dropped his phone and Rolex on the deck beside a railing at the stern of the Nebula, the engines below softly churning the dark waters.

He gazed back at the boat. He had never been in love. He appreciated women, their beauty, enjoyed sex. But *love?* He hadn't been raised on love.

But the Nebula—that was a beauty to be loved. His design, his testament to everything he had accomplished and would do. He stared at it as a man would a lover on her death bed.

Then he climbed the railing, standing unbalanced at the corner of the stern, as far from the engines as possible. The lights of New Jersey and Manhattan formed a dizzying panorama of radiance around him. Placing his hands out to the sides, he leapt forcefully into the darkness.

The harbor was frigid, and he gasped for air as he struggled to tread water. Fortunately he had been a talented swimmer at Harvard, and despite the numbness creeping over his limbs, he was able to orient himself onto his back, his feet pointed back toward the Nebula, its music and soft lights fading as it sped away from him. A minute passed. Then two, and he worked to keep his arms and legs moving, the circulation flowing, retarding the hypothermia that had begun to freeze his muscles.

What sounded like a series of humming hornets' nests streaked over his head and toward the boat. He spied small shadows cross over the lights of lower Manhattan, but he could not be sure it was anything more than his imagination.

But then the Nebula erupted in flame. A series of fireballs ignited around the boat, consuming his lady in a hideous light. The sound rushed over him, one-two-three punches of compressed air and ear-splitting detonations. Burning debris flew into the sky, then rained back down on the dimming skeleton of the boat.

Robert Avram wept. He knew in that explosion he had lost not only the symbol of his greatness, but everything. Confirmation arrived with little delay as he felt hands grasp his shoulders and lift him out of the water, dumping him harshly onto the deck of a small motorboat. Burly shadows manhandled him like livestock, binding his arms and legs, toting him to one end of the vessel, and casting him painfully into a corner. His captors revved the engine, and turned the boat southward toward Staten Island, racing into the darkness.

OCTOBER 20

10

WRECKAGE

Savas watched the faint light of the morning grow over the East River. He sped down the FDR en route from La Guardia airport in an FBI vehicle, retracing part of the path Goldman CEO Craig had taken right before he died. The lights of the Queensboro Bridge were still bright enough to be easily seen in the creeping dawn, the tram lifting sleepy commuters into Manhattan from Roosevelt Island like a floating cabin in the sky. To his right, the concrete redwoods of the city flew by him with trails of light.

He was hardly awake himself. Last night an explosion had occurred in New York Harbor, before the eyes of Lady Liberty herself. Another CEO of a powerful multinational financial company was dead, his luxury liner blown to pieces where the fresh water of the Hudson mixed with the sea. The agency branches in Washington could work on their disappearing governmental employee problem themselves. New York, *his* city, was under siege again.

He had spent the better part of a night arranging his travel and for Frank Miller to stay in DC to coordinate between the coupled investigations. An early plane landed him in New York with the first businessmen. His driver flew down the East Side highway, traffic still minimal at this hour, their destination lower Manhattan. Cohen was waiting for him there.

The thin tower of the UN building darted past on the right, the reddening sky casting an infernal hue across its glass facade. For Savas, it seemed prescient, foreboding. His instincts told him that something subterranean and evil was brewing. He only hoped that they could find a break in their endless game of catchup with these dark forces and find a way to prevent further attacks.

The car passed NYU Medical Center and soon entered lower Manhattan. Lost in his own ruminations, he failed to notice as they darted into the Battery Park Underpass and emerged on the western tip of the island. He was surprised to sense the car slowing as it pulled into North Cove Marina.

Cohen was immediately at his side as he stepped out of the vehicle.

"God, John, you look like crap."

He laughed and fingered the lapel of her coat. "Always good to be home." They walked toward the dock and the Coast Guard boat waiting there. "We've lost three CEOs in a week."

"There's still no claim for the attacks or abductions. The JP Morgan CEO, Robert Avram, is presumed dead, although his body hasn't been found. Most of the bodies on the ship manifest haven't been found."

"But Senator McDougal?" He asked. "I heard that he was found."

"Confirmed an hour ago at the morgue."

"*Jesus*. I've heard talk of the National Guard, although I can't imagine what good it would do outside of giving the public and news shows some sense that we aren't sitting here helpless."

"But we are, John."

They neared the boat and several members of the Coast Guard approached them. He gritted his teeth. "Let's see if we can change that. Gentlemen!" They walked forward and shook hands. "Agents Savas and Cohen."

"You're the man who took down Gunn," said one of the sailors. "Honored to meet you, sir. I know about your son. I was here on 9/11, evacuating folks trapped on the south end after the towers fell."

Savas swallowed. "Then *I'm* honored. You guys moved more than half a million, if I remember right."

"Maybe more. Papers said it was bigger than Dunkirk in WWII. Somehow feels like we're always at war."

Savas understood completely. "Let's get out there and see what we can see."

They stepped onto the boat, the sailor gave instructions, and they pushed off from shore. "We towed it to Governors Island. Used to be a

Coast Guard base. Boat was sinking, even with all the technology built into it to prevent that. I read up on it. The owner was a paranoid son-of-a-bitch."

Within minutes they had arrived on the small island. The wreckage of what had once been a luxury yacht was awkwardly tethered to the dock, wisps of smoke still trailing upwards from her, the smell of melted plastic overpowering. It was obvious why no one had survived.

Police and fire crews worked with investigators combing the remainder of the vessel. A sharply dressed man, attired in a suit, with black hair and a French nose walked up to the FBI agents.

"JP," said Savas. "What do we have?"

Rideout squinted in the light of the rising sun. "Well, this is big league forensics. Half the evidence is at the bottom of the harbor. But from what we've found and working with witnesses on shore and in other boats who saw the explosion, we're talking about multiple detonations spaced a few seconds apart. Odd for a bomb planted on the boat, but there you go. The fireball was hot enough that we can assume synthetics and a big payload. But it will take some time to analyze the residue and debris." He indicated a small boat pulling out nearby. "We're still relocating the bodies, the remains. It will take some time to identify them all. In some cases DNA matching might be the only way—there isn't much left to go on. NYPD and several university labs with the required equipment are pitching in. Avram threw a big party."

Savas shook his head. "Grim work."

Cohen shuddered and rubbed her hands together in the morning chill. "You said multiple blasts. Could it have been explosives delivered externally?"

Rideout nodded. "Drone idea again? I think it's likely. Missiles are out, as crazy as it is to even say something like that. Avram had a pretty sophisticated radar system that not only detected incoming birds but automatically would send the data out encrypted on military and police frequencies. I guess he had some issues, but the fact is that the boat didn't squeak last night. But I don't think it could pick up fliers as small as many drones. They'd be invisible to the radar."

"I guess he didn't modernize his paranoia," said Cohen. "Who would have thought to protect their assets from drone strikes?"

"Why aren't there more agents here?" asked Savas, glancing around the dock.

"It's a bit chaotic," said Rideout, "and you've been in transit for the last two days. Commands from on high have all agencies scrambling to put bodies on people and places. The Bureau is like a ghost ship, if you'll excuse the juxtaposition."

Cohen turned to Savas. "It's all been in the last twelve hours. The kidnappings and killings have a lot of powerful people very frightened. Pressure is being put on all governmental and state agencies to secure them. Favors are being called in. People are starting to panic."

Savas nodded. "Should have seen it coming. You'll have to excuse me —I'm running on about negative three hours of sleep. Hopefully I can get some shuteye soon, that is if nothing else goes FUBAR in the next few hours."

His cell rang.

Rideout and Cohen stared at him. He just sighed. "Here we go." He tapped the screen and placed the phone to his ear. "Hi, Angel. What blew up now?"

BEFORE:
THE ANONYMOUS EVENT COMMISSION

DEPOSITION IN THE MATTER OF:
UNITED STATES ARMED FORCES SPECIAL TRIBUNAL, Plaintiff,
versus
JOHN SAVAS, Defendant
Case No. M120039E-007X

Continued DEPOSITION OF:
Jean Paul Rideout

MR. RIDEOUT: John had just flown back. He and Rebecca met me at the dock and we got our first look at the boat. What remained of it.

[REDACTED]: Is this when Agent Lightfoote became involved in the investigation?

MR. RIDEOUT: Angel? No.

[REDACTED]: Statements from other members of your division state that she was.

MR. RIDEOUT: Why would she be involved in the bombing case? She was cybercrimes.

CBD: But she called at the dock? We have cell phone records and the testimony of Agent Cohen.

MR. RIDEOUT: Yeah, she called. So what? The virus was completely unknown to us at that point. Angel didn't know why they were calling. She took the call and passed the message on to John.

CBD: Is that normal?

MR. RIDEOUT: NSA called. She's cybercrimes. What's the mystery?

CBD: But Savas took her along with him to the meeting?

MR. RIDEOUT: Of course. Again, she's *cybercrimes*. Why wouldn't she go?

[REDACTED]: But you said you didn't know about the virus.

MR. RIDEOUT: That's what the NSA meeting was about! So, no!

[REDACTED]: So, why bring your cybercrimes leader?

MR. RIDEOUT: Because NSA, duh? Angel is our digital guru. We're retreading this thing like you've never heard of a circle.

[REDACTED]: And now she's AWOL.

MR. RIDEOUT: AWOL? What the hell? She's not conscripted! She doesn't owe you guys anything. Just because your goons failed to grab her doesn't mean she's up to anything bad. If I hadn't been shot, I might be out there with her, deep in hiding from this mess.

[REDACTED]: She's breaking the law.

MR. RIDEOUT: Not any laws I know about. But you all have new laws now, don't you? Just making them up as you go. Christ, I had a bad feeling when martial law was declared. Little did I know!

[REDACTED]: There have been extraordinary events. Unprecedented threats to the nation. We are doing what we can to preserve order.

MR. RIDEOUT: Don't you think I know that? But you're shooting at friendlies, dammit!

CBD: Then you can understand our need to get to the bottom of things. Tell us about Lightfoote.

MR. RIDEOUT: Why are you so obsessed with her? Don't you have one hundred dossiers and film surveillance and case records? What the hell am I going to tell you that you don't know?

[REDACTED]: How about where she is?

MR. RIDEOUT: If I knew, that'd be the last thing I'd tell you.

11

EPIDEMIC

"Joe, Jesus, it's the middle of the trading day. What the hell is this about?"

Two men huddled underneath a pedestrian walkway in a quiet London park. They had both approached the location independently, secretively, without informing anyone of their destination. Both had exercised extreme vigilance in their journey, checking for pursuit or other surveillance, doubling back and changing routes several times, increasing by three-fold the amount of time it would take to reach the rendezvous. One man was dressed in a suit and sported closely cropped gray hair. The other, a younger man by two decades, wore slacks and a button down shirt as well as sunglasses. Both appeared anxious, their British accents cutting like daggers through the conversation.

"I'm taking a huge risk even showing up here," said the young man.

"And I'm not? Spit it out. Is it this virus you've been talking about?"

"Worm," he corrected.

"Whatever."

"The difference is important."

"That's because you're a computer programmer."

He shook his head. "It *matters*. Look, a virus is a file, you have to execute it, infect your computer with it. A worm digs in by itself, and can lay a lot of viral eggs and do other things. But it spreads itself. This worm is spreading *everywhere*."

"What's everywhere?"

The programmer's arms danced through the air. "By now, half the machines on the London exchange are likely infected. By next week, nearly all of them will be."

The older man straightened slightly. "What will it do?"

"We don't know!" he shouted, quickly catching himself and lowering his voice. "Look, my division at Interpol got the first information from Singapore a few days ago. Since then, all hell's broken loose. We're finding it everywhere, chasing it everywhere. No one has a handle on it, not the Americans, the Chinese, or the Russians. Hell, if the Russians can't take it down, we're in a fucking boatload of trouble!"

"Brilliant. Let's calm down. What do you know?"

The Interpol programmer wiped his brow, sweat glistening and beginning to pool in his eyebrows despite the cool autumn day. "It's global. Initially we thought that it was only a finance worm, now we're finding it other places. It actually seems to have used NSA backdoors and code as gateways to infiltrate the machines the damn Americans were already spying on. It hides well. We mainly find what it leaves behind."

"Which is?"

"Lots of really nasty code. The thing is injecting subroutines and entire programs into existing software or between two pieces of software and handshaking them. Gave itself away when large sums of money started to funnel through the infected systems into offshore accounts."

"How much money?"

"I don't know. Billions. Maybe more. But that's one thing. Billions from the derivative market isn't going to be missed, really. But recent findings are looking a lot more scary. Your machines, your trading algorithms that run the damn exchanges, they are all compromised."

The older man narrowed his eyes harshly. "Compromised? How?"

"We're still trying to figure that out! We'd need full access to your machines, *today*, to get to the meat of it quickly. We can't lock this down with you running the programs. You're going to have to halt trading."

"Out of the question! We aren't going to shut down the London Exchange so Interpol can go rummaging through our systems."

"You don't get it! This is preliminary, but if it's verified, if what we're seeing is real or even looks like it might harm the exchanges, Downing will pull the plug on the exchanges anyway! A stop in trading on purpose is better than a system meltdown."

"There isn't going to be a system meltdown!"

"We don't know *what's* going to happen."

"Every few years you fools cry wolf over some Millennium bug, Heartbleed this, or Shellshock that, and all manner of bloody apocalypse is about to descend on us. Every time the markets kept going just fine and the only thing hurt has been your reputations."

"You know, most of the time the money you guys send my way is all I need for motivation to talk to you. And I've more than paid for myself in the information I've delivered. But this is *different!* I'm scared shitless right now by this thing, and so are half the people in my division. The Americans are scrambling and the Asian markets as well."

"And I don't see them shutting down in panic, do you?" The programmer said nothing, but stared toward the other end of the tunnel, exhaling a cloud of vapor. "Look, we'll do a complete IT sweep, antivirus everything. We've handled these types of things before."

"I'm telling you, this isn't like—"

"Bring me back something *concrete*, with concrete effects and predictions, and then I can make a financial assessment of how much is to be lost from the thing as compared to the absolutely huge losses that we'll be *sure* to take for shutting down the exchange. *Shut down* is the panic button. The fail-safe. Bring me real data, not doomsday maybes. Understand?" He fired a harsh gaze toward the programmer and stormed off into the park.

The man remaining in the tunnel shook his head and lit a cigarette. He smoked it under the walkway for several minutes before leaving, spacing his exit with that of his contact at the exchange. He also needed to clear his head and calm down. It was always like this, he told himself. Investors had profit on the brain and a foresight of a goldfish. All that mattered were next quarter's returns.

I could be wrong. The truth was that they really didn't know what this thing was yet or what it would do. He *hoped* they were all wrong about the dangers. He dropped the bud on the concrete and crushed it out with his shoe, turning up his lapels and entering the chaos of children's shouts.

~

A BOY STARED toward the man as he exited, his gaze focused slightly above him and the bridge under which he had stood for the last half hour. He tugged on his mother's arm and pointed into the sky. A small, blurred ball danced in the air above the park.

"Look, mummy. It's a helicopter! It's remote control!"

His mother nodded her head and tapped onto her smartphone. "Yes, dear, that's nice."

The boy continued tracking the object as it moved away from the bridge. "Herman has one. It's wicked. It can do anything and...oh no!"

"What is it, dear?" his mother asked, her eyes never leaving the screen in her hand.

"It's just going up and up. It's too high!" He looked frantically around the park for the child who was trying to control it. His face dropped. "It's going to be lost."

And soon enough it was. The small object disappeared from view as it ascended into the sky. It did not return. The boy continued to look around the park, but there were no children in distress or racing after an out-of-control toy. His shoulders sank and he dug into the soil with his shoe.

The woman looked up from her phone. "What was that you said, dear?"

12

VIRTUAL MONEY

"So it seems the internet is going to blow up."

Savas sat in front of a table in the computer science department at NYU. The academic setting was made all the more surreal by the presence of NSA staff, Interpol officers, and members of the Secret Service alongside several professors and students.

The NSA man tried again to assume command of the conversation. "That's a rather dramatic way to put it, Agent Savas." The representative of the agency was stiff in his gray suit, looking down his nose at the students and especially Lightfoote. However galling, Savas had to admit, she looked the part of a freedom fighter from some post-apocalyptic dystopian teen film. Eyes tended to wander toward her.

Savas was still trying to parse the odd collection of people around him. The NYU students had stumbled upon something. Fine. They had called, of all places, specific *NSA branches*. Why? Because along with Homeland Security, the NSA was funding their research. They were a "National Center of Academic Excellence in Information Assurance and Cyber Defense." *Information Assurance.* He liked that.

Then there was the presence of the Secret Service which had been explained by the financial end of this story. Yes, Agent Savas *was* aware that the Secret Service was responsible for investigations into financial fraud, in addition to its protective function for governmental VIPs. *But still.*

Finally, *Interpol!* But that is where things really got interesting and expanded from a local to a distinctly global problem. In fact, it was the Interpol officer who cut in on the NSA suit.

"Drama, Mr. Teller, may in fact be warranted here." His thick Scottish brogue worked as an aural spotlight. "Our offices in Singapore have this worm penetrating systems all over the world, including major financial institutions and governmental entities. We believe upwards of ninety percent of machines exposed to it are vulnerable."

The NSA man cut in quickly. "There hasn't been time to ascertain how widespread it is."

"With all due respect, I think the NSA has a lot of reasons to minimize the threat of this code." The Interpol and NSA representatives stared each other down.

Savas leaned forward toward the European. "Why is that?"

"Because the worm has gotten the most mileage out of piggybacking on the NSA's own spyware—*their* worms—used for hacking and stealing the secrets of everyone from the UN to foreign leaders. And don't even try to deny your agency's actions," he said, cutting off an attempted protest by Teller. "Snowden let that cat out of the bag a while ago."

The Secret Service agent spoke. "It's a financial instrument," she said. "Once into the system, there are a set of specific programs it looks for. When it finds them, it adds modules of code that relate to options trading on the derivative market."

"What does this code do?" asked Savas.

The Interpol officer spoke. "From what we can tell, it's funneling enormous sums of money from the off-market derivatives trading."

"Off-market?"

"Yes," he continued. "Contracts, *bets* if you will, that do not show up on any exchanges and are poorly regulated. In fact, we don't even know how much money is tied up in those deals. But it dwarfs the imagination. Estimates are in the hundreds of trillions of dollars."

Savas tried not to let his jaw drop. "I didn't know that much money even existed in the world."

"It's all in bits and bytes, not in gold or cash," said Lightfoote.

"Virtual money that isn't so virtual." Savas leaned back in his chair. "And how much money is being stolen?"

A white-haired professor from the computer science group flipped pages on a notepad. "We've been following the thing for three days now.

There's no way to know how much was siphoned before that, but our estimates are in the hundreds of millions of dollars."

"That's a hell of a lot."

"Per *day*."

A silence filled the room. Savas looked at Lightfoote, who just laughed.

"Does you intern think something is funny, agent Savas?" asked Teller.

Lightfoote spoke for herself. "You *idiots*. Did you ever stop to think that if it was so easy for you to tear through the world's firewalls that others couldn't? Did you stop to think how fragile everything is now, everything online, everything in bytes—money, electricity, nuclear power systems? And now someone is using your own black hat code to leech from an underground financial market that should have been shut down after 2008? You're like a bunch of fucking twelve-year-olds wandering around an arms factory and pushing buttons."

"Your division has been included in this briefing because of your track record, Agent Savas," said the NSA official, "but the disrespect and frankly treasonous attitude of your staff cannot be tolerated."

"Are you insane?" asked the Interpol officer. "This is not a US governmental matter only. You aren't in authority here, whatever God-complex your organization has developed. The lady is right. This is *big*. This is a disaster!"

"Look, people," said Savas, standing up. "I'm inclined to agree with that assessment, and I thank you for including us in this briefing. Our team will get to it immediately. Anything we find with we'll pass your way. But, you may have noticed that we have our plate full right now. Matters of life and death, not just money and taxes. Our resources are stretched to the breaking point." He turned to the Scot. "This is a big threat. We'll help, but we're going put out the fire in our house, first." He turned to leave.

"We need countermeasures," said Lightfoote. Eyes turned toward her. "This is something new. Something truly dangerous. You can't just rely on the software companies to develop and issue patches. There isn't time."

"What do you mean there isn't time?" said Teller.

"I mean that whoever is behind this is not playing for a criminal unit or nation-state. Those groups have long-term ends in mind, stability of the system. You can't make a living off the system as a criminal if you bring it down."

"The *system*, whatever that might be, isn't going down!" Teller looked incredulous.

"That's where you're wrong." Her green eyes burned. "This is major artery damage. You can't wait to patch it. The patient will bleed to death. Organ systems will malfunction. You've got to go in aggressively and root the damn thing out. If you don't, at the rates the professor mentions, come November you're going to have an economic *catastrophe* on your hands."

13

WATCHING THE WORLD BURN

A four-by-five panel of giant flat-screen monitors covered a wall in a dark room. News stations spanning the content of the major networks to cable providers flashed a diversity of images. One by one, sound was associated with a given monitor and channel, large speakers on the sides of the array of screens projecting audio, the brightness on the other nineteen monitors dropping dramatically to emphasize the featured screen. Centered before the dizzying display was a lone chair containing a shadowed figure.

"This is Monica Grayford from CNN," began the short-haired brunette standing before the Capitol building in Washington, DC. "Chaos has swept over the House of Representatives as a rebellion in the GOP threatens to bring the legislative branch to a standstill. Key members of House committees have suddenly switched their votes on multiple issues central to several pressing pieces of legislation. Among them are a host of financial reform bills including raising the marginal tax rate on the wealthiest Americans, legislation to remove corporate tax loopholes, and challenges to overturn the Supreme Court rulings on campaign finance reform and the personhood of corporations. In addition, numerous laws aiming to regulate the internet have found their support shifting dramatically, with numerous Democratic and Republican Congressman now supporting net neutrality and opposing governmental regulation and internet monitoring. For more on this developing story, we go to—"

The screen dimmed and the audio cutoff. A monitor on the upper right brightened, and a panel of men and women on Fox News were yelling at each other across a common table. A stout man in a suit centered in the middle screamed over the group.

"None of these theories makes sense! With elections nearly here, you aren't going to see members of both parties suddenly reversing their long-held positions on important issues! I think that we need to step back and ask what is really going on here. What backroom deals are being made and has the White House been involved to try and throw the results in November into chaos? We all know the polls show that the midterms are not going to go their way, so they have to be involved!"

A woman near the end of the table on the left cut in. "Based on what? Why do you always have to turn everything into a conspiracy of foul play by this administration?"

A black man near the center raised his hands in the air. "This is all speculation at this point. We don't know what is going on. Neither do the leaders of *either* party. Until we can get explanations from the members of Congress themselves, all this is just hot air."

The viewpoint shifted, jumping to a monitor on the lower level in the middle of the array. A heavyset man in a suit with gray hair paced about a television stage, waving his arms and gesticulating. Behind him was an enormous chalkboard, names of important political figures and organizations written and boxed in various locations, numerous arrows studded with short phrases and comments connecting the various names. The commentator was shouting.

"A Democratic Super PAC with ties to a billionaire is suddenly bankrupt? Why? Where did all that money go? A week later, we find one member of Congress after another switching their votes, always in the direction of the liberal agenda. Always decreasing our ability to monitor communications for terrorist activity and attacking the earnings of the job-creating class. Am I the only one seeing this? I mean, could it be more obvious? My fellow Americans, we are poised on the edge of a terrible cliff, where the terrorist sympathizing, Marxist left-wing agenda has put our very freedoms in the crosshairs." His voice caught, and he wiped his eyes. "There might not be much more time. I don't know how many times I'll be allowed to address you when the new world order is imposed. I've never said this before, but I'm scared. Scared for America. Scared for the world. Because, in the end, it is we Americans that stand between order and chaos on this planet."

The image and sound jumped to the upper left of the screens, a dour, bald man centered in the camera before a microphone. A woman's voice spoke over the images.

"The Russian president has just begun a press conference. This is Russia Today with an exclusive video feed of the event called in response to reported violations of international treaties this week by the US Congress."

The sound switched to the figure behind the podium. An angry voice speaking in Russian, muffled beneath the words of a man translating the speech into English.

"...are extremely destabilizing and foolish. We urge party leaders in US House of Representatives to stop extremist wings and put stop to many bills now on floor. We call to United States President to veto laws passing. Russia will not tolerate more US imperialism over regions and resources international law has divided."

The focus point shifted to a monitor in the middle of the array, a young woman of Middle Eastern appearance interviewing a cabbie on the streets of New York.

"Miss, what's to say? It's open season on the one percent. It's bombs and guns in New York. All the VIPs are disappearing or going nuts in Congress. You know what I think? I think it's the antichrist. I think it's the goddamned end of the fucking world. First we're gonna eat each other and everything's gonna fall apart. Then all those angels with fire and lightning are gonna come down and fry us. You know what I'm gonna do tonight? I'm gonna go to church. I'm gonna light some goddamned candles and pray my ass off that God's got a place for me in heaven."

The man rolled up his window and the cab sped off. The reporter turned to the camera, her face troubled, her words stuttered.

"This is Maryam Tavazoie, Al Jazeera America, in New York."

All the monitors went dark and the figure in the chair brooded in silence for several moments. From the faint afterglow of the screens, a weak line reflected off a hard surface.

A toothless smirk.

OCTOBER 21

14

EYE IN THE SKY

Angel Lightfoote poked her head around the doorframe. "John, the kids—they're not all right."

Savas sat behind his desk and held up his index finger with one hand and cradled the landline receiver in the other. The digits of his free hand also tapped onto a cell phone as he texted.

"Right. Ronald, look, I have to go. Thanks for the report and I'll share it with the group." He hung up the phone.

"Forensics?"

Savas nodded. "Yes. Residues found at the car and boat bombings match. Synthetics. Nothing special that we can trace."

She nodded, the fluorescent lighting reflecting brightly off her scalp. "Come with me. We need to talk."

~

FIVE MINUTES later they were exiting an elevator and stepping onto the basement floor. Savas smiled as he looked around the maze of monitors and racks of computers.

"Love what you're doing with the place, Angel. Looks more and more like the Bat Cave."

Lightfoote gestured toward several rows of servers. "That's the Hernandez pile, all Manuel's machines that can still keep up. Most of the connections to law enforcement and other agencies—not to mention the satellite uplinks—are now ported to the Great Wall." Her hand swept toward a much large bank of computers racked in metallic girders, floor to ceiling.

"Glad to see the money's well spent."

Lightfoote shook her head. "Everything's been augmented, enhanced. More aggressive than the old crises center. *Militarized.* It's cyberwarfare out there now." Lightfoote sat at a long table with several monitors. "We've been stalking both of Senator Moss' girls. One is at UCSF, the other Georgetown."

He sat down next to her, watching windows displaying two young women's faces. Video footage streamed and maps and other surveillance software recorded locations and other information. "So there's a problem, or I wouldn't be down here. Disappearance?"

"No, it's a lot more subtle. The women are fine. So far. No sign of anything on their social media, personal emails, or phone conversations. We correlated their routines to video surveillance footage over the last few months. Nothing to indicate that they are functioning under duress." She turned toward Savas and winked, the piercings running across her face inches from him. "But we're playing with some inside information."

She cleared the active windows and opened several CCTV montages displaying footage from numerous cameras. There seemed little relationship between the locations, angles, or time the video was captured. Lightfoote stared at one intensely and then hit a key, freezing the playback.

"There. See, that's Anna Moss, right there, backpack, ponytail. She usually takes this route on Wednesdays. This is footage from two weeks ago. Look there," she indicated on the screen.

Savas squinted. A dark blur was above and behind the student, but he could not make out what it was. "What is it?"

She stared at him with her eyes angled upward, nearly rolling them. "Watch." Frame by frame, she advanced the footage. The Moss daughter moved jerkily as if caught by a strobe light, pedestrians and cars around her as well.

And so did the blur. Savas felt his pulse quicken. "It's tracking her," he whispered. "It's a drone."

Lightfoote smiled. "He can be taught! Watch closely. It shadows her up the street and then, *there*, lifts off into the air and is gone. We've got hundreds of hours of footage of the sisters. That let us catch the drones in ten or fifteen events. No doubts, John. We've tried to use image enhancement but didn't get much. We're also taking known drone models and creating cross-sections at different angles and using image recognition software to score similarity. But whatever the models, these women are being stalked. By drones."

"That's it, then," he said. "Imagine the kinds of photos you could get with these things. The kind of photos that when sent to a parent with the right note attached would petrify them."

Lightfoote nodded. "And you don't even have to put organic assets in play or touch the ground around the targets."

"Wouldn't someone notice these things?"

"Probably, but what would they think? There are kids' toys as big as some of these, and in several states law enforcement groups are beginning to use drones. And whoever is behind this isn't stupid. They don't hang around long. So, somebody sees one? Then what? Before they can do much it's gone. Not much to report without sounding like a UFO nut."

"No wonder she jumped when I asked about drones. She's a smart woman. She would have connected the bombing and these drones shadowing her daughters. And it's almost a certainty that Craig from Goldman was calling her about her vote flip-flops. If it hadn't been for the other CEO murders and kidnappings, I might have thought he was killed for that."

He stood up and placed his hands on his hips. "That's great work, Angel. You've linked the killing to the threats on Congress. With the meltdown there yesterday, it looks like she was the canary in the coal mine. We can use this to pressure the rest, make them open up about the blackmail."

"You'd think that the victims would have noticed their peers' behavior. Teamed up. Gotten some crowd bravery and brought the blackmail to the attention of someone by now."

Savas nodded. "Maybe. But it just happened. They probably thought they were the only ones, working in a panic, tunnel visioned and focused on whatever personal nightmare was threatening to consume their life."

Lightfoote stood up as well, continuing to stare at the blurry drone images on her monitors. "Drones of all sizes exist. Some able to handle large payloads. Some able to be mounted with weapons. And they're invisible to radar. They could fly right up to the president with a bar of Semtex strapped to them. Or pop over to the Indian Point nuclear plant. They can go anywhere, John. They can photograph people's bedroom windows, follow their kids, spy on the routes of world leaders. I'd be worried if I were you."

A chill ran through him. "I am, Angel. I think we need to find out who is making drones in this country, what they're making, and who the hell they are selling them to. Look for patterns in purchase and shipment. *Anything*."

"Already beginning that search. What I'm worried about is that our drone-master is too smart for that. He wouldn't have left such an easy trail, but would likely buy them in small amounts and change shipping locations, payment methods. Or under the table purchases from dealers who aren't listed in the Better Business Bureau. That's what I would do."

"You know what Angel," said Savas, eyeing her suspiciously. "You are frighteningly good at thinking like a psychopath."

Her face darkened in a manner that unsettled Savas. She spoke hoarsely. "Thanks, John. It's good to be noticed."

"Well, I want you to keep doing that. In fact, you have my explicit permission to go full madwoman down here and follow any idea you think might be interesting. Don't tell me when you fail. Don't tell me missteps. Just do it. Find out what in the name of all that's holy is happening."

15

COUP D'ETAT

"No fucking *way*, man."

Two young men sat in the middle of a nearly empty warehouse, a dense clustering of high-tech equipment forming an isolated island in the middle of the space. Three to four rows of nested black towers formed a maze around them, the cabinets housing shelf upon shelf of computer banks. A thick series of cables and power cords snaked across the dusty cement floor like an obscene vasculature bringing nutrients to a gestating embryo. In the center of the maze was a set of tables holding five or six large flat screen monitors.

"No way, Chen."

The contrasting pair sat in front of the monitors, typing on keyboards, staring at a scrolling data stream. Chen was dressed in fatigues, close-cropped hair topping off a thin and angular frame, a tight tank-top revealing tattoos painted across his arms and back. He sat upright, tense, tapping the screen in front of him.

"I'm not shitting you, Dave, these are *his* accounts! Offshore, unregulated. It took me this whole week to get to them."

Dave swept his long, unruly hair out of his face, a tangled mass of brown and blond, greasy and unwashed. His general appearance was slovenly, and he slouched forward gazing at the screen. He shook his head in disbelief.

"Can't believe Fawkes left a security hole."

"Well, he's not running the bank servers, now is he?" said Chen, his voice defiant.

"Five hundred million? I mean, *what the fuck?*"

Chen shook his head. "I dunno, man. Something's up with this. Something really not cool."

"Yeah, how does Fawkes get half a billion dollars? You think it's related to all this shit going down?"

"Look at the withdrawals!" Chen scrolled through the banking records. "It's like five million here, ten million here. Restore Our Future. American Crossroads. Strong America Now."

"Sounds like student council assholes," Dave said, upturning a bag of chips into his mouth, his words garbled.

"They're conservative SuperPacs, you fuck."

"SuperPacs?"

Chen rolled his eyes. "You're such a fucking pothead, Dave."

"Amen and praise Jesus, you bet!" said Dave, smiling.

"Whatever. Look, there are transfers to Europe, China, India. It's like he's some multinational! These transfers are totally laundered. No transaction codes, no IDs, nothing!"

"Ain't no money for nothing, dude."

Chen nodded. "Something is *really* not cool here."

A loud scraping noise startled the pair. They spun in their chairs and looked behind them, through an opening in the maze of the server farm. The large door of the warehouse had been yanked open, and three men walked into the cavernous space. In the middle was a young man, thin, nearly gaunt, dressed casually in a black T-shirt and jeans. His short-cropped black hair and pencil-thin goatee were offset by a pair of shaded smart glasses. He constantly fiddled with a smartphone affixed to his belt. Flanking him on either side were two much larger, muscled men. They wore nondescript business attire, their eyes hidden behind black sunglasses. Their expressions were indecipherable.

"Shit," said Chen under his breath, spinning slightly to position his hand over the keyboard and enter several strokes. The windows on the screen disappeared. He turned back quickly to the approaching men as they neared. The three stopped a few feet in front of the hacker pair, silence lingering for several moments.

"Yo, Fawkes!" said Dave awkwardly. "What's this? Fucking Terminator Ten?" His smiled floundered against the stony gazes of the three men.

Hands continuously tapping the smartphone, Fawkes appeared to stare straight ahead at something outside the room. "You were always such a fucking waste, Dave. You could've been the best black hat to ever crawl out of 4chan. You know, when that shit-hole was actually worth something."

Dave flipped him the bird. "Up yours. I still am."

Fawkes ignored him. "Chen. It's too bad you had to be so curious. Killed a lot of cats. I thought you'd be more grateful after I gifted you this little playground."

Chen licked his lips, glancing between Fawkes and the two men on his sides. "What's up, Fawkes? We're just hanging."

Fawkes finally took off his glasses, his gray eyes burning into Chen. "I've had a tick on you for weeks, Chen. I know you've been poking around the offshore accounts."

Chen sat utterly still. The large room was silent except for the constant hum of the server farm around them. Dave broke the eerie stillness.

"So the fuck what, man? It's not like you haven't hacked your way through a hundred accounts."

"But those are *my* accounts, Dave. Accounts that are too important to be messed with. Or for anyone to know about."

"Fawkes, what's going on?" asked Chen, his face grave. "Hundreds of millions? What are you up to? What's with the bodyguards?"

Fawkes laughed. "You stupid fucks still don't get it. You actually think a hundred million is a lot! Try seven-hundred *trillion*—that's the size of the derivative market. Did you know that? And it's *all* virtual money." He gestured vaguely to the walls of computers around them. "It doesn't exist except inside investment bank computers and people's very active imaginations. When things are bytes in compiled data structures, they are *meant* to be hacked. It's fucking righteous deeds." He laughed. "I've got *trillions* of dollars, you clueless ass. Those accounts you stumbled on were early, poorly secured penetration tests."

Chen blinked. "Trillions? That's not possible. What's the game, Fawkes? This doesn't make sense. We were against all this stuff!"

Fawkes fit his glasses back on, his voice growing slightly distanced. "I don't have the time to explain to you losers. You never had the balls, Chen. None of you did. We hacked our way to the truth, but it didn't set us free. We found out their dirty little secrets, and all of you panicked. *Pissed your fucking pants!* You wouldn't dare do what had to be done. You hit *MasterCard* or outed bad cops."

Dave and Chen looked at each other anxiously. Chen spoke again. "What has to be done?"

Fawkes began fiddling with his smartphone, staring off into space. With his other hand, he lifted a black and white object, a tight string hanging off the back. Placing it on his head, he pulled downward, the elastic string tightening around the back of his head, the object fitting tightly over his face: a mask of a smirking man stared back at them.

"What the fuck?" whispered Dave.

Fawkes motioned toward the two men beside him, who nodded. His voice was muffled. "Core dump, bros. The system software is too corrupted. Time for a reboot." He turned his back on them and began to walk away.

Chen shifted nervously in his chair as the large forms of the bodyguards approached the two hackers. "My God, it *is* you! All of this!" His voice rose dramatically in pitch. "Are you insane? Do you understand what will happen?" Silence. "That's not what we were about! No one reboots the fucking world!"

Fawkes stopped and sighed, his fiddling paused. The mask turned back toward them. "I do. And nothing is going to get in the way of that, not even Anonymous. *I'm* Anonymous now—what you all should have been." He laughed. "You'd be amazed what you can do with a trillion dollars."

Fawkes resumed his distracted gait and headed for the exit. The bodyguards who had entered with him reached into their jackets and removed pistols. Bulging suppressors were attached to the ends.

"Ah, man, no way, no way, no way! This isn't happening!" cried Dave, his eyes large. He stood up trembling in his chair, looking around the wall of computer cabinets hemming them in. Chen didn't move, but simply closed his eyes.

A sudden scream ripped through the warehouse, punctuated by a series of sharp spits. The following silence was disrupted only by the echoing clap of shoes on hard concrete.

BEFORE:
THE ANONYMOUS EVENT COMMISSION

DEPOSITION IN THE MATTER OF:
UNITED STATES ARMED FORCES SPECIAL TRIBUNAL, Plaintiff,
versus
JOHN SAVAS, Defendant
Case No. M120039E-007X

Continued DEPOSITION OF:
Jean Paul Rideout

CBD: And so this was the first hard evidence that drones were being used?

MR. RIDEOUT: Right. But we all believed it was drones from the start. Nothing else fit.

[REDACTED]: And yet your division, led by Savas, still refused to share this information with other FBI divisions and national agencies.

MR. RIDEOUT: Refused? We didn't refuse anything. This was all unfolding in real time. Do you understand how that works? We'd barely get a chance to breathe before the next shock wave hit. We had barely just put this together. And the evidence wasn't going to win any court cases. I'm sure John would have been happy to share more. In fact that's what we did!

CBD: When he contacted NSA?

MR. RIDEOUT: Exactly. Angel made a breakthrough.

[REDACTED]: This is when Lightfoote broke numerous cybercrimes laws and released dangerous viral codes into the internet?

Mr. RIDEOUT: Worms. They were worms. Yeah, damn. She sure as hell did. And it worked! But the damned NSA just blew us off, right when the whole thing went to shit.

OCTOBER 22

16

MADWOMAN

It was past midnight, and the basement at the FBI building was staffed only by three people. Two women and a man hunched over monitors as the steady buzz of computer servers churned around them. The bald woman stared across at the other two, her expression grave.

"Well, John, there was something about 'explicit permission to go full madwoman.'"

"I didn't know you were going to turn everything back on us!"

"It's a logical byproduct of the search algorithms."

Cohen placed her hand on Savas' shoulder and yawned. "Can we just have one night without another crisis?"

Lightfoote stood up, a short tank exposing her midriff and rows of chiseled abdominal muscles. She walked over to the banks of servers and ran her hands over them like a nurse would a sick child.

"That meeting at the NYU computer science department spooked me. They weren't coming clean with how bad things were, and what was said was bad enough. I knew then we couldn't trust any of the other agencies to handle this. Worst of all was the NSA. They know the most and share the least." She patted the metal shelving holding the individual units of the server farm. "So, assuming the worst, I let loose some worms of my own."

"What?" said Savas, his eyes wide.

She turned her green eyes toward them. "*Full* madwoman, remember?"

"Yeah, breaking Federal law?"

"Well, that's all not going to matter much longer anyway if we don't get this under control soon."

Savas swiveled in his chair to face Lightfoote. "Angel, what are you talking about?"

"My little wigglies reported back. It's *everywhere*, John. Gone fucking viral is the phrase. All my babies," she leaned her head against the machines, "they're all infected. We're infected—FBI is infected."

"Damn." Savas rubbed his temples. "Okay, so what—"

"The whole goddamned world is infected! This thing has simultaneously exploited every known security whole in the underlying operating systems. It's like a MIRV missile for the internet with multiple warheads. Each one hits something, somewhere, in every system. And that's all it needs. One weakness. Then the worm is in."

Cohen whispered softly. "What is it doing?"

"Nothing yet. Nothing active. Or, whatever it's done was done before we began monitoring it and it has covered its tracks. There's a bunch of encrypted code that comes along with the thing in every infestation. That's got to be the heart of it. Whatever it's up to, I'd bet it's contained there."

"Can you get into it?" asked Cohen.

"Not yet. But I'm worried that when I do, it won't be straightforward. Whoever did this has made an attack that is sophisticated beyond anything the internet has ever seen. The code isn't complete or standardized."

"I don't understand," said Savas.

"Those encrypted modules? They're really diverse. Not one the same size on each system. I think it's distributed. It's like a P2P system where pieces of the file to be shared are stored all over the internet in different places. When you download your pirated film, the software at the end assembles a composite file from hundreds, sometimes thousands of independent file elements. *That's* what's going on here. The worm has spread to tens of thousands, probably millions of computers. Each infection is one of a large set of different worms—let's call them strains like for viruses. Each strain carries a different piece of the code."

"Then if we can kill some of the strains, it can't put the full program back together and we stop it?" asked Savas.

Cohen shook her head. "If I understand this, then each strain will have thousands of copies of itself all around the world. We'd have to hunt every one of them down."

Lightfoote nodded. "Exactly. It's too distributed. It's like having a million backups on different servers where literally every computer is a potential backup system once infected. We'll never stop it that way."

"Then how?" asked Savas.

Lightfoote shook her head. "I don't know."

"Okay, then what does that code do when assembled?"

"I don't know that either. I haven't cracked any of the encryptions, and there are already hundreds of different packages I've found with the worms. We need the NSA computers to be working full time on this."

"You think they know?"

"Yes. Definitely. They're poking around infected systems, just like I did. So many computers are poorly secured, it's easy to get into them and find things out. They *have* to know by now, or they shouldn't have the keys to their computer arsenal."

Savas stood up. "Then it's about damn time they opened up and worked with us. Tomorrow morning we'll get this moving."

Cohen grabbed his arm. "Are you sure about that? I think you might be overestimating the influence the FBI has on the NSA. They're so frighteningly close to Big Brother, we're not going to have much pull."

Lightfoote nodded. "And they aren't going to look at my little enterprise as anything remotely useful compared to the fleet of processors they have. From a certain perspective, they're right."

"So, what then? We wait here helplessly for the NSA to formulate a cure and perhaps share it with us? If this thing shuts us down, we're crippled to investigate the killings and abductions, anything at all really. We can't remain that vulnerable!"

"Try the NSA, John," said Cohen, walking up to Lightfoote. "Meanwhile, I suggest that you leave the leash off Angel. Don't rescind your madwoman decree." Cohen took Lightfoote's shoulders in her hands, squaring up to face her. "Angel, why don't you see what you can do about this thing. Assume we're on our own. Assume it's a matter of life and death."

Savas nodded. Lightfoote stared between them and then back at her server.

"Okay. But be careful what you ask for."

17

HEADLINE NEWS

CHAOS ROILS WALL STREET AS WORLD MARKETS SHUTTERED

By Christina Patrikia, *Washington Post*

In an unprecedented turn of events, the major world stock exchanges were forced to suspend trading as markets oscillated wildly and company fortunes were obliterated and made in instants.

Beginning almost immediately after the opening bell was rung at the New York Stock Exchange, and despite normal after-hours trading the night before, chaos hit the floor as share prices of everything from Fortune 500 companies to bundled options on the futures market dropped or increased thousands of percentage points in seconds. The changes swung back and forth, even on individual stocks, at the speed of the electronic trading computers.

"The system went haywire," said Brian Gunter, an analyst from Brookmans. "It was faster than the human mind could follow. All in electronic trading, across the board stock dumps and purchases, seemingly at random."

It appears that automated trade-halting safeguards designed to prevent massive stock fluctuations either did not function as expected or were unable to handle the volume and nature of the spurious trades.

"We are assuming a major malfunction," said Gordon Jones, a technical support specialist working for the NASDAQ exchange. "Either the safeguards to prevent market meltdowns failed or something more systematic occurred. With current software, trades are executed in less than a half a millionth of a second. Feedback loops at those speeds can lead to major problems on time scales human beings can't react to. It's a very nonlinear system."

While there had been previous scares such as the rogue program from Knight Capital that nearly halted trading in 2012, no glitch in the now-ubiquitous trading computers had caused anything approaching what took place today. Representatives from the world exchanges have been in conference calls since trading was halted in the early morning.

Washington Post financial correspondent Angela Kong explained: "World leaders are involved. It is an unusual crisis. You have a majority of the largest companies in the world now worth pennies on paper, or rather, worth nothing in the digital systems storing their valuations. We're talking IBM, Apple, Google, GE—you name it. They're wiped out. Meanwhile, there are a host of nothing companies, green energy, solar, drug companies in India that have instantly grown to the size of Google. It's economic chaos. There is talk of a market reset."

Kong quoted several sources within the administration stating that, once the market software had been fixed, there were plans to resume trading at the prices on shares at which the exchanges had opened this morning. The move would be unprecedented, and is not without vocal critics in the government and private sector. However, consensus seemed to be building that only through such action could an unparalleled market collapse be staved off.

In an ominous repeat, the malfunction of the trading software that led to the trading halt in the US markets spread to every exchange across the world. One by one, as each of the major exchanges opened, chaos ensued and trading was stopped. Markets in Asia have not yet opened, but already the Nikkei and Shanghai Stock Exchange are being prepared for an unscheduled shut down to prevent further chaos in the world financial system.

First term senator and political firebrand Nathan Schelot—who rose to power on an election in California rocked by accusations of fraud—was vocal on Capitol Hill following the Press Secretary's minimal statement on the crisis at noon.

"And is this the leadership we need in a time of turmoil? Now you see the product of a runaway, capitalistic system. When will we regulate the bidding bots, the electronic microsecond trading that has turned our once human economy into a cyborg market? Robots take our jobs and now they are taking over our corporate structures. We are not in control anymore, and if something isn't done soon, everything this nation has built will come crashing down."

BUGS IN AUTOMATED WRITING SYSTEMS FLOOD ONLINE NEWS

By Anna Zeabee, *Wired*

They have been heralded for years as the next wave in machine displacement of human workers. They are the programs that have been written to produce news articles, financial reports, sports summaries, even law briefs. Light years ahead of the clumsy text and speech generators of a generation ago, they are now increasingly used by all the major media outlets to fill the seemingly insatiable appetite for online content.

They are even the seeds of new businesses, as Image Council's Jeff Philips has deluged the publishing industry with manuals and fact guides created only by computer algorithms that write books based on the contents of databases and fact lists.

But today a major bug has turned these time-saving tools into seemingly independent intelligences as thousands of unapproved and propagandistic news stories swamped online publishing sites, hijacking a significant fraction of the news reported.

While the chaos on Wall Street was the story of the day, for several hours the *New York Times* sported a headline criticizing income inequality in a thousand-word manifesto.

"It's clear that we have some hackers playing with our system," said Executive editor Jerry Wilbur. "The writing seems to be similar to taking a fourth grader's dictionary and throwing it into a dishwasher. Nevertheless, it took some time to pull it."

Despite the high profile nature of the breach, the *Times* was hardly alone. Most of the major news feeds and even news flagship websites were drowned in a cascade of articles focused on financial statistics and world economic problems. The automated systems adopted a Marxist bent that seemed funny to many except for the problems caused.

"Income inequality? Corporate welfare? Lobbying and money? All very interesting to some left-wingers and it was cute to see the *Wall Street Journal*'s editorial page moaning about the evils of capitalism," said a source at a competing publication. "But this shut down our news systems as well. This was a global problem that cost man-hours and will total in the millions to fix. We're still flushing these bot-articles out. They haven't stopped. Only when the companies running them shut things down will it end. Meanwhile, we're unplugging from their services. Right now, they're drowning us."

18

MASKED EXECUTIONS

Evening had fallen on the crowds in Times Square, but the streets were bathed in electric hues from multiple monitors displaying ads and streaming video from numerous locations. Horns blared as cars piled along curbs waiting for an opportunity to turn into adjacent streets through the flood of pedestrians. Some walked in groups. Many seemed tuned out and into their digital devices. All were dressed in jackets to ward off the late October chill.

One by one, those walking the streets began to slow down, staring at their phones or tablets. Others began to crane their necks upward, interrupting their conversations, staring puzzled at the glowing behemoths of dancing images around them. Within a minute, nearly all the motion in the square had come to a halt, and the blaring of horns increased ten-fold as roadways were completely blocked.

Like dominoes, all the monitors in the square flipped jerkily to the same static image: a circle with a globe depicted in grid lines, leaves of a plant along the sides, the figure of a headless man in a black and white suit with a question mark over him.

Out of a window, a taxi driver stuck his head and gazed up at the bizarre tiling of images across the buildings around him. He tugged on a baseball cap.

"What the hell?"

~

"JOHN, you'd better come with me."

Cohen stood in his doorway, a sharp glint in her eyes. Savas prepared for the worst. "Another attack?"

She shook her head. "Something different. But I think related. Media across the country, maybe worldwide, is being hijacked. It's cable, network, online streaming sites like YouTube and Hulu. It's systematic."

"Systematic? The worm?"

"Don't know. But this sure sounds like something it could be up to."

Savas sprang from his chair and followed her into the floor's common room. Normally a place for coffee and a break from work, the small space was packed as agents and staff stared up at a flat-panel screen. A strange black-and-white image of a headless man in a suit took the place of all programming on nearly all stations. Savas and Cohen stood outside the door looking in.

A man's voice came up over the din of buzzing conversation. "That's Anonymous!"

Cohen turned to Savas. "He's right! I knew I had seen it before."

"Anonymous? Those kids who do social justice hacking?"

The voice of Lightfoote startled them from behind. "Kids, maybe. No one really knows who they are, how they organize, where they are. A few caught were high schoolers. Others older. Some established, even corporate. They're everyone and no one. The name really does mean something. Unknown, distributed anarchy. Probably why they never achieved anything really big."

"Until now, maybe," said Savas as he started at the disconcerting image.

"Uh oh, there it goes," said Lightfoote.

The screen pixelated horribly, and then locked onto another video feed. The crowds at FBI, in Times Square, and in millions of homes across the nation stared at two rows of chairs in a dark room. Harsh lighting fell directly on those seated in the chairs, the space behind them and to their sides too dark for any details to be made out. The men and women were tied to the seats, their arms and legs lashed with rope, gags in their mouths, and terrified expressions on their faces as their eyes darted.

"Oh, my God," whispered Cohen. "The abductions."

Savas felt his stomach drop as he began to recognize faces. The CEO of GE. Congressmen. The Chair of the Federal Reserve. Luminaries in business, finance, and politics. What the hell was happening?

Lightfoote spoke. "I'm going to the basement. They've compromised major digital distribution hubs. I bet it's the worm. We might be able to catch it in action and see what it looks like!" She darted from the crowd and headed toward the stairway.

A mask appeared in front of the screen. Black-and-white, smirking, a thin goatee etched across the upper lip and chin. Savas had seen it before. It was a symbol of underground resistance to established powers—the mask of Guy Fawkes.

"Greetings sheeple of America, Europe, and beyond," came a digitally distorted voice. "We are Anonymous and today is a day of judgment."

The masked speaker stepped back from the camera. The figure was of indeterminate frame and size, dressed in a black suit and tie. It walked confidently toward the double row of hostages. Their eyes looked hopeless and panicked.

"Already we have targeted some of the worst criminals in our malignant society. Robber barons, plutocrats who pull the strings of the drugged masses. The architects of a feudal world increasingly of a few elements of royalty standing on the backs of millions of slaves."

"Jesus," said Savas. He picked up his mobile phone and dialed. "Yeah, Angel. You got *anything* on this? Location?" He grimaced. "I *know* there hasn't been time! But what I'm seeing—it's *not* good. I think these people are in danger."

The masked man continued. "Today, as a taste of things to come, we again pass judgment on a group of criminals whose status in society is the only thing separating them from the mafia. Because in their greed they have killed like common thugs."

He slapped the face of a man next to him. Savas recognized the captive as CEO O'Kelly.

The masked man continued. "They have poisoned our world, our rivers, our air, our very bodies as they profit. They have drilled and dug and burned and buried. They have denied health and home and peace to billions so they could luxuriate in ten thousand times more than they could ever require."

Several shapes in dark clothing moved into the view frame of the camera. They wore Guy Fawkes masks. They carried automatic weapons.

"Oh, Christ," whispered Savas. Murmurs ran through the crowd at FBI.

Several of the hostages in the chairs let loose gagged screams, twisting and wrenching their arms and legs in attempts to free themselves. Others seemed resigned, staring forward blankly.

"Today, we reject the weakness of fools. Of the failed Occupy Movement. Of the false Anonymous. Of corrupt nation-states who claim to serve the people but serve only their masters. Today we reject the foul words of the pundits, the professors, the activists, and the politicians who spout lies about change as they bathe in the status quo. Today, a real change comes. Today, we begin to put down a sick and broken system."

There was a pause. He nodded toward the gunmen. "Remember! Remember the fifth of November. This time there will be no providence of God."

The men raised their weapons. Shouts came from some of the FBI onlookers.

Cohen turned to Savas. "John, tell me he isn't—"

Bursts of light erupted from the muzzles of the automatic weapons, blurs of static from the flatscreen. Puffs of fabric and blood exploded outward from the clothes of the hostages, their forms shaking from the projectile impacts and reflex action, muffled screams bursting from their gagged lips.

Then silence.

The murderers with guns were gone. Only the bodies of the dead stared back into the camera with vacant eyes or tortured final expressions. The grinning plastic of the man with the Guy Fawkes mask approached the camera, until the mocking face filled the entire screen.

"We are the *real* Anonymous. We are indeed Legion. We do not forgive. We do not forget. Expect us."

The video feed switched to a set of multiple views arranged in an array across the screen. In each case, the camera floated above the ground at what seemed to be disparate locations, darkness punctured by the lights of cars and buildings in the cities below.

The viewpoints descended. With increasing speed the ground dashed upward toward the viewer as the land sped by underneath, buildings whipping past. A disorienting collection of sub-screens careened wildly together.

But there was guided purpose to the movements. A zeroing in towards defined goals. Familiar and famous objects swam into view. The Capitol. The New York Stock Exchange. The Citibank building.

Savas gasped. "Oh, my God, Rebecca. They're drones. They're drones flying in for the kill."

The screens went black. Outside the FBI windows, light pierced the darkness. The crowd turned toward the flash, an orange fireball climbing in the evening sky from Midtown. An explosion rattled the windows of their building.

OCTOBER 23

BEFORE:
THE ANONYMOUS EVENT COMMISSION

DEPOSITION IN THE MATTER OF:
UNITED STATES ARMED FORCES SPECIAL TRIBUNAL, Plaintiff,
versus
JOHN SAVAS, Defendant
Case No. M120039E-007X

CONTINUED DEPOSITION OF:
John Savas

[REDACTED]: Again we remind you that you are under oath, Mr. Savas. You understand that this is not a Federal or Civilian court, that the jurisdiction of this case is considered outside the Constitution and to be part of the armed forces in a service in time of war and public danger?

Mr. SAVAS: I have been made to understand that all too clearly, [REDACTED].

[REDACTED]: Please answer the question posed. Do you understand the law as it pertains to you in this tribunal?

MR. SAVAS: I forfeit my rights to the 5th Amendment and others. No grand jury or due process. And I can be compelled to be a witness against myself.

[REDACTED]: Counsel may continue the questioning.

CBD: Mr. Savas, let's pick up where we left off yesterday, shall we?

MR. SAVAS: Or why don't you go fuck yourself, instead?

CBD: Cooperation will save you time and mitigate further inquiry.

MR. SAVAS: Inquiry? Is that the latest term? I thought it was enhanced interrogation.

CBD: [Inaudible] Would you please just continue your account from yesterday?

MR. SAVAS: Remind me. My brain is a mush. Isolation for a month, sleep dep. Just staring at gray walls. Messes with your mind. So will near drowning.

CBD: The executions.

MR. SAVAS: Right. Jesus, yes. The executions. [Inaudible] Live and HDTV for all to see. Well, as horrible as that all was, it was our first real break.

CBD: How so?

MR. SAVAS: The worm. Angel's spyware reported back. The television hijack was tied directly to it. So, there it was. What we had been pursuing as unrelated cases, the murders, the kidnappings, and the financial meltdown. It was all tied together by the worm. By Anonymous. It was part of the same thing. And it all made sense.

CBD: What made sense?

MR. SAVAS: I mean it all fit together. Anonymous had set its eyes on bringing down the world financial system. It was fighting on several fronts from the virus wrecking the markets to the drones killing financial tycoons. The blackmail of congressmen changing laws was another front. It was incredible, really. Amazingly orchestrated. Diabolical genius.

[REDACTED]: You sound inspired.

MR. SAVAS: You sound like a goddamned Nazi. Inspired? Well, we all had to be. The world had been caught with its pants down and effectively castrated. Anonymous had played us like fools.

CBD: And you are so sure it was the hacker group Anonymous? Who was their leader again?

MR. SAVAS: I've told you already, there isn't one Anonymous. There are legions. It's more an idea than an organization. And Fawkes, well, he was the inevitable, the instability that takes over any distributed authority.

[REDACTED]: Fawkes. This is the one found in your office. That you claim you caught and who single-handedly masterminded the Event?

MR. SAVAS: Yes. It was his worm. His plan. His signal that was to bring it all down once and for all. But I didn't know that then, when he murdered them all.

[REDACTED]: And that is when you contacted Lopez?

MR. SAVAS: That is correct.

[REDACTED]: Can you tell us why you thought it prudent, let alone legal, to search for and enlist the aid of the nation's most notorious outlaws? Murderers of hundreds, including some of the most important persons in our nation?

MR. SAVAS: Because I knew they weren't murderers. I knew that they had been framed.

[REDACTED]: This is ridiculous. You only reveal your own involvement with these terrorists!

CBD: This is not a trial, [REDACTED]!

[REDACTED]: There isn't going to be a trial.

CBD: This is a deposition and we are instructed to take it. [Inaudible] May I continue? Thank you.

CBD: We will ascertain how you knew the pair later. For now, can you tell us please how they got involved?

MR. SAVAS: We had setup a safe house for them.

[REDACTED]: Who is we?

MR. SAVAS: You'll have to waterboard me some more to get near that. Let's just say there are many forces at work here that you don't know about. Forces that believe in this nation. What it used to be, anyway.

CBD: Mr. Savas, look. As your counsel I am trying to help you, but you are making that a challenging assignment. Can you help this panel understand why you would bring in two wanted terrorists and murderers?

MR. SAVAS: After we put together the bigger picture, when I saw where Anonymous was headed, I knew then what was at stake. So did my team.

CBD: And what was at stake, Mr. Savas?

MR. SAVAS: Civilization itself.

19

MARTIAL LAW

Chaos stormed through New York and the world.

After the feed from Anonymous, network programming returned to something quite different than normal. Broadcasters replayed the carnage over and over, whipping themselves and the public into a frenzy.

At FBI, Savas had steered his people back to work. They would be slogging through the night. Schedules, family, *health* would suffer, but until the crisis could be controlled, he didn't see any other choice. His phone rang constantly. From his superiors came a barrage of commands. Most of these came from above as the governmental apparatus went into war mode. Contacts and numerous agencies checked in with him, provided small pieces of useless information, and asked for favors of investigation and protection in return. He had nothing to give. His staff was already depleted even before the televised mass assassination.

In the middle of the chaos, he received a message on his private cell. He stared at the number. It made sense. In all that was happening, now was one of the greater periods of danger from a government eating itself, going too far, forgetting its principles. Now would be a time for the Watchmen to call.

The group had formed during the Bush years when some in the FBI and CIA had grown concerned about the powers the executive branch and other governmental agencies had begun to assume under antiterrorism laws.

Under the increasingly paranoid Obama administration, they had only redoubled their efforts to exert a more sane response to threats. Indefinite detention and torture were one thing, but secretive decisions for assassination of Americans without trial, endless spying on citizens by governmental organizations—for some of them, it had gone too far. With the national scandal of the Priest and Whore last year, they had finally pooled their meager resources and acted. And thus had Gabriel been created.

"Alice. To what do I owe the pleasure?" His smile faded. "What? Are you sure? *When?*" Savas looked around the floor. "Jesus. What will that mean? How far is the decree?" He nodded scribbling on a notepad. "Understood. Right. Thank you."

He put the phone away and stared forward, seeing nothing except images of the city in his mind. A New York surrounded by military vehicles.

Savas jumped from his chair and exited his office, finding Cohen on the floor. She was coordinating with several agents on the requests—or rather *demands*—for even more of his staff to be reassigned to protective functions for VIPs. Very soon, they would be running Intel 1 on pure air.

"Everybody listen up," he said, cutting into the middle of their conversation. "Very serious newsflash. I just got a call in from some sources, reliable ones. The president is going to declare martial law."

Cohen blinked. "*Martial law?*"

Savas nodded. "Within the hour. In the city for sure, maybe the whole tri-state area. They're panicking. I guess I understand that, although I don't know how locking down the city is going to help much. They must know about the worm, and now with additional threats of terrorist bombings and killings, they needed to act. They decided to lock everything down."

"Anonymous isn't stuck walking the streets of New York, John!" shouted Cohen. "This won't achieve anything except to cause a real panic. People are going to start bolting from the city."

"They won't be able to."

"And you know how that's going to turn out, right?"

"God, I hope not. We can't let this panic us, too, okay? At the root of this is a core organization, people orchestrating everything. If we can find that core, flush out or corner those people, we can put a stop to this. And for that we need—"

"Here, Commander," said Lightfoote, panting from a run.

"We need Angel."

"It's probably going to be both New York and DC," said Lightfoote, catching her breath. "I'm intercepting a lot of chatter. People aren't using secure lines. They're freaking. They've also got a lot of the Cabinet and Congress going underground, presuming continual threats."

"Word on the Capitol?"

Lightfoote nodded. "You've seen the footage on the news. Main entrance and steps are blown to hell and back. Few were hurt at this time of night, but the point sure was made. The building is structurally sound, however. It would take a lot more firepower than these little drones can carry to seriously damage it."

"And what if they have bigger drones?" asked Cohen.

Angel bit her lip. "Then it could be a lot worse. But the scurrying of governmental staff is creating power vacuums. Basically, we're moving to a crisis mode unlike anything except during the Cold War. Not even 9/11 approached this. The apparatus is gearing up for siege."

"This is not going to end well," muttered Savas. "Update me on the worm."

"It had to get visible, and wow, what a beauty." Cohen arched her eyebrow. "Seriously, Rebecca, this is the Michelangelo of hackers. The damn thing *self-assembled* from thousands of computers around the world on some mysterious signal."

"Self-assembled?" asked Savas.

"Yes! We thought that it was hiding on various computers. Only *parts* of it were. Like the distributed code I mentioned? I didn't realize that the *entire worm* was networked. In other words, it doesn't exist as a single piece of code on *any* computer, but like a neural network that's the sum of a bunch of minor worms on millions of computers. It's incredible. Powerful. Unstoppable."

"Unstoppable?" said Cohen.

"Well, *I* don't know how to stop it. I don't think anybody would. It's unprecedented. It's a distributed AI that's taking over the distributed brain we call the internet."

"But it was activated with the Anonymous broadcast?" asked Savas.

"It *ran* the damn broadcast, John! I tried to get inside the code that activated, but it quickly detected my efforts and erased itself from my computer and shut down the computer's internet access. Wiped the hard drive. I'm reinstalling from backups."

"Wouldn't that cutoff part of itself, if it's some distributed thing over computers?" asked Cohen.

"Yes, but it's like killing some of your brain cells by a night of heavy drinking. The brain overall isn't hurt much by that afterward. And the thing is everywhere from finance to military computers. We can thank God that the nuclear arsenal is still mainly run off five-and-a-quarter inch floppies and machines from the 1970's. But every other damn thing is infested. We don't control the digital world, anymore. The worm does."

Savas felt his head pounding. He needed something concrete, something practical. "Tell me what the threat is."

Lightfoote looked at him in shock. "John, it can do anything. Write any code, erase data, create data, shut systems down, modulate system function. Turn off the water and lights. Open the Hoover Dam. Drop half the airplanes from the sky. Delete the world's money supply. *Anything*. What's the threat? It's fucking digital Armageddon."

Cohen turned to Savas. "John, this is too big for us."

He nodded. "I'll call in every contact I have at the CIA and NSA with what we have. We'll run a shadow agency. Meanwhile, let's see what's left here."

"We're down to the core group and a few extra hands," said Cohen. "They've pulled all the assistant agents and trainees. It's mostly us. We're the boutique group. Expendable in this crisis."

His mind raced. "Let's break this down into tasks. Overall, we need to provide some kind of quick break into the worm and who is behind it. We're a small team, a talented team. We can move quickly whereas other agencies will just be reactive. We need to go after the worm first." He nodded to Lightfoote. "We'll get JP down with Angel in the basement, and they'll try to trace the origins of this thing, find out its weaknesses. Rebecca, you, me, and Frank will find everything we can on this Anonymous group. But Intel 1 doesn't have much firepower right now."

"We do have an ace-in-the-hole," said Cohen.

"Yes," said Savas wearily. He rubbed his hand across his brow. "I'm not sure they're ready to wade back into things—they're still radioactive. But we don't have a choice. Once they defied an entire nation. Maybe now they can help us save it."

20

GABRIEL AND MARY

Sara Houston, wrapped in a dark coat, trudged across a white field carrying a pile of firewood. The pines behind her circled a small cabin, smoke rising from its chimney, a warm yellow glow spilling through the windows, reflected on the snow crunching under her boots. Clouds of vapor escaped her lips as she marched forward, a serene expression on her face, crisp blue eyes peering outward from a face framed in brown hair.

She climbed onto the porch and dropped the wood into a bin. She ran a gloved finger across the door, tracing the vines that trailed up the wood. The leaves had fallen, and only cordons and trunk remained, hardly more than thin stems. But Houston had planted them only a year ago and was satisfied with the progress.

Dusting off her boots and coat, she opened the door and stepped into the warmth of the small cabin—a single room with bed, table, and miniature kitchen. A sofa beside the window overlooked the porch, and the fireplace crackled loudly on her right, casting red and orange light across her chiseled features. She lowered her hood, chin-length brown hair dancing in a disheveled mess about her face. She smiled at Francisco Lopez walking toward her with a pair of tumblers holding caramel liquid.

The light showed the breadth of him, muscles filling out a black sweater, short and curled black hair and a dark beard masking much of his face. His features were a sharp contrast to hers, his skin a rich copper, features Aztec. He held a glass toward Houston and smiled back at her. She brought the drink to her lips.

"Mmmmm, Francisco," she said, downing a quarter of the two inches in the tumbler. "Cask strength?" He nodded. "Nice and warm. That shed is going to get further and further away as the winter comes."

Lopez grunted. "I think we'll spend a lot of time just clearing a path to it. I didn't realize the snows came so early here. The mountains in Alabama weren't all that high or cold."

"How's the buck?" she said, walking into the small kitchen. "Biggest one we've bagged. You've got your work cut out for you to top that one."

"You're one competitive girl, Sara," he said, laughing and shaking his head. "But he's coming along well. Should be dinner for two weeks with the last veggie run."

She nodded. "Runs are going to get harder with the weather. We need a strategy for supplies. I don't think the Outback can handle what might be coming on these lousy roads. Next trip into town we need to make sure we have enough fuel for the generator."

"By then we'll have natural refrigeration and drain less power. We can fill the shelter with things. We're remote, Sara, but not that remote."

Houston placed her tumbler on the table and walked up to Lopez, draping her arms around his neck. "I'm getting used to a certain rustic luxury up here, Francisco. Nothing ruins rustic luxury like a few weeks of rationing."

They kissed. Houston wasn't sure what felt warmer, his lips or the whiskey. As his hands moved over her waist, she realized that both could spin her head around in the most delicious ways.

A device buzzed from a table beside the sofa.

Both Lopez and Houston turned quickly to the sound, the warmth draining from their faces, softer expressions replaced with intense eyes and set jaws.

Lopez rumbled deeply. "My guess is that it's for you."

Houston smirked and walked toward the landline. It looked like a receptionist's business phone, rows of buttons and an LCD display glowing back at her. The phone cable ran through a black box with a pair of lights. The red light glowed. "They sure know how to ruin a girl's evening."

Lopez downed the rest of this whiskey and followed her to the phone, ignoring the device and staring out the window. He seemed to focus on objects thousands of miles away.

"Mary here," said Houston, using the false identities they had been given. "Gabriel's fine." She pushed a button and the device went to speaker. A woman's voice spoke from the other end.

"It is said: 'Do not meddle in the affairs of Wizards, for they are subtle and quick to anger.'"

Houston replied. "And it is also said, 'Go not to the elves for counsel, for they will say both no and yes.'" She watched a series of numbers changing across the LCD. They locked in a particular sequence, and she continued. "Handshake completed. Hi, Rebecca."

"Hello, Sara," said Cohen, her voice strained.

"This isn't going to be a good call, is it? Are we blown?"

"No. Nothing like that. Something much worse."

Lopez turned his head and met Houston's eyes. His voice was curt. "What's going on?"

There was a sigh and long pause on the line. "Be glad you're in the mountains. Down here, it's chaos. Short story is that there seems to be a hacker group called Anonymous that has suddenly mutated into a full-bore terrorist group. Attacks have ripped through the virtual world and bombings and assassinations in the real world."

Houston crossed her arms over her chest. "What's that got to do with us?"

"Sara, this is a national security threat. We've had major figures in business and finance and in the US Congress blown up or gunned down in the last week. At the same time, some kind of Armageddon worm has been secretly eating its way through world networks, siphoning off huge sums of money, controlling international media, and insinuating itself on every computer from academia to the Pentagon. It's already caused havoc and we're pretty sure it's just getting warmed up."

Lopez leaned over toward the phone. "That doesn't answer the question. Why on earth are you calling us? What could we do? If we show our faces down there, we'll just end up in a cell. More likely just dead."

"The President has declared a state of martial law in New York and Washington."

"What the fuck?" said Houston. "Are you kidding me? It's that bad?"

Cohen sounded tense. "They've used drones to bomb the Pentagon, Wall Street. They took over the networks to televise the execution of business and political leaders. Military units are already moving into the city. Curfew is in place. So yeah, it's pretty damn bad."

Houston shook her head. "How does the world go to hell in a week's time? You were just here!"

Lopez pressed her. "Look, if what you say is true, then what could we possibly do? Seems better that two hunted fugitives wait it out in hiding. Law enforcement will be looking suspiciously at everyone. That's some attention we don't need."

"Most of our staff has been annexed by Homeland Security and put into bodyguard roles for the powerful. It's the same all over NYPD and other FBI divisions. All kinds of 9/11 laws are getting dusted off and put into use. HS is calling all the shots. It's ludicrous!" Cohen barked a laugh. "Right now, all we've got is the core of Intel 1: me, John, Angel, JP, and Frank. The other agencies seem paralyzed. We need you. The *country* needs you."

"The country needs us," said Lopez. "Would that be the same country that wants us dead? The same government that slandered our names and has us on *your* most wanted list?"

"Francisco, today's not the day to seek justice for what happened to you. You know there are plenty of good people who deserve our best. Some of those risked their lives so that you and Sara could find a new life up there."

"And now you want to take that away from us."

Cohen sighed. "If we don't stop Anonymous—I don't know how far they'll go. I'm *afraid*, Francisco. Soon, there might not even be a country to establish your innocence in!"

"This is crazy," said Houston.

"I know it is, but aren't most disasters as they unfold? 9/11? The attack on Mecca with one of our own nukes? Please. You two have unique skills. Highly valuable skills. And you're ghosts. You have no obligation to the US government or anyone else. You can do what we can't. Even Anonymous can't find out who you are. Tools we can use to turn this around."

"Tools," said Lopez.

"Dammit, Francisco, you know what I'm saying! You've been screwed, yes. But don't you feel the least bit of obligation to the people of this nation?"

Houston looked painfully toward Lopez, who turned his head away as he spoke. "You know I do. I was a priest once."

"Then help us! We need everything we can get right now!"

Lopez looked at Houston. He nodded and closed his eyes.

"The activation protocol?" Houston asked.

They could almost hear the relief in Cohen's voice. "Yes. I'll rendezvous with you at the specified location. Thank you. Both of you."

"You're welcome," said Houston.

"And Sara, make sure you come prepared."

The light on the phone switched to green and the LCD went blank.

Lopez grabbed his coat and walked to the door. Houston followed suit and took an LED lantern from the mantle. Together they walked outside and around to the back of the cabin. Lopez approached the cabin wall and knelt down. He brushed away several inches of snow, revealing a set of padlocked doors embedded in the ground. Houston removed the key from a chain around her neck and inserted it into the lock. They pulled together on the doors, the sound of them swinging on their hinges muffled by the deep snow around them.

A short flight of steps ended at the bottom of what appeared to be a surprisingly large wine cellar for a mountain getaway. Houston stepped from behind him and held up the lantern, pressing a button to intensify the light. Sharp shadows were cast across the room. The light spilled over crates and suitcases, canisters and body armor.

Lopez flipped open one case. Dark vestments, black gloves, and masks were folded neatly into sections. Houston ran her fingers over one of the masks and sighed.

"Never thought I'd be wearing these in the States. Never dreamed we'd be activated here."

"Well, it'll shoot facial recognition to all hell and back. We have to assume the targets will all be wired with a hundred cameras, and half of them might be governmental for all we know."

"Blended in better in Islamic countries. That's where all the action is these days. Or used to be."

"From Rebecca's tone, disguise will be the least of our issues. We'll need something more serious than clothes."

They both turned to an open wooden box, the top of the crate slightly off position. Houston tossed the lid to the ground and they stared inside. The light of the lantern glinted off black metal.

The interior was filled with guns.

PART II

FAWKES

Guy Fawkes, Guy Fawkes, 'twas his intent to blow up the King and the Parliament. Three score barrels of powder below, poor old England to overthrow —English Folk Verse (c.1870)

21

COMING OF AGE

"Why do we have to call you Fawkes, anyway?"

Three teenagers crouched in a dark hallway, whispering sharply to each other. Mark and Violetta slunk behind the third, a lanky boy with unkempt hair. He turned back to them with his finger on his lips.

"Because I said so," he whispered. "Now, be quiet. Boot camp library is around the corner."

"But it's locked," said Violetta. Fawkes reached into the back pocket of his jeans and removed several small, metal rods. "You're gonna pick it?" Her eyes widened.

"Come on."

The three moved quickly down the hallway. The building was still and silent, only the emergency exit signs providing light in the corridor. At the end of the hallway a set of double doors framed by windows on each side awaited, a soft glow from computer monitors in screen-saver mode spilling through.

Fawkes knelt down beside the lock and quickly worked the tools as the other two watched in awe. Less than a minute and the mechanism clicked. He reached up and pulled the handle down and the door opened.

"Inside."

The three rushed in, Fawkes closing the door quietly behind them. He motioned with his hand for them to follow, and he led them away from the windows toward the recessed counter where the librarian worked. He went behind a computer monitor at the book checkout and wiggled the mouse. A login screen appeared.

"What are you going to do?" asked Violetta.

"I told you. Get us all out of here," he said with a smirk.

"With the computer? Come on."

He used one of his tools to open the chassis of the machine as he spoke. "These old junkyard machines have BIOS holes you can drive a truck through." He toggled from working on the circuit board to typing at the login prompt and back again.

"I hate this place," said Mark, looking around the dark room. "All I did was one joint. I didn't even want it. Then it's undercover cops and detention and mom sending me to this stupid place to save me, or whatever. It's all my brother's fault."

"It seriously sucks," Violetta agreed. "Caught me with a boy in the attic. Shamed the family, you know. I'm fifteen! They think I'm a baby."

Mark swept his eyes over her body. "You're not a baby."

She ignored him. "So, Fawkes, why are you here? You never said."

The computer beeped and he typed furiously at a prompt on a black background. "Stepdad. Got tired of beating on me. Decided the ex-marine who runs this place would get my ass straightened out." He clacked the enter key and the screen went dark. A second later it lit up with a bright image of a field of green grass. "We're in."

His companions crowded around the screen. Fawkes worked quickly, searching through file systems and applications.

Violetta continued questioning. "How can you do anything from the library computer?"

"It connects to the others. See, look. I'm using this terminal window to remote login on the other system. They're so stupid. All the passwords are related. So I'm in there, too. Admin office computer. And these," he said smiling as text scrolled through the window, "are files on all of us. What's your last name, Violetta?"

"Rayon," she said.

"There you are. Born in Mexico City? What, you illegal?"

"Shut up."

"Maybe you were born in LA."

The girl gasped as the text changed at his keystrokes.

"You can do that?"

"And, looks like you're here for the month program. That's a long time."

"Yeah." Her face fell.

"But since the last day is tomorrow, you'll be going home."

She squinted at the screen. "You changed the dates!"

Fawkes opened another window and keyed in lines of code.

"Take too long to do this by hand," he said. "This little script—wait, gotta save it—it will do them all." He typed the name of the new file into the other command window.

"What's it doing?" asked the boy.

"Reading all the files in this directory, looking for the dates, and changing them. There, all done. Everyone goes home tomorrow."

"Fucking awesome!" The boy shouted.

"They'll figure it out, dumbshit," said Fawkes. "Don't get too excited. But we'll have a few days of chaos. I wonder how many parents will get calls and show up?" They laughed.

"What else can you do? Can you like put naked pictures on the screens or something?"

"Yeah, sure. We'll need to download some. And—wait, what's this?" Fawkes stared at the screen and the file he just opened. "Oh, this is good. See the dollar signs? This is budget stuff! Financials! Same format my stepdad uses for his accounts. Okay. We can do some serious damage here."

The girl's eyes darted. "Fawkes, maybe we should leave. We could really get in big trouble for this."

"Hold on, hold on." He tuned her out, opening other files, scanning the numbers and accounts at light speed. "What the hell? Ah, no, no, no, no, no. Ah, man. Tonight's fucking lotto. Oh, Mr. Harrison, you've been a very bad man!"

Mark backed away slightly. "Mr. Harrison? Don't mess with him, Fawkes. Scares the shit out of me."

Fawkes laughed. "Boot camp marine man? Yeah, but right now, I got his balls in a vice. Oh, man. My stepdad's gonna love seeing where his money went! The tuition? All the fees? It's all transferred. It goes from the school account to this one. And look whose it is!"

"Wait," said Violetta. "Mr. Harrison is stealing?"

"What's stealing? Dumbass parents send them the money. Fix us and all that. He already stole it. But that's not how the world works. I've seen my stepdad with his money. Taxes and shit. You have to do it right or the FEDs come down on you. You can go to jail, even. Mr. Harrison's gonna be in a world of hurt if this gets out—which it's going to!"

"Don't!" said Violetta. "Fawkes, don't. He'll do something. The man is messed up or something."

"Yeah," said Mark. "Look man, this was fun, but I don't want to end up somewhere worse than this. You get him in trouble, then what's he gonna to do?"

Fawkes froze a moment in thought, a half-smirk on his face.

"Excellent points, friends. But it's a crime to let this go. So, there's only one option left. And I think it's a much, much better option."

"Get the hell out of here?" said Mark.

"No. Blackmail."

BEFORE:
THE ANONYMOUS EVENT COMMISSION

DEPOSITION IN THE MATTER OF:
UNITED STATES ARMED FORCES SPECIAL TRIBUNAL, Plaintiff,
versus
JOHN SAVAS, Defendant
Case No. M120039E-007X

DEPOSITION OF:
Tyrell Sacker
called for examination by Counsel for the Defendant, pursuant to Notice of Deposition, at the Independent Council Offices, located at [REDACTED] Washington, D.C., when were present on behalf of the respective parties: [REDACTED]

CBD: Will you please identify yourself for the record?
MR. SACKER: Tyrell Sacker, Detective, NYPD.

CBD: And your background? How long have you been with the NYPD?
MR. SACKER: Four years. I signed up after my Iraq tour. Promoted to detective two years ago, detective second-grade this year. Military service and cracking cases clear a lot of paperwork.

CBD: Congratulations to you, Mr. Sacker. Can you tell us how you came to know the defendant, Mr. Savas?
MR. SACKER: Professional interactions. I served as the point of contact between FBI and the NYPD on the kidnappings and murders by Anonymous.

CBD: How did that come to be?
MR. SACKER: I was on site at the bank kidnapping of Mitchell O'Kelly. Agent Cohen from Intel 1 led the FBI team. I worked with her and her division from that point on.

CBD: You worked exclusively with Intel 1? No other agencies at FBI?
MR. SACKER: That's right.

CBD: Why is this? Why only Intel 1?

MR. SACKER: I'm not sure. With all the chaos, it was just easier to set up a clear protocol to pipe information back and forth between the agencies. Things seemed to fall into place. You know, it was all getting crazy and manpower was being sucked up for a hundred security cases and events. Ladner, my captain, barely had time to go for a piss. The setup was working, so why fix it?

CBD: So you were exclusively shuttling information from NYPD on the events to Intel 1?

MR. SACKER: That's right.

CBD: Do you know whether they shared this information with other divisions?

MR. SACKER: I assume so.

CBD: But you have no evidence for that?

MR. SACKER: No. But why wouldn't they?

CBD: Please take a look at these photographs. In your interactions with the FBI, did you ever come across either this man or this woman?

MR. SACKER: No. I don't think so. Who are they?

CBD: Known terrorists. Francisco Lopez and Sara Houston. You might know them better as the Priest and the Whore.

MR. SACKER: [INAUDIBLE] Why would they be with the FBI?

[REDACTED]: I'll be frank with you, Detective. You have been summoned to this tribunal to help us figure out some highly irregular actions on the part of the Intel 1 division led by Mr. Savas. It is for some of these actions that he is the subject of this inquiry.

MR. SACKER: Irregular?

[REDACTED]: Illegal. Treasonous.

MR. SACKER: No. I don't believe that. These were good people. I didn't work day-to-day with them, but I interacted with them enough to see their dedication. Look, I don't know what was going on, but they aren't traitors.

[REDACTED]: But as you noted, you were not closely involved with them. You need to understand the seriousness of this inquiry, and the consequences for not being completely forthcoming.

MR. SACKER: What does that mean?

CBD: The site in Connecticut—how was NYPD involved?

MR. SACKER: That was a coordination between New York and local police, as well as FBI. Most of the victims were from the city financial district. We had been filling our offices with new case files on their disappearances. We had a pretty big stake in it. FBI helped bring some of us on board in Bridgeport.

[REDACTED]: But neither you nor the local police handled any evidence?

MR. SACKER: No, it was local and NYC FBI forensics teams. Mostly the New York guys, I think. They were much better equipped to do the work.

[REDACTED]: So NYPD never saw any of the alleged evidence?

MR. SACKER: Alleged?

[REDACTED]: Can you answer the question, please.

MR. SACKER: No. Like I said, the evidence was all handled by FBI. They kept us updated on the results.

CBD: You mean the Intel 1 division?

MR. SACKER: I don't know whose forensics team was involved. I think the results were handled by that division, yes.

CBD: But Cohen kept you informed?

MR. SACKER: She did. I mean, with everything going down, it wasn't like I had her piping information to me on an hourly basis! But all things considered, they were pretty good about keeping us in the loop.

[REDACTED]: But you knew nothing about the fugitives Lopez and Houston?

MR. SACKER: No, I didn't.

[REDACTED]: Or about the Intel 1 division hacking into governmental agencies?

MR. SACKER: Sorry, what?

[REDACTED]: Or about the disappearances of the fugitives and the head of their cybercrimes division after these hacking events?

MR. SACKER: No! What are you talking about?

[REDACTED]: Would you characterize all the NYPD interactions with FBI in this case in a similar fashion?

MR. SACKER: I'm not following you.

[REDACTED]: The raid on the Anonymous group. The capture of the hackers. The hit on the warehouses and ship. NYPD had involvement, but is it not true that all evidence, all prisoners, all aspects of the case were tightly control by Intel 1?

MR. SACKER: Yes, but—

[REDACTED]: And in all of this, you would describe John Savas as masterminding all the activities at FBI during this crisis?

MR. SACKER: He was head of the division. I don't think masterminding is a good word, but he—

[REDACTED]: Thank you, Mr. Sacker. We appreciate your time in this inquiry.

CBD: [REDACTED], there are still several questions—

[REDACTED]: That will be all, Mr. Sacker.

MR. SACKER: But wait a minute! What's this all about? What hacking? What treason? You can't just drag me in here and ask me questions without telling me anything!

[REDACTED]: The tribunal reminds you that the entire proceeding is classified under past and more recent national security laws: The Patriot Acts, the Terrorist Surveillance Order, the Obama Doctrines. You are to be reminded that we are at war and under martial law. You may not speak to anyone about any of this or even acknowledge that you have been here or that this tribunal exists. The recent NSA authorizations for tracking and recording citizens means that you will be monitored via your new nation identity card through all electronic devices, both public and private. Failure to abide by these instructions will be discovered and may be construed as action hostile to the United States of America. Do you understand?

MR. SACKER: Jesus.

[REDACTED]: Do you understand?

MR. SACKER: Yes.

CBD: You are free to go.

OCTOBER 24

22

SCENE OF DEATH

Miller blasted through the left-most toll lane with lights flashing as he and Savas raced down Interstate 95 on their way to Bridgeport, Connecticut. The NSA finally seemed to be playing nice with the other agencies and had come through in a big way. With their eyes nearly everywhere in the digital world, they had been able to trace the feed for the streaming video of the assassinations to a boardwalk section of the port town.

"Near Captain's Cove," said Savas, mapping the location on his phone. "Seems to be some minor touristy location by a marina. Move a bit out from it and things deteriorate quickly. A lot of abandoned buildings."

"Buildings with serious bandwidth, it seems," said Miller. He cast a sharp look toward Savas. "Rebecca's where again? We could use her today."

Savas sighed. "Tell me about it. Look, I know I've been keeping this in a black box, Frank, but there are some very good reasons. Things will be clearer soon. Current events have complicated things, but she's tending to something important."

"Your call, John. But I can't say there hasn't been a lot of interest and speculation."

"Answers are coming. Meanwhile, we focus on today."

Miller stared a moment more at Savas, then turned his eyes back to the road. "Sure."

Savas continued. "We're going to have local and state police at the scene, and some agents from the New Haven Division. But they've saved the crime scene for us, and I've got a forensics unit en route. This is our first real physical connection to Anonymous."

"Well, let's hope these digital ghosts leave real-world footprints."

THEY STEPPED out of the car in front of a faded orange building. Sandwiched between several dilapidated and shuttered structures, it hardly seemed the location for the broadcast of the most devastating video in the history of the internet. They were met by representatives of the local FBI division and surrounded by police. Bystanders stood behind police tape, gawking at the uniformed presence, cell phones raised like torches, beaming images around the world.

"Assistant Special Agents in Charge Jimmy Onda and Maggie Linven," said a tall woman wrapped in a coat and indicating a wiry man with thinning hair. Both of the New Haven agents appeared anxious and fearful.

Savas shook their hands. "John Savas and Frank Miller, Intel 1. I take it you've been inside?"

Their wide-eyed expressions gave Savas his answer.

"Yes, agent Savas. The bodies are still there. They haven't been disturbed. I was told your New York crime units are coming."

He nodded. "Yes. They should be here any minute. Mind if we have a look ourselves?"

"No. But it's pretty grim."

The four of them entered the building, a narrow hallway leading back to what might have been a storage room for a small business decades ago. Photographers continued to take pictures, and the strobing of the flashes in the dark space created a strange, discontinuous visual effect as he and Miller snapped on nitrile gloves.

Even walking in the space was hazardous. Clotted pools of blood had seeped from the center of the room outward, coating the floor in an expanse of red goo. The staging was as it had been in the video: two rows of ten chairs, corpses tied to them, stage lights affixed to stands around the massacred, and a dark cloth framing the nightmare in a semicircle of black.

"There seems to be some rigor mortis remaining in the bodies," said agent Liven. "That's consistent with the timing of the broadcast last night."

"So it was live," mumbled Miller, a scowl on his face. "Like to tie down the bastard that did this and see how he likes the treatment."

The accompanying agents eyed Miller cautiously. Savas turned the conversation back to Anonymous.

"That speech on TV sounded like talking points from a manifesto. They truly hated the people here, saw them as criminals and murderers that deserved their punishment."

"Sounds like you're empathizing with them," growled agent Onda.

"Not at all," said Savas. "But we can't sit here getting off on righteous indignation. We need to understand them, get in their heads. We need to anticipate them. And we can't do that if we can't think like they do. Basic criminal psychology 101."

A glint of light caught his attention. Moving in a wide arc around the crime scene to avoid the blood, he approached the left side of the chairs and crouched beside a white object on the ground. One side of it was dyed red from blood that had run alongside the plastic.

"The Guy Fawkes mask," said Savas.

The head of the New Haven division stared between Savas and the mask. "I wondered what that was all about in the video. Who's Guy Fawkes?"

Savas shook his head. "Too much FBI training is still in the analog years." He stood up and continued to move parallel to the chair rows, examining the layout. "Historically, he's a figure from British religious wars in the sixteenth century. Led a failed Catholic rebellion against the English. Fast forward. Now, amazingly, he's become a general symbol of resistance to oppressive systems. Started with a graphic novel. The hacker community in particular has adopted him as a symbol. Anonymous often uses iconography of him—the mask in particular—when putting a public face on their activities. It literally keeps them anonymous and gives them some kind of mythic power."

The New Haven agent shook her head. "That doesn't make any sense."

"Yeah, well, since when do sociopathic revolutionaries have to make sense?" asked Miller. "But the idiot left the mask here."

"Exactly," said Savas, a glint in his eye. "And look, behind the chairs," he pointed with a blue finger. “Some masks from the shooters. They wore them for the entire video.” He smiled. "Maybe Anonymous is made up of geniuses, but their intelligence is limited to the digital realm. They’re rookies here.”

At that moment, several additional agents entered the room carrying equipment and evidence bags. One waved to Savas as he approached.

“Just in time,” said Savas. “Our NYC crime unit. And it looks like Anonymous has left some interesting Easter eggs for us to open.”

OCTOBER25

23

FUGATIVES RETURN

An unremarkable blue sedan pulled up to a tollbooth on the George Washington Bridge on the Jersey side. The booth officer watched as a man with blond hair and a youngish face shoved a fist out the window, offering a ten and a five from inside. The officer could see her face reflected in his mirrored glasses. She glanced inside at his companion as she took the bills, glimpsing a woman with short black hair and dark sunglasses. The man looked away as the gate swung upward, and the car dashed off, lost in the traffic swarming onto the bridge.

Lopez rubbed his hand across his face as he steered the vehicle toward the right lanes, glancing upward to a sign for the Harlem River Drive.

Houston smiled. "Miss the beard?"

"Not sure. Just getting used to it. Nervous habits and all." He took the offramp from the bridge and forced his way into the gaggle of vehicles queuing up for the East Side Highway. "I'm sure we got our photos taken back there."

Houston stared outside the window at the merging traffic. "The image-recognition solutions still struggle with facial hair, so I'm the bigger danger. We *are* number one on the most-wanted list. Anyone would want to make their career bringing us in." She looked behind them and studied the vehicles. "These giant sunglasses should mask my forehead and cheekbones some. I kept the visor down as well as we approached the toll booth. Which reminds me: fifteen bucks for a car?"

"Getting a bit ridiculous. Cheaper with EZ-Pass, but we have to stay off the grid." Lopez grunted. "So how do we fight a digital terrorist group when we stay off the grid?"

"First, they stopped being digital. Rebecca's encrypted data was informative: Bombings, shootings—nothing virtual there. Second, there are ways to get online without alerting the world to your presence. We've done it."

"*You've* done it. But these guys put the Feds to shame. It's different."

"They aren't omniscient. They don't know what to look for. We don't exist for them. Not yet, anyway. We'll be targeted later."

"They seem pretty good at that."

Houston turned her body toward Lopez, swinging a leg onto the seat to stabilize herself. "I've been thinking about that, Francisco. How the hell did these guys remotely pilot these things so skillfully? They aren't drone operators."

"Maybe they recruited some. Besides, it's not like people don't know where the Capitol is. Just punch in the GPS coordinates and off you go."

"And how do you explain hitting a moving vehicle like the CEO's car?"

Lopez nodded. "Got me there. They'd have to steer it. In real time."

"Pretty tough with an evasive target. I doubt the best drone pilots in the CIA could do that."

"Then how?"

"Same thing you said. GPS coordinates."

Lopez furrowed his brows. "I see. Mobile devices."

"Right. Even CEOs have their damn smartphones these days. If they could hack into one or more of the Big Brother databases out there, they might be able to get the target's phone GPS feed. It's like shining a laser beam for a missile. Even a *moving* target. Individualized. It's perfect. They were using this in Pakistan and other locations for al-Qaeda honchos. But it should work even better in Western nations."

"You're right. It's perfect for assassinations: auto-piloted drones coupled to the real-time coordinates of the target."

Houston spun back around as Lopez exited the Harlem River Drive and entered the streets of Harlem itself. "For now. If this is what is happening, you can bet every figure of importance will ditch their GPS-enabled tech."

"By then, it might be too late."

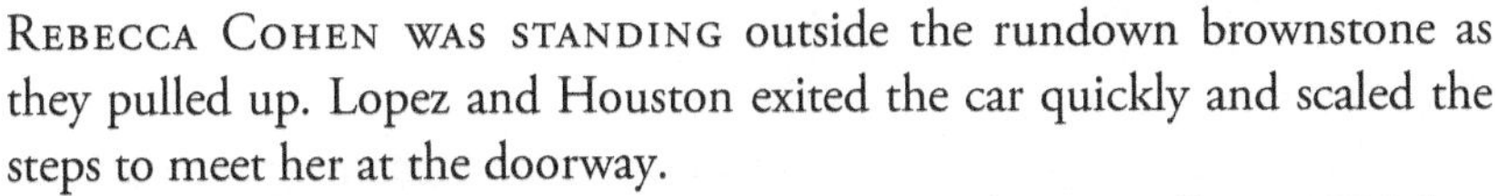

Rebecca Cohen was standing outside the rundown brownstone as they pulled up. Lopez and Houston exited the car quickly and scaled the steps to meet her at the doorway.

Houston glanced around them. "You're on a burner cell? No GPS?"

Cohen nodded. "As you asked. It's a cheap model, but it makes calls. You might be right about how the hits were made. It's so simple it's frightening." She motioned them to the entrance. "Let's get in and I'll let John know you're here." Cohen unlocked the door and the three entered rapidly.

"What a dump," said Houston. Cohen shut the door behind them.

The wreckage of the former living room was strewn with broken furniture, blankets, and litter. Grime coated the walls and floor. It stank.

"Former crack house that was shut down and left to die," said Cohen as she handed Lopez the keys. "Gentrification hasn't made it this far north yet."

He nodded. "It's perfect. I'll be right back."

The ex-priest returned quickly with a heavy suitcase in each hand and a backpack strapped over his shoulders. Cohen glanced briefly at the bags as she dialed. She didn't need any guesses as to what they held within. She punched a key on her phone.

"John? It's Rebecca. They're here. Yes, okay. Go ahead."

She was silent for a few moments as muffled sounds came from the speaker. Meanwhile, Lopez and Houston opened one of the suitcases, removing body armor and firearms. They stripped to their underwear, Houston with a tight sports bra, Lopez's rippling musculature distracting the FBI woman. They donned tight black tanks and black pants, strapping on shoulder harnesses with holsters for handguns and knives. Cohen thought she saw stun grenades as well in the suitcase, but it was closed before she could be sure.

She hung up the phone and approached the pair. "Some interesting news."

Houston slipped a loose black shirt on, the rough fabric concealing all evidence of the weaponry within. "The crime scene?" Lopez seemed to be tying together a long robe or coat of some kind.

"Yes," said Cohen. "The executions. Looks like our hackers left considerable physical evidence behind in their getaway. The crime unit just went through things and it's preliminary, but there are prints and hair."

Houston's face was set. "Well, it's a start. How soon until we have something?"

"This is priority one. John and Frank are on their way back with them. They'll do this right. Best people, best labs. Everything is nearby. Bottlenecks should be travel time to the labs and lab work. We'll get the fingerprints first. DNA tests in some hours plus time to search databases."

"If things go well," said Lopez. He stepped beside her.

His demeanor had changed completely. Outwardly, he was covered in black vestments, modified and tightened so as not to restrict his movements. Along with the monastic garb came a stern expression on his face, one Cohen had never seen before. For the first time, she noticed clearly the scar on his forehead, branded there by the hot barrel of a weapon held by a vengeful madman, a circle of white tissue with a cross from the site at the top. It almost seemed to glow.

Cohen cleared her throat "Yes, if things go well. Listen, I want to thank you both for coming. I know you didn't have to."

Lopez slammed a magazine into the butt of a gun and holstered the weapon within the folds of the vestments. Even his gloves and boots were black. As Houston unconsciously moved to his side, Cohen noted how similar they seemed, how coordinated their motions, like two black cats stalking prey.

"Let's get to work," Houston said. "When do we get to meet the gang?"

24

RENDEZVOUS

The location was ideal. The overpass was large, the tunnel and space underneath deep and shadowed. They were concealed from nearby residential windows by the thundering highway above and from other eyes by the East River at their backs. The dark evening created numerous pockets of gloom away from any direct lighting. There had been a contingent of homeless, but at the sight of the figures entering the dark underpass, they seemed to sense danger, and one by one they filed out and seemed to dissolve into the flow of the city.

Savas had used Intel 1's access to city camera systems and determined that the area was poorly covered, a patchwork of lenses crossing nearby but leaving considerable holes, including the space underneath. It was not difficult to arrange for separate approaches that would avoid nearly all surveillance.

Miller, Lightfoote, and Rideout stood like statues in the cool air and watched three shadows approach from the opposite side of the tunnel. The distance was only fifty yards, and it was easy to identify one of the shapes. Cohen walked at a brisk pace several paces in front of the two other figures, her eyes locked on Savas. Behind her glided a lithe woman with a confident, feline gait, her body remaining shrouded in black even as she approached close enough for light to spill over her form. Her face was covered completely by a veil or mask. A slit in the dark fabric revealed a pair of intense, blue eyes. Beside her strode a powerfully built man, also black-clad but with his face uncovered, dark eyes and raven hair blending into the night. He seemed to possess an underlying tension that caught on the air like static.

Miller spoke quietly to Savas as the three neared. "Is that a cassock?"

"Maybe," Savas growled.

Rideout cut in. "If you mean the one next to the hot burqa-ninja, I would say yes. Definitely a cassock."

Miller shook his head. "John's mystery project. Who are these ghosts?"

Lightfoote laughed, tipping her head to Miller's. "Avenging spirits, Frank."

The pair behind her stopped several feet in front of the others. Cohen stepped up to Savas and placed her hand gently on his shoulder. She glanced backward.

"They weren't happy to come, John. But they're here. They're ready." She slipped alongside him and turned to face the ciphers.

Savas spoke to his team. "I'm sorry for this secrecy, but it was necessary for reasons I can't go into. But they're here to help." He gestured toward the pair. "Gabriel and Mary. You're to know them by these names. They're professionals. They are off the radar. They have no ties or allegiances to anyone. But they're allies."

Savas saw Miller and Rideout appraising the pair. Lightfoote only smiled.

Cohen continued the introductions. "Mary is an experienced field operative. She's smart and can handle herself in just about any situation. Gabriel has a unique history, but he is unparalleled in combat and crisis."

Rideout cut in. "Gabriel and Mary? What's next, the Holy Spirit? Christ child?"

Lopez walked up to Rideout, who could not suppress an instinct to step backward. As Gabriel, he offered his hand. "We'll need all the help from God we can get, if what Rebecca has told us is true. You can trust us."

Rideout extended his hand cautiously. The two men shook. There followed a repeat of the ritual with the other members of the team. Houston paused a moment looking Lightfoote up and down.

"This the one? Your white hat hacker?"

Savas nodded. "I don't know what color she is. Red, by the color of her butchered hair." He gestured toward Houston. "Angel, meet Mary. You and JP will be paired with her and Gabriel to form a team to look into the drones and computer end of this case. The rest of us will pursue the human angle and try to dig out the members of Anonymous."

The two women shook hands.

Houston stared quietly a moment longer. The fabric around her mouth pulled tightly from a smirk. "I like this one. She's hardcore."

Lightfoote looked deeply into Houston's eyes. "We all have to be. Now the nightmare really begins."

Lopez moved between Savas and Lightfoote. "You said she was special."

Savas shook his head. "You have no idea."

"Now that we're one big, happy family," said Lightfoote, "Let's get the hell out of here. Meeting together is a bad idea. For all of us, because of Anonymous. For you," she said, indicating Lopez and Houston, "because of, well, everyone else. Right, Fearless Leader?"

Miller and Rideout looked over sharply, but Savas ignored them. "As usual, Angel is correct. But I felt to get us through this email wouldn't cut it. Sometimes face-to-face is required. So, the drone data?"

Lightfoote pulled out a black binder filled with paper and handed it to Houston. "Mary, your homework for tonight."

"What is it?" Houston asked.

Savas answered. "Angel's been digging into the drones. Records of the sales and trades of the major manufactures in the country. Hardcopy in case we'd transfer the worm to your computers. You said yours are scrubbed?"

Houston nodded. "Re-virginized."

"I think you'll find this interesting," said Angel, a sly look on her face, indicating the binder.

"Once you've had a chance to digest it, we can plan the next steps," said Savas. "Meanwhile, we split up again, contact only through burner cells without GPS. Anonymous may have compromised telecommunications, and we can't afford to tip our hands."

Miller grunted. "Or you may find a drone up your ass with an unfriendly payload."

"Who's our contact point?" Lopez asked.

"You'll have all our numbers, and should we need to dump a phone we'll update as we go. But you'll funnel all communications through Angel. The rest of you, outside of an emergency, straight to me. We believe Anonymous is using the NSA-developed snooping tools, piggybacking on US surveillance. That means anything and everything is possibly an eye or ear for them. Angel is monitoring those tools for any hint that we've been compromised. Unlikely given our precautions, but we need to be careful, so let's keep communication minimal."

"See, you aren't the only ones hiding from Big Brother," said Lightfoote, smiling toward Lopez and Houston.

Lopez arched an eyebrow and Savas cut in. "Frighteningly intuitive, as I mentioned. I'm still calling it a feature, not a bug."

Houston half turned to leave. "Okay then. Let's break and communicate when we're ready to move."

Savas nodded, and with a last look across the members of Intel 1, Lopez and Houston walked back through the tunnel and disappeared into the darkness.

Rideout let out a long breath that condensed in the air. "Well, that was intense!"

"Trusting your judgment on this, John," Miller said. "But I know death when I see it. And it was just standing in front of me."

"They've been through hell and back," said Savas. "Believe me, you wouldn't want to walk in their shoes."

They turned to exit the tunnel in different directions, each to take a different path and avoid detection. Before leaving, Lightfoote dropped alongside Savas and pecked his cheek with a kiss.

"Explanation?" Savas had known her for too long to hope to guess.

"The Priest and the Whore." She nodded approvingly. "Good catch, Aging Overlord."

Savas sighed. "Damn, Angel, sometimes I don't know whether you're our only hope or our doom. How the hell did—"

"And it's really something that you did for them." Her expression turned serious. "But don't forget—I'm the only Angel."

25

FINDING THE TRAIL

It was three in the morning, and a bleary-eyed Sara Houston lay back against the filthy wall of the abandoned brownstone. Small lamps were placed on the floor around a crouched figure in front of her. Cords ran to outlets in the wall at her left. Lopez sat cross-legged in the middle of the circle of light, his dark features giving him the appearance of some ancient priest petitioning the gods. Instead he bowed over reams of paper and rubbed his eyes.

"It's so obvious if anyone had been looking." His voice was deeper than usual, rough from lack of sleep.

Houston spoke over the wailing of an ambulance siren as the flashing lights played across the windows. "So, we've got records for six major drone manufacturers in the US. Every single one of them has seen a marked increase in sales over the last six months. No wonder Angel thought we'd find it 'interesting.'"

Lopez nodded, stood up, and stretched. "But we could be jumping to conclusions. Maybe the market has picked up for drones? More and more police and news stations want to get their hands on these things. Doesn't mean it's Anonymous-related. Would they even shop local? Leave that kind of trail?"

"I don't know, but they haven't shown the same talents in real world crime as they have online. Anyway, we can't visit all these places across the country. Not in time to hope to contribute meaningfully to this case. But from what I can see, four of the six plants only ship smaller scale drones. I think we can forget those. The drones carrying explosives—they'd have to be much larger."

"Agreed."

"There are only two providing models of that size in any number in the US. And guess what? One of them happens to be across the Hudson in New Jersey."

Lopez stared down at her. "I suppose you're interested in paying that place a visit?"

Houston smiled. "And there's no time like the present. What do you say we make a little excursion to Jersey?"

Lopez began to pace. "We're not ready. We need to do recon. Find out what this place is, try to determine the security, what we'll be up against. And what's our target? We won't have access to the guided tour."

"We'll need to be in and out in under half an hour to be sure the police don't arrive. We need their records. What they've been selling and to whom. Hopefully, we can use that to trace the drones to Anonymous. In the real world, you always leave footprints."

"So we need to identify their offices, determine how to penetrate their perimeter and security, how to get into the records, all from outside with no computer access."

"We can't do it without online access."

Lopez raised his hands. "But that opens our computers to the worm. Right now they're wiped. Pristine. Who knows how long before we're infected online."

"From what Angel said, not long."

"Then we might as well be televising what we're doing. At some point we risk opening ourselves to discovery by that thing. Best case they blow our data. Worst case they send assassins."

"So we don't use our computers."

"Then what?"

Houston stood up, stretching slowly in different yoga positions as she spoke. "Public library. We'll disable some of their safe-browsing settings, install TOR for anonymity, and get what we need and hope for the best."

"All those computers are infected."

"Yes, but the worm isn't omniscient. It's also latent until activated. Is there a trigger keyword in every strain on every computer about everything that might be a threat to them? Anonymous can't anticipate all the threats."

"And if they have anticipated that one?"

"We'll lose the computer and connection as the worm is activated. Then we go back to the drawing board, or head into the plant blind."

"With somebody alerted to our interest."

She sighed. "A risk we have to take."

Lopez nodded. "We need building specs. Satellite info. How do we get that from the library computer connections?"

Houston laughed. "More than you think is publicly available. But for the details, we need governmental access." She picked up her phone. "Angel must not be getting much sleep these days." She dialed.

Lopez walked to the window and stared out into the night. The streetlights took on a hazy blur from the soiled glass. The occasional passing car was enveloped in a glowing fog that seemed to give it a phantasmal quality. Sleep deprived and anxious, the images stirred his primitive emotions. To add to the suspense, a whistle rose and fell from a wind picking up and blowing through the alleyways.

"Hi Angel. Mary here." Houston made her way to their weapons cache. "We have a lead on a manufacturing plant in Jersey. No, not far. South of Newark. Yes. Look, we need to do some serious recon before we hit that place. We need access to FBI databases, satellite scans, building schematics. Anything on the site." She paused, listening. "We don't have time to wait until John's back. Yeah, I know you'd like his approval, but he's not my daddy. You're point for us, remember? And don't tell me permission from the boss ever got in your way!" Houston picked up a large handgun, a Browning 1911, and sighed. "Look, can you do this, give us access or not? Okay, then just do it." She nodded and checked the magazine on the weapon. "Thanks. And tell John we'll be careful."

She closed and pocketed the phone as Lopez approached. He glanced down at the weapon in her hand.

"Tell your dad to watch over us."

She smiled at the .45 caliber, semiautomatic. "He always does. Believe that."

Lopez checked his watch. "So, what time does the library open?"

BEFORE:
THE ANONYMOUS EVENT COMMISSION

DEPOSITION IN THE MATTER OF:
UNITED STATES ARMED FORCES SPECIAL TRIBUNAL, Plaintiff,
versus
JOHN SAVAS, Defendant
Case No. M120039E-007X

CONTINUED DEPOSITION OF:
Rebecca Ruth Cohen

CBD: And it was at this point that you began to question the individual members of Anonymous.

MS. COHEN: Yes. We had compiled a list of known and suspected members that were in custody, serving time for hacking-related crimes. Other offenses. We could get immediate access to those.

CBD: How many were in custody?

MS. COHEN: In the tristate area? At that time, four. Three were minor hackers. One was a central figure in the underground community, Laurens Hanert, who had just been transferred from FCI Manchester in Kentucky. We focused on him.

CBD: Who is Hanert?

MS COHEN: An online activist, mainly. Started a hacker site open to the public. Criminal record consisted of a few Mary Jane possessions and participation in protests. Riled up a bunch of people by working with Wikileaks. Then in 2012 he was busted by the FBI in a sting operation using an informant who was a former member of Anonymous. Basically, he was set up for a hack of an intelligence company. Borderline entrapment but it worked. Pleaded guilty and got fifteen years. Longer than most murder sentences.

CBD: Did you speak to the other hackers in custody?

MS. COHEN: No. We were low on personnel. We didn't have the manpower to question them all. We thought that Hanert was our best bet.

[REDACTED]: And so the other members of Anonymous remained free.

MS. COHEN: Free? Those we knew anything about were in lockup! Free from our rushed and crazy inquiry as the world fell apart, sure. But Hanert was important. We were right to zero in on him.

CBD: How so?

MS. COHEN: He led us to some of the local hacker cells, cells that were unknown, underground. And he was the first to clue us in to Fawkes.

[REDACTED]: The mythical Fawkes, again.

MS. COHEN: I don't know what this witch hunt is about, but you're missing the elephant in the room. It's not John! Fawkes was real and nearly got us all killed as we hunted him down. If you want to understand this thing, you'd better start taking that seriously.

CBD: And where did you meet this Hanert?

MS. COHEN: FCI Ray Brook, up in the Adirondacks. Long five-hour drive from the city.

CBD: Why drive? Why not fly?

MS. COHEN: We considered it, but with the risks of the worm to air traffic and guidance systems, if we were blown it seemed an easy way to get us out of the picture to bring an aircraft down. Paranoid, sure, but staying off the grid as much as possible, that was our plan. We tried hard to stick to it. Which makes the end result so ironic. But Hanert was worth it, even if it almost cost us our lives.

OCTOBER 26

26

QUESTIONING MASKS

The guard sat the prisoner down across from them on the other side of the plexiglass. There was a voice activated speaker that did away with the antiquated two-phone system of the past. Cameras were perched on the ceiling in multiple locations. The armed guards did not leave.

Savas and Cohen had driven north from the city into the heart of Upstate New York, the scenic Adirondack mountains. Miller remained at Intel 1, serving to coordinate the division's activities in their absence as they waited for the results of the forensics. On the way up, Lightfoote had informed them of the progress on the drones and Lopez and Houston's plans to infiltrate the New Jersey plant. It was reckless, but Savas had to concede that it was necessary. The finer points of legality and admissibility seemed to matter little when the city was locked down by the National Guard. It had taken them an hour simply to get permission to leave Manhattan.

The prisoner stared across the composite glass with apparent bemusement. He was lanky and his posture slovenly, body nearly vanishing in the folds of his overlarge gray and tan uniform. A baby face aged by a short growth of beard grinned at them as his fingers drummed incessantly.

"Laurens Hanert?" began Savas as the pair of FBI agents settled into chairs. Cohen swiped across her tablet and opened several files.

Hanert smiled. "Who wants to know?"

"FBI Special agents Savas and Cohen. New York."

Hanert leaned forward with a smile. "Federal special agents. Well, well, well. What brings you two all the way up here? Don't you have a national crisis to solve?"

Cohen scowled. "I'm sure you can imagine why."

"An-on-y-mous." He broke out each syllable in slow motion, seeming to relish every moment. "Remind me why I'm locked up in here?"

Cohen set her lips in a line. "Hanert, the judge slammed you, no doubt. But you weren't a nihilist. You were an activist. You can't tell me you approve of what has happened."

"FBI girl with a heart. I like that. You must be good cop. In fact, you remind me of the lady that cuffed me when they flash-bombed my bong-session at home. America is lucky to have you folks on the job."

Savas cut in. "Why do you have any loyalty to Anonymous? They ratted you out."

"Please, at least pretend you're not as stupid as you sound. It's a distributed group, Einstein. Anarchist. There isn't *an Anonymous*. There are as many as there are people and groups within it. I was sold out by one motherfucker who decided to protect his own ass when he fucked up. He set me up to cut time served. *You folks* gave him that deal. I don't blame Anonymous for this," he said, rapping on the glass and gesturing around him. "And you shouldn't blame them for what's happening now."

Cohen tilted her head to one side. "What do you mean?"

"I mean, pretty agent girl, that you need to take that bloodbath broadcast seriously. One very disturbed dude with an *I'm-the-real-Anonymous* delusion of grandeur. The rest of us are as *Oh Shit!* as you FEDs are."

"Do you know who he is?" asked Savas.

"We all know who he is. Those of us who were in deep. There is only one nut job with the chops to pull this off."

Savas leaned forward. "And who is that?"

Hanert smiled. "What's Batman say? 'If you make yourself more than just a man'?"

"That was Ducard," said Cohen. "And it's *a legend*."

"No fake geek girl here!" Hanert paused and looked between them. "Interesting. There's some chemistry between you two! Tell me, gramps, you banging this one? You getting some? 'Cause she's hot."

"What legend?" asked Savas, his voice strained.

The prisoner's smile fell. "Right now I should be asking for early parole or something. But honestly, I think this damn place might be safer than being on the outside from here on out." He leaned forward, his expression serious for the first time. "You know why communism never worked?"

Savas blinked. "I don't see what—"

"Because it's based on perching society at the top of an unstable equilibrium. I mean, forget all that 'give to those in need from what you have' Marxist ivory tower bullshit. Sounds nice. Would be a good Sunday school lesson if people understood a fucking thing in the Bible. But it's a god-damned local maxima!"

"I'm not following," said Savas, who looked to Cohen. She was staring intently at Hanert.

"Jesus, don't they teach even basic math to you *special agents*? How are you going to understand the economy or cybercrime? Look, for an economic system you want stability. Communism ain't it, because all it takes is one person—a single fucking non-saint—to start being a selfish asshole and the whole thing collapses. Of course, usually you get groups of selfish assholes that form parties and blocks and structures to protect their power. But I digress. It's inherently unstable! Like a car perched at the top of a hill. Release the brakes and zoom! That's Anonymous."

"How's that?" asked Cohen.

"It's a leaderless, structureless anarchy. That's nice for flexibility and isolating different cells when you Feds come knocking. But its weakness is in the Selfish Asshole. One person can assume control of it before it can be stopped. This new *real Anonymous* of live televised massacre notoriety. And that person is Fawkes."

"Fawkes?" asked Savas. "As in Guy Fawkes?"

Hanert slumped back in his chair. "Yeah. I mean who takes that handle? Mt. Everest ego. But this wacko was like Mozart. He could play the hell out of the code."

Savas shook his head. "You're telling me that there is a single individual—this Fawkes—who is responsible for what is happening? I don't believe you."

"Look man, I don't care what you believe."

Savas continued. "Who is he, then?"

"Hell if I know. It's not like we all got around and passed the hash pipe. It's called *Anonymous* for a reason, you know."

Cohen pressed. "Doesn't this Fawkes need other members of Anonymous to help? An infrastructure? You can't orchestrate multiple bombings, kidnappings, and hackings without money and people. A small army."

"No doubt."

"And so?"

"So, it isn't Anonymous. None of the main players anyway."

"And how would you know that?" asked Savas.

Hanert smirked. "I have my ways of knowing. Even in here. Believe me when I tell you that the main hacker groups aren't involved. It's a ridiculous idea, anyway. They aren't terrorists. Most wouldn't know which way to point a fucking gun."

"I want contact information on all of these groups."

"Fuck you, man."

Cohen spoke. "Hanert, one of them might know something that can lead us to this Fawkes. We're not interested in them right now. They may have broken one hundred federal statutes, but in the larger context that's background noise. You can see how serious this is. You know about the worm, I assume?"

He nodded. "Yeah. We all do now."

"Then you know what's at stake. *Please.* You have to trust us. And we need to trust you to tell us what we need to know. Anonymous was about changing a corrupt system. But right now the entire system is about to be blown up."

"That's Fawkes. His conclusion. Some agreed with him."

"Do you?" Cohen locked eyes with him.

"No. Far more damage than gain. We could go back to the Stone Age."

"Then you'll give us names?" asked Savas.

Hanert looked at him and back to Cohen. "Yeah, but only because she's so damn pretty. I wouldn't give grandfather here jack."

"Go to hell, Hanert," said Savas.

The hacker smiled, tapping his index finger, nail to vinyl on the short shelf between him and the glass. "I said we didn't know each other. That was mostly true. But there's online and there's the real world. Some of us did pass the hash pipe. Maybe more."

Cohen tapped on her tablet and looked up. "Well, I'm ready when you are."

27

NEVER SAFE

Cohen sped down I-87 toward New York City, the black Dodge Charger clearing one hundred without seeming to break a sweat. She glanced from the speedometer over to the impressive LCD screen flashing information on the cellular signal as Savas continued to speak through the hands-free system. The hidden flashing lights had been activated, but she had left the siren off—she'd have a migraine by the time they entered the City otherwise.

"Several of the prints returned with hits." It was Miller's voice. "They're all over the place—security firms, prison guards. One was ex-military, then worked for a contractor that provided muscle in Iraq and Syria for VIPs."

"I'm smelling mercenary," said Savas, his expression grim.

"Possible. But it's not very helpful. No recent addresses. We'll fish with relatives and last known residences, but—"

"But we don't have the time for that. What else?"

"The mask was better."

"How so?"

"Hair. They got DNA sequence—likely the mask ripped out some strands with roots."

"A match?"

"No, and that's the interesting part. Doesn't match the prints. The DNA sequence is an unknown. But some genotyping gives us a first sketch of the leader: Caucasian male, brown eyes, black hair that matched the hair color found, so a good control."

"Fawkes," whispered Cohen, staring ahead at the blurred road. The dash display flickered oddly. She hoped that she wasn't pushing the car too hard.

"Sorry?" asked Miller.

Savas answered. "We'll fill you in soon, Frank. Thanks. I'm getting an alert of an incoming call from Angel. We'll get more details in an hour when we arrive."

"Right. Out for now."

The connection was severed and Savas punched the touch screen on the dash to take the call from Lightfoote.

"Shoot, Angel."

"John, pull the damn car over!"

"Sorry—repeat that, Angel?"

The dash screen pixelated and froze. Cohen spoke coldly.

"John, the steering wheel is locked."

Lightfoote's voice still came in over the speakers. "The worm! You're on a system with an online connection. Your car cell is tracked. Worm activity lit up on my monitors and it's you two!"

Savas felt his stomach clench. "The car?"

Cohen gasped. "Oh God."

Savas didn't have to see the needle on the speedometer begin to spin clockwise, he could feel the acceleration in his gut. Cohen frantically stomped on the brake.

"Nothing's responding!"

The speed climbed toward one-hundred and twenty. Cohen flipped the switch to engage the sirens. They were not part of the car's system, installed independently, and they blared out. Cars in front began to swerve to the side as the blue and red lights bore down on them.

"Disconnect the motherboard!" came Lightfoote's voice. "Under the steering wheel, wires lead to the circuitry. Yank them! You'll get manual, maybe. Or the car will shut down. I don't know! But disconnect, now!"

There was a loud pop from the speakers. The control panel went dark.

"Angel?" called Savas. There was no response.

"No time, John. Connection's severed. Do what she said. Get over here."

The car shuddered and Cohen gasped. Her hands were white with pressure and her shoulders hunched as she struggled with the wheel.

"John, hurry! It's trying to turn!"

Turn? At that speed, they'd flip over and roll to their deaths.

There was no time for finesse. He removed his sidearm and fired several shots into the casing of the dash near Cohen's legs. He saw her flinch as the plastic exploded only inches from her knees. His ears rang. He released his seatbelt and fell onto his back toward the driver's seat. His feet worked their way up the window and he pushed himself between the steering wheel and the floor board, body crushed into the tight space.

"One forty! It keeps trying to turn! John, hurry!"

Jesus. Grasping the smoking and shattered plastic, he ripped with all his strength. Toxic fumes from melted insulation choked him, but he reached in and grasped elements of the circuitry and wires, praying that he wouldn't electrocute himself.

Cohen screamed and he felt the car lurch back and forth and barely remain under her control. He felt sick from the motion and stench, but forced himself to focus. He ripped backward from the electronics, snapping wires and yanking pieces of the computer boards out with them, static pops exploding beside his face.

The car stalled.

"John, no control. No brakes, no wheel. Key is locked! I can't start it!"

"Is the computer control dead?"

"I don't know!"

Ahead of them construction arrows indicated a merge of traffic. Cohen could see a small bottleneck approaching and a single-file line of cars. The car continued to slow down, but it wouldn't be enough.

"John, hotwire it. Now. Construction!"

"Shit! Can you hotwire these cars?"

"Try!"

In his wild efforts to disconnect the computers of the dash, he had smashed part of the paneling around the steering column. He reached up and beat on the loosed parts, crushing several elements and the ignition cover. By now his hands were bloody, but he hardly noticed, running on pure adrenaline.

Three wire pairs. "Battery, lights, ignition," he spoke numbly as his slick fingers worked to strip the wiring, bring the leads to this mouth where his teeth ripped at the insulation.

"John, now!"

He didn't have time to figure it. He'd have to guess. He grasped two wires which he prayed were the power to the car. He disconnected them from the cylinder, twisting them together.

Cohen cried out. "We've got the dash and lights. Start it, John!"

He took the two remaining wires and touched them together. There was a spark and the engine roared. Cohen slammed on the brakes and steered the Charger. The car shuddered and leapt into the air. From his vantage point he could see nothing, only imagining her veering away from the obstacles ahead and likely off road. If the shoulder was not forgiving, they were likely dead.

A machine gun sound beside his ear announced the engagement of the antilock brakes, and the car began to spin. Cohen screamed. They wrenched sideways, glass shattered, and everything went dark.

28

LATENCY

"John, can you hear me?"

A woman's voice. Probably his mother's.

He was at the seaside. A strong wind was blowing, waves crashing, muffling sound. No, he was in the water, floating on his back, incoming waves smashing against him, up and down, right and left. Dizzy.

His whole body hurt.

"John?"

"Please, ma'am." A male. "You shouldn't even be here." That would be dad.

Sirens. Why were there sirens at the sea?

Another jolt and his eyes opened. He was staring up at a ceiling, a blurry sphere above him condensing slowly into a fluid-filled bag. A tube ran from it to his right arm. Across from him was a shape on a gurney. A woman with brown hair. Her leg was immobilized with a metal shell of some kind. Blood soaked bandages on her head and shoulder.

"Rebecca."

He tried to sit up but found himself unable to move.

"Hold still, Captain Overlord," came the woman's voice again. "You're strapped down or you would have bounced all over the place. Highway infrastructure deterioration and all that."

"Angel?" he turned his head painfully to the side. The motion was restricted and stiff. There was something fitted around his neck.

"Rebecca's banged up, but she's okay. Well, broken leg, I think. Maybe a concussion. We're inbound to the hospital and will be there in twenty if the traffic opens some. Frank will meet us there. I was lucky to catch a ride. Not policy you know, but with the world going to shit the plumbers get some perks."

Savas looked down at his body on the gurney. A few bandages. Ripped clothing. Otherwise, he seemed to have escaped any serious injury. He let himself settle back into the padding of the gurney. He closed his eyes. "What the hell happened?"

"You don't remember?"

"They hacked the damn car. Nearly killed us. We spun out and crashed."

"That's about it," she said. "You were lucky she steered into a row of construction barriers and attenuators. Course you were going nearly seventy at that point, so it was still a mess."

"Yeah, that part I don't remember."

"Frank and I followed the last known GPS pinging from your car and alerted local emergency responders. We got up here as they were extracting you from the car. A really twisted cage you two were stuck in."

"Jesus." He looked toward Lightfoote, her bald and pierced image surreal in the sounds of the siren. "And the worm?"

She smiled. "Well, it was likely not your plan, but that act of crazy on the highway may be a breakthrough."

"How?"

"The worm in the car's system—it never got a chance to go into hiding again, to erase itself from memory and go latent. Bang, you cut the power and froze everything in place. We've got a crew extracting the computer elements from the Charger. We might get lucky."

"What does latent mean?" He just wanted to sleep.

"It's like Herpes."

"Herpes."

"Yes. Cold sores come out every now and then. Not from new virus you get exposed to, but from virus hiding out in your cells. The genetic material is dormant, *latent.* Waiting to be activated. Usually for herpes it's stress of some kind. For the worm—well, we don't know all the things that might wake it. But the programmers have established some flags.

Apparently investigating Anonymous members like Hanert was one of them."

"Wake it up?"

"Well, not really wake. It's not sleeping. That's just scientific vernacular. For viruses, there are proteins that react to signals or stresses and then go and start making the virus again from the genetic code hiding out in the cells. That's waking up."

"Uh-huh."

"For the worm, the signals are detected by smaller pieces of code floating about, placed there by the initial infection, and they wake up the worm, which then assembles, like the parts of a mature virus particle, from various pieces of code across the net."

This would have given him a headache on a good day. Now it was torture.

She continued. "Usually, after that, the worm disintegrates, so the active, fully functional copy is lost, and the encrypted genome hides out latent. That's the problem getting at it. I couldn't get my hands on anything functional. Until now. Just maybe your automotive catastrophe trapped our little monster in a cage."

"So you can study it." His voice was hoarse.

"It's going to be tricky. As soon as I try to connect a live computer with functioning operating system to the thing, the worm is going to try and go active. Like melting the ice off *The Thing*. Look out. I've got to prevent that, prevent it from taking over whatever system I'm using to study it. And prevent it from erasing itself before I can look inside."

"Can you?"

Lightfoote stared into space. "I don't know." She turned her intense eyes on Savas. "But I'm going to try."

He was beginning to drift off. He fought the currents dragging him under.

"Lopez, I mean Gabriel and Mary. Have you heard anything?"

Lightfoote shook her head. "They've gone dark since we gave them the keys to the databases. My guess is they're prepping."

He nodded. "How's the world doing?"

"A few days of martial law sure has an effect on a town. It's like some apocalyptic thriller. But no zombies, sadly. The worm's been quiet since the massacre. Well, quiet is a relative word. It's still spreading, penetrating more and more systems. No one has a solution to that yet. But so far no direct attacks. No other mischief."

Her voice seemed to fade. He was staring up a deep well, trying to communicate. "That's good. That's good."

"But I think everyone knows it's a calm before the next storm. Someone has a grand scheme. Phase one is done. Phase two will be worse, I bet."

She looked down at Savas, but he was already back under. Her hand found his. "Goodnight, John. Rest up. We're going to need it."

29

COGNITIVE DISSONANCE

A lanky adolescent male slouched in a baroque chair, the office around him out of a seventeenth-century painting. He sported shoulder length black hair and rumpled denim attire, square prescription sunglasses masking his eyes. Across from him, a young woman with a shawl over her bare shoulders scribbled notes and nodded her head. The boy hardly looked at her.

"I will have to submit my evaluation next week, Tony," she said.

"That's not my name."

The woman nodded. "And I will continue to use it as per the juvenile privacy laws. Tony. I will not know your real identity. We protect those under custody."

"Jesus Christ. How long do we play this game?"

The therapist sighed. "You do want me to write you a good report, I assume? You want to go home?"

"Home? You've got to be kidding. Don't you read the files they send you?"

"Foster home. You ran away from home and your mother is a recovering alcoholic. Yes, I know. I meant, don't you want out of here?"

The boy completely repositioned his frame in the chair, whipping a leg across the other and folding his arms across his chest.

"It doesn't matter. I'll be out very soon no matter what you write. I've made sure of it."

"Hacking the city council's computers is a serious offense. Hasn't this experience humbled you at all?"

The boy laughed. "It was an experiment. Not for the hack. That was all too easy. For the effects. Learned a lot about cybercrime investigations and protocol. I'll follow up on the outside. But I've gotten all the data I can from this, so there isn't much of point in continuing here. And, you know, what I found on their servers was a thousand times worse than anything I've done. And they know it. I squirreled it all away where they can't touch it. They're not going to fuck with me."

The woman stopped writing. "I'm worried about you, Tony. You manifest a collection of antisocial behaviors and extreme, nearly delusional idealizations."

"Don't forget boundary issues. I think you still show too much cleavage for a doc. Go with the more discrete pushups from Victoria's. I like small and well-made. You don't have to look like you have implants, you know."

The woman buttoned the top of her blouse and angled her body to the boy. "Yes, that is what I mean. You are alienating. Hostile. Even to those you know mean you well. Psych profiles place you in the top percentiles for intelligence. If you would have cooperated on the examinations we could have placed you more accurately. But you don't use that intelligence wisely. You purposefully lash out and degrade those around you."

"Or, you could just be more honest and say that people want to maintain the facade of comfortable lies and masks they use. Jesus, don't you all get tired of it? Or is it that you're all just so fucking scared all the time? Fuck all your boxes. Fuck all your strata and rules and cages. Look at you! Borderline anorexic, overly made-up, over-slutted, and probably thinking to get a boob job. Honestly, did you sign up for this shit when God handed out the double X's?"

The woman looked away from him. "Is that why the girl left you? Did you treat her like this?"

The boy turned to face her for the first time. "Seriously? You know my fuck-buddies? Is that why they picked you?"

"We receive detailed dossiers on our patients. Personal relationships are often part of that. All anonymous. We try to understand and we need backgrounds to see the big picture."

He laughed, throwing his head back. "You lying motherfuckers. You're a goddamned Fed! I should have known it. All this therapy for juvenile offenders! You're profiling me!"

The woman froze slack-jawed but said nothing.

"I can't believe I didn't see through it sooner. I guess they picked you for that. I kinda trusted you. It was like instinct. All those pheromones and those boobs and the neural pathways—zap! They fuck you up. You really want to know? Zap! That's what the girl was. Lots of research you can read online. It's like heroin, you know? Same brain pathways. Same high. Same addiction and withdrawal. Except it also plugs into all these emotional pathways. So it's a hundred times worse than heroin. Hormones and receptors and neural pathways designed over ten million years to get chunks of meat to fuck and make more chunks of meat."

The woman paled and pulled back slightly in her chair.

"These thoughts, Tony, I am concerned—"

"You are concerned," he barked, chuckling. "You don't give a fuck except for what kind of checklist of personality traits you can enter into a database for your puppet masters. Fingerprints, blood type, you likely got my DNA. Now it's gonna be some kind of brain-print. You need a pattern, profiles, data for the algorithms to train on. Not really there yet, are you, though? But let me help. I can tell you all about our relationship." He leaned forward toward the woman. "I think you like talking about sex. I think it arouses you." He held his face steady in front of hers. "Maybe that's why you do this."

The woman licked her lips.

The teen pivoted his body again and looked away from her. "Anyway, that fucking girl. I can tell you, heaven and hell, love and loss. All that. Damn, that panic. Lost, lost, lost." He replaced his glasses. "But that's the withdrawal. You're sick, all the hormones fucked to hell. Then, you finally come out of it. Then you see. You finally know the truth."

"Which is?" Her voice was hoarse and dry

"That there is no love. No destiny. No meaning to these stupid feelings. That's the delusional thinking, doc. Then you understand that emotion is the problem."

She shook her head vigorously. "Don't you see, Tony? This is just another form of extreme idealization. You went from an extreme belief in transcendent love to an extreme disbelief in all love, a rejection of all meaning in human emotion."

His voice turned cold. "Look, dogs love us. Cats nurture their young. Birds have emotions. The only thing that distinguishes us from the rest of the animals is a small first step in abstract thought. That's it. With emotion, we're puppets to our dicks, our ovaries, some asshole with a shiny car or a promise that you'll live forever. Cut the emotion! Engage the fucking homunculus."

He stood up and pressed his jacket flat, buttoning it closed.

"We're done here," he said. "You go write your report. Like I said, they're not going to do anything with me. They wouldn't dare. File it. It won't matter. In ten years, it won't even exist."

The woman's eyebrows arched upward, but he didn't pause to consider her confusion. With confident steps, he walked to the door of the office and left.

OCTOBER 27

30

VULNERABILITY

It was one of the largest water filtration plants in the United States. Twelve acres, drilled through bedrock to a depth of over four stories in the Bronx's Van Cortlandt Park, it sat over one of the main supply lines feeding water from the Croton Reservoir into New York City. Water flowed from the force of gravity upstate through two eight-thousand-foot-long tunnels into the plant, where particulates were removed, solids dewatered by centrifuges, and the filtered water disinfected with ultraviolet light and chlorine. Chemical alterations were then made to control corrosion and add fluoride.

The entire process utilized several networked controllers, twelve workstations, five separate operator interfaces and numerous 'intelligent' devices, including flow meters, pressure and temperature sensors, transmitters, and automated chlorination analyzers. Everything was networked, highly modernized, automatic, and requiring far less human oversight than anything else like it ever produced.

On the evening of October 27th, the first sign of problems was detected by a skeleton crew manning the equipment to analyze the quality of the final water to leave the facility. A young woman with Indian features and lush black hair gazed at the readings from a dilapidated sensor, a relic from the early testing of the computer systems. Her body was tense, the white of her lab coat contrasting with the deep caramel of her skin. The readings from the other sensors were normal. She felt that she shouldn't care about this artifact of older tech, one that management had never given the order to remove. While it had never acted up before, common sense told you that someday it would fail. It shouldn't bother her when all else appeared normal.

But it did. She spoke into a mobile phone.

"No, Larry. Everything reports nominal. It's only the older ovation monitor. It's screaming on the chlorine and fluorine levels. Look, I didn't want to get you out of bed for this. Probably just the old unit has finally gone senile on us."

There was a pause in her speech as she listened intently. "No, really, no need to come in. Look, I know your close, it's just I...Okay. All right. Fine. I'm happy just to log it, but if you want...Okay. Yeah, I'll call the chemists on three."

She walked up to the bank of computer monitors to check once more the readings from the chemical sensors. Satisfied that all was within normal parameters, she sat down to open a video call with the staff upstairs.

"What the hell?"

The computer was unresponsive. She moved to a nearby terminal, but it too had completely locked up. The unease that had buzzed in the background of her mind at the anomalous readings came much more strongly to the fore. *Is there a computer problem?* In all the years she had worked here, there had never been a glitch affecting more than one unit. Multiple computers down alongside the dangerous readings coming from the other unit—she whipped out her cell phone and called the upstairs number directly.

"This is Deepta from Analysis. Look, are you guys having any computer problems?" Her brow furrowed and she listened. "Yeah, me too. Look, I need to ask you a favor. I'm getting some ridiculous readings on an older sensor. It's not networked with the others; it's probably just failing. But all this has me nervous. Is there a way you can monitor your additive levels? Yeah? Sure, I'll wait. I'll put you on speaker while I recheck that damn unit."

She pressed a button on the mobile phone as she walked to the far wall and crouched in front of the older equipment again.

A voice erupted with distortion from the small speaker of the phone. "Okay, Deepta. Give us a few minutes here. There is a panel of sensors directly on the additive pipes. They *should* be read by the main software—

and all that looks good—but they also display the values on the sensor units themselves. We can read them off directly. Hang on."

"I'll be right here."

She shook her head. The anomalous readings had not normalized. In fact, they were shooting up. It was like they were unloading their entire store of toxic chemicals into the New York City drinking water!

The door to the operations center burst open. A middle-aged man with a crop of silver hair dashed into the room. He was roughly dressed, clothes obviously thrown on in a hurry, hair uncombed. He rushed straight to the computer monitors as he put on his glasses.

"Mike, wait that's no good. There—"

"Deepta! What the hell's wrong with the interface?"

"It's down! I'm trying to tell you. All the machines! And not only here, but on other floors."

"But the software's still running. I just can't access anything. God, we'll have to reboot everything!"

"Mike, come look at these readings." Her superior shuffled over and bent down to examine the older unit. "Please tell me this is malfunctioning."

His face paled. "I grew up on these things, Deepta. When they fail, they don't give readings like this. The checks are too thorough in the logic. This is not failure behavior. We need to find out what's going on with the treatment chemicals."

"Right. I'm on the line with—"

The phone popped. "Deepta? Mike? This is Herman Richards upstairs. We have several people double-checking, but your aberrant sensor is *not*, I repeat *not* malfunctioning. Our pipe sensors are screaming. The valves are completely open. We're dumping everything into the supply!"

"Can you shut things down from there?"

"So far no! All computer control is locked. We can't get into the system. We're force rebooting a few to see if that clears the problem. Meanwhile we're poisoning the water supply for millions in the city! We've got to get a public health message out. Get this on the news. Something!"

"Calm down! We follow protocol. Deepta, get the manual open and let's go by the book on this."

"We went paperless three months ago, Mike. The hard copies were recycled."

"Jesus!" He shook his head. "Then go from memory! Meanwhile, we've got to shut it down before too much gets out there."

The voice on the phone sounded panicked. "I know! What if we can't?"

"Then we're going to have a hell of a lot of sick people come tomorrow."

BEFORE:
THE ANONYMOUS EVENT COMMISSION

DEPOSITION IN THE MATTER OF:
UNITED STATES ARMED FORCES SPECIAL TRIBUNAL, Plaintiff,
versus
JOHN SAVAS, Defendant
Case No. M120039E-007X

CONTINUED DEPOSITION OF:
John Savas

CBD: And what was the result of the filtration plant failure?

MR. SAVAS: Minor. New York only got about 10% of its water from the Croton pipeline. They manually shut off the flow before much of the tainted water got into the main supply into the City. What did was diluted out. We got lucky.

CBD: And this was the worm?

MR. SAVAS: Yes. The computers running the plant were all infected, of course. They lost control of them. Like with our car. Everything is plugged in now, even things that are life and death. Something as basic and driving, as basic as water.

CBD: So, it's your belief that Anonymous tried to murder you by hacking your car?

MR. SAVAS: Not Anonymous. We were learning better than that. Fawkes.

CBD: But you have said that he called himself Anonymous.

MR. SAVAS: I could call myself the Pope, but it wouldn't mean I could lead services at the Vatican.

CBD: You claim you were nearly killed by this Fawkes. How could he hack your car?

MR. SAVAS: Turns out it's not that hard. We were in a brand-spanking new Dodge Charger model outfitted for police work. One of the most powerful engines in a production model—seemed some great wheels to make time upstate. What a bunch of idiots we were. Like the civilian models, it came standard with a new high-tech digital interface. Everything from GPS navigation and mobile apps to handsfree phone calls. Probably would do your dishes if you asked nicely. Used the latest mobile phone tech to connect to the internet. Ran one of several operating systems vulnerable to the worm. QED. Infected.

[REDACTED]: And how would you know all this?

MR. SAVAS: You do remember I have a cybercrimes group? Angel filled us in once we got back, as luck would have it in one piece. We went back to older Crown Vics from the garage after that. They weren't networked and so were isolated from infection.

CBD: How would Anonymous know to target you?

MR. SAVAS: *Fawkes*, not Anonymous. And that one is a bit of a mystery. Maybe by pairing our FBI origin coordinates with the prison destination. Hanert could have been a trigger, a flag, and once raised, they could monitor our phone calls made from the car system. We were really stupid. So much for off-grid. We ignored the OS backdoor in the car we were sitting in. And we knew that wasn't going to be the end. The clock was ticking. Fawkes knew we were poking around. It was just a matter of time before they tried something else to slow us down.

CBD: Wouldn't the break-in at the drone factory have had the same result?

MR. SAVAS: No. Lopez and Houston, they were ciphers. No ties to anything. Sure, it would have given Fawkes a jolt, but nothing to bring FBI, and our division in particular, into the cross-hairs. They were in and out like ghosts. And thank God Houston took the paper copies.

CBD: Please elaborate.

MR. SAVAS: On what? The break-in?

CBD: Yes.

MR. SAVAS: This is second-hand, but they had the same problem we were facing, this dependence on digital technology for nearly everything, and now behind it all, the worm, of course. So, they worked off public computers, I think the library. Angel gave them temporary codes to the federal databases, access to names, locations, sat imagery, and more.

Down to the positions of the guards on an hourly basis as I understand it. They even had the specs on the security system. Not sure what happened, if anything, to the computer systems they used to do all this research on.

CBD: And they used this information to break into the factory?

MR. SAVAS: Yes. They had schematics for the buildings, and Angel had put a trace on orders coming in and out to verify the likely center of operations and data storage at the facility.

CBD: Which was your target?

MR. SAVAS: If we could get the buyer info, we might find leads. Those drones had to go somewhere. Someone had to get them at a specific address. All this would leave a trail. It was worth a shot.

[REDACTED]: So you ordered a commando-style hit on a civilian manufacturer without authorization of any kind?

MR. SAVAS: I did. But since the fugitives didn't work under me or anyone else, you might say that they acted on their own recognizance.

[REDACTED]: Are you saying you had no authority in this? Didn't you lead the investigation and bring these criminals into this?

MR. SAVAS: Lopez and Houston helped bust this case open. They were instrumental then and later in bringing Fawkes to justice. Just who do you think the criminals were in all this?

[REDACTED]: Well, that indeed, Mr. Savas, is why you are here. And until you give us what we want, we have no option but to assume that you are implicated in a bigger conspiracy.

MR. SAVAS: What is this nonsense? I've told you—you've made me tell you over and over—I don't know where Angel is. I don't know where Houston and Lopez are. When you sent the cavalry to pry us out of our own offices, by the time the smoke cleared they were gone.

[REDACTED]: We want the file.

MR. SAVAS: You have it! It was on her damn computer! I don't understand any of this!

[REDACTED]: A copy was made. A thumb drive was connected to that computer and the file was copied.

MR. SAVAS: I can't help you with that. You have your copy, you can try to decrypt it as well as they could. Unless. Wait a minute. [INAUDIBLE] This isn't about trying to figure out what Fawkes was trying to tell her, is it?

CBD: Let's proceed to the next set of questions, Mr. Savas.

MR. SAVAS: I'll be damned. It's about the file! You don't want that file in her hands. In anyone's hands! You're trying to bury the information!

CBD: Let's take up what you have said Houston found in the factory records. First—

MR. SAVAS: That's it, isn't it? What the hell is going on here? What are you trying to cover up?

OCTOBER 28

31

HARDCOPY

A heavy cold front had rolled in a thick layer of clouds, and the evening was without moon or starlight. Lopez and Houston lay prone at the top of a small hill overlooking a factory. Inside, thousands of drone unmanned aerial vehicles were assembled for governmental and civilian buyers, loaded at a wide dock, to be shipped across the country. The factory was isolated in a relatively undeveloped region in New Jersey east of Newark, nestled in a minor valley. The small facility was surrounded by tall fences and wire, imaged by numerous cameras, and protected by a small crew of five security guards at several stations scattered around the compound.

The two fugitives wore dark clothing and gazed down through night vision scopes mounted on rifles. Houston pulled her head back from the lens and whispered.

"I think we've got shots at three guards from here."

"Should be four," grumbled Lopez. "The info is outdated, so our guard count is wrong. Other things could be off."

"You didn't expect a briefing from them, did you?" she smirked. "Three down is a big win. I doubt they'll have added many more guards. Maybe one is out to piss."

"Things could get messy. These guys are naive hires. They don't deserve a grave for this gig."

Houston sighed. "So we'll do our best, Francisco. Right now the big game is threatening many more lives. Even theirs."

"I know. So, let's bring them down. One should do it. Two for sure with plenty of margin for safety on the overdose."

They bent to the rifles, aiming down the hillside. The sounds were soft, muffled expulsions of pressured gas. Each of the guards jerked when hit, twitching again from a second impact. Within seconds, each fell to the ground, unmoving.

Houston pressed a button on her wristwatch. "Clocks running."

Lopez donned a ski mask and they sprinted down the hill, arriving at a central transformer near the fence line. Houston removed a small pack, placed it on the metal casing with a clang as the magnet took. They dashed away from the location as a red light blinked on and off behind them, putting several hundred feet between themselves and the pack when it blew. A small explosion lit the dark night orange with a shower of sparks. The facility lost power, and they quickly cut through the fence and raced toward the central office building.

The structure was the size of a residential home, lined with corporate dark glass, dwarfed by the manufacturing buildings and warehouses around it. They passed two guards on their way in. Large darts in their thighs left them unconscious, drugged. As they neared the entrance, the door opened and two figures stepped out.

The two guards were disoriented, the blast and light drawing their attention. The blurred motion of their assailants was glimpsed too late, part of a distraction of violence and prone figures, two shadows blending into the night.

The intruders engaged without weapons. In a flurry of hands and feet, the guards were disarmed, their weapons sent flying, sudden blows to the abdomen and head stunning them. Before they could even cry out, both were down, unconscious in front of the doors of the office. Lopez emptied the guards' weapons, slinging the ammunition into the night. Removing wires from their belts, the two shadows secured the guards, tying their arms and roping their ankles together. Duct tape sealed their mouths. Houston grabbed a keycard from one of the men and tried it on the front door. It opened.

"Emergency power's up," Lopez noted.

They headed inside. Weak illumination spilled from corners in the room and green lights from some of the older cameras.

"Smile pretty. Just keep your mask on," said Houston.

Passing the reception desk and moving down a hallway, they stopped in front of a door labeled 'Records.' An alphanumeric keypad was embedded in the door beside the handle.

"I don't recall any of the files mentioning a code for this, do you?" she asked. Lopez shook his head. "Didn't think so. Hinges?"

Lopez reached behind his back and unslung a short-barreled pump-action shotgun. Houston stepped backward as he aimed. He fired blasts near the top, middle, and bottom of the door across from the handle. Wood splintered and metallic fragments rained around them. He spun and kicked the door inward, the wood hanging to the frame weakly from the keypad and lock mechanism, then ripping free and thudding to the floor.

Inside were a set of computers and floor to ceiling filing cabinets. They moved quickly.

"Grab all the hard drives," said Houston, pulling out what looked like a large pocketbook. She unzipped the leather and removed several tools. "We'll deal with them later. I'm going to go for paper."

Lopez knelt down and pulled the chassis off one of the computers. "That wasn't part of the plan."

Houston went to work with several microtools on the locks of the cabinets. "Neither was the fact that they still had paper records."

"The disks will be fast! It will take you forever to get the records."

"We've got twenty minutes. A little more if they're out for donuts."

The shell popped off one of the units as Lopez reached inside to disconnect the wires to the hard drive. "Cutting it close, Sara!"

There was a click, and the large cabinet door was slung open. Houston shone a small flashlight on the folders and began scanning their content. "Paper, Francisco. No bytes. No worms. No worries. I'll be done before you."

Grunting, he dropped one drive into a bag and moved to the next computer. Within ten minutes, Lopez had removed all the drives and placed them in the bag. Houston called him over, showing him regions in three cabinets where purchase orders over the last six months were filed.

"That's three full boxes!"

"So, a transport!" she said, pointing to the far end of the narrow room.

Lopez rushed over and wheeled a wobbly cart to her side. Together they hefted three large boxes full of files onto the slight metal surface.

"This is definitely not my idea of stealth. I hope this doesn't collapse."

They sped out of the building as fast as possible, Houston with one hand stabilizing the boxes, Lopez pushing the cart from behind as they navigated prone bodies, ramps, and the sharp rise of the hill. They were forced to remove the boxes and fit them through the hole in the fence one by one, bringing the cart awkwardly through at the end.

"It's no good. We can't get that thing up the hill," said Lopez.

"Okay, bring the car around. Tape the plate, but we'll have to lose it tonight."

He nodded and sprinted up the hill. Houston waited in the cold night air, her fogged breaths coming quickly. She heard the engine cough.

Lopez rounded the corner of the hill and braked hard beside her, popping the trunk. They worked quickly, flinging the boxes in, the car bouncing with each impact. Houston slammed the trunk and ran to the passenger side, Lopez already seated. He gunned the engine.

Red and blue lights flickered in the distance, reflecting off the low lying clouds.

"Wait, Francisco! We'll need a back road. Listen!"

Sirens. The police were converging on their position from the main route. Lopez spun the car in a one-eighty and tore down the road in the opposite direction.

He laughed ruefully. "Well, this sure feels familiar."

BEFORE:
THE ANONYMOUS EVENT COMMISSION

DEPOSITION IN THE MATTER OF:
UNITED STATES ARMED FORCES SPECIAL TRIBUNAL, Plaintiff,
versus
JOHN SAVAS, Defendant
Case No. M120039E-007X

CONTINUED DEPOSITION OF:
John Savas

CBD: And so the computer records led you to the warehouse on Long Island?

MR. SAVAS: No. The hard drives melted down.

CBD: I'm sorry?

MR. SAVAS: Well, not literally. But all the facility's computers were infected. Turns out, the worm was indeed monitoring the records of the drone sales, so Fawkes at least saw that as a potential vulnerability.

CBD: The worm erased the files?

MR. SAVAS: Nuked all the drives. One after the other as they tried to access them. Maybe Angel could have prevented it, although I doubt it. But Lopez and Houston didn't have the digital chops to even try.

CBD: Then it was the paper records you mentioned.

MR. SAVAS: Yes. Can you imagine? Two burglars with the police bearing down on them toting six months of paperwork out of a secured facility? I don't know if Sara guessed there might be a problem or it was just instinct to get everything they could get, but it saved our investigation. They must have spent hours going through that crap. But they knew what they were looking for: shipments of large drone models, likely in quantity. And they found them.

CBD: So, all of them went to the Long Island facility.

MR. SAVAS: No, they weren't that reckless. In the end we'd find that they ordered multiple drones from several facilities, using a series of aliases for each order, often multiple orders under different names from the same facility. Then they'd ship them to one of five or ten storage locations, then re-mail them.

CBD: How did you discover this?

MR. SAVAS: You'll have to ask Lopez and Houston. Too bad they aren't here.

OCTOBER 29

32

ANONYMOUS REMAILERS

A misting rain partially solubilized the grime on the gray Ford Taurus that pulled alongside a nondescript brick warehouse in Long Island City. Lopez and Houston exited, both dressed in dark trench coats and shades. Passing underneath the "Your Storage!" sign and the security cameras, they entered the small business.

The office was more a glorified hallway outfitted with a narrow countertop and secretarial equipment on the right side. Behind the counter was a receptionist, a slight African American woman, with thick glasses and makeup obscuring much of her face. She spoke into a microphone on a headpiece as she motioned for them to sit. Houston turned to look behind her at a small and uncomfortable looking bench. She shook her head at Lopez.

Reaching over the counter, Lopez removed the headset in one quick motion, tossing it to the side. The receptionist looked stunned.

"Hey! Just what do you think you're doing?"

Houston placed a hundred dollar bill on the counter. "We'd like to purchase the expedited service."

"The expedited...?"

"Just get your manager out here now and you'll get another one."

Grabbing the bill in her hand, she stood up slowly, her eyes ludicrously exaggerated in the strong lenses, her bright purple eyeshadow giving her features a slightly alien quality. "Just a second." She stepped out from behind the counter and clicked to the end of the room in impossible heels. She opened a flimsy door. "Hey, Ryan. A man and a woman need to speak with you."

"What do I pay you for, bitch? You deal with it!"

The receptionist startled as Houston handed her another hundred. "Go on back to the call. We've got it from here." The woman took the bill and scampered away.

Lopez opened the door and stepped into a crowded room. Likely an addition to the hallway, the walls were a temporary attachment, the flooring added over part of the cement below it. He canvassed the ceiling and corners, the desk surface and walls. There were no cameras.

A bald man sat over a terminal and flashed them a puzzled expression.

"Who the hell are you?"

He gasped as Houston pointed her Browning at him. Lopez closed the door.

"We're the ones with the guns. Don't scream. Keep your hands over the desk."

"Oh God, oh God, oh God. Please. Take what you want. I have a safe, there!"

"Shut up," said Houston, ignoring his gesture. "I'm going to ask you a few questions. You are going to answer them truthfully and quickly. Or I'll let my partner deal with you." Lopez held a hunting knife in his hand.

The man swallowed, struggling to speak. "Yes."

"So, Ryan," she began. "What do you do here?"

"We, ah, store things."

"What things?"

"We don't ask. It's like a remailing service. People ship here, we get another address for the item and ship it there. Keeps buyers and sellers separate. Anonymous."

"Anonymous?" said Lopez.

The man stared at the knife, terrified. "Yeah. Private. That's why we don't ask what's in the boxes. It's all perfectly legal."

"So you don't know where the boxes come from. How do you know where to send them?"

"Paired codes. The sender has a code that has to match the buyer's code before we ship to the buyer's address. They get those from whatever exchanges they make their deals on. That way nothing can be traced."

"But you put the items in the mail. In their original boxes?"

"Oh, yes. We never open a box."

"Then you must know the weight of the items. For postage."

He nodded. "Yes."

"And you have records of that?" Houston asked.

"Of course. That's our main expense. Why are you asking this?"

"The people with guns ask the questions, Ryan."

The man shrank into his chair. Houston removed a set of folded papers from inside her coat and looked them over. As the seconds ticked by the manager began to sweat. Beads of perspiration dripped down his forehead, and his underarms stained.

Houston grabbed a pen and circled several regions on the paper. "Ryan, I need you to find shipments that match these weight specifications."

"Now?"

"Yes, now."

The manager typed furiously on his computer keyboard. Within seconds, his face relaxed. "Yes, I have a bunch of them. Lots of orders match those specs exactly."

"Where are they shipped to?"

"Um. That's interesting. All shipped to the same place. Some address in Jersey."

"We would like you to print out one of those records, Ryan, with the address."

"Yeah, okay." He clicked several times with his mouse. A small printer behind Houston whirred to life.

She grabbed the printout and stared at it. Nodding to Lopez, she grabbed the papers she had given the manager and then pocketed all of them. A wad of cash thudded on his desktop.

"You wouldn't lie to us, would you, Ryan?"

He looked at the knife again. "No way." He licked his lips.

"We were never here, and you can enjoy the fee for this priority service." The man nodded dumbly, taking the money. "But this is a discrete service, right?" She glanced at Lopez, who twirled the knife slowly, staring at the serrated edges. "There isn't going to be any need for us to come back and register a complaint that our privacy has been violated, is there? Nobody would like that."

Again the man swallowed. "No. I never saw you. I never want to see you again."

"That's good," she said smiling, opening the door.

Lopez sheathed the knife, staring fixedly at the bewildered man. "It was a pleasure doing business with you."

33

RAID ON ANONYMOUS

"You sure you're up to this, John?"

Savas shifted his position in the car once again. It didn't help. He was bruised all over his body, several lacerations still quite painful to the touch. He stared at Miller and ground his teeth. Of course he was *up to it.*

"Frank, I'd have to lose a leg or worse to have an excuse not to be on the ground in this crisis. Are you going to tell me otherwise?"

"You are literally the boss, so okay." The ex-Marine continued to focus ahead as he drove. "And Rebecca?"

"Tibia was snapped. Soft tissue damage from the bone as well. It's set, she's stitched up. But it's going to be a serious cast and crutches for a couple months. She'll heal. She's tough."

Miller nodded. "It always seems to get personal with us, doesn't it?"

Images of a gray-haired man swept through Savas' mind. They came with explosions and collapsing buildings, a sniper round buried in the shoulder of the man driving next to him. A massacre of an FBI division. A threat to Rebecca's life.

"Yeah, and I'm getting kinda tired of it."

"We sure know how to make friends." Miller's smiled faded as they pulled alongside a black van in an abandoned parking lot. "Don't think this club is going to be very taken with us today. I hope this intel is worth it."

"Highest level contact in Anonymous we have. Rebecca seems to trust him. Let's see if she's right."

A commuter train rumbled overhead along the Queens subway line. Nestled underneath, a rusted warehouse waited before them. Heavily armed FBI agents in body armor stepped out of the dark van and grouped around them.

Savas limped toward the group. "I'm sorry to pull you from every which division, but you know what we're up against. FBI—now the damn Federal Bodyguard Institute." The men laughed. "Thank you for coming on such short notice. We might already be too late, but we have to try. Police are inbound, but we'll be without their backup for the dangerous parts. I'll let our vet from Kabul fill you in."

Miller stepped forward. "There was no time and no data to recon this right. I don't know what we'll find in there. Might well be empty. Might be an armed engagement with as many as ten hostiles. But if our intelligence is right, it's going to be a bunch of hackers scared shitless about what's going down. We don't need them dead—understood? We need information. They need to be able to talk, and dead men don't. Defend yourselves but keep a level head. We'll go in through the main door with a volley of flash bangs and tear gas. Unless they're trained militia, that ought to have most of them rolling on the ground crying for mommy. Bag them and into the van. Make sure you canvas the interior and clear it. We don't want any surprises. Questions?"

"Yes, sir," came a voice of a young blond to the right. "Is this Anonymous? Are these the guys?"

"We don't know, but not likely. But we think they can get us to the real criminals. So remember—*alive*. Understood?"

The men nodded. Along with Savas and Miller, they donned gas masks. Savas drew his weapon. "Okay, boys, your show."

The SWAT team filed off in a quick jog, splitting into two groups on either side of the door, weapons at the ready, quickly reaching the wall of the warehouse and using it as cover from the building windows. They slid along the sides, Miller and Savas at the far end of the lines. An officer nearest the door pulled slightly on the handle near the ground. The roll-up door moved slightly, and he gave the thumbs up. Miller nodded, the other officers set, and the door was raised.

The men dashed inside and out of sight. Savas ran forward and could just discern the arc of canisters being lobbed into the air and over a set of dark obstacles inside the building. The flash bangs flashed and banged. It was nearly stunning even from their position. Several canisters of tear gas filled the space inside with a cloud of burning vapor.

For a moment, there was no other sound. Then the screams began.

THE SWAT TEAM pulled out the last member of Anonymous just as their police backup finally arrived. They had never been in any danger. The disoriented and snot dripping youth that were dragged out of the warehouse were never going to put up any kind of a fight. Some of the SWAT team administered first aid to those who had suffered most from the chemicals and shock. It looked to Savas that the agents felt sorry for them.

The blond leader of the SWAT team came out of the warehouse, mask in hand.

"Secured?" asked Miller.

"Yeah," he said, coughing. "Most of the gas is gone. And you need to come and see this."

Savas arched an eyebrow. "Right behind you."

He led the special agents into the warehouse. The dark obstacles Savas had seen were revealed to be rows of computer hardware stacked six feet high in places. The SWAT officer zig-zagged through it like a maze and brought them to the center, a space occupied with several large monitors. And two decomposing bodies.

"Jesus, that ruins your lunch," said Miller, scowling.

Savas stepped forward and stared at the bodies. Flies danced around the forms and maggots were slithering over the decayed faces. "They've been here a while. Likely rules out a killing by our friends."

"Today, anyway," said the SWAT officer.

"I doubt they'd have come back here," said Miller. "Division in the ranks?"

Savas nodded. "Looks like a hacking bunker. I'd say these poor jerks pissed somebody off."

"Fawkes," said Miller. "He's turning out to be one ruthless bastard."

"Okay, let's get a forensics team in here and see what we can find. My guess is the computers are all wiped. But we need to check them all. Meanwhile," he said, turning toward the door, "I've got a few questions for our hogtied friends outside."

He strode back out the door, Miller close behind. The members of Anonymous were placed in a circle in front of the FBI van facing outwards. Their eyes were red, faces flushed, one with bandages over his head. Groups of NYPD and SWAT officers mingled in haphazard groups around them. He stopped in front of the circle.

"I think you know that all of you are fucking screwed," he began. "Basically anyone connected to Anonymous right now likely goes straight to jail without their $200. Not to mention, as you surely saw inside, the real problem is still out there on the loose turning you folks into corpses."

He could tell the last remark struck a raw nerve as several bodies jerked and heads turned toward him. He hoped to God he could reach the sane part of someone in the group.

"Now, we have a global catastrophe looming. We know about the worm." More heads turned. "We know about Fawkes. But we don't know where he is or what the endgame is. But I think it's clear it's going to be ugly. As in civilization-ending ugly. We're going to get you all back to lockup to question you there, but time is not our friend. So I'm going to give you the opportunity to talk right here, right now. Right now there's no Miranda. There's just me and you and getting us all out of this mess."

"Fuck you, pigs!" yelled one of the group, a long-haired man across the circle. He spat at Savas.

"Anyone else? Anyone else with parents? Friends? Kids? Anyone who wants to help us stop this before it's too late? Right now I couldn't give a rat's ass about you, your amateur cybercrimes, or the Anonymous Manifesto, or whatever you have. I need answers now! I need to stop this. Help me."

There was only silence. Police red and blue flickered over them like washed out club lights, the setting sun beginning to dip below the taller buildings in midtown across the river. Officers in heavy gear shifted weight, the friction of thick Kevlar on rubber popping around them. Savas looked up into the sky with his hands on his hips. A crimson scab ran down the left side of his face.

"No one?" He shook his head and turned to the SWAT team. "Okay. Load them up. We'll try again back home."

"Wait!" A female voice. Savas turned to his right. A black-haired woman with deep black eyeliner stared back at him, the goth makeup running down her face as her eyes watered.

"Yes?"

"Shut up, Poison! Don't make this personal!" said the long-haired man.

"Up yours, Protos. Fawkes is into some fucked up shit. Pig's right. Somebody has to end this."

Savas crouched down beside her, several agents stepping forward with weapons at the ready.

"You know Fawkes?"

She laughed. "Yeah, you might say. Better than all these losers here, anyway. Better than you Protos and your group of ass-wipes."

"Fuck you, Poison. We'll remember this."

She laughed. "Remember this? You gonna remember Dave and Chen? Yeah? You don't get it. He's burning everything to the ground. Us, too! There ain't gonna be nothing to remember, you dumb fuck!"

Savas tried to control his voice. "How do you know Fawkes? What can you tell me about him?"

She looked Savas in the eye and smiled. "What do you need to know? His favorite food? Fetishes? Size of his dick?"

Several members of Anonymous laughed. Some of the police officers smirked as well.

"Look, if you want to help, I need you to be serious. What can you tell me about his whereabouts? How do you know him?"

"Whereabouts? I don't know jack. He's too careful. But how do I know him? That I can tell you. I was his lover."

"His lover?"

"Yeah, you know, Anonymous cock. Hackers do it through the back door. Fawkes' fuck buddy. On top, underneath, sideways." She angled her head to the side and ran her tongue over her teeth, leering at him. "Fucking yoga position. I was his right-hand girl, you know what I mean? That answer your question?"

Savas stood up. "Yeah."

"Then let them go, and I'll tell you more than you want to know."

34

POISON

Lightfoote and Poison were hitting it off charmingly.

Savas had agreed to release the other prisoners if and when she responded to their questions back in Manhattan. They had carted the entire crew back into the city, once again subjected to the delays and authority conflicts from the declaration of martial law. However, having claimed to have bagged key members of Anonymous opened the gates more quickly, and they soon had Poison isolated in an interrogation room. The rest were being held in lockup.

Poison was actually Tabitha Ivy, 'Poison' her own hacker handle used from the time she was fourteen. A quick database search revealed that she was now nineteen, a repeat offender having been busted for several hacks of corporate websites, having served nine months behind bars for one job on Pepsi. There was an additional list of minor infractions from possession to vandalizing a parking meter.

It was no wonder she hit it off so well with Angel.

"From what I can tell," said Lightfoote, "about half the code is just to execute this biological like replication and camouflage system." She sat next to Poison at the table, Savas and Miller across in a more standard adversarial position. "Another quarter is still just a black box. Finally about another quarter for ending the world as we know it."

Poison sounded impressed. "How the hell did you get all that? We couldn't even get near the thing."

Lightfoote looked at the battered visage of Savas and smiled. "Mr. I-tried-to- shave-during-an-earthquake over there trapped a live worm for me."

Poison's eyes grew wide. "How the fuck did he do that? I'm surprised he can log into his own computer."

"An unusual technique, but it worked. I have an activated worm trapped on a hard drive. The hardest part was dissecting it without it sending everything to hell and back. That's when I thought, oh, *VMS*."

"VMS? Like your great-grandfather's OS?" The hacker looked confused.

"It's 1970s stuff, for sure, but it kicks serious ass. It's a hacker's worst nightmare. Amazon uses it for shipping. Some stock exchanges. Pretty rare and pretty secure."

"And the worm wasn't designed to hack those machines?"

"Bingo!" Lightfoote beamed.

The two men stared at each other in confusion.

"I don't get it," said Miller.

Poison scowled at him as Lightfoote elaborated. "Fawkes found hacks into a bunch of the world's computer operating systems: Microsoft, all the flavors of UNIX including Apple. The worm bundles all the tools to hit each of them. But he didn't waste his time finding security holes in something so rare and hard to hack as VMS."

Miller shrugged his shoulders. "And?"

"So it's fucking *immune*, you thug," spat Poison.

"Wait," said Savas. "So you could use it to look at the worm? The worm can't operate in this VMS machine?"

Lightfoote clapped her hands together. "Correct! But interfacing with the hard drive was a nightmare. We only had a few 1990s era VMS machines left around here. They weren't designed to handle modern hard drives. I practically had to solder half the spare parts we owned, and cannibalize several perfectly functional computers, to rig something to read the data. Piece by piece. The older machine doesn't have a lot of memory. But we're doing it. JP is down there now with some of the rest of the unit. Active worm, but frozen on my lab table!"

"What else have you learned from it?"

Lightfoote's face fell. "Nothing good. Names. Important names. Politicians. More CEOs. I think they're targets."

"Jesus, here we go," said Miller.

"We need those names now, Angel," said Savas.

"JP's getting the list. But just wait. This is only one active worm, and every worm is different, remember? These were the names we were lucky to get. And we don't have dates or other information. Just names."

"There could be other targets?" asked Miller.

"Almost certainly. But there's more. I don't think the main course has even been served."

"And that means?" asked Savas.

"That last 25%. The really bad part? It does a lot of things. It infiltrates, copies, and reports out to address that are relays to relays: I can't track them, but it's pooling information somewhere, likely ending at his terminal. But the weird part is that this region *always* has empty space. In the code, nonsense. It's filler. But no way this guy would write junk code. That code is something else. I think it's a marker for new code. The virus is waiting for new command modules, something that is going to come down the road."

"Why?" asked Savas. "Why not just hide it all around like the rest of the code?"

Lightfoote shook her head. "I don't know."

Poison rested her head on the table and spoke through a mumble. "Fawkes. It's Fawkes. He's paranoid. A total douche about it, too. Never get involved with a paranoid. Fucking misery."

"What do you mean?" Savas asked her.

"It must be the kill shot," she said, her eyes closed. "He's too paranoid to ever trust his code. He thinks he can hack anything—that anything can be hacked. So he's worried he'll get hacked."

Miller looked at Lightfoote and chuckled. "He was right."

Poison's eyes flashed open. "So, he's saving the best for last, just in case."

Lightfoote nodded. "Now I see. The relay system to the worm. He's going to use it to upload a final code sequence."

Poison slammed her hand on the table, causing the others to jump. "And then we're fucked. Once he sends that signal, it's over. You can't let him send that signal. You've got to stop him or the worm will carry out his final instructions."

"And what might those be?" asked Savas.

"Who the hell knows?" said Poison, her arms out to her sides. "But seriously, Einstein, after all this shit, how do you think his kill shot is going to go down?"

Savas looked toward Lightfoote. “I hope you have some good news about stopping it.”

“Sorry, John—no. That’s a whole other story. But, I’ve sent out my little spies to find out as much as they can.”

“Little spies?” asked Miller.

Lightfoote beamed at Savas. “The virus I used to discover we’d been hacked? Well, I’m a few generations down the road with it and it’s spreading across the net. The worm gave me a few ideas of using NSA backdoors and we’re using them. They’re looking for worm activations and taking what snapshots they can, sending them back to me. Real time. You should come down and see the data. Like some war going on out there.”

Poison stared at her. “Beautiful.”

Miller held his hands up. “You’re infecting computers now? That makes us hackers, too?”

“You’re amateurs compared to the NSA,” said Poison. "As American as apple pie."

“Too true,” said Lightfoote. “But we’re not looking for stealth or long term stability. We’re going in full bore. But don’t worry, Frank. It’s a good virus. A pet virus. It’s on God’s side.” She smiled.

Miller stared incredulously at her. “Jesus. John? What do you say to this?”

Savas appeared not to have heard him. He stared intently at Poison, his eyes focused, seemingly both near and far away.

“John?”

He glanced toward Miller. “Yeah. I’ve green-lighted Angel’s shenanigans. Paying off, I’d say.” Then he turned back to the hacker. “You stopped seeing him?”

Poison frowned. “Fawkes? Yeah. Look, I told you, I don’t know his real identity. He only trusted me with his dick.”

“But you said he pursued you.”

“Jeez, yeah. And you know, when you have the world’s best hacker stalking you online, it’s a fucking nightmare. I spent months shaking him off. I mean, he said it was over, so get the fuck out of my life, right? I think he finally gave up.”

Savas held up a small cylinder. “Are you sure?”

She reached over and grabbed it from his hand. “What’s that?”

“GPS tracking device. An agent pulled it off your car at the warehouse. It’s not in our records. Not a model we use.” Savas stared intently at her. "Anyone else you think might be interested in following your every move?"

"Oh, Christ, that fuck!" She stared furiously at it.

"He likely knows you're here by now."

"Yeah, well, so what? He won't be tracking me anymore."

"He might try to get you out."

Poison laughed. "You're kidding right? Why would he do that?"

Miller leaned forward. "Because he's obsessed with you. Maybe he thinks it's love. But it's obsession for sure."

Savas nodded. "And that makes me wonder just what we're going to do with you."

Poison shook her head. "You really think he'll come after me?"

Savas smiled for the first time. "I'm counting on it."

OCTOBER 30

35

PRAYER BEFORE BATTLE

A deep voice chanted in the darkness beside the candle flames.

"God of power and mercy, maker and lover of peace, to know you is to live, and to serve you is to reign."

Houston observed the flickering light from a distance, giving Lopez space as he dressed. Body armor under vestments, belts and holsters for guns, magazines, knives, and grenades. All the while he chanted. She would never understand. He reached out to a God who had rejected him. He sang the song of a priest when the Church had cast him out. It was his way.

"Through the intercession of St. Michael, the archangel, be our protection in battle against all evil."

Michael. The older Lopez brother. The man whose death had brought her together with Francisco. The man whose life had upturned theirs and so many others. The man whose actions had created a monster of terrible vengeance that had burned like acid through the Central Intelligence Agency. T*he wraith.* A killer whose life ended before the barrel of the man before her.

Michael. An archangel. Like his brother, *Gabriel.*

"May our cause be just. May we have clear vision. May our courage not falter. May our efforts bring lasting peace. Should we perish in the struggle, may God embrace us and find for us a place in His Kingdom. Amen."

Crossing himself in front of an icon of St. George slaying the dragon, he blew out the votives and turned toward her, his black cassock a flowing shroud over layers of death. She waited as he approached, a shadow herself in dark camouflage, an energy anticipating the coming violence burning within her.

Lopez spoke softly, staring into her eyes, black to blue. "Everything will depend on removing the sentries on the roof. Those snipers will pick us off if we try to enter. We'll have to be fast and accurate. The diversion will buy us only moments."

She smiled beneath the covering of the mask. "Amen."

Lopez frowned. "Let's hope our recon remains accurate, that they don't change anything."

"Lord hear our prayer."

He watched her silently for a moment and then pulled down the fabric of the mask covering her mouth. He kissed her, lingering until they pulled away for breath.

"In case it's the last kiss," he said. "I want to make it count."

She reached her hand up to his face and cupped his cheek. "Every mission you do that. And every time I want you to. Because one day, we won't come back, Francisco."

He nodded, turning with her toward the door. "But let it not be this night, O Lord."

36

WITHOUT MERCY

They called him simply Alpha. He was the point man, the de facto leader of this group of men wrapped around and above, guarding the warehouse. The building was a squat little thing, about half a city block. Isolated in the northern New Jersey countryside, it attracted little attention, was not easily accessed, and unregistered in any business directories. It was a ghost.

Like they were. All their real names were scrubbed. They adopted spy thriller handles. Former soldiers and contractors, all of them, hired secretively by a company many in his team began to suspect was involved in some of the attacks occurring around the country. That suspicion led some to leave. But most stayed. The company had done its homework. Like Alpha, most of them would point the gun for whoever paid them the most.

But tensions had escalated dramatically. Five additional guards had been added bringing the total to fifteen. Powers that be were getting rattled about what was inside the metallic walls of the structure. Alpha didn't know what was in there, and he didn't want to know. A few times each month, a small convoy of trucks would show up and pull into what he presumed was an enclosed loading dock, the doors closing and sealing off everything from view. Shortly afterward, the trucks would drive off, whether having unloaded or loaded a mystery that was not part of his job description. A job that paid ridiculous money for guard duty in the states. Iraq had been one thing, but Jersey? Retirement gig.

Until things started blowing up. Until more and more trucks had come. Until more former soldiers had been brought on to fortify a rural building like something in the green zone. Just the presence of that many guns raised the temperature.

"Main gate, clear," came a voice through static on his headset.

"Roger that."

It was Delta. There was only one way by vehicle into the building, through a gate lodged in the electrified fence, then down a broad, truck-friendly road to the loading dock. Three guards patrolled the gate, two at the dock entrance, four moving about the perimeter fence. Six took to the roof, four at the corners and two on the longer sides of the building. Those on the roof were trained snipers. Alpha was one of them, positioned at the front on the right-hand side facing the gate.

"Perimeter report."

Several voices spoke in order of established protocol. The roof snipers followed suit. The space was clear. As it was half an hour ago. As it was at dusk. As it was every night for the last six months that he had worked this job.

That's why when he spotted the headlights at the top of the hill in front of the gate, he didn't quite believe his eyes.

"Delta, check scheduled arrivals."

It looked like a smaller delivery truck, not the massive eighteen wheelers that they tended to get. He zoomed his night-vision goggles. The truck was nondescript, no insignia, the plate damaged and unreadable. The windows seemed opaque or blacked out. Something was wrong.

The vehicle began to accelerate down the hill. Alpha didn't hear the telltale sounds of torque in the engine, the changing pitch as the rpms increased. The steering was odd. His alarm bells were ringing

"Log's empty, Alpha. Nothing due until tomorrow afternoon."

He powered up his scope and set his transmission signal to maximum. "Unidentified vehicle approaching from the road. Treat as hostile. Repeat, treat as hostile!"

Automatic gunfire erupted from the gate. The flashes lit the dark night, strobing the gatehouse, glinting off the chain-links in the fence, reflecting back from the glass in the truck that was now barrelling down the hill. The windshield of the truck exploded, glass spraying inwards, the metal of the hood pocketed with bullet holes. It only accelerated.

"Perimeter guards move forward to engage. Anyone up top with a view, take a shot if you have one. Gamma and Omega, hold the dock!"

The maniacs! Whatever crazed assault this was, it was only going to end one way, and that was with the occupants filled with holes. A foregone conclusion that didn't give him any comfort—madmen always maimed and killed. How many men would he lose tonight?

He settled into a crouch on the roof's ledge, stabilizing his rifle, knowing that the snipers around him were doing the same. The night-vision scope zoomed in on the rushing vehicle. Alpha focused on the cabin, determined to take out the driver himself.

The cabin was empty.

Shit! "Delta, all crews, break off! Repeat, break off!"

But it was too late. His eyes were seared by a bright light and a blast of air that nearly knocked him backward. Stunned, he shielded his eyes as an orange fireball climbed into the sky, quickly darkening in a blanket of smoke and falling embers. The screams hit him now. Just like he remembered. Just like in Mosul when the trucks came and the bombs blew and men and pieces of men lay strewn in the street.

The afterimage of the blast partially blinded him, but he strained to see the gate below. It was gone. The metal ripped and melted like cotton candy, flaming chunks of truck and gatehouse scattered radially around the scene of destruction. Only those bodies that were not close to the explosion were visible, but all of the men he had sent to converge on the intruders were now corpses, or as good as. Three at the gate, four wrecked forms from the perimeter guards. It was a slaughter.

"Roof report." His voice was strained and husked.

Silence.

He spun around the rooftop, dropping the goggles over his eyes again. Motionless forms were draped in various positions across the asphalt. They were all dead. Sniped themselves while distracted by the commotion and chaos at the gate.

Alpha stood up fully now, heedless of the danger, removing his goggles. It was just a matter of time now. Light flickered from the burning debris behind him. He stared up into the sky, looking for some heavenly object, the moon, even a single star to glimpse before the final darkness came.

But it came without mercy. His head snapped backward, a bullet tearing through the soft flesh of his face, a clean hit to the brain stem that unplugged his basic physiological functions in an instant. For a second, his eyes empty, he stood staring stupidly forward. Then the electrochemical signals ceased completely, and he dropped straight to the rooftop with a thud.

Then, only silence.

37

MOTHERLODE

Lopez and Houston entered the burning compound. Their forms wrapped in black, packs strapped to their backs, and pistols in their hands as they jogged cautiously among the scrap and human remains scattered before them. They paused over several bodies, checked them, and moved on toward the compound's entrance.

With weapons raised they approached, stairs on either side leading to a loading platform in front of the enormous roll-up shutter door. Two bodies lay on either side of the stairway, blood pooling underneath them. Houston sprinted up the right-hand steps and examined the large locks barring entrance. Lopez continuously scanned around them with his weapon raised.

"Francisco, it's no good!" she cried. "We're going to have to blow it."

"I counted fifteen. They can't have had more, could they?"

Houston sprinted down the steps, unstrapping her pack. "I don't know. Paranoid as all fuck, so I won't put anything past them. We need the charges from your pack."

Lopez slung his bag to the ground and removed several gray blocks with detonators. He handed them to Houston who returned to the door as he resumed his scanning. Placing the explosive on the locks, she set the charge and sprinted down the steps. They grabbed their bags and rounded the corner of the building, constantly alert for hostile movements or sounds. Houston raised a controller.

"Three, two, one..."

She pressed the bottom and a blast shook the building. After several seconds, they came back around the wall and ran to the loading platform. Twisted steel and smoke greeted them, as did an enormous hole in the shutter door the width of a small car.

Houston laughed. "Just meant to break the locks. I need a course on explosive yields."

She removed a flashlight and they stepped into the building through the hole, careful to avoid the sharp and smoking edges. The air inside the place was stale, almost metallic tasting, the acrid smoke from the blast mingling with the stored smells of machines and dust. The echoing of their footsteps made it clear that the space was vast and open, but it was too dark to see much beyond the direct beam of the light, which only revealed the reflective hulls of large shapes.

Lopez led her arm. "Try the wall. Lights."

Houston scanned the beam across the nearby wall and located a set of switches. Lopez faced away from her with his gun raised in anticipation. She flipped the switches together in one motion.

Ceiling-high bulbs winked to life with a buzz. Dim at first, the bulbs slowly waxed to full brightness, their combined numbers across the length of the warehouse causing the pair to squint as their eyes adjusted.

"Holy shit, Francisco."

They stared down rows and rows of enormous bladed aircraft. The machines were variable, all devoid of a cockpit or other indication of a pilot's chair. Some of the smaller units sported large cameras. The larger drones were outfitted with an array of cargo, all of it dangerous.

Lopez walked up to one of the larger ones, bulbous, metallic shapes strapped to its underside. "Bombs."

"Looks like," said Houston. "And those are aircraft sized machine guns on that one. Can you imagine the bullets?" She swung her gaze across the interior. "There's got to be forty or fifty in here. It's the drone motherlode."

Lopez got to one knee and crossed himself. "At least it wasn't for nothing." Houston placed her hand on his shoulder.

"It had to be done," she said, staring across the warehouse, seeming to see beyond it.

"It makes us as much murderers as them."

"And the alternative?" She knelt down beside him. "We knew the moment we canvased this place that the drones were here. Stupid to put the place surrounded by hills, but it was muscled up. We weren't going to be able to convert them to our cause. It was either more drone attacks or we fight this war."

"Killing in war only makes it necessary, not moral." He stood up, his composure returning. "It's still killing, and we just left the biggest body count we ever have."

She placed her hand on his face and looked into his eyes. "I know. I know it hurts you. And I know you do this only because you see that we had to. You'll ask your God for forgiveness. And I know you'll mean it. But, meanwhile, we need to bring in the cavalry."

"FBI?"

"Yes. This changes everything." She held up a plastic bag with several phones. "And we got these."

"You don't think they'd be stupid enough to leave a trail?"

Houston shook her head. "Not Fawkes, but he's got an army now. You're only as secure as your weakest link." She looked back outside toward the carnage. "Lots of bodies. Lots of hires. Lots of potential weak links." She pulled out her phone.

"How much time do we have?"

"I don't think the local police or fire will be out here quickly. It's the middle of nowhere, and these guys weren't plugged into their systems with a burglar alarm. No, just the opposite. I bet this place is off the grid completely." She punched a number. "I think our Intel 1 pals will be the first on the scene."

A voice crackled on the other end.

"Angel? This is Mary. We hit the jackpot. Tell John and the others to get to the address we sent you. And bring fire and a cleanup crew. And body bags. Lots of body bags."

~

HOURS LATER AN ARMY of police cars, FBI vehicles, SWAT vans, and emergency response crews were stationed around the smoldering scene. Spotlights were trained around the compound, and forensics teams darted around the bodies like fireflies with their flashlights and cameras.

Cohen slowly exited one of the black Crown Victorias. She hopped beside the door, removing a pair of crutches, and then proceeded to swing herself toward the stairways. Refusing the aid of several agents and police, she forced her way clumsily up the steps and into the warehouse.

Inside, a group of men stood marveling at the building's inventory. Flashbulbs exploded around them, documenting the scene.

"John. Frank. Sorry I'm late."

Savas turned around and the lines of his mouth tightened. It was hard to see her like this. The bruises had only begun to leave her face, the hideous black and green fading to a sickening yellow, scabs slowly being absorbed, hair lost from her left side where stitches ran over her scalp like laces on a game ball. Cohen limped toward them, her breath ragged, her eyes fatigued, yet a light burning within them.

"You didn't miss anything," said Savas, taking her arm. She relented and let him help her. "Or rather, we all missed the same thing. Hell of a fireworks display. And just look what Pandora's box has inside it."

Cohen whistled. "And no one noticed that someone was piling up large drone orders like this?"

Miller shook his head. "It didn't look that way on paper. Our two shadows tracked it all down, like tributaries piling into a big river. Then they came here and did this," he said, gesturing outside. "Who did you say those folks were?"

"I didn't," said Savas.

"Mmmm."

"We've counted twenty-five of the largest models," said Savas, "most equipped to bomb or shoot anything to smithereens. The rest are reconnaissance setups, smaller models with different imaging equipment ranging from cameras to infrared, audio—you name it."

"The bodies outside?"

Savas nodded. "Need to confirm, but facial recognition from snapshots IDed two of them. Former contractors that worked in the Middle East, one ex-army."

"More mercenaries," growled Miller. "Fifteen of them, it seems. Your ghosts are better than Jason Bourne."

"Moving on," said Savas. "We'll ID all we can and see what we can find from it."

"Meanwhile, we've put a dent in their attack plans," said Cohen.

"I hope so."

"What do you mean?"

Savas sighed. "Fawkes used a bunch of shell companies, crisscrossing aliased orders to stock this place. It was to hide his tracks, hide this place from prying eyes. But I'm starting to think that he's not the kind of guy to put all his eggs in one basket."

Miller looked gravely at him. "You think he has more drones."

"I know he does."

Savas didn't want to believe his own words. He needed a win, the kind of win that would let him believe he had declawed this nebulous monster. But the truth was too obvious.

Cohen changed tact. "You said there was a call from Gabriel?"

"Yes. They have a bag of phones. You can guess from where. Angel's on it now, but it's beyond her resources. I'm going to go long on this and bring in Simon."

"Fred Simon of CIA?" she asked. "We haven't contacted him since—" She caught herself. "Not for a while."

Miller smiled. "Who's he?"

"Someone who might can help," said Savas. "We might also need the NSA to work those phones."

"More Watchmen?" asked Cohen.

He nodded to her and stared at Miller a moment. "Why don't you fill in Frank a bit on the group while I get this show wrapped up here. I think the usefulness of certain secrets has diminished greatly given the current circumstances."

"About damn time," whispered Miller under his breath.

Savas smiled wanly. "Be careful what you ask for, Frank. Ignorance can be bliss."

OCTOBER 31

38

WEAKEST LINK

Savas and Cohen sat in the back of one of the old Crown Vics as it sped toward Manhattan on I-80. The sun arced over the factories and former swamplands, pouring a bronze coating over the buildings and waterways. Savas found it increasingly difficult to keep track of the days, one rolling into another on minimal sleep and maximal stress. But now, finally, there were some real breaks in the case.

They had insisted that the car be swept for digital technology, and screened their drivers, allowing only those who agreed to leave their smartphones and similar equipment behind. There was no point in spending the time to explain why. The turn to Luddites had hampered them severely, however, as the attempt to establish a conference call with Fred Simon had demonstrated. They had tried to have two phones on speaker, Lightfoote on Cohen's phone, Simon on Savas' cheap model. But it had proved unworkable, the sound quality rendering much of the dialogue incomprehensible. They had settled on speaking to Simon alone.

The CIA agent's voice was energized. "Our mutual contact at the NSA has managed to make rapid progress. All the calls and texts from the numbers you gave were grabbed over the last week. There wasn't much to go on. They were careful, but not careful enough. Two of the phones had sent text messages to the same number. I don't think it was because they were brothers and contacting mom."

"What was that number?" asked Savas.

"An unregistered phone. Likely a burner. But we don't need a name to track it."

"GPS?"

"No. They weren't that careless. But with enough activity, we can triangulate from the cell towers. They didn't check the fine print on this model. It checks with the home company a lot for service performance. Pinging back on an hourly basis. They might as well be flashing a light."

Savas sat up in the seat. He turned to Cohen. "Do you think it could be Fawkes?"

"I doubt it, John." She swept the crutches from between them and leaned them against the window. "You never know, but my guess is a mid-level operator. But he could lead us to the boss."

The speaker crackled. "My thoughts exactly."

Savas nodded. "So where is this phone?"

"Long Island Sound near Glen Cove."

"In the water? They ditched it?"

"Unlikely," said Simon. "It's moving. Speed and direction consistent with a maritime vessel following the coastline."

Savas and Cohen exchanged glances as she spoke. "Well, that isn't likely for some low-level grunt. Maybe we have something interesting."

"Want real-time footage?"

"Are you serious?"

"Soon as we had the coordinates, we dispatched a chopper."

"An agency chopper in the US? Where from?"

"Need-to-know basis, John."

"I thought the CIA didn't operate within US borders."

"Clinton said it best: it all depends on the definitions of words like 'is' or 'operate'."

"Mmm-hmmm. You bet your ass I want footage, but we're pre-smart-phone era here, Fred. When the AI in our car tried to kill us, we decided to go Amish."

Simon barked a laugh. "I understand. NSA has found a way to fire-wall the damn worm. Slowing them the hell down to fence everything off, but they've got server farms now with serious prophylactics. I'm watching real time. It's a nice boat."

"I bet it is."

"With a bunch of folks on it. Hard to make out high-res detail—the bird is at a distance and altitude that won't give it away. But I can tell you they aren't milling about socially. Positioned strategically."

"Bodyguards," said Cohen.

"Who needs a ship full of muscle?" chipped Simon.

Savas felt the adrenaline kick in. "Fawkes." He turned to Cohen. "We need a rapid response team. They'll lose that phone or the owner soon."

She nodded. "That means air. We're out of choppers. Too busy flying the VIPs out of the city still."

"Dammit!"

Simon cut in. "Well, remember those contractors that the CIA doesn't hire under aliases for work inside the country? Well, why have one chopper when you can have three for ten times the price? The fact that they don't exist creates some budget magic."

"You've got a spare bird?"

"Already routed toward you."

Savas punched the seat in front of him, startling the driver. "I owe you big, Fred."

"Don't think so, John. I've got a ways to go on that other debt I owe you. Speaking of which, how are my kids?"

"They're good. Spooking my team with their ninja-assassin program. Even Frank was impressed. But they're delivering big time." He glanced at Cohen. "We're a bit busted up and we've got a full plate of hackers in the City. I think I know who I'd send for a rendezvous with the boat."

"I agree," said Simon, "but we're pushing them. They're human, whatever they seem to accomplish."

Savas sat back in the chair and closed his eyes. "I know, Fred. But right now we all need to be a little superhuman. There's a monster to fight. I don't have the manpower to do this. Maybe Frank, but he's one. And there are some important people we need to question as of several hours ago."

"I'm with you. Tell them the chopper's been loaded with some useful gear. But getting on that boat and surviving isn't going to be as easy as the warehouse."

"Easy. Right. I'll tell them. I'm glad you're with us, Fred."

"I'm not the only one, John. The Watchmen still have some kick left. Until soon."

The connection was closed. Savas dialed and held the phone to his ear.

"Yeah, Mary? This is John. That bag of phones? Well, they might have bagged some big game. The guards called a number. Fred Simon traced it.

It's zipping along the Long Island Sound as we talk. We need you two to intercept a boat."

A muffled voice sounded through the other end. Savas nodded.

"Not to worry. Give me your current position. We've got that covered."

BEFORE:
THE ANONYMOUS EVENT COMMISSION

DEPOSITION IN THE MATTER OF:
UNITED STATES ARMED FORCES SPECIAL TRIBUNAL, Plaintiff,
versus
JOHN SAVAS, Defendant
Case No. M120039E-007X

Continued DEPOSITION OF:
Jean Paul Rideout

CBD: I want to read for you some documentation from the archives of the NSA. Prepared specifically for this inquiry.

MR. RIDEOUT: This should be fun.

CBD: As of 30 October, more than a third of the agency's computers were wiped and placed behind a newly designed firewall, code-named ROUNDUP. This firewall successfully prevented further infections and those machines took on the bulk of NSA computing tasks, both internally and externally. This was not a "cure" of any kind. It served as a preventive measure for infection and allowed the agency to resume increasingly normal levels of operations. However, due to national security concerns, it was decided not to share this information with outside agencies, private or public institutions, or the personal computing world for fear that release of the code would allow Anonymous to develop countermeasures.

MR. RIDEOUT: Hang on! So they had a block—they could fence it out—but kept it to themselves? Genius! How did the asses there feel when the Boeing plants blew themselves to bits? Robots slinging parts every which way, killing hundreds of workers, crippling aircraft construction for years? Jesus! Or the General Dynamics tanks and trucks? So sophisticated with their fully wired innards! The worm had them turning on their operators and blowing holes in the army bases! Bet those guys would have liked a peek at that firewall!

CBD: There was debate. For example, it says here—

MR. RIDEOUT: Debate! I love it. How about the farm belt catastrophes? Irrigation and treatment systems poisoning tens of millions of acres? Chinese air traffic control going to shit and nearly leading to a launch of missiles? Taiwan is lucky to still be here, honestly. And of course, who can forget the digital money supply of the world banks literally disappearing before our eyes?

CBD: The NSA isn't the focus of this inquiry!

MR. RIDEOUT: Then why bring them up at all?

CBD: I was getting to this point. The document continues.

CBD: Debate on this topic intensified during the next few days as the worm caused accelerating damage to civilian and governmental infrastructure. However, increasing concern developed over a second, and unrelated series of malicious code attacks that were eventually determined to have originated from offices of the FBI in New York City.

MR. RIDEOUT: Oh, here it is! Angel. Now I see what this is about. So the NSA began to spy on the FBI as well.

[REDACTED]: Because your division had gone rogue and was releasing viral code into the internet!

MR. RIDEOUT: Because it was the only way to fight the damn thing! Fight, well, that came later. At this point, we'd only begun to see the worm's activity through Angel's code. We didn't have time to get permissions or test the friendliness of this stuff! As you read so eloquently, the damn world was falling apart around us!

[REDACTED]: Many find it intriguing that at the same time as Anonymous was bringing down the world's digital economy, military, even food and water production, your group at FBI was engaging in a simultaneous release of hostile code.

MR. RIDEOUT: It wasn't hostile to—

[REDACTED]: And that it was your small division in an obscure branch of the FBI that managed to bring in the leader of Anonymous. A hacker who personally communicated with your chief programmer before and after the arrest—

MR. RIDEOUT: Communicated? He fucking wiped our server farm!

[REDACTED]: leaving her, and her only, encrypted messages and files.

MR. RIDEOUT: You're serious? You think we're in league with that fuck? He tried to kill us multiple times! We were trying to save the nation!

[REDACTED]: Did saving the nation require you to provide aid and comfort to enemies of the state?

MR. RIDEOUT: Aid and comfort? That's treason. What the hell are you talking about?

[REDACTED]: Francisco Lopez. Sara Houston. The Priest and the Whore. Surely you have heard of them?

MR. RIDEOUT: The Priest and Whore? [Inaudible] Oh, my God. Gabriel and Mary! Are you telling me those ciphers were Lopez and Houston?

[REDACTED]: It's charming that you are so ignorant of this.

MR. RIDEOUT: I didn't know who they were and I don't believe anything coming out of your mouth! All I know is that those two risked their lives over and over to bring Fawkes in. And they did! You should pin a fucking medal to their chests.

[REDACTED]: Perhaps they'll receive what's coming to them if you would tell us where they and Angel Lightfoote are hiding.

MR. RIDEOUT: I have no idea! Neither does anyone else in Intel 1. For all I know they're dead in the chaos. The city was on fire when you took us underground, when your thugs knocked our doors down and grabbed us. They were already gone into that mayhem. From what I'm seeing here, I'm thinking that was maybe the best outcome.

CBD: You say this Mary and Gabriel risked their lives several times. Can you elaborate?

MR. RIDEOUT: I've told you about the warehouse raid. Jesus, that was straight out of Call of Duty. That's where we found the drone stash. They took down a bunch of armed guards to get into that place. Of course, that fuck had more than one location. But I can at least say that there is no way their raid didn't save lives and infrastructure. Some bridges are still standing and some people still walking around because of that raid.

CBD: Who else was in on it?

MR. RIDEOUT: No one. Two on like fifty, I don't know. Bodies were everywhere. I saw the photos. Of course, the craziest was the boat.

CBD: Boat?

MR. RIDEOUT: Yeah, the very next day. Airlifted them like battle bots and dropped them in. And we almost had him, dammit. We could have prevented so much if they had caught him. So many deaths. But it wasn't to be.

CBD: Fawkes? How did you know he was there?

MR. RIDEOUT: We tracked some phones. Dead guards had contacted people. Led to the boat.

[REDACTED]: How was the FBI able to track this boat without computers, without the technology? Where did you get the vehicles to airlift the fugitives?

MR. RIDEOUT: John had connections. In fact, I think some were in your vaunted NSA. Some good guys. I don't know. But they made it happen, tracked the calls, got Mary and Gabriel in there. Would have been something to see in the flesh, I have no doubt.

39

BOAT PARTY

A dark-haired man handed Lopez a tablet and swiped through several photos. Although dimmed, the glow of the screen was nearly blinding in the dark interior of the aircraft, the thundering sound of the blades and engine suffocating auditory senses as well. They were flying just over the low cloud cover on a moonless night, shadowing the boat by matching speed and direction, remaining well out of earshot.

The two men were young, barely out of their twenties, and Lopez wondered where Fred Simon had found them. Breaking agency protocol, even in this crisis environment, likely meant they were not mere tools, but a part of the loose network united by Savas and Simon. *The Watchmen.* Lopez didn't know whether to respect their efforts or consider them hopeless idealists.

He turned his attention to the tablet. The images showed increasing zooms toward an unusual-looking boat. Lopez strained to hear the CIA man over the sounds of the helicopter and the strong headwind that rocked the craft mercilessly. Even with the headphones, he found himself using hand signals to get Houston's attention as he handed her the device.

The CIA man repeated what he had said. "It looks like one of the newer anti-pirating vessels. Aluminum hulls and cabins designed to withstand small-arms fire. Dual-engines to bring top speeds of around sixty miles per hour. They can turn on a dime and chase down anything that isn't a speed boat. Or outrun it."

"Good thing we're in a helicopter," said Houston, smiling.

The CIA man wasn't amused. "Look, I don't know who you are and what strings you pulled, but his isn't a day trip. Look at these."

He scrolled past several photos that centered on the boat and its hull, pausing over a pair that focused on the deck.

Houston interrupted. "We see them. Guards fore and aft, automatic weapons, even a fairly large machine gun mounted there," she pointed. "If I were you, I wouldn't bring this bird in too close. The gun might almost qualify as anti-aircraft depending on the rounds."

"But if we are going to have you near enough that thing, the approach is going to have to be close," he scowled. "They'll make us for sure by sight as well as sound. There's nothing identifying on the outside, especially at night, but that in itself will likely send up flags."

Lopez nodded to the side door. "What is this thing? I assume it's for us?"

"The best we could manage on extremely short notice. We aren't the Navy Seals, and to be quite honest, this is our first and I hope only sky-to-sea assault mission. Usually we do things with a bit more stealth."

The man edged over and unzipped one of the bags. Black fiberglass gleamed back at them, reflecting the light of the tablet and cockpit instrument panel.

"But this will get some points for that."

"It's a jet ski?" asked Houston.

"Yes," said the CIA agent. "Electric. Good for the environment."

Houston nodded. "*Silent*, in other words."

"Next to the motors on the boat, most definitely. It's pitch out there on the open sea and they're not running all that dark, so you should almost be invisible. We disabled the safety lights. It's a two-seater, so you'll both fit with some minimal gear. You stay in their wake and you should be able to grapple on before they know you're there."

"Except for the thundering helicopter drop-off, of course," said Lopez.

"We'll try to keep as far out as possible, so there will be some distance. You can hit 50 on this thing. Boat tops off at 60 and they aren't pushing it that hard right now. Nowhere close. You can close the gap." He looked Houston up-and-down. "It's not us I'm worried about. Getting on the boat is one thing. Then what? I hope Simon hasn't lost his mind."

Houston used the silence to loudly slap a fresh clip into her browning.

"Just get us on the water and watch your own ass. We aren't outfitted for a sea mission. Put us low to avoid a bath and we'll preserve more function in the gear."

The CIA man motioned to a rope and pulley. "Thirty feet already laid out. In this blackness, well, that's pushing it, and the downwash is going to be a problem."

"We'll make do," she answered, wrapping a tactical vest around her.

The pilot spoke through the noise. "Target has decelerated. Down to 30 miles per hour."

"We do it now," said Lopez.

The CIA man nodded. "Drop us down, Charlie."

They felt a tug inside and the helicopter buried itself in the cloud layer, additional turbulence rocking the small craft back and forth violently. The pilot was flying dark except for instrumentation. They plunged below the clouds and the sea swelled into view. Light from the boat ahead bobbed like a beacon.

Houston and Lopez removed the remainder of the tarp on the jet ski. Without a combustion engine, it was surprisingly light, and they positioned it in front of the door. They were dressed in black with protective vests, ski masks and dark gloves, packs on their backs and weapons strapped to utility belts. Night vision goggles dangled from their necks.

The helicopter plunged toward the sea, the pilot speaking in their headsets. "Wind's a bitch! Be quick."

They lurched to a hover. The pair removed the headphones and fastened the rope to the jet ski. The CIA man opened the side door and they lowered the watercraft quickly. The gears on the pulley hummed as the rope flew through the mechanism, the smell of burnt leaves filling the small space. Far below, they watched the water splash outward from the impact on the surface.

"Go, go, go!" cried the pilot.

Houston leapt onto the rope and wrapped her feet around it. She descended swiftly down its length and vanished below. Lopez paused a split second to give her space to clear, then dropped straight into the wind and night.

It was all completed in less than a minute. The pilot was skilled and held the helicopter in position. Feet firmly planted on the jet ski, they detached the rope as Houston slipped into the driver's seat and fired it up, the engine purring softly.

The craft leapt forward toward the dancing lights of the yacht. Lopez removed a high-powered assault weapon and focused ahead as the helicopter darted upward, heading back toward the cloud bank and safety.

Only it would not make it. Operators on the boat had seen the craft. Through the washed-out green of the night-vision, Lopez saw a volley of infrared tracers converge on the aircraft. He remembered the large weapon in the recon photos. He removed his goggles and stared helplessly.

A bright light erupted above them, painting the ceiling of cloud-cover in orange and white, the water reflecting the growing fireball. The sound shook them as they sped forward, the rending of metal and air pressure from the ignited fuel. In the dimming fireball the wreckage could be seen to careen toward the open sea and slam into the water like the surface was made of concrete, the helicopter crushed and sinking. It vanished below the waves.

Lopez felt all ambivalence evaporate.

"Let's get these bastards."

40

GETAWAY

Their target accelerated. Houston gunned the jet ski and pushed it to the breaking point. The boat took no evasive action and even angled toward them to narrow the distance somewhat of their approach.

"They haven't spotted us," screamed Lopez behind her. "Running from the crash site!"

Houston nodded vigorously and continued to push the ski full out. The high waves gut-punched them as they sliced through the water, but they gained on the yacht. Lopez began to see just how fortified it was. *Anti-pirate, indeed.* While it possessed a superficial resemblance to the luxury powerboats decorating many docks, the fiberglass was replaced with thick aluminum, the windows black and refracting light unnaturally, the bullet-resistant composition altering the optical properties. And of course the guards and their weapons, in addition to the churning motors kicking a spray like a comet's tail behind the craft.

They were within ten yards and still gaining on the starboard side. Now came the true insanity: The boat had accelerated beyond fifty miles per hour and the jet ski was barely holding together. The angle had decreased, reducing their relative velocity, but also affording the only way to try to board. Lopez shouldered the automatic rifle and removed two stun grenades.

"Flash bangs ready!" he called to Houston. They were nearly alongside the yacht.

She nodded and he flung the bombs one at a time toward the bow of the ship. Both landed and rattled across the surface, ricocheting off the gunwale, then exploding. Even from the side of the ship, the sound and light were startling.

Lopez heaved a grappling ladder against the side and it caught, the roped steps unfurling against the hull. Just then the boat lurched starboard slamming into the jet ski. Instinctively, both of them leapt off the doomed craft and grabbed the sides of the ladder, one on each side, their legs half-submerged in the sea. The friction of the water threatened to pull the grapple from the boat and deposit them into the propeller blades.

Lopez placed a foot on the roped ladder and violently swung himself toward the gunwale, grasping the side of the boat with his hands. He tucked his legs underneath his torso like a gymnast and planted his boots on the uppermost portion of the hull, a powerful thrust of his legs propelling him over the side to land in the stern on top of the engine box.

Two men were positioned near the cabin looking ahead at the commotion caused by the still smoking flash grenades. At the sound of his awkward landing, they turned too slowly, the shock of the unexpected attack leaving them off guard.

The distance was only a few feet, and Lopez placed his hands on the engine box and swept his leg through the air like a switchblade. His boot connected with the head of the leftmost guard, the neck snapping to the side, teeth raining sideways against the metal. The man fell with a crash and didn't move.

But it left Lopez open for a strike from the second guard. He prepared for the worst, hoping Houston would be there in time to engage.

And she was. As he spun away from the guard and onto his feet, he crouched and pulled a handgun from his belt. In front of him there was a blur of hands and feet as Houston's lithe form pummeled the thick hulk of the other guard. The results were devastating. Blows to the neck and groin incapacitated him while she drew a knife. Using the momentum of his failing retreat, she toppled him onto the prone form of the other guard and plunged the blade into his neck, wrenching it several inches, sidestepping a jet of blood that bathed the floor of the boat.

It was over in seconds. In the cacophony surrounding the boat, the melee had barely risen above the chaos.

"I'll take the cabin," she said, twitching her head toward the interior.

"There are two guards at the bow. I doubt the flash bangs did much more than knock them sideways."

"Be careful, Sara," said Lopez. "I don't want to lose you now."

"Move, priest," she said and darted toward the door.

Their actions played in counterpoint. Lopez sprang forward, his weapon raised, back sliding along the wall of the cabin. The acrid smell of smoke from the lingering grenades burned in his nose as he approached the front of the ship. He turned the corner of the cabin and crouched to one knee, steadying the pistol with his left hand as he scanned the deck.

One of the guards remained positioned on the gun turret, checking the skies as if awaiting another attack. The other had tossed one of the smoking remains of the grenades over the side of the boat, aiming his weapon downward, anticipating an assault from the water.

The assault came from behind. Lopez fired two shots before the man could turn. Both connected. The guard slipped over the railing and disappeared into darkness.

The other guard heard the shots. Lopez walked casually toward the turret, his weapon aimed at the man, the guard releasing the controls of the large machine gun, realizing it couldn't be used at close range. He desperately tried to draw a pistol.

Lopez blasted his right shoulder, the man's obvious gun arm. The guard screamed and clutched the wound, terror in his eyes as the masked assailant approached.

Lopez grabbed the wrist of his uninjured arm and twisted. Again the man screamed, his body paralyzed in pain, eyes shut harshly.

"How many guards?" yelled Lopez. "Don't think! Tell me! How many guards?"

Like a programmed machine, the man stuttered his answers: "Two here. Two in the back. Two in the cabin with Fawkes." Tears streamed down his face.

Fawkes? It wasn't to be believed. The architect of Anonymous was *on the boat.* "Sara's in the cabin with him," he whispered, the frightened man looking on in distress.

Lopez brought the handle of the pistol down on the man's temple, the body collapsing into the turret. He sprinted back to the stern of the boat.

~

AT THE SAME TIME, Houston stood over the bodies of two men.

She had entered the cabin forcefully, kicking in the flimsy door to find three men looking through the front window at the aftermath of the flash bangs. Two were obviously hired protection—broad in the back, towering over the middle figure who could otherwise have been mistaken for a scrawny teen. They turned at the sound of her entrance.

Fawkes. It was the glasses that sealed the identification. The female hacker's words—her *lover*—the lanky body, the darting motions, the smart glasses: it was Fawkes. But she had no time to consider the implications.

The men held guns in their hands. They turned to engage, but she held the advantage. She fired twice, each shot aimed quickly at the moving targets across from her. The first shot hit true to rip through the forehead of the bodyguard on her left, his blood splattering the window and ceiling. The second shot drifted right from her momentum. The bullet hit the man in the chest, too high for the heart, but he cried out, dropped his weapon, and careened toward the window.

But he wasn't down. As Fawkes screamed and darted left, the guard faced her and rushed, the crazed look of a wounded animal on his face.

She pivoted, side-stepping, and grasped his outstretched arm, using his momentum against him. He missed, and she thrust him toward the window in the back of the cabin. His face smashed the glass, a spiderweb of fractures erupting from the bullet-resistant material. Leaving nothing to chance, Houston fired once into the back of his head. She turned quickly to subdue Fawkes.

But he was gone. Wind and a salty mist poured in from an opening in the roof. A short ladder led from the cabin upward. Fawkes had gone up.

She ejected the magazine and pulled another from her belt. Slamming it in place, she darted to the stairway, weapon raised to the ceiling. She could see no one. At the same time, the whirring of an engine could be heard, changing in pitch from low to high.

"No!" she whispered under her breath and sprinted up the ladder.

A LOUD VOICE exploded throughout the cabin as Lopez charged inside.

"Sara!"

She was climbing a ladder across the room and didn't hear him. Her feet lifted from the steps and out of sight. Ignoring the bodies around him, he dashed to the ladder and ascended. Houston was there, firing her gun madly as she aimed out over the open water.

He followed the barrel of her gun. In the distance, a form was suspended over the ocean, legs dangling and kicking, arms grasping desperately above him. Overhead, a shadow hummed, a black object the size of a bed, the pitch dropping as the man accelerated away and faded into the blackness.

"*Fuck!*" cried Houston as the object disappeared, her mag emptied.

They both stood there in silence, spindrift coating the dead bodies scattered below them, the boat hurled back and forth in the wind.

All for nothing!

Fawkes had escaped by drone into the night.

BEFORE:
THE ANONYMOUS EVENT COMMISSION

DEPOSITION IN THE MATTER OF:
UNITED STATES ARMED FORCES SPECIAL TRIBUNAL, Plaintiff,
versus
JOHN SAVAS, Defendant
Case No. M120039E-007X

CONTINUED DEPOSITION OF:
Rebecca Ruth Cohen

MS. COHEN: We almost had him. It could all have ended right there. But we had the boat. And a lot of bodies to examine. Also one survivor to question.

CBD: They killed the others?
MS. COHEN: Yes.

CBD: You don't look okay with that.
MS. COHEN: [INAUDIBLE] Not really. Violence isn't really my thing, you know? But sometimes there isn't another choice. Those were hired guns that would have killed them—tried to kill them—without a second thought. God! Why am I explaining this?

CBD: I'm interested in understanding the motivations behind each member of your team.
MS. COHEN: The motivation was the same: to stop what Fawkes was doing!

CBD: Did the survivor provide any useful intel?
MS. COHEN: Not much, but some. Once isolated, it was clear to him that the money he had received wasn't worth what he was going to get. We didn't even have to lean on him.

CBD: And?
MS. COHEN: Unfortunately, most of it was what we had guessed, but confirmation was nice. Hired mercenaries. Paid ridiculously well.

Never privy to anything important—Fawkes kept them completely in the dark. They were there to follow his direct orders and serve as protection. He was one paranoid monster. Anyway, we learned that Fawkes was spending more and more time at sea.

CBD: Why was that?

MS. COHEN: The bodyguard thought it was to avoid law enforcement. I think it was more than that. I think Fawkes was planning to ride out offshore the societal chaos he was inducing. With everything Angel began to put together, it was clear that he was planning some big event, and it would go down soon.

CBD: What else?

MS. COHEN: Print and DNA samples linked two of the men onboard to the public assassinations. And we matched Fawkes' DNA as well—same as in the mask in the Bridgeport scene.

CBD: Where the shootings occurred?

MS. COHEN: Right.

CBD: But you still hadn't found him in any database?

MS. COHEN: No. Might be he was off the radar. He was young, maybe never caught in criminal activity. Another possibility we considered is that he scrubbed his files.

CBD: Scrubbed them?

MS. COHEN: Fawkes was a master hacker. Databases are often too easily accessible online. Really—do you know of a single major private or governmental organization that *hasn't* been hacked in the last ten years? If he knew he was in certain systems, he might have found his way into them and deleted all information about himself. He could do it, I don't doubt that. Either way, we had nothing. And now we had stirred the hornet's nest.

CBD: Meaning?

MS. COHEN: Until that point, we had been only a blip on his radar. Someone probing too much in the wrong places. Even that was enough to try and kill us. But now—we'd entered his space, killed his bodyguards, nearly grabbed him off that damn boat. If he didn't have that escape drone on the roof, we would have. Now he was pissed, and he came after us.

CBD: First with Angel?

MS. COHEN: Well, she was the thorn in his side that kept getting worse. But everything just began to escalate at that point. Within the next few days we'd be hit, and absolutely devastating attacks happened across the world. And if it hadn't been for the information Angel obtained from the worm dissection, we would have lost even more.

CBD: So she was key.

MS. COHEN: [INAUDIBLE] Here we go again. Yes, she was key. So were John, and Frank, and JP. And certainly Gabriel and Mary.

CBD: The aliases—

MS. COHEN: Just stop. I'm not going there. Look, we worked as a team. A damn good team. What happened next just motivated us more. That's when John's idea took root, when we agreed to try it. Fawkes was hitting the world where it hurt. This time, we were going to hit *him* where it hurt.

NOVEMBER 1

41

MAN IN THE MASK

He spoke to them on five different encrypted video conferencing calls. They were hired guns and bombers, assassins trained under diverse conditions spanning the military to organized crime. He'd baited them through the underground online marketplaces with money few could refuse. He'd filtered through information searches, background checks, and video chat interviews. He'd tested each of them with small-scale operations, sifting the wheat from the chaff, identifying the unreliable, the unstable, the less competent, and those who reported back to others and revealed themselves as informants. Sometimes he was forced to erase those who could pose a threat.

The few who survived the process were moved like chess pieces, directed remotely so that groups were formed, hierarchies established, rules set and punished harshly when broken. And always there was money. Hard to comprehend amounts of money, accounts protected from the worm scattered across the world. Houses and lands were purchased. Protected lives and identities created and promised. All for the taking should a final set of missions be accomplished. And all to be snatched away once the missions completed. He was fighting against the plutocracy and he was sure as hell not going to create another one.

Fawkes adjusted the mask over his face. A mask of a smiling, goateed madman from another age, always in place, his identity revealed only to those bodyguards who worked directly with him. He prepared a final address. Now he would move the strikes forward quickly in time. Now he would give a last set of instructions for the beginning stages of the end. Dangerous people at the FBI and other agencies had forced his hand sooner than he would have liked. He preferred careful probing of systems and weakness, test shots and stress tests that allowed him to screen his people as much as the target systems. He liked to thoroughly debug the code.

But the time for precise experimentation was gone. The time for drastic action had revealed itself. He could not afford another near disaster like that on the boat. How had they found him so quickly? Attacked him so easily? He had taken every precaution! Every trace erased from the digital world. But he was clearly not careful enough. Which meant he had to hurry. There was no telling from what direction they were coming, what flaws in the program were still lurking, waiting to collapse like poorly designed walls under siege.

Chaos was his ally. The more dysfunctional the world became around them, the less the governmental apparatus could use its considerable firepower to find and kill him. The attacks would begin there with the heads of the hydra in Washington. They thought they *had* been attacked! But they had seen only the weak pieces, a feint to test the strength of their defenses. And those defenses had been found lacking.

But the hydra's handlers were not in Washington, but Europe and Asia. And so he would begin the dismantling of the European society and destabilization of China and the lesser economies. There could be war. These disturbances might be enough.

Otherwise, he would bring the final direct attack. He would darken America and plunge the nation into complete anarchy. Moments before the lights went off in the centers of power in the United States, the signal would be given for the worm to complete its final function. The digital mind of the planet, on which all the modern societies rested, that calculated trade and commerce, that built buildings and cars, that became nearly a higher order organism of parsing ideas and thoughts in a fiber-optic neural network, a brain beyond anything the solar system had likely ever seen—it would die. Erased. Unmade in a cascade of deletion that would render them beyond salvage. Once the signal was given, the mad mind of Earth would die.

Only then might there be a chance for something more worthy, more pure to rise from the ashes. Fawkes didn't care if it was Humans 2.0 or the dolphin beta release. It had to be something new. Utterly new. The corrupt, cancerous, and insane thing called modern culture, what the deluded called modern civilization, had to be sterilized. Every cell wiped to prevent reinfection.

The worm would do that. The final cargo to be uploaded was designed and long perfected. It would exploit the enormous security and logical holes in the neuronal system of the world mind and scramble it, then like an acid eat away at the fibers and proteins until even the very DNA was digested.

Fawkes smiled behind the mask as he spoke to his blind tools. The FBI group had nearly ended it, but had only accelerated the date of doom.

He would start with them. He would pay that bitch in the bowels of Manhattan a short visit. Then he would show her who really ran things in cyberspace.

"Knock, knock, Angel."

42

MELTDOWN

The names unfurled across the screen like entries in some doomsday book.

It was the new month, November first at three in the morning, and Angel had spent it deep in the basement of the FBI building. She rubbed her eyes. The holes across her left ear were swollen and red from the piercings that had been squashed as she slept during the last worm decryption job. Running one hand over the orange stubble of hair on her scalp, she clicked with the other to silence the alert tone from the computer that had called her out of some murky dream—only to stare at another nightmare.

She read through it again. The list was a who's who of the power brokers in Congress and business.

"Oh, look—there's the president herself!"

Of course. If you're going to bring down the US in one blitzkrieg, you ought to have her on the list. That made sense.

But did any of it really make sense? Angel knew her brain was close to oatmeal at this point, but were these really hit lists? What madman would try to off that many high-profile people? What lunatic could ever think something like that was even possible? And to what end?

Chaos. She shook her head. It all seemed to point in that direction. The banking meltdown. The attacks. This list of powerful names. Fawkes had made no demands. He hadn't tried to leverage the threats into anything. He seemed to be running by a playbook no one had ever seen before. No one could anticipate his moves.

Until now. Her virus was functioning, reporting on the worm's activities. And her little digital operating room had revealed more and more of the inner workings of the worm. Like any code, it was a series of instructions, fragile logic and loops calling out to be hacked. All she needed was time. But there was precious little of that left.

Angel sat upright and gulped down a wash of cold coffee. She'd bring this directly to Savas in the morning. Those names had serious protection, especially after events of the last two weeks. But was it enough? Could the secret service, the military, private contractors, could any of them anticipate what attacks might come from a man that was as diabolical as he was creative? Could anyone?

Her screen went dark.

"What the hell?"

She clicked on keys and the mouse, but there was no response. *Wonderful.* It was a very bad time for a device failure. She began to reach around for the power switch to forcibly reboot the machine when a line of green text ran across her screen.

"HELLO, ANGEL."

It was like some old mainframe terminal, letters appearing left to right revealing words, then phrases. Carriage returns advancing text. A knot formed in the pit of her stomach. Someone else had hijacked her computer, and she had no doubts about who that was.

The GUI was gone, but she found that she could type.

"HI, FAWKES."

She jumped up and disconnected the VMS machine from the internal network. She hoped to God he didn't have any inkling of what she was doing with it.

More text appeared.

"LIKE THE MATRIX, RIGHT? IT'S BEEN INTERESTING WATCHING YOU WORK. BUT I'VE GOT THINGS TO DO AND YOU'RE CRAMPING MY STYLE."

A green light appeared on the upper lip of the screen indicating that the camera was on. She ignored it and the video image that appeared on the screen. She raced toward the bank of computers along the wall.

A mocking voice came over the speakers.

"No use, Angel, baby. I've turned all the drives to goo already. You don't think I'd give you the chance to shut them down first, do you?"

She reached the first machines and scanned for the main power connector.

"Thorough, aren't you? Look at your pretty little ass wiggle! Here, I'll just put a stop to all this unnecessary work so we can chat a little bit."

The cluster of computers switched off. Machine-gun like clicks of the system shutting down, the lowering pitch of hundreds of disk drives spinning to a stop—it was like some sonic rush of wind through the room.

"There. That's better."

She turned to face the only active monitor left. A masked figure stared back at her, smile frozen in place. She walked up to the terminal and sat down.

"Practical. I like that," came the distorted voice. "Butch, too. You swing both ways?"

"I'll be swinging at you."

He laughed, the sound crackling as the distorted audio maxed out the dynamic range of the electronics.

"Feisty! I should'a known that, though. I knew right off that those bugs crawling up my ass weren't NSA. Not close to their style. Crude, self-taught. More clever. You weren't raised in some dot gov hacking camp."

Angel resisted the urge to look at the VMS machine. Everything might depend on whether he had discovered it. It loomed like a presence behind her, some spirit that waited for her attention that she had to ignore. Until this asshole had his gloat and finished the wipe.

"It's not over, Fawkes."

"That's where you're wrong, Angel Lightfoote, special agent Intel 1. Angel Lightfoote of the scrubbed records."

She bit her lip and tried to keep her composure.

"What? You thought I wouldn't do my homework? You got *history*, girl! Most of it wiped. Somebody wanted you cleaned up and made presentable. Would that be this Savas guy? No? Probably the other one, Kanter, the one blown up a while back?"

"Fuck you," she hissed.

"Oh, emotions, Angel. Not a girl's best friend in this game. Don't get attached. Don't feel bad for Blown-Up Man. Slows you down. Blinds you."

"Makes you human. He was a hundred times the man you are."

"A man who was into other men, huh? Hundreds of times, I bet."

She flipped him off.

"Well, good old *Larry* must have gone the extra mile. I was scraping the digital basements. *Nothing*. But then I found all that stuff on dear old *dad*."

Tears welled in her eyes as she ground her teeth.

"That all had to suck, yeah? Tell me, were you really there, in that cage when he bit it? Yeah? I thought so. Fucked you up good, didn't it? Did dear old dad have to watch what they did to you? Every little thing? I can imagine the next few years. No wonder they had to bleach your record! Is that what they did upstairs in that shiny little head of yours, too?"

The sly face on the mask, the smirk of Guy Fawkes, the tormenting knowledge this sociopath had about her life, it was too much. Angel reached down and picked up a metallic wastebasket from the ground.

"Angel, darling, let's not fight."

"It's not over, you bastard. I promise you. *Never* make it personal? Well, you just sure as hell did! And I'm coming for you!"

She swung the basket at the monitor. Again and again she pummeled the screen, plastic cracking, pixels shattering. The monitor fell to the ground, a black circle from the impact in the middle of the masked face, blocking it out. Still she smashed it. Over and over on the ground, a fissure opening in the screen, the dark circle expanding like some black hole to swallow the entire image.

All the while, laughter.

Fawkes' wild laughter spilled like acid from the speakers into her ears. Finally, she turned to the power cord and grabbed it with both hands, yanking it from the socket, releasing a tormented scream.

The sound ceased. What little was still glowing on the screen went black. The room was plunged into near darkness, the glow of the EXIT sign over the side door painting the room dimly in an infernal red.

She wiped sweat and tears from her face and stumbled over to the VMS machine. Her right hand was bloodied. She crouched and touched the surface of the old computer with her left, resting her head against the cold metal.

Her head nodded rhythmically as she began to rock back and forth on the ground. She repeated words over and over, her voice much higher, nearly that of a child's.

"I'm sorry, Dad. I'm so sorry. I'm so sorry."

She wept.

43

BILDERBERG CALLING

The marine contingency posted around 1600 Pennsylvania Avenue had swelled beyond anything Elaine York had ever experienced. A former army field officer, one of the few women to be deployed into live hostilities in the first Iraq War, she didn't shrink from conflict, armed or not. But to see the White House nearly obscured by flak jackets and fatigues was to enter into the kind of nightmare reserved for over-the-top Hollywood blockbusters. That it could become real had never truly entered into her imagination.

President York stepped away from the window and turned back to her desk. Her last images of a figure sprinting down the circular roadway in front of the main doors—George Tooze, her Secretary of Homeland Security. She sat down and tried to compose herself. Her head throbbed from two straight days without sleep. Her mind still reeled from continuous updates, each more alarming than the last, from every corner of the globe. And now Tooze racing over like a high school sprinter, his sixty-five-year old body likely straining under the duress. This was not going to be good.

And yet, what had been? The latest report from the NSA couldn't have been worse. The damned worm had begun to disrupt vital elements of the world's infrastructure. Haphazardly, to be sure, but her advisors, and her own gut, spoke to the possibility that what they had seen so far had only been feints. *Tests* to optimize the monster running through the cortex of the modern world and yet which had, even on their own, produced planetary chaos.

Food and oil supply chains were disrupted from agribusiness farms to the international shipping systems on which a hungry world depended. Sea and air systems were scrambled, systems that transported the world's goods, including the ever-critical supply of oil. Hospitals were running out of supplies. Telecoms were unreliable. The world was losing its collective mind.

She half-expected red lights to be flashing around her and sirens wailing. The National Terrorism Advisory System threat assessment was at "IMMINENT." All branches of the military were at DEFCON 2 or higher, the birds in international airspace with different flags buzzing around each other nearly an invitation to a catastrophic mistake. The Force Protection Condition was DELTA nearly everywhere. INFOCON was at 1 and might as well have just put up a white flag and shut down.

And here was Tooze.

The flushed face of her trusted adviser burst into the Oval Office. He held an envelope in one hand that he brandished before him like a radioactive substance.

"A number," he gasped, resting a hand on the other side of her desk. He held up the letter again. "Limited lifespan. It's from Bilderberg."

Time seemed to stop and she felt her mind disengage. She remembered the first time that she had experienced death. Her mother had been braiding her hair one morning, and by afternoon she had been a seven-year-old raised by a single-parent father. The moment had been just as immediate as the rush of Tooze into the room. One minute, she could hear the sounds of her mother talking on the phone in the kitchen while she played in the living room. The next, a crash and house-jolting thud. She had run in to find her mother unconscious on the floor. She would never wake. A brain aneurysm, or a big balloon that popped in her head as one of the doctors had tried to explain it to her. She had feared balloons ever since. It could happen so fast. Pressure. Weakness. Then—pop.

She rose, turned away from Tooze, and walked back to the window to stare at the troops outside. So much firepower. Such an apparatus in the nation's military. And, in the face of the forces that truly controlled the world, so powerless.

Had it come to this? This new land and new dream of not even three centuries, of miracle cures, trips to the moon, supercomputers in your pocket—had its time come so soon? All because of this terrorist and his devil worm?

Pop.

"Ms. President? Elaine?"

She turned back to Tooze and felt the room sway, barely keeping her balance. "Thank you, George," she said, pulling the paper from his hand and trying to remove a tear discreetly. "I will need to be alone for this call."

He nodded, his face telling her all she needed to know, that he too understood the significance of what she was about to do.

"I'll be outside," he said. "Don't lose hope."

He turned and walked out of the room, closing the door softly behind him.

Sighing, she approached the grand desk and pressed her thumb against a fingerprint-reader on a drawer, then entered a code into a keypad next to it. There was a clear click, and she pulled the drawer open. Inside was what looked to be a bulked up cellular phone from decades past. She knew it to be a special device, engineered to work through a covert collection of satellites, encrypting transmissions through means not even the worm could break. At least some things were beyond its reach. In the realm of monsters, the worm was just another fiend.

Bilderberg. So it had finally come to this. Like ghosts, powers that many felt but never saw, sometimes they became incarnate. Like the beginning of her presidency, they had come and impressed upon her their reality. Sometimes the phantoms moved objects around a haunted home. Or a nation. Sometimes they killed.

She read the number off the paper in the envelope and keyed it in. A series of strange sounds of static and digital processing harshly burbled from the speaker. Then a loud click.

She exhaled slowly.

"This is Elaine York calling from the White House."

BEFORE:
THE ANONYMOUS EVENT COMMISSION

DEPOSITION IN THE MATTER OF:
UNITED STATES ARMED FORCES SPECIAL TRIBUNAL, Plaintiff,
versus
JOHN SAVAS, Defendant
Case No. M120039E-007X

CONTINUED DEPOSITION OF:
John Savas

CBD: And it was at this point that you put your trap in motion?
MR. SAVAS: Yes.

[REDACTED]: Why did you trust this criminal?
MR. SAVAS: To be quite honest, I didn't. Maybe the trap was going to be reversed and sprung on us. I was flying on instinct, and something resonated as truthful about her dislike of Fawkes and what he was doing. Anyway, I didn't feel I had much of a choice. We had to act fast or things might get beyond the point of fixing. The disaster with Angel just confirmed how vulnerable we and the entire world were to this maniac.

[REDACTED]: The purported accident with your computers.
MR. SAVAS: Not accident, sabotage. It was a cyberattack.

[REDACTED]: Conveniently timed to cripple you at a moment, to use your words, where things were so serious that they might not be fixed.
MR. SAVAS: Which is exactly what Fawkes would have wanted. We'd shaken him. He responded to protect his plans.

[REDACTED]: But no one else was with agent Lightfoote when the alleged hacking attack occurred?
MR. SAVAS: Alleged?

CBD: Why don't you tell us about Angel Lightfoote, Mr. Savas.
MR. SAVAS: Can you be a little more vague, please.

CBD: Why did you put her in charge of your cybercrimes unit? Her records do not indicate any experience in digital technology or training of any kind.

MR. SAVAS: She showed an aptitude. After we lost Manuel—agent Manuel Hernandez—we needed someone in the chaos of the time to handle the system he had set up, our operations room at Intel 1. Angel was one of those to step up. After a short time she was running things by herself.

CBD: Is it common practice at FBI to promote people into positions for which they clearly have no training, no experience?

MR. SAVAS: Of course not. But it wasn't common occurrence to lose half your people to a vengeful tycoon plotting a global genocide. John Gunn and Mjolnir massacred half our division. The regs didn't mean a hell of a lot in those moments. We were battered. We survived as a team. More than a team. As a family. Screw the fucking protocol.

[REDACTED]: Again, we are to understand that you were able to *ignore* policies and procedures because of your division's vaunted status at FBI and elsewhere?

MR. SAVAS: We were cut a lot of slack.

[REDACTED]: Which you used to promote an unstable personality into the prime position overseeing your cybercrime investigations just as the world was to suffer an unprecedented digital terrorist attack.

MR. SAVAS: Unstable? Look, Angel was weird, but she was a damn fine agent. Became a better one after Mjolnir. The trial by fire chars some, brings out the gold in others. She was gold.

[REDACTED]: These photos, Mr. Savas. This is Lightfoote?

MR. SAVAS: Yes.

[REDACTED]: How can you possibly justify this?

MR. SAVAS: So she's got short hair and some piercings. She saved the damned world, you idiots! You want to turn that back so you can dress her like a Stepford girl?

[REDACTED]: Saved the world. Only she could do it. Only she had the power to stop the virus, a virus she was instrumental in discovering, that she claims wiped her computers and all previous records of cyber-activity in your division. A woman contacted by the very man you assert was the prime terrorist in the events last fall. A woman with a diagnosed mental illness, hired and promoted without following basic FBI protocols.

MR. SAVAS: What do you mean a diagnosed mental illness?

[REDACTED]: Don't play ignorant with us now.

MR. SAVAS: What diagnosed mental illness? There's nothing like that in her file.

[REDACTED]: Of course not, because as our research has uncovered, FBI computers were used to wipe national databases, medical records destroyed. Or so it was thought. But you were not thorough enough.

MR. SAVAS: Deleted records? [INAUDIBLE] Larry. Dammit, Larry, you should have told me.

[REDACTED]: Now you wish to pass the buck to a dead boss, is that it?

MR. SAVAS: Never mind. You're going to twist and fit everything into your preconceived notions in this witch hunt. I can tell you I didn't know, but I don't much care even knowing now. Larry made some unorthodox hires, including yours truly. Those choices wouldn't look good on paper in front of a committee like yours. And those choices put together a group of damaged yet exceptional people that have saved all your asses on more occasions than we have time for!

[REDACTED]: So you would justify this?

MR. SAVAS: I'll justify it with our record.

[REDACTED]: That is exactly what we are here to examine. Not the fantasy you put forth as you actions, but what really happened.

MR. SAVAS: What really happened.

[REDACTED]: Yes. And we know that Angel Lightfoote is at the center of this. Placed at the center of digital operations immediately before the chaos by you, escaping from custody with two known terrorists and enemies of the state that you sheltered and aided.

MR. SAVAS: Oh, good God.

[REDACTED]: You might ought to pray to your God, Mr. Savas,

because as things are shaping up, that is the only place you can expect to find any mercy.

CBD: Can we turn this back to the so-called trap?

MR. SAVAS: [INAUDIBLE]

CBD: So, this "Poison", real name Tabitha Ivy, she agreed to serve as bait for Fawkes?

MR. SAVAS: Yes. She was bait. We'd make it clear we were holding her, that we would extract information by any means necessary, threatening to expose Fawkes, to harm someone he possessed an emotional attachment to.

CBD: And by any means you mean torture?

MR. SAVAS: We faked interrogation scenes, placed them on poorly secured servers. Sent unencrypted emails revealing that we held her, provided information that we could possess only if we did. We believed this would get back to him and he would respond.

CBD: Which you claim he did?

MR. SAVAS: With a vengeance. We weren't actually prepared for how swift and devastating the response would be. We were naive about just how much manpower he had amassed and how obsessed he was with Poison. But afterward, we knew the plan would work. He gave us the confidence to set it up by those actions.

CBD: And so that was the next event in the chronology, the warehouse in Brooklyn?

MR. SAVAS: The plans for that were set in motion, but everything was exploding at that point. Lopez and Houston were sent to D.C. You know, your two terrorist enemies of the state? They *volunteered* to try and stop the assassinations we deduced were coming. They saved the president.

[CBD]: Let the record show that Mr. Savas refers to former president Elaine York.

MR. SAVAS: Former?

[CBD]: She has been charged with treason and is a most wanted fugitive under the current authorities.

MR. SAVAS: Current authorities? What does that mean? Who is running the damn country?

[CBD]: We are not at liberty to convey such information to you.

MR. SAVAS: Jesus Christ! What the hell is happening topside? What have you people done?

PART III

ANGEL

By God's providence he was catched With a dark lantern and burning match. Holloa boys, holloa boys, God save the King! Holloa boys, holloa boys, make the bells ring! —English Folk Verse (c.1870)

44

DO NO EVIL

"Look, you need to understand. This comes from way up—from Sergei. We need those users in China. If we don't expand into those markets, we're going to end up on the wrong side of history in tech."

The bald suit behind the desk looked down at his desk as he spoke. Across from him, a dark-haired man with smart glasses stared forward with intense eyes. His fingers drummed on the armrests of the chair.

"Wrong side of history? What the fuck is 'Don't be evil' then? We censor and keep information from people? Information should be free for everyone! You know, even the Chinese! I thought that's what this company was about!"

"We have to make compromises. Find the right balance."

The young man stood up, his voice seemingly focused on the conversation, but his fingers on a smartphone and tapping furiously. He began to pace the small office space.

"And what about the backdoors to NSA and others?"

The superior finally did look at the younger man. "What are you talking about?"

"Don't play dumb with me. I've got enough access to source that I can recognize a backdoor when I meet it. Fucking sloppy code too, if you asked me. Some Russian mobster is going to rape you up the ass for it someday if you don't clean it up."

"I think you're definitely poking around in places you don't need to be," he said, swiveling around in his chair to fully face the young man.

The pacing continued. "Oh, look at that. Suddenly we're all serious like. Well, I'm into free information. Nothing is off limits."

"Then you're going to have to find yourself another job. I don't know why we tolerated you as long as we did."

"Because I can code circles around anyone here."

"No one is irreplaceable."

His step uninterrupted, the youth laughed. "Oh, a threat. From the internet's biggest, baddest company."

"You should take that seriously. We can make you. Or break you. Don't fuck with us or you'll never work in the valley again."

Finally the pacing stopped and the man stood over the desk, facing his superior. "Make me? What, move up the ladder? To what? Chief of sucking China's dick? You dumb ass, I can make more money hacking clueless banks than you pay me here. I thought maybe there was something good in the corporate cesspool. Man, you guys have let me down."

The man behind the desk looked stunned. "There will be no more talk of illegal activity in my office."

"'Cause the NSA is on the line, you mean. How much of your soul did you sell for this shit?" He laughed and shook his head. "Let's get this straight. You're actually upset about me tapping the evaporation *off these big companies while you prostitute yourselves to a dictatorship? Keeping information from its own people? Allowing our government to spy on its own citizens? Okay, this place is actually* seriously *evil. God, I didn't see it. I didn't want to see it. I mean, what's left? I can be a legal criminal here or a black hat out there? This whole tech industry is in deep with the devil." He threw a chair across the room. "Fuck you! And fuck the slave masters. The entire system's corrupt."*

The bald man stood up behind his desk and pointed to the door of his office. "Get out of here. You're fired! No, as of today, I can promise you, you're finished in this industry."

The youth laughed again. "You fucking moron. I'm just getting started."

NOVEMBER 2

45

WASHINGTON BURNS

Sara Houston stared through the window of the helicopter at Washington, D.C. The familiar landmarks were gone. The bejeweled arteries of transportation dark, the lights extinguished by a city-wide blackout. Along with the loss of the grid, the monuments vanished as the spotlights winked out—the Capitol, the Lincoln Memorial, the pillar of the Washington Monument. Gone.

But there was light—orange, glowing in a primitive anger rising from the ground. *Fires.*

The pilot's voice rang in her headphones.

"I'm going to put you down as close to 1600 as I can. I'm broadcasting on all frequencies—if anyone is listening we've got the codes to prove we're friendlies."

"Maybe they're shooting first and asking for ID later," mumbled Lopez beside her, his words barely discernible in the thunder of the blades above them.

"Might be," said the former Blackhawk pilot. "But the rest of the city is chaos. The food riots from the lockdown last week exploded earlier tonight when the power cut. It's like something out of a zombie flick. You'll never make it through the streets."

Houston shouted over the noise, "The President is still there? Are we sure?"

"As of twenty ago, yes. They've had a marine contingent keeping the mobs at bay."

"Why hasn't she been evac'ed?" asked Lopez.

"Got me. Word was filtering through that they were going to. They were flying missions in. Marine One should have choppered her out, but something happened."

Lopez looked at Houston and mouthed, "The Worm." She nodded staring back down to the patches of red and orange flickering below.

The pilot continued. "But I don't know why they haven't been able to get a military mission in there. Someone must be running interference."

Houston gasped, pointing vigorously below. "Maybe those?"

Lopez and the pilot glanced downward. Over the dark city, underneath and in front of them, structured like a migrating flock, small objects reflecting the moonlight sped along their vector. The outlines of the White House could be made out, approaching quickly, the building still illuminated by emergency power. The objects raced straight for it.

"Look!" cried Lopez. "The ones in the back—they're carrying people."

"Drones," said Houston. "They're dropping in a hit squad. Can you outrun them?"

The pilot shook his head. "We're too close. This old shit heap you forced me to fly can't compete with the new birds. It's too slow."

"Gun it!" she yelled, releasing her safety harness and grabbing a machine gun from the back. "Just gun it. Bring us into firing range."

The pilot accelerated sickeningly. Houston was nearly thrown against the back of the cabin. Lopez leapt up and steadied her, pulling her forward beside him near the side door. They mounted one of the weapons on a makeshift turret, Lopez slinging the other weapon against him.

The helicopter darted forward, closing the gap between it and the flock of drones. They approached the back rows, human forms dangling from the larger machines, a strike team of nearly ten black shapes descending with the flock toward the growing form of the President's house.

Houston slung the door open. "Keep it steady!"

They fired. At their distance accuracy was poor, but they compensated with a full spray of bullets. Houston worked the larger, mounted gun, the ordnance dramatically blowing apart machines and men. Between them, they managed to take down more than half the team before the killers realized their peril. The rest dove straight to the ground and out of range.

The remaining drones ignored the helicopter and accelerated downward. Houston and Lopez fired maniacally at them, but only managed to down a handful more. The remaining plunged like kamikazes toward the White House.

"Aerial strike!" said the pilot.

Around the property, explosions erupted. The fireballs lit the drone's targets—military trucks, fortified gunners, the power generators. The building was plunged into total darkness.

"Setting you two down!" came the pilot's frantic words.

The chopper dropped like a brick, the lurch in their stomachs only matched by the strength of the crush to the ceiling. They held on for dear life. The aircraft came to a bone-shaking stop as the landing skid struck the grass on the front lawn, hopped, and slammed down again.

"Go!"

They leapt out of the helicopter and crouched, automatic weapons at the ready. The chopper climbed quickly to an altitude the pilot hoped would be safe from the madness below, prepared to return and retrieve them once Houston and Lopez had located the President.

They'd taken no friendly fire on landing, and it was quickly obvious why. Flames raged around them and smoke filled the air. The initial wave of explosive drones had more than neutralized the military defenses, leaving no one to guard of the nation's First House.

Lopez pointed to the blasted remains of the fence in front of the building. Bodies of rioters were strewn everywhere. It was unclear whether they had been killed by the deceased marines or by the blast that had torn the barrier down. He screamed over the cacophony around them: "The assassins landed back there! They'll be coming through the front gate."

Houston nodded, motioning for him to follow. They sprinted forward, and she made a beeline for the blasted remains of a military barricade. Soldiers and their remains littered the makeshift rampart. Houston heaved one off a mounted machine gun, pointing the weapon toward the street.

"They wanted shock and awe," she said, looking around. "They got it, but we punched a hole in their plan. We can stop them."

Lopez crouched beside her and removed pieces of a weapon from a backpack. He quickly assembled a rifle and attached a night-vision scope. Placing it on the cement barricade in front of him, he aimed through it.

"They're here!" he said. "Four. No, five! I can get several before they react."

"Wait!" said Houston scanning around them. "Let them get through the fence."

"That's too close, Sara!" he said. "Less than a hundred feet. Anything could happen!"

"But if some rabbit and come at us from other directions, we might be sitting ducks hunting for York. Draw them in," she said, pulling out two grenades. "Pick off as many as you can. The others will hunker down for a few seconds before making a run for shelter."

He nodded. "Throw deep, girl."

They didn't have to wait long. In the dancing light of the flames, Houston was soon able to spot the shadows approaching. They were moving swiftly, in a tight formation, cautious yet still seemingly confident of the outcome. *Overconfident.*

Lopez squeezed the trigger. One of the five arched backward, paused a second frozen, then tipped like a bowling pin to the ground. Before he'd hit the asphalt the man beside him took a shot to the head as well.

The others dropped quickly to the ground. Houston hurled one grenade after another at their location. Her motion drew the attention of the attackers, but she continued to throw, even as shots whizzed by. She'd launched four grenades in quick succession when Lopez tackled her before she could remove more. As they fell, the explosions began.

"Dammit, Francisco!" she screamed over the series of detonations.

He ignored her and aimed the rifle again, staring through the scope. "All five down, you crazy fool!" he said, removing the weapon from the barricade and planting the butt on the ground beside him. He sighed. "What a mess."

She smiled and grabbed him roughly by the cassock. "No more foreplay. Need to find POTUS."

They turned to the entrance, preparing to run into the damaged building. A rapid fluttering sound whipped over their heads and two shadows dropped to the ground in front of them, catching them unprepared. They stared into gun barrels.

"Sara, down!"

Automatic fire erupted as they dove for cover. Houston felt two rounds slam into her stomach, the flak jacket absorbing the most dangerous energies. She rolled desperately away and then sprang to her feet, leveling her weapon. She expected to die.

A pair of women stood in front of them, the bodies of the assassins at their feet, smoke trailing upward from their weapons. One was a female

Marine, bloodied, and with a fire burning in her eyes. Houston moved her finger off the trigger and raised her gun skyward. She stared at the other figure, an older woman in a dark suit, short gray hair in disarray, a gun in her hands.

"Well, I'll be goddamned."

It was the president.

46

MADAM PRESIDENT

"Madam President," said Houston as she stood up, grass stains and soot plastering her face. "You look like you know your way around a war zone."

Elaine York scowled and handed the weapon to the marine. "*Ms.*, please. I don't run a brothel. Your friend's hurt."

Houston's eyes darted across to Lopez. He sat on the ground holding his left arm. "Shit!" She dashed over to him.

"It's okay, Sara," he said, seeing her wild eyes. "Just a graze. Not even my gun arm." Blood soaked his shoulder and dripped through the cuff of his sleeve.

"Dammit, Francisco, you're too much a linebacker to dodge!" Houston ripped open the fabric of the cassock and revealed an ugly laceration across his upper arm. "Graze or not, you're going to bleed out if we don't close this up."

"Get York out," said Lopez, glancing up as the president stood over him. "Call the pilot. We'll deal with it after."

A pained look in her eye, Houston pulled out a handheld radio. It cracked with static. "Extraction 1. Target is acquired. Retrieve immediately. There are wounded."

There was a short silence, then: "Roger that. On your position. On the ground in half a minute."

Houston thrust the handheld to the president who took it with stern eyes. Pulling the dark mask off her head, she ripped it lengthwise and wrapped it into a tight mass, pressing it to Lopez's shoulder wound.

The marine beside the President looked grimly over the field of battle. "Let's hope to God that's the last of those fucking deathbots."

The deep throb of the helicopter blades grew quickly. Lopez stood up as the craft hovered above the building, kicking up debris and nearly blinding them. It set down on the lawn fifty feet from their position. The pilot waved them over frantically.

They ran. There were no more surprise landings. No shots fired or bombs detonated. As Houston slammed the door, the four of them still moving to take seats, the bird rocketed up, the sound of the rushing air muted as the latches sealed. She reached over and pulled a first aid kit from underneath the seat. Within seconds it was open and she was dressing Lopez's wound.

"I was going to offer some help," said the marine, eyeing her carefully. "I'm certified as a medic. But it looks like you know what you're doing."

Houston didn't take her attention from Lopez, who grimaced unmoving as she worked the torn flesh. "We've had some experience."

The President spoke. "Okay, so who the hell are you people? I don't usually jump into moving aircraft with just any pair of armed personnel, but today has been a bit unusual."

Houston continued working on Lopez's shoulder. "The pilot will drop you off at Mount Weather. Plans were likely for NAOC or something, but given the buzzing drone armies, I think feet on the ground is the place to be."

The President furrowed her brow. "You aren't coming? What's going on here? Who are you?"

Houston paused a moment and turned her head toward York, expression strained. "We don't exist, Madam—Ms.—President."

"Let's not get cheeky, darling. Out with it. There are no government ciphers to me."

"We aren't government. We don't exist. Friends called us in. But we're out before the light of day." Houston returned to treating the bullet wound, hands covered in Lopez's blood.

York eyed her silently for several seconds. "Friends called you in, huh?" She shook her head. "Damn prescient friends you have and I'm not going to second guess them. Not after what just happened. I assume you're legit or I'd be dead by now."

Houston chuckled. "I wouldn't go so far as to say we're legit."

Lopez opened his eyes and fought to smile. "I'm Gabriel," he hissed between clenched teeth. He twitched his head at Houston. "This is Mary."

York nodded. "Praise the Lord. Whoever you really are, I'm pleased to meet you." She shuddered. "I thought we were goners down there. I hope to be able to thank you properly someday. Consider me very intrigued."

Houston spoke flatly. "Who else is left?"

York closed her eyes and sighed, the fatigue apparent on her face. "A few staff. I hope to God they retreat to the bunker. We were cut off from escape by the explosions. Caved in a good part of the White House. Killed most of the soldiers. Nearly killed us." She looked to the bruised and bloodied face of the marine. "We're barely standing up again and it's gunfire, more explosions, your helicopter in the mix. I thought you were the bad guys until the drones dropped off the last two." She looked at Lopez. "Saved your life right before we mowed them down. Anyway, I judged you were friendlies. The Vatican look might have helped."

"I meant, who's left in the government?"

York's face hardened. "It's not good. Confirmed killed are the VP and the most of the leaders of Congress. The cabinet is MIA." She opened her eyes and stared out at the receding flames below. "Damn. Look at her burn. Should take a photo for my presidential library." The others stared at her in silence. "Meanwhile, Mount Weather makes a lot of sense. It's close enough, secured like all hell, puts me in contact with all the governmental emergency systems. Better than airborne right now. Speaking of which, how safe are we?"

The helicopter began to descend. Houston finished taping off Lopez's shoulder and slumped next to him on the chair, drenched in sweat.

"We're not Air Force One, Ms. President," said Houston. "Just another helicopter flying around on doomsday. Who's to care?"

Lopez steeled himself and sat up as the craft neared the ground. "This is our drop off, Ms. York," he said with difficulty. "The pilot is in our circle of *friends*. He'll get you to the emergency operations center, assuming the little flying demons don't pick you off."

"Reassuring," muttered York.

Lopez smiled. "Oh ye of little faith."

The helicopter touched down and the pilot called out to them. Houston opened the door and prepared to jump. York grabbed her arm.

"Good luck," said the president, holding Houston's eyes in an intense stare.

She returned the gaze. "We're all going to need a lot of that."

47

EVAC

They watched the helicopter disappear into the evening sky. Tall grasses spread over the remains of an abandoned farm and a dilapidated barn rose behind them, the property encircled with trees.

"Let's get moving, Francisco."

He nodded and they turned toward the barn, moving as quickly as the former priest's fatiguing body would allow. There wasn't a door to secure the building, the remains having fallen off and laying rotted to the side. Much of the ceiling had collapsed as well. The rank smell of rotting wood was overpowering.

In the center of the barn was a jeep, a canvas thrown over the vehicle hastily, barely covering the sides. Houston walked up to the driver's side and yanked it off, tossing the fabric behind the truck. She helped Lopez remove his backpack and stripped his body armor.

"Don't worry about it," she said as he began to protest. "We should be done with commando activity for the night. You need to conserve energy."

He acquiesced and entered the jeep, stowing the gear in the back. Keys were sitting in the ignition. "Savas has some connections," said Lopez, staring ahead of them as Houston started the vehicle.

"I don't think anyone is keeping score on favors right now," said Houston, gunning the engine and racing out of the structure.

She felt conspicuous with the lights on, the clandestine and dangerous mission still locking her mind into a paranoid state. But it was too dark to drive without them, too dangerous on this poorly kept country road to risk ending their efforts for something so irrational. The jeep leapt and shuddered over holes and mounds in the dirt road. With each impact, Lopez gasped, his face a mask of pain.

Near the rusted gate to the field, Houston pulled the jeep to a stop. She removed a mobile phone from her shirt pocket and switched it on.

"No signal," she said.

"Location bad?"

"No, this area was supposed to be blanketed, remember?"

"So the towers are dark. What's even functioning, do you think?"

She shook her head. "Not much. Washington's completely dark." She released the belt and turned to the back, digging through one of the packs. She spun back in her seat holding a large handheld device. "At least we have this. Unless the damn worm fried the satellites, it should work."

She switched on the device and let it power up. Within a minute she had punched in a call and was waiting for a response. A low click sounded as she put it on external speaker.

Savas' voice burst into the crisp, Virginia air. "Gabriel? Where the hell are you two? What happened? It looks like an invasion in DC!"

"Mary here, John. Gabriel's close, nursing a blasted shoulder."

"Jesus! The president?"

"POTUS is secured. En route to the agreed upon location. She's shook up, but okay. The lady can take care of herself."

"You should see the footage on the city."

"We were *there*, John. It's worse. Look, I'm heading to the landing strip. We need immediate evac for Gabriel. I'm not going to wander into a local hospital, I hope you'll understand. He needs stitches. Maybe some blood."

"Roger that. We'll get you two back here, however we can. It'll be a bitch, though. You think the lockdown was serious before? Right now it's not clear to anyone who's running the damn country. The Guard is not ready for this. Folks are going to get killed."

Lopez motioned to Houston for the phone and grabbed it with his good hand.

"John, Gabriel here. Look, we need to regroup. This is moving too fast. You need to circle the wagons and get that crazy idea of yours in motion. Something. *Anything*. I don't think there's much time left."

"Agreed. Damn! We need to get her out of here to a different location, one where they'll feel confident to make a move. FBI headquarters is likely not going to encourage them. We're scouting some places, but it's hard to imagine how to get around the way things are."

Houston took the phone back.

"Look, John. We'll figure that out soon enough. I'm closing this call and beelining to the strip. Please tell me something is waiting for us there and it has airfoils."

"Fueled and ready. Go. There's no way to say it right, but thanks to both of you. And I'm sorry. The worst is still coming."

The line went silent. Houston flung the device into the bag behind her, released the brake, and hammered the accelerator. The jeep jumped forward onto the main road, tires screaming as Houston veered sharply right. Within a minute the vehicle was lost from view, red tail lights winking like mad eyes in the dark, leaving the pastoral hills of Virginia to cricket song and the glow of distant fires.

48

IRRECONCILABLE DIFFERENCES

A morning glow seeped through the filthy window and spilled onto two naked forms entwined on a bed. The woman lay with her head on the chest of the man, short-cropped hair like a sea-urchin next to his long, black strands. Both rested unmoving, eyes half-lidded. The man spoke.

"You know, Poison, it's finally hit me."

The woman frowned, her brow creasing, and sat upright in the bed, small breasts decorating the sculpted ribs of a thin body. She moved her hand down the man's torso.

"What's hitting you?"

The man grabbed her hand and sat up as well.

"I'm serious."

"Yeah, that's obvious." She turned away, to stare out the window.

"I finally realized something about us." Poison didn't say anything, just watched the growing light. "You want to know what that is?"

"Fuck you, Fawkes," she said rising from the bed and wrapping a tattered robe around her. "No games."

"Not a game." His eyes were intense. Almost wild. "I finally realized that something incredible has happened. Something I never, ever expected. Something that should be impossible for me. Really, man, if you knew. Should just be impossible now."

"What, dammit?"

"I realize that sometime over the last month I've fucking fallen in love with you."

Her face froze and then a smile crept outward, shyly.

"Yeah?"

"Yeah. I mean, it's happened once before. But I thought that was it, never again. I'm pretty much all fucked to hell and back, you know. Emotionally retarded and all that. Psych-ward material. But whatever. I'm fucking nuts about you. Suddenly, I don't care anymore about all that shit, all these damn plans our stupid groups have been putting together. I don't care. Right now, I realized all I want to do is just take off with you. Disappear. Live in some trailer somewhere and forget the goddamned world."

She moved toward him with her hand extended, but he stood and turned away from her, slipping tight underpants on, grabbing a t-shirt from the floor.

"It came into focus and explained so much. Why I couldn't concentrate. Why I was losing motivation."

Her hand dropped to the side, her smile fading.

"And then I realized what I had to do."

He turned toward her, the shirt pulled down over his thin frame, yanking on a pair of jeans.

"So what do you have to do?"

He sighed, snapping his fly closed. "It's over, Poison. I'm leaving and not coming back. It's been fun." He held her eyes.

"I don't understand. Her tone rose, the pitch quavering, her eyes large. "Why?"

"Don't make it any harder. For either of us. Just let it hurt and die." He threw things into a duffle bag. "This is the hardest thing I've ever done."

"Then why are you doing it?" she shouted, tears in her eyes.

"Because it is so hard! Because I know! I know that all our feelings, this love and joy and soaring hope and wonder is all a lie!" He looked at her as some despised thing. "Bubbling broth of chemicals in our minds that will lead us astray. That will end in hurt." He zipped the bag and walked to the door as she stood rooted, turning her head stiffly to follow his motions. "Worse. It'll wreck my plans, erase my desire to achieve my goals, to impact a lasting change. And why? For love. *For limbic lies. I will destroy everything I've worked so hard on, only to lie dazed and happy with you under some tree somewhere. Justice demands so much more."*

"Justice?" her face was a mask of confusion.

"It will not be stopped. Not even by you, Poison. I will go, our love will die, and I can finish what I started. I'm sorry for the pain. But it's just withdrawal. Just your brain missing its biochemical fix. It'll be over soon."

With that he stormed out of the room, leaving Poison to sit on the bedside, her eyes red and wet, a snarl on her lips.

BEFORE:
THE ANONYMOUS EVENT COMMISSION

DEPOSITION IN THE MATTER OF:
UNITED STATES ARMED FORCES SPECIAL TRIBUNAL, Plaintiff,
versus
JOHN SAVAS, Defendant
Case No. M120039E-007X

CONTINUED DEPOSITION OF:
Franklin Joeseph Miller

CBD: So then, these fugitives were sent to rescue the nation's president?

MR. MILLER: Which they did. Poke any holes in your dumbfuck theory?

CBD: And what were you doing during these hours of chaos in Washington?

MR. MILLER: If only it was just Washington! You seem to be forgetting the hand basket Europe went to hell in.

CBD: Yes, the nuclear plants.

MR. MILLER: You want chaos? There you go! Chinese party leaders blasted, too. When the TV news wasn't streaming video of DC on fire, it was showing ten different reactors smoldering in France. All from aerial reconnaissance photographs, of course, because it was a radioactive clusterfuck on the ground. Did you know that the Germans were nearly nuclear free?

CBD: I'm sorry, I don't see the relevance of—

MR. MILLER: They had made it a fucking law that they'd end nuclear power in Germany by 2020 or something. You know those Krauts, damned if they didn't figure out how to do it! Nuclear free. Fossil fuel free. Sustainable energy. In five years they'd be there. No worries for meltdowns. Unless, of course, some psychopath flies a bunch of drones into your neighboring country's reactors, blowing that shit into the atmosphere. Ain't nuclear free no more.

CBD: Mr. Miller, let's get back to—

MR. MILLER: So, when you say 'what were you doing?', try to remember that, first of all we were all trying to stay sane. Stay focused. On task. Every single one of us was struggling not to lose his shit as the world literally burned right in front of our eyes.

CBD: Yes, as I said, it was chaotic.

MR. MILLER: And in our own backyard. The food riots were spreading. No deliveries into or out of the city for days. Even if the worm hadn't FUBARed the distribution economy, the lockdown of the city made things ten thousand times slower. People were hungry. What's that saying, even a good man is nine meals away from murder? It was getting scary just to go outside. Everyone was panicking about a blackout like in DC. But we didn't have time for that shit. John's plan. That's what was on our minds. We spent sleepless nights setting it up. Filming interrogation scenes worthy of a goddamned Oscar. Feeding it out through Angel's digital feints.

CBD: I thought her system had been sabotaged by Anonymous.

MR. MILLER: Yeah, that set us back. She quarantined the computers from the internet and wiped them to make sure all traces of the worm were gone.

CBD: How?

MR. MILLER: I don't know. She's the code-head. I just shoot stuff.

CBD: Her system was brought back online?

MR. MILLER: A part of it. Enough to hook back up to the net. By then John had gotten some of the code for the firewall from NSA, and Angel fortified our position, whatever that means. She had more space now to breathe, but we didn't seem to have much time.

CBD: These feints?

MR. MILLER: Right. So, she put the interrogation videos on some unsecured boxes, other shit. To piss Fawkes off. The idea was to find a location offsite that looked vulnerable, move the girl there, leak that we moved the girl there, then wait with the bait for that fuck to show up.

CBD: Sounds like a good plan.

MR. MILLER: Yeah, you try to find a way to net that ghost in a few days while everything went to shit. But it *was* a good plan. The only problem was that Fawkes had his own plans. And we hadn't anticipated them.

NOVEMBER 3

49

BAITING THE TRAP

The elevator opened and Savas saw the broad form of Frank Miller filling the space between the doors. The ex-marine's suit bulged on each side and his shirt strained from the pressure of body armor underneath.

"Suiting up for a rough game, Frank?"

"Time to move," Miller said.

Savas stood beside Cohen and the woman who called herself Poison. No one moved for a moment, the air charged with the potential of what was to come. They were crossing a threshold, setting events into motion that could not be recalled.

"FEDs first," said Poison, grasping a USB disk hanging around her neck like a talisman.

Savas followed as Cohen limped into the car and turned around, watching the hacker intently. Poison continued to face them as Miller pressed a button to hold the doors open.

"It has to be done," said Cohen. "You know that."

Poison nodded, looking sideways around the room as if for an escape. "Yeah, but when it comes to it, leading the prick to the net seems low even for slamming your ex." She looked at them harshly. "Try not to hurt him."

With that she walked into the elevator and turned her back on them as the door closed. Savas felt it better to leave her last request unanswered.

"Gabriel and Mary?" he whispered to Cohen.

"On their way. He's okay, patched up."

"Once we're outbound, I'd like to talk to them."

Cohen nodded. Miller was silent, and the remaining ride to the basement garage was eerily quiet.

The doors separated to reveal an underground parking lot—gray walls, flickering fluorescents, and row upon row of vehicles blurring into monotony. Standing out dramatically from that background was a black FBI van. It was built for undercover work, devoid of any insignia or lettering, the communications equipment inside visible through the open side door. Only the telltale bulge of the black antenna by the back doors would announce an investigative presence to the trained eye.

Alongside the van was a row of four uniformed SWAT officers. They were fitted in black uniforms and external body armor with weapons at their sides. Poison looked them up and down with a scowl.

"I'm part of the matrix now," she said bitterly. "Is this all you could get?"

"You think Fawkes will throw worse at us?" asked Miller.

"I don't know what he might do anymore," she said. "I hope these Storm Troopers know what the fuck they're doing. He won't mind wasting any of them."

Cohen handed Savas her crutches and faced Poison, her brown hair like a shawl offsetting the angry fire in her eyes. Cohen startled the hacker by reaching up to her shirt collar and straightening it.

"Look, Ms. Ivy—*Poison*—whatever you want to imagine yourself to be *in the matrix.* A little appreciation for putting ourselves in harm's way would do you well. Appreciation for dedication, duty, public good and all that. Inside the suits are human beings, just like you. Try to remember that."

Poison stepped back from the intensity in Cohen's glare, but the agent had turned away. Savas tried to rescue the moment.

"We were lucky to find anyone. Fawkes has pressed all the panic buttons. Washington's on fire and New York might be next. We have what we have. Most importantly, we have you. I just hope Fawkes wants you badly enough to do something stupid."

Miller motioned to the SWAT personnel. "Poison will go in the van with the team. There shouldn't be any issues along the way, but if there are, they'll need a small army to get to her out."

"Assuming they want me alive," she said.

"That's the basis of the entire plan," said Cohen. "Otherwise, he'll just drop a drone on you when he gets your position."

Poison looked terrified.

Miller continued. "The rest of us will follow in the car. I've put through all the channels we can for clearance, without revealing exactly what we're doing of course. Hopefully we'll make it through the checkpoints without issues. There are a lot of ways to get to Brooklyn. If we're held up at one bridge or tunnel, we'll try another. Hopefully we won't waste too much time."

Savas nodded. "What this means, of course, is that we're on our own. No backup. This entire operation would never fly with the brass if they knew what we were trying. It's too unorthodox, too poorly planned, too risky."

Poison laughed. "You're giving me a whole lot of confidence."

Miller scowled. "You should worry about the warehouse. You'll be dug in with no place to go there. Like I said, I don't anticipate any issues in transit today. Fawkes doesn't know what we're up to, he won't know where you are without his GPS device. Angel will leak the location once we're ready."

"Unless he knows a lot more than you think he does," said Poison.

Tires screeched. The group turned toward the sound. From the exit ramp two white vans rushed recklessly into their level and came screaming to a halt. Savas cried out as the doors of the vans swung open and dark shadows leapt out, weapons drawn. Cohen grabbed onto Poison and fell with her to the ground behind a car as the FBI SWAT team faced the oncoming figures.

Miller drew his gun and concealed himself behind the back of the van. Savas rushed forward beside him, pulling out his Glock and crouching. The SWAT team remained exposed, flanking their right.

In the sudden chaos, the sounds of automatic gunfire echoed madly through the underground chamber.

50

FIREFIGHT

The haphazard positioning of the participants ensured that the firefight would be quick. The SWAT team was exposed and took the brunt of the initial offensive, unable to find cover. They responded by advancing into the fray and opening fire. Despite their protective gear and powerful weapons, they were outnumbered, and the attackers cut them down mercilessly.

But not without cost. Savas had kept the van between him and the assailants. He swung his gun arm into the line of fire just as the last SWAT man fell in front of them. Multiple bodies of their attackers lay on the asphalt as well, shell casings littering the ground beside him and in front of the vans. Gunshots exploded above his head as Miller fired, and Savas saw a shape fall as it ran, a body striking the concrete only feet from the shelter of parked cars.

His peripheral vision caught other forms dashing for cover on his left and right. A magazine dropped to the ground beside him as Miller reloaded, sliding down the side of the van.

"How many?" Savas asked.

"Four or five more," Miller panted. "They're spread across."

Savas spotted movement behind a blue pickup. He blasted its windshield for effect more than any hope to strike a target.

"Right idea," Miller said. "But it won't stop them for long. They've got the firepower on us. And still the numbers. How the hell did they know?"

Savas shook his head. "No time for that. Take point."

Miller swung into position and fired several shots. He ducked back and a barrage of gunfire chased him, blowing out the tires on the far side of the van, the windows exploding. Glass rained down on them.

"So much for an escape," Savas muttered.

He had turned back toward Cohen. She was propped on one knee and the car, poised with a pistol, head barely over the hood. Poison crawled behind the Crown Vic, terrified. Savas wondered if she could be the target. Was Fawkes there to terminate her?

Harsh words disabused him of the notion.

"Send the girl!" a man's voice cried. "All we want is the girl!"

Savas saw Cohen shake her head vigorously in the negative. Miller sighed.

"We *might* bring them down, John," he said, "but not before we're bloodied up good."

"Any ideas?"

"If I had a few minutes, maybe."

Their assailants wouldn't give them thirty seconds.

"We've got one of your men!" came the voice. "He's wounded but not dead. Send the girl or we waste him!"

There was a scream and Savas thought he heard the word "name". A rattled voice could barely be heard.

"Agent Longwell. Special Weapons and Tactics."

The voice was gasped, in pain, heavy breaths between the words.

Savas dropped to the ground and slightly forward. For a moment he was able to see ahead, the presence of an armed intruder pointing a gun at the slumping body of a SWAT officer, a trail of blood across the floor from where he'd been dragged. He rolled back behind the van just as shots ripped open the asphalt where he'd been. "Hurt bad but still alive," he said to Miller. "*Damn!*"

"You got ten seconds!"

"John, whatever you do, don't negotiate with these killers!" Miller looked furious.

Savas looked back. Cohen had dropped her head, defeated. He had a second to make a decision weighing a man's life and a possible stop to a world terrorist event. He closed his eyes.

"Frank, take my gun and—"

"I'm coming!"

He opened his eyes and saw Poison standing up behind Cohen. The hacker moved her hands upward and danced around Cohen's clumsy attempt to grab her, trotting forward awkwardly with arms raised.

"Anyone else move and this pig is dead!" cried the voice.

Savas cursed. The girl had taken things into her own hands. They hadn't killed her, which ruled her out as a target. It looked like Fawkes had sent a retrieval team to get her out of FBI custody, that he wanted her alive and was willing to invest significant resources into saving her. *Dammit!* The plan would have worked!

Poison was now just in front of the van, walking slowly, eyes wide and face frozen. She was beyond the team's reach now, any actions they might take could be countered devastatingly.

"They've got her," Savas said to Miller, hand clenched into a fist.

Miller nodded. "She made the call. Damage control, John. We need to create a distraction."

"A distraction?" he asked, the truth dawning on him.

"To get Rebecca out," said Miller grimly. "No way we all walk. Not after those videos. Not after this bloodbath. We need to draw fire and get her the hell out of here. Somebody has to walk away and try to get assets on that van."

Savas nodded, the implications hitting him like a sledgehammer. "Maybe we can take enough of them down, damage the van. Trap them, slow them down."

"Good a plan as any," shrugged Miller.

"But she can barely walk."

Savas looked back toward Cohen. Her attention was focused on him. He motioned with his eyes to the stairwell, a bright EXIT sign over the door. She followed his gaze and nodded, grabbing the crutches beside her.

They heard a scream and thump. Savas assumed it was Poison being thrown into the van. They had only seconds now.

"Go!" he hissed to Miller, and the two spun toward the attackers, weapons drawn.

They opened fire.

51

BUGGED

Weapons discharge filled the reverberant chamber. It was several seconds before Savas could fully process what was happening. He'd locked on the shapes in front of the white van, the form of Poison glimpsed momentarily within as he took aim. From both sides figures were rushing toward the van in a blur of motion.

But something was wrong. The mass of figures was too large, and the flow of bodies counter to what would be expected of their attackers. Shapes were moving down from the access ramp, black fabric fluttering as they dashed.

They were firing on Fawkes' team.

"Friendlies!" screamed Miller beside him, his combat vision parsing the chaos more quickly than anyone.

Lopez and Houston. Savas didn't have time to consider how they had arrived and found their way to the conflict. That would come later.

"Sideways, John," Miller yelled. "Watch the cross-fire!"

They darted away from the center. The team sent to snatch Poison was caught between hailstorms of bullets. Lopez and Houston had drawn their attention, wounding several, just as Savas and Miller opened fire. In less than a minute, the firearms were silent. Shell casings tinkled to a stop on the hard surface below. The charred reek of gunpowder burned in their nostrils.

A mass of bodies was scattered around the white vans. Two of the forms jerked helplessly, one screaming in agony. The rest were silent and still. It was over.

"Poison!" cried Cohen. She hobbled on her crutches straight to the van.

Miller and Savas moved cautiously, training their weapons on the bodies below them while Cohen disappeared inside the transport. Lopez and Houston rounded the right side of the vehicle, the former priest's left arm in a sling, his right clutching a submachine gun. Houston holstered a large Browning.

"Fuck, Savas!" she said, out of breath. "This was supposed to be where we recuperated!"

He frowned at them. "Thanks for saving our asses. Now get topside and check that we aren't going to get another surprise. Call Angel when you get back and let's try to figure this out."

"Francisco can wait it out here," she said. "Doc isn't going to be happy with his recent exertions." She sprinted away and up the ramp, weapon drawn again.

Lopez looked toward the fallen men around them. "I'll see what's left here. Go check on our bait."

Savas nodded and ducked into the vehicle. Inside, Poison cowered at the far end, shaking, wedged into a corner by the back doors with her legs pulled up and her arms around them. Cohen crouched next to her, one hand resting on the hacker's arm.

"Poison," Cohen said. There was no response, just a wide-eyed and distant look on her face. "Tabitha." She turned to Cohen, still not speaking, and Cohen continued gently. "It's over. We need to get you out of here, now, in case more are on the way."

"He knew," Poison whispered, clutching her necklace. She grabbed Cohen's vest. "How did he know?"

Cohen shook her head. "I don't know, but we need to move."

"We aren't safe anywhere! He'll know. He'll follow." Her eyes were wild. "How could he know?"

Savas' baritone rumbled from the front of the van. "Maybe I can shed some light on it." He spun from the front seat to the pair in the back, holding up a smartphone. "Look. GPS app."

He held the device toward them. On the screen a bright sphere blinked on their position.

"You're bugged, Poison," Savas said grimly.

"Bugged?" Poison looked perplexed. Then a light flared in her eyes.

She jerked her necklace hard enough to break the clasp, leaving two ribbons dangling from her hand. Inside her palm was the USB stick.

"The drive?" asked Savas.

She laughed bitterly. "My first hack. Backed up. Like a trophy for luck. He knew. The prick! He knew. He must have switched it with a tracking device. *Jesus!*"

With a wild motion, she flung herself through the van, forcing her way past Savas and outside. The two agents followed her out and watched her fling the device to the ground. She picked up one of the assault rifles beside a dead man and aimed the butt of the gun toward the USB stick.

Cohen extended one of her crutches and stopped her. "We want him to know where we are, remember?"

"You want another bloodbath?" Poison said, indicating the bodies at their feet. "He'll come again. Can't you see that?"

"No," Cohen said. "We'll shield it, jam it until we arrive at the warehouse."

Poison nodded. "Yeah. All right." Her breathing slowed. Her eyes flashed downward. "I still want to smash the damn thing."

The edges of Cohen's mouth twitched upward. "I'm sure you do."

Cohen reached down awkwardly and scooped the stick from the ground, her face momentarily lost in a cascade of brown hair. Houston came jogging around the two vans.

"All clear," she panted. "The guards at the front are dead and the gate mechanism's smashed to hell and back. I used the phone there to call for some backup. This building must be ghosted. There hasn't been any response!"

Savas nodded. "We're spread so thin across the city that we're losing function."

"I also got Angel on the phone. She says she's got some interesting news."

Savas turned his head. "What news?"

Houston shrugged. "Something about immune code or something for the virus? I have no idea. I turned the conversation to our little problem down here. She'll get some reinforcements to us soon. "

"No need for a medkit, though," said Lopez, stepping back into their circle. There was blood on his hands. "Too much iron, too many holes. They're all dead. Your men and those from Fawkes. The last just bled out."

They all turned to look out over the bodies scattered around them.

Savas grimaced at the sight of the downed FBI agents, and the pools of blood clotting underneath them.

"This bastard is building one hell of a body count."

Cohen held up the USB stick. "Yeah, and he still thinks he holds all the cards. But not this one. Not anymore. We make it go dark, move to the location, and set up. Then we switch it back on. After all this, is there any doubt?"

Houston smiled. "Moth to the flame."

BEFORE:
THE ANONYMOUS EVENT COMMISSION

DEPOSITION IN THE MATTER OF:
UNITED STATES ARMED FORCES SPECIAL TRIBUNAL, Plaintiff,
versus
JOHN SAVAS, Defendant
Case No. M120039E-007X

CONTINUED DEPOSITION OF:
John Savas

MR. SAVAS: Everything was happening at once. We worked to clear the parking level. There wasn't much point in turning it into a crime scene. The whole planet already was one. The bodies were moved, some of the mess fire-hosed away. Found another van, but that was it for a SWAT presence. We were on our own.

CBD: Who then headed to the warehouse?

MR. SAVAS: Me, agents Cohen and Miller. Lopez and Houston. Finally, the woman. Poison.

CBD: The convicted hacker?

MR. SAVAS: That's the one. Agents Rideout and Lightfoote stayed behind to handle the digital angle of this.

CBD: How did you prevent Fawkes from tracking you?

MR. SAVAS: Simple. We bagged the stick in a shielding case—no signal in or out. For good measure we brought onboard a jammer. We checked it carefully. It was gagged. We sent out three vans in different directions in case any of his drones were watching. Janitors drove them around the city for a while. Not sure what was the key element, but it worked. We weren't followed.

CBD: And you know that because?

MR. SAVAS: We're still alive.

CBD: So it was during this time that agent Lightfoote designed the prototype code that infected the entire internet?

MR. SAVAS: Her immune cells. Yes.

CBD: What does that mean?

MR. SAVAS: Go ask a biologist. I don't know. [INAUDIBLE] All right, look, the idea is simple, at least. Our bodies have immune cells that recognize different bugs and kill them, right? These cells float around inside us waiting for an infection then do their business. The way Angel explained it, she couldn't attack the worm directly. It was too distributed or something. All over the place. A hundred million computers. If you don't get all of them, all the parts, it reinfects and spreads like wildfire again. So, her idea was to mimic the immune system. Design programs that would spread themselves like the worm, copying themselves, hacking into computers. But their purpose wasn't going to be to fuck things up like Fawkes. Her worms were single-minded in going after his worm. She called them immune cells.

[REDACTED]: Then let me get this straight. Your agent created viral, self-replicating code that would break into computers all around the world, including classified networks, including governmental systems?

MR. SAVAS: It was the only way. Like an infection where you only kill 99% of the bugs with an antibiotic, it can come roaring back. We had to get close to sterilization.

[REDACTED]: And you gave her permission to release this code?

MR. SAVAS: You bet your ass, I did. I had no idea if it would work. I'm not sure she was confident it could work. But it was sure worth a shot. What was the downside? It fails? Back where we were. We accidentally blow up the internet with her code? Well, that's *where* we were *already*!

CBD: Why did she think it could work?

MR. SAVAS: You know, I'm not a programmer or a biologist. She used the worm she had trapped in-house and some other bits of it she had captured across the net, used that code as some sort of matching-recognition system. All of her immune cells, her worms, were randomized with different bits of the code. They would search for matching elements, worm signatures, on any computer her code infected. Match meant two things. Her code would copy itself like crazy and spread the recognition element, amplifying it. It would also erase the worm on that computer, but not before copying the code of *that* worm for identification elements to spread. The idea was to find new bits of all the different, variable worms around. Over time it should recognize them all and erase them all. Fawkes' worms had to sit around and wait for his signal. It wasn't designed to fight off something like Angel was making. If she did it right, and if we had enough time—if it spread fast enough—we might sterilize enough computers so that whatever final action he was planning would fail.

CBD: Sterilize. How can the computers be sterilized if they are infected with her code?

MR. SAVAS: Okay, sterile as far as the Anonymous signal was concerned.

CBD: The Anonymous signal?

MR. SAVAS: Yeah, what we were calling it, the activation Fawkes was going to send to take down civilization.

[REDACTED]: Sounds very far-fetched.

MR. SAVAS: Does it? You saw what was happening. All the attacks on online systems from finance to manufacturing—did all that not happen? And those were test runs! Used to assess and refine the hammer stroke. It was just a matter of time.

[REDACTED]: Yet now all that remains is a wrecked computer infrastructure the world is trying to patch together again. And your agent's code is the only thing on every computer! No other malware. Nothing from some imaginary mask-wearing global vigilante named Fawkes. No Anonymous Signal.

MR. SAVAS: So now you're going to condemn her because she made the damned thing work?

[REDACTED]: She isn't here, Mr. Savas. Which is damning enough. Last seen in the company of the two most wanted fugitives in this nation, murderous terrorists the likes of which we have never seen before. You are the one who has orchestrated every element of this. It is not Angel Lightfoote who is on trial now. But you.

MR. SAVAS: Unless I tell you where she is, right? If I hand her and her damn file from Fawkes over to you, then you'll cut me some deal and I walk.

[REDACTED]: You won't be walking, Mr. Savas. Not from this. But there are sentences and there are sentences.

MR. SAVAS: You idiots. If she took the file, it could be copied a million times by now and in a million hands. The horse is out of the barn. Closing the door won't matter now.

[REDACTED]: One fire at a time, Mr. Savas. One fire at a time.

52

REVENGING ANGEL

"Well, hi there, Fawkes!"

Angel stared at the computer screen and smiled. Once again buried in the basement of the Javits Federal Building late in the night. Again the mask of Guy Fawkes stared back at her, floating on the screen in front of her.

But this time, the gloating was gone.

"You fucking cunt!"

She laughed. "Don't you swing that way, Fawkes? Or can I call you Guy? I thought you liked cunts. I *know* you liked Poison's cunt. She says you visited all the time."

"Fuck you!"

"And your pathetic attempt to grab her was as clumsy as your code, which, by the way, my programs are eating through right now. You notice?"

"You think you're safe behind the firewalls of your NSA overlords, but you aren't. I can't reach you right now, but it's just a matter of time before I'm back in and burn your fucking house down."

Angel nodded as she typed. "Not before I hunt down every last one of your worms, you mean. Dissect the motherfuckers. I know you've been keeping score out there. See that tide rising?"

"You're interfering in things you don't understand!"

"Really?" She shook her head. "You going to mansplain the situation to this poor, clueless little cunt?"

"Damn you! You don't know what I know. The power isn't where you think it is. It hasn't been for hundreds of years! I've hacked my way to it."

She put her chin on her hand. "Fawkes, seriously. Is this where you try to tell me how we can rule the galaxy together if I'll just embrace the dark side?"

The masked face in the video stream turned to the side. A scream sounded over the monitors.

Angel clicked her tongue. "You have major anger management issues."

The face was back.

"Every nation, every corporation, every standing army is marching to hidden orders. Events—they're all part of a big game board! Pieces—disposable pieces—moved by the few that really hold the power. We can't change it from within. We can't defeat them on their terms!" The face panted. "But they've made themselves dependent on the modern information system—and they can't control it. For the first time in hundreds of years, they've made a fatal mistake!"

Angel stared silently for a moment. "You're really a mental case, aren't you?"

The scream again. "No! I can show you. Prove it! Your fucking code—it's threatening everything! You have to listen to me!"

"Listen to you go full tin-foil-hat on me as you try to destroy the world? This crap's not even up to the bottom suckers of the worst chat room. If you wanted to make a good first impression, you lost the chance big time when you screwed over my servers, when you brought my dad into this!"

"I will bring your shitty code down!"

She was standing now, palms down on the table. The light of the monitor reflected off her scalp and the metal in her face. "And we still got your girl! She's singing, singing, singing like a fucking bird. Well, really, it's a bit more like screaming. Honestly, so far—it's just screaming. But we know we'll get enough out of her to come after you in the real world."

The mask hovered in the center of the monitor without speaking. Angel could hear his labored breathing. She twisted the knife.

"I can send you a live feed the next time we go at her. But do you really want to be there when we break her? Might fuck you up good, yeah? Watching what we do to her? Every little thing? Believe me, I can imagine how that'd make you feel."

His next words were slurred—hissing. "You're not the only one who can reach out in the real world."

She laughed again. "You hit us with everything you had and I'm back. It's worse for you than before. Really, Fawkes, you were an inspiration to write this code! Thank you for that."

"I will make you hurt for this."

"Oh, Guy," she said dismissively, "I'm not scared of you. And neither is my code. Expect it, fucker."

Lightfoote hit ENTER and sent a video feed through the connection. She watched a mirrored window on her monitor display the content—a young woman strapped to a table, men beating her, blood on her face and pouring from her nose. *Poison.*

She closed the connection and walled Fawkes out with the NSA module. The monitor went dark. She sat down and leaned back in the chair, disgusted with the lies they were sending him.

"But you made me get dirty, you fuck," she whispered. "Now, come get her."

NOVEMBER 4

53

MOUNT WEATHER

For Elaine York, the "SF" was as comforting as it was alarming.

The acronym-smiths of the bureaucracy had called the Mount Weather retreat the High Point Special Facility, HPSF, but the human beings it was designed for had digested that down to something more manageable. *High* in the Virginia mountains to be sure, it was *special* in ways only a self-contained, doomsday hideout could be. Replete with self-sustaining environmental processes for waste and water, military grade rations lining underground storage silos to feed hundreds for weeks to months of isolation—its soldiers, weaponry, and communications systems were rivaled only by NORAD. Prime vacation estate for the nation's leaders when the world went to shit.

And the world was definitely going to shit.

The Colonel—*which one was he?* She'd lost track in the chaos—droned importantly about the precariousness of their plight.

"Without the logistics software, Madam President, we risk an entire breakdown of the supply chain. Our recommendations are to secure all of the major air, land, and sea routes immediately for governmental use only."

President York stared outside the reinforced glass window at the color explosion of the surrounding forest. The morning sunrise crested over the mountains and flooded the compound with light. Waves of flaming red and orange, bright yellow and dim browns blurred in her mind with impressionistic artists' canvases. Patches within the tapestry, like flaking paint in a poorly maintained van Gogh, revealed the skeletal tree branches buttressing the display and hinted at the coming hardness of winter. York knew that this winter would be one of the hardest in memory.

The bald man behind her continued, his ghostly reflection in the glass distracting her. "It's not just food and fuel anymore. We're looking at a prolonged deficit in nearly every category needed to maintain defense functionality."

She now presided over a nation teetering toward dissolution. The major neural networks controlling the modern world were misfiring, clogged with corrupt code like amyloid plaques, rendering the body of the nation as disoriented and confused as an Alzheimer's patient. Beyond the psychological damage of losing most of the modern computer infrastructure—a loss utterly traumatizing to generations now raised on its presence and dependent on the very idea of a world entirely connected, ubiquitously digitized—the very tangible losses of computer regulated transport, manufacturing, scheduling, communications, and medical care had left increasingly large swaths of the country reeling.

"As per NSA analysis, the projections from the last few days, the attacks are intensifying, likely to reach a climax very soon."

Remember, remember the fifth of November.

It was November fourth, and York dreaded the passage of time like the helpless descent of a sleeper into a nightmare. "What about this anti-worm virus they were talking about?" she asked, turning around momentarily to face the officer.

"There's too much contradictory data, Ma'am. No one knows where it's coming from, who's behind it, if it even *is* working against the worm. Some are convinced of it, but others aren't. It might even be a feint by Anonymous to distract us. It is spreading, though. Pretty rapidly."

"And the drone attacks?"

"Those have tapered off. The worm is a replicating resource, but the drones are finite. Anonymous is running out of them."

"They seem to have done enough damage. And what of the reports of a lone mastermind—this *Fawkes* from the FBI data?"

The man shook his head. "Unconfirmed and isolated reports to a single division of FBI. Analysis casts a lot of doubt on the hypothesis."

"Intel 1, if I'm not mistaken."

The soldier nodded. "That is correct. But the consensus—"

"They trumped the consensus five years ago. You might remember." She rubbed her temples. "I wish we had more time to consult with them."

The lights flickered momentarily, then steadied. York glanced around the ceiling and then back at the Colonel.

"They're still working out some kinks in the new electrical regulators," he said.

York shook her head and turned back to the window. "Decades of prep time and what do we do? Repeat the same mistake the world over! The pretty digital magic, all wired up here, the Pentagon, White House! Look at the damn walls! Everything gutted now! 1970s wiring is our salvation! Sophisticated environmental, solar-powered-what-have-you duct-taped to rusted generators. I'm starting to think that when it's all said and done we're going to blow it all up and the damned forests out there are going to swallow what's left of us."

She tried to focus, but the crushing weight of the crisis and the lack of sleep was breaking down her will.

"It's not just us," the Colonel answered. "Every country is struggling with this. Some have it easier: North Korea was so damn paranoid that even the worm is slowed there. And the third world doesn't have enough of a modern architecture that they're relatively intact from the direct effects. But the indirect effects are equally crippling, Madam President."

"Yes, yes," she said, waving him off. "The world is *flat* as the pundits like to say. A sneeze in Beijing or Washington gives a cold to the world. You know what it feels like now? Not like a cold, but like that plague Ebola is eating its way through the arteries of civilization! It's like the world were a giant hive, and now it's degenerating into thousands of isolated and panicked islands." She tried again to focus. "Market report?"

"Securities trading restrictions have effectively brought them to a standstill. The viral bidding is completely out of control. Destabilizing. The evaporating monetary base, huge capital movements into and out of banks by the worm—they've frozen lending and shut down more and more banks. Liquidity is gone. Commerce has come to a standstill. The food riots are growing and taking root in some of the most populous regions of the globe. Hell, right here in America."

"More reports?"

"New York. Chicago. Atlanta." The Colonel paused. "We're losing control."

Remember, remember the fifth of November.

When York didn't answer, the Colonel coughed. "It is the consensus of the Joint Chiefs and what remains of the military advisement panel that we should implement Directive 51."

York glanced sharply over her shoulder to glare at the Colonel. The rest of her body followed and she walked deliberately to her desk. The temperature in the room seemed to drop several degrees, the scarred walls of hanging circuits and controllers feeling like violated strips of her own body.

"So it's come to that."

The Colonel spoke quickly. "The situation is critical. Standard Constitutional protocols are hampering our ability to respond to this crisis. It's urgent that we temporarily suspend the government and act under the emergency directive."

York nodded. "It's frightening how well prepared the United States government is to abolish the United States government."

"You would be overseeing all the branches, Madam President. Nothing is abolished. Power is only concentrated."

"Yes, with the executive. With *me*, as you note. That is exactly what frightens me." She sat down behind the desk and sighed. "I know about REX84, Colonel. You remember the Readiness Exercise of 1984? My father served on the Senate panel that authorized and buried it."

The military man stiffened. "That was an important first step, Ma'am, the first real plan to cover something outside of nuclear war. It was needed! We weren't ready for every contingency."

She nodded, her fingertips pressed against each other. "I know. We'd seen it happen to other nations. Well, after REX84, all a president had to do was declare a *State of National Emergency* and bang! The machine would kick into full gear. Martial law. Military control of state and local governments. Detention of citizens who were scored as national security threats."

"Simulations were run. It's the best way to contain such crises. Maybe the *only* way."

"But Directive 51 goes one step further, doesn't it? Bush and Cheney made sure of that. At least with 84 we had a Constitutional structure, a president answerable, in theory anyway, to Congress and the Judiciary. But here comes 51, *paying respects* to the three branches of government, to separation of powers. But bottom line? The president has unlimited power." She coughed. "At least I won't be called *chancellor*. But we don't kid ourselves, do we, Colonel? Not when survival is on the line."

Concentration camps. Military rule. Dictatorship.

"Everything's temporary. Reversible once the crisis is resolved. Meanwhile, we can have some breathing room. We can act without the delays of Congress and the fiscal limitations! The only other option is to invite collapse of this government!"

The man was red-faced. York arched an eyebrow.

"So the analysts predict," he said, passing his hand over his scalp.

"Here's a mouthful for you, Colonel: *Ermächtigungsgesetz*. German for Enabling Act. You heard of it?"

"No." His face appeared strained.

"Passed by the Nazi-controlled parliament in 1933. They called it the 'Law to Remedy the Distress of the People and the State.' My father also taught about it in law school. It suspended constitutional authority and placed absolute power in the hands of the Chancellor, whom you may have heard of."

"Ma'am, we aren't Nazi Germany."

"Neither was Rome, but it was easier for them, too. In hard times just turn over power to a strong leader. Doesn't usually end well." She laughed, closing her eyes. "Here we were the last twenty years, repeating the mistakes of the Weimar and serving as a script for George Lucas and Alan Moore. Do I make a better Susan or Palpatine, do you think?"

"This isn't fantasy. This is serious. Look what's happening! There's a lot of concern about how to maintain order and preserve the nation through this catastrophe, Madam President. There are growing and serious divisions in the military."

Her head cocked to one side. "Is that a threat, Colonel?"

He paled. "No, Madam President, what I mean is—"

She stood up from her desk, gripping its edge. "What you mean is that order—more to the point, *loyalty* to this office—is being lost. Whether you want to admit it to yourself or not, Colonel, what you're telling me is that the military no longer has confidence in civilian rule. I see the beginnings of a coup."

"You misunderstand—"

"Out!" she shouted, walking around the desk. "Go back to your handlers and tell them that they had better not underestimate my support. We're at a precipice, Colonel, both externally and internally. And I'll be damned if I'm going to bow to any pressure to burn our Constitution. Go back and tell them that I will ignore Directive 51. Tell them that they need to make their choices, and that those choices will define them for the rest of their lives!"

After a final, panicked stare, the man dashed out of the room. York stood in front of the door, trembling, pressing her fingertips to her temples again.

NORAD. The command structure there was solid, loyal. At least she *hoped* it still was. The location was even more secure. She would make arrangements to relocate the principle elements of government. But she had to move quickly. They were at a tipping point. *The irony.* She was as vulnerable here in this doomsday locker as anywhere.

Remember, remember the fifth of November.

The second line of the old song danced rebelliously in her mind.

Gunpowder, treason, and plot!

54

END GAME

The bright light of the sunrise was smothered by thick shutters that plunged the room into complete darkness. In the center of the space was a lone figure in dark robes, a shining Guy Fawkes mask reflecting the artificial light in front of him. The wall-panel of flat-screen monitors displayed multiple locations, scenes dim and sequestered. Figures stared back through the screens, their eyes wary and unsure, weapons and military-issue equipment surrounding them.

"What good is all your money if there ain't nowhere left to spend it?" came one voice.

The mask spoke. "Have you forgotten the plan? When power is taken from the forces controlling our world, my software will orchestrate a new order. An order where each of you will preside like kings over lands and treasure and people. Kingdoms for kings, if you want. Or whatever you want. There will be no interference. I hold the keys to this new order. Have you become such terrified children at the destruction we have spread that you long for the safe chains of your former lives?"

The groups could be heard talking in a cacophony amongst themselves. The mask waited patiently. Several screens clicked off, the images gone, the fearful opting out of this terrible and all too real multiplayer game. The mask keyed in codes. A few remaining solo drones switched on in their hidden hangars. They were preserved for just this contingency, this betrayal and danger to his efforts. Along with a sortie to finish the game, they were all that was left of a once impressive fleet. Images flashed on the darkened screens, a God's eye view of a takeoff and flight. The man behind the mask smiled. *Once in, never out.* They would be dead within minutes.

One by one, the remaining groups committed to the final missions or were similarly dispatched. The final plans were rehashed. Ports and landing strips. More nuclear power plants. Dams and oil rigs. And finally, a team recommissioned to the US electric grid. The mask closed all the connections save this last one.

"You have your new target?" it said.

A bearded man with a green army cap nodded. "I thought your damn worm was going to shut the grid down."

"It was, but the anti-worm code has substantially weakened our capabilities. I can't risk failure. The grid must fall and never rise again. America must be plunged into a final night."

"Some speech you gave," said the man, an automatic weapon in his hands.

"You are my most trusted allies. We have shared goals from the beginning. We do not hope to live as kings or queens. We know how vile and rotten the system is, how deeply the roots of the octopus dig. There is only one way to burn it out—wither the thing to the core."

"You like to talk," laughed the man. "We don't give a fuck about your politics. For us, it's just the high! Mutilation. Dissection. Destruction!" There was a loud cry in unison from the group. "You are the Dark Angel, masked man. You're the power to bring Hell to earth! See you in the flames!"

The figure pressed a button and a screeching recording of death metal thundered in the room. The masked man switched it off and sat silently in the darkness.

The gore-grinders weren't wrong. If all went according to plan, the nations would eat themselves. The violence would consume all power structures. Modern civilization would be laid waste by the very wires it used to hoist itself.

But it was of course not enough. True anarchy could not be achieved until they had erased the heart of corruption. And only his worm could achieve that. Only by completely liquidating all the modern elements of control could there be true freedom.

It was this very goal that was now in doubt. The FBI woman was tweaked, that was for sure. Only a deeply twisted mind could conceive of such a violent cure for the dying human enterprise. It broke all their laws. It was off leash and could possible turn on healthy systems. It was reckless and wild.

And it was winning. He had not counted on anyone with the talent or audacity to unleash the monsters that she had. She had his respect. He would not turn from the truth of it. Truth was the only thing left. *The truth of human corruption.* The truth of what needed to be done.

A screen opened revealing a set of black-clad men.

"Are you prepared?"

A man with intense eyes nodded onscreen. "It's a small unit. There isn't much left now. But it should be enough. We've been watching the building for days via the surveillance drone you spared us. Some boots on the ground, too. We could walk into the place without a problem. They're decimated."

"It must be done right. They have proven far more resilient than we imagined."

"We aren't taking this lightly after what happened to Bravo team."

"You're sure that several members of Intel 1 left the building?"

"Yes. Immediately after our extraction team failed. They sent decoys and used multiple evasive strategies. We didn't have the manpower to follow everything. We lost them."

"And Poison?"

"Signal was lost. They could have discovered the device. Or maybe they're underground too deep. There are mazes of old tunnels on this island. Rumor has it there's some kind of Fed bunker, too."

The mask nodded. "One they will need soon. I have other plans for dealing with Poison. Stay on mission. You have the blueprints."

The man laid out a building plan on a table, pointing to the lower portion of the paper. "Lower basement. These three rooms."

"Your priorities?" asked the mask.

"Seize the mainframes," he said, holding up a UBS stick, "and inject this code."

"And the personnel?"

"We're to kill them all, especially the bald woman."

"Then go. There isn't much time."

The screen went dark. Fawkes removed the mask and exhaled, his features hidden in the darkness. Everything was coming to its final iteration. His ammunition was nearly spent. Ten years of preparation, weeks of assault on the world, and now the final activation. A signal to be sent to every active computer on the planet, one that would induce a final and unstoppable chaos.

He smiled. He *did* respect the girl. That's why when he silenced her, insured her talented hands would not continue to wreak havoc on his plans, he would broadcast the signal from her very machines, thwarting her counter-code and symbolically triumphing over her impressive resistance.

He twirled the mask in his hands.

He was, after all, quite taken with the dramatic.

55

RACING TO POSITION

"Attacks on the power grid?" Cohen shouted into the phone as the car sped along the Shore Parkway, the waters of the Lower Bay tinted orange by the rising sun. Savas had engaged the switch boxes, running quietly unless hitting traffic, the red and blue flashing lights beginning to give Cohen a headache. Poison sat in the back of the vehicle with Miller, in silence. Behind them a second Crown Vic with Lopez and Houston followed closely.

"What's happening?" asked Savas.

"Okay, Angel, hold on. Let me tell John." She turned toward him and sighed. "Looks like the November fifth theory is right. Angel says all hell is breaking loose and major manufacturing and resource systems are under attack by the worm. The scariest is the power grid. You remember the briefings after 9/11?"

He nodded. "Yeah, craziest situation. What, ten critical power stations stand between us and the Stone Age? Six month black out?"

"Pretty much," said Cohen. "It was nine of them. Out of fifty thousand. Which ones were classified of course, so no terrorists could get them. Unless—"

"Unless you've hacked into every computer on the planet and gotten your paws on the files."

"Right. It would likely be down by now just from software attacks, but her crazy code seems to be slowing it. Maybe even turning the tide, she says."

"That's good, right?" He wove in and out of traffic, switching on the sirens to prompt cars out of their path.

Muffled sounds from the phone mixed with the wailing pitches. "Hold on, Angel. Yes, John, that's good. And a lot of good news on that front. Angel says she's working on a new iteration of her immune code, one she thinks will erase the worm once and for all. It can spread anywhere the worm has gone, using the worm to do so, and sterilize any machine that's infected."

"In time?"

Cohen shrugged. "She not done with it and Fawkes is putting things in overdrive." There was more screaming from the phone as Cohen held it away from her ear. "Right! So, the *bad* news is that she's convinced there'll be a physical attack on the power grid, at what she's calling a weak node."

"And she knows this how?"

"She's intercepting more and more information from Fawkes' data stream, hacking more worm strains. She found blueprints, schematics for an assault strike on the power plant. It's in Jersey, routes huge amounts of power from the US and Canada." Angel called out loudly over the phone again. "And like Angel says, it was one of the weak links in the 2003 Northeast blackout. Caused by a software bug at a power plant, she reminds my battered ears."

"Great," said Savas, accelerating unconsciously. "They could already be there."

"And at who knows what other *weak nodes* across the country," said Miller from the back.

Savas shook his head. "No. I don't understand how he built up the resources to do as much as he did, but they're finite. It's clear his supply chain is gone. I don't think he planned to strike every weak grid point with a commando team. He couldn't. Angel's code might have just saved the lights."

The ex-marine shook his head. "Nothing is certain, John."

"We'll see. But I do think this is because of Angel. I think he meant for the worm to throw wrenches into all the electrical machinery like the industrial plants. Machinery tearing itself apart, transformers exploding. But now he's not *sure* anymore. His code might not be there or at enough locations. So he has to make sure, and the East Coast is the seat of government, finance. He's sending all his assets to make sure."

Holding the phone away from her ear again, Cohen nodded. "Angel agrees. She says you need to get Bonnie and Clyde on it."

"Bonnie and—right. Okay, tell Angel we'll call her back after we've explained things."

Cohen smiled, closing the phone. "No need. She called them first. They've agreed and were waiting for your instructions." The headlights of the car behind them blinked repeatedly. "I think she just informed them of your consent."

Savas shook his head. "She'll be running the damn place soon."

The car behind pulled right and exited at an approaching turn-off, the black vehicle disappearing behind an overpass. Lopez and Houston were gone.

Poison spoke from the back of the car. "So, wait. Now it's just us? I'm the bait for your trap and you three are going to face down all his killers?"

Cohen looked back in the review mirror at the frightened woman. "That's right."

"Well, fuck! Can't you call in some cops or army or something?"

Cohen turned around and placed her arm on the chair. "In case you haven't been paying attention, we're in a war zone. There *isn't* anyone who's going to hand over troops or police to some obscure FBI division because they have some unsubstantiated theory about a crazed madman and are unilaterally going to test it by playing a dangerous trap-the-terrorist game with his ex-girlfriend."

Poison simply gawked at her.

Cohen sighed. "We're betting that he's about out of muscle, and that most of it is headed to a power plant in Jersey."

"Betting with our *lives*," stressed Poison.

"Well, probably not yours, dear. He's trying to rescue you from the monsters at the FBI, remember? You'll be fine as long as some stray bullets don't find you." Her tone was impatient. "We'll be the ones filled with steel."

"Not if I can help it," said Savas. "We're going to set up carefully before we let that beacon out of the box. We'll make them come to us and take heavy damage. If he's as weak as we're hoping, that might be enough."

"Fawkes might not even come," said Poison. "Could all be for nothing."

"He'll come," said Savas.

"Why? He didn't last time. He sent people, but he didn't come. Why now?"

"Because you're off site. Because of the last failure he won't want to repeat. Because it's almost over: The fifth of November is tomorrow. I don't think he had much of a plan after that. Besides watching the world burn."

Savas hammered the accelerator, Coney Island and the New York Aquarium flying past them. The engine howled.

"He'll come."

56

POWERGRID

The electrical substation was located on the outskirts of Elizabeth, New Jersey. Houston had raced across Staten Island through a surreal apocalyptic landscape. Fires were raging around the ports, and Lopez thought he had seen Blackhawk helicopters launching missiles at boats and opening fire at the docks. Military vehicles from the National Guard were positioned at gateways—toll booths, tunnel and bridge entrances, certain exit ramps—but eerily, all were abandoned. News on their radio confirmed that rioting had spread through the tri-state area as essential functions continued to break down in the public and private sector. Law enforcement was completely overwhelmed.

They had crossed two bridges without incident and were now speeding past Elizabeth and into a decayed urban wasteland of rusted warehouses and closed factories. The power lines around them were beginning to converge. The substation was near.

Lightfoote's voice came over the speaker. Houston had wedged her phone inside a cup holder, the conical shape funneling the sound upwards and acting as a small megaphone.

"Power's still up, so they haven't hit it yet. Latest military data indicates a contingent of Guardsman are assigned there, maybe ten. The site was on a list to lock down in a national emergency. I don't know if they made it or are still there, but if so, you have to warn them, prepare them."

"And how do we do that without getting arrested?" asked Lopez.

"They won't let us get near, and if anyone tries to get our story verified, too many questions will be raised. We'll be in a cell before nightfall."

"I don't know how!" cried Angel, "But we need all the help we can get. We don't know how large Fawkes' strike team is."

"Mother of God," whispered Lopez. "How many enemies do we have to fight?"

"Look, we'll improvise," Houston said. "Meanwhile, you were saying they would hit the transformers?"

"I've given myself a crash course in this the last few hours," said Lightfoote. "Power from several coal and gas plants, and the nuke plant south of you, are funneled through the substation. To handle it, they have these enormous transformers that link up the lines coming into the lines going out. Match up the power on them. For the size of the loads they're dealing with here, these are giant things. We're talking hundreds of tons, tens of thousands of gallons of fuel. This is one of the biggest in the country."

"Fuel?" asked Lopez. "Why does it need fuel?"

"To run all the coolant systems," said Lightfoote. "Ever had your outlet or computer heat up?"

"I think this phone is about to explode," said Houston.

"Well, just imagine this transformer that's bigger than a house and all the current running through it. Fawkes could take it out just by blowing the cooling units and waiting for the thing to burst into flames."

"Jesus," said Houston. "So, big as a house. Lots of big wires going in. We can't miss it."

"No, it will be obvious. And, from what I could find out, relatively unsecured. A chain link fence and some concrete barriers to stop suicide trucks."

"Wait," said Lopez, shaking his head. "Our electrical grid is dependent on a few of these behemoths and all we've done to keep modern civilization running is slap some cheap wire around it?"

"Pretty much, Holy Man," said Lightfoote. "Lots of congressional hearings after 9/11. Not much done. It's a sitting duck. If we lose it, it could be the entire Northeast and parts of Canada."

"That's unbelievable," Lopez said.

"They *did* fortify the transformer in 2015. Says here it's bullet resistant."

"Bullet *resistant*? What, to protect from transformer snipers?"

"In part," Angel continued. "There have been several incidents of lone wackos shooting at them. One guy caused an explosion that blacked out part of Texas for hours. Anyway, this one has reinforced concrete around it."

Lopez pointed ahead of the car. "That's it, Sara. Take that road."

The substation opened up in front of them. Several football fields in surface area, it looked like something from a dystopian film. Wires sprouted from it like tentacles, only to be contrasted by the harsh steel and Frankenstein-esque electrical devices that neither of them had names for.

The transformer was obvious. Enormous. It dominated the other structures within the compound. Thick, metallic arms erupted above a sloppy concrete girdle around the thing, giving the object the appearance of a colossal robot design project gone terribly wrong. Thick wires connected to the transformer through the ends of the arms to the chaos of wiring overhead that linked the substation to the rest of the grid.

"You found it?" called out Lightfoote.

"Yes," said Houston flatly.

"And the transformer? You see it?"

"Oh yes," she said.

"Great!" Lightfoote's relief was palpable.

"Not so great," said Lopez as Houston slowed the car in front of the twisted and mangled remains of a chain length fence.

"Why? What's wrong?"

Two National Guardsman lay by the wrecked gate, their bodies riddle with bullets. The gatehouse windows were shattered and the wood pocked with holes.

Lopez spoke in a rough baritone. "It's on fire."

Black smoke poured into the air in front them.

57

TARGET PRACTICE

"The transformer's burning?"

Lightfoote's voice rang out desperately over the phone. Lopez exited the car and stared forward, shielding his eyes from low-lying morning sun. Houston shut off the engine, grabbed the phone, and followed.

"I'm not sure," said Houston. "Lots of fires and smoke. Some around the transformer. But, no, it doesn't seem hit."

"Then there's still time!" cried Lightfoote. "We still have power. You still have a transformer. I need power to get the last code out! Hang up, get in there, and stop them!"

"Yes, ma'am." Houston closed the phone. "She's right. There's still a chance. They haven't managed to bring it down yet."

"Could happen any moment," said Lopez. "We don't know their numbers or how they're armed."

Houston removed her Browning and pulled the mask over her smile. "I'm a lady who loves surprises." She jogged down the small road from the gate, toward the flames.

Lopez reached inside his vestments and grabbed the submachine gun. His left shoulder was screaming, useless to help him aim his pistol. The submachine gun would blanket his targets and help compensate. He ran forward, chasing Houston.

They passed grassy lawns on both sides of the road. Ahead, rows of wired equipment intersected above them. In the middle of it all lay the concrete slab with the transformer inside. Keeping alongside a row of utility sheds, they remained concealed from anyone around the object. Apparently, the idea had occurred to others. The bodies of three men—not Guardsman—were strewn along the path of the sheds, gunned down while moving toward the transformer. The bodies of several soldiers were across from them, near the far corner of the sheds.

"They must have used the shelter of the sheds for a last stand."

Houston pressed her back against the cold metal, stepping over the body of one, and peered cautiously around the corner.

Her head snapped back and her eyes locked with Lopez. "More dead guards. Looks like grenades."

"The strike team?"

"They're there. Alive. Right next to the concrete around the transformer. One had his hands on the wall, fiddling with something. The other seemed to be yelling at him. That's all I got."

"Bomb," Lopez said.

"Likely they're wiring it up now. From the argument, we can only hope some of the dead bodies were their demolitions experts."

"Assuming those two are the last."

She nodded and spun around again, keeping her sights forward for several seconds before whipping back around.

"You think you can get me on top of that shed?"

Lopez frowned. "It's over fifty yards, Sara. That's a good shot, even for you."

"You have better ideas? It's all open field from here to the transformer. No way to sneak up on them. We could go in blazing and hope for the best, but odds are not good for a clean win. I'll stabilize on the roof edge. Three shots or less and you owe me a drink."

Lopez frowned and got on one knee. "Just don't step on the left shoulder, or you forfeit any winnings. I'll be ready for a sprint."

She holstered the weapon and he hoisted her toward the roof. She grabbed the edge, swinging herself over. Lopez couldn't follow with his bad arm, so he returned to the corner and crouched, weapon readied.

Houston kept low and crawled to the end of the shed overlooking the transformer. She could see the two men facing the concrete wall, oblivious to her actions as they worked on the explosives. She removed her Browning. The edge of the roof rose several inches from the base and she used it to steady her weapon. She sighted the two dark shapes, focusing on the one who seemed to be taking the lead. She calmed, steadied her breathing. His torso fused into an extension of the barrel. She felt the metal tube reach outward towards him, connecting, closing the space between them. She stopped breathing and pulled the trigger.

There was an explosion. The figure before them shuddered, hands jerking outward and away from the bomb. He fell to his knees, then onto his side. She repositioned the gun.

The man next to him froze for an instant and then wheeled in their direction, weapon raised. He scanned a small arc across the sheds, then centered on the roof, and Houston. He dropped to one knee and aimed his gun in her direction.

Two more shots burst in the compound, the sounds reverberating off the concrete and metal, echoing and blending in a dispersing chaos of noise. The man in front of them buckled but did not fall. He began to turn toward the wall slowly, gait lumbering, face toward the device fixed to the transformer.

A fourth shot rang, a third bullet embedding itself in his torso. This time he fell, his weapon dropped. His legs jerked as he tried vainly to rise. Houston saw the broad form of Lopez race toward the shape.

"Four," she said, sitting up and scanning around them for hostiles. The place was empty but for the dead and Lopez, who now stood beside the explosive device, waving her over. "Perfectly good glass of whiskey shot to hell."

58

HAVE BOMB, WILL TRAVEL

Houston sprinted across the lot toward the concrete security barrier. Two bodies lay beside the house-sized transformer, unmoving. Lopez had laid out several of their items: firearms, cell phones, and, most crucially, detonators and radio-controllers. He was studying an array of what looked like beige clay blocks taped across the concrete. Detonators and wires ran down from the blocks to a metal box.

"C-4?" Houston said, catching her breath.

"That, or something similar. Twelve blocks."

She examined them closely. "I'm guessing M112—military issue. Uncle Sam needs to keep his shit off the arms markets."

She crouched and examined the wiring. Above her, the huge expanse of two transformer arms cast a long shadow in the early light. The hum of the electricity flowing through the area was almost nauseating. Thick wires like oak limbs sprouted from the arms many tens of feet away.

"Look at this shape," she said, turning back to the molded plastique. "It's going to funnel the blast inward and up. Twelve blocks? Shit, this concrete wall will be turned into a weapon. Those humming arms are coming down, probably the whole thing will take major damage. No way this thing survives. Game over. Power gone."

"No timer, so we don't have to deal with that," said Lopez, eyeing the metallic box.

"Is it trapped?"

He shook his head. "Doesn't seem so. They didn't have time and weren't planning to leave it here long. Set it up, reach safe distance, maybe behind those sheds, radio the signal into this control box. Boom."

"Should be easy to disarm then." Houston frowned. "Why does that make me nervous?"

"Because nothing is ever for free."

Houston centered on the far-left block and placed her hand around the blasting cap wires. "Let's make sure and remove the detonators from each."

Lopez mirrored her actions. "Here goes."

They pulled on the wires. Thin metal tubes resembling smoothed hinge bolts came out of the soft material. As the end of the tube was cleared from the explosive, they paused and locked eyes.

“No boom,” she said.

They repeated the process until all the detonators were removed, and tossed the blasting caps onto the ground beside the dead men. Lopez removed a large knife and cut through the thick tape sticking the blocks to the barrier. Soon there was a stack of clay blocks on the ground as well.

“All right,” he said, wiping sweat from his face. “Always exciting. Let's call this in to Angel. We did our bit to preserve the lights.”

Houston punched her contact number for Lightfoote's burner cell. She frowned and looked at the phone.

“Zero bars. No signal.”

Lopez looked around. “This place should be blanketed. We had signal when we arrived.”

“Check yours. Maybe this cheap thing's failing.”

He removed his phone. “Nothing. No signal.”

“Shit.” Houston folded her arms over her chest. “No coincidences. The towers are down. Probably the worm.”

“Or more of these guys,” he said, nodding toward the bodies.

“I doubt it. No way he has an army. This was a strategic target. Too many towers for physical strikes on the cellular system. That's got to be the worm.”

Lopez nodded. “Maybe it's just some of the carriers.” He reached down beside the corpses and grabbed two phones.

“Everything's down. AT&T. Verizon. This guy had T-Mobile.”

Houston scanned the horizon back toward New York City. “Everyone's cut off now. No voice, no data. I think this will trigger a real panic. After a few hours, it's going to be mayhem.”

"There's more here," said Lopez working on one of the phones. "Messages. All about this raid. Has to be from Fawkes."

Houston stepped beside him and looked at the screen. "With those kind of details? Fawkes for sure. They were getting sloppy." She took the other man's phone and examined it as well.

"Well, tomorrow's the fifth, right?" said Lopez. "The end of the world as we know it. Security is so pre-apocalypse."

Houston continued scrolling intensely through the phone's messages. "Or maybe not. *Fuck*. Francisco, tell me you don't recognize this address."

The former priest stared at the small screen, brow furrowing. "That's the warehouse in Brooklyn. Where they're taking Poison. How—"

His eyes widened.

"They know, dammit!" said Houston. "Look at this message. 'Heading to the site. When finished double back there for backup.' They've known for a while!"

Lopez glanced up toward the car. A line of dark clouds was moving in from the south, promising to bring showers and possibly thunderstorms.

"Savas isn't setting the trap. Fawkes is."

"Jesus! No cell phones. We can't reach them. We have to get over to that warehouse!"

"We took out their strike team. That helps."

"Judging from the message, he wasn't counting on them. They're backup. He's got others."

"But what do we do with this mess? Dead men? Bombs?"

Houston stared down at the bodies with disgust. "Leave these assholes to rot." She began stuffing the plastique inside a bag lying on the ground beside them. "But we take the bomb. Could prove useful."

59

MUTAGENESIS

Lightfoote stared at hundreds of lines of code on her screen. She spoke in a distracted monotone. "All the carriers are down?"

Rideout nodded, tossing his phone on the table next to five others. "I checked them all. He's nuked the cellular system."

"Damn," she said. "Cut off from everyone. Power's still up so our Dynamic Duo hasn't let us down. But we need the coast power up or we'll never get this new worm out there with enough time to spread."

He grabbed two of the phones and held them up. "You guys want your phones back?"

Across the room three men were arguing animatedly over the scrolling text of a computer screen. They waved him away to continue their heated debate.

Rideout leaned over the computer desk and whispered into Lightfoote's ear. "I don't trust those yahoos."

She smiled, never removing her gaze from the screen. "John does. The older one, anyway. *Simon.* They have some kind of history. And to be honest, the coders from the NSA are really good. I'd never have gotten this finished in time without them."

"Thanks for the vote of confidence," said Rideout. "And *are* you finished, anyway?"

Her face clouded. "Getting there." She returned her gaze to the screen and typed furiously.

A stout man, near sixty, ambled over toward them and dropped heavily into a wheeled chair. He looked at Rideout.

"Ah, John-David?"

"Jean-Paul. Just call me JP. And you're who again?"

"Fred will do," said Simon, rubbing his eyes. "*Angel* I do remember. I'm getting too old for this shit." Lightfoote ignored both of them as Simon continued. "Look, Dietrich at NSA lent us these two programmers. Technically, they're not under our authority. I'm CIA. You're FBI. But with our connections, and dangling your project in front of them, they ate it up. But they're stuck on something now."

"Can't keep up?" asked Rideout.

"It's not a pissing contest, son. It's the new bit, the code randomizing thing."

"The mutagenesis," cut in Angel absentmindedly.

"Whatever you call it."

She turned to him. "It's important! It's key. I call it mutagenesis because the whole thing is based on mimicking biology."

"Is this going to be a graduate school lecture?" asked Simon, his face weary.

Lightfoote continued. "Look, we have code that hunts and recognizes Fawkes' worm like a white blood cell. In the body, one thing those cells do is *mutate* the parts of them that recognize the foreign invader. For some mutants it screws them up. They don't work anymore. But for a few, the mutations make them better or create variant cells that recognize mutant pathogens. And when you combine that with recognition-based replication, you quickly select for optimized cells and make lots of them. It's evolution!"

"I think I'm gonna fail this test, professor," said Simon.

The two NSA men stood behind him. One interjected. "Yeah, but you know what happens when you get a lot of mutants in a population? You get cancer. Or autoimmunity. *Bad* changes with the good. Things go south, you know?"

"Sometimes," admitted Lightfoote.

"And so what are we doing?" continued the man. "Unleashing rogue code, independent of any controls, that's designed to replicate and mutate? We could lose control over it."

The other coder chimed in. "We probably *will* lose control over it."

Rideout waved his arms animatedly. "Does what is happening now look like an abundance of *control*? Sounds like you're scared this thing might actually work, take down the worm. How about we put that fire out first, before it burns everything to the ground? We can worry about Angel's mutants afterward."

Simon nodded. "That's about how I see it. We either fire the new weapon and hope the collateral damage is low, or we watch as that thing out there tears our world apart." He stared at the two men. "But we need you two on this. Angel's nearly done, but she needs those modules from you. You in?"

They looked at each other. One sighed. "Yeah, I guess so. We have to do something."

The other nodded. "Okay. But we are literally letting a genie out of the bottle here. Remember that a year from now."

Lightfoote nodded. "If there still is a digital world left over for this code to haunt, we'll work on it."

"How close are you two?" asked Simon.

The men were back at their terminals. One called over. "We're done. That's the fight. We built a bomb, we're just pissing our pants about arming it."

Simon turned to Lightfoote. "Angel?"

"I'm debugging the mutation code. I don't have the time to fine-tune it, and that worries me. Too much and it will fuck itself to oblivion. Too little and it won't adapt fast enough to identify all Fawkes' worms. But I'm almost there! Then I just need to assemble the modules and fire it out."

An explosion rocked the building and the lights flickered.

"What the hell?" cried Rideout.

Dust filtered down from the ceiling and the lights completely cut out. Emergency lighting clicked on while the computers continued to hum. Shouts from floors above erupted, followed by gunfire.

"Fawkes," said Lightfoote, her face grim. "He's going to shut us down the old fashioned way."

"Jesus," mumbled Simon, rising stiffly to his feet.

Rideout unholstered his pistol and checked the magazine. "Thank God you put the servers on generator power. That explosion blew the main lines."

"But not the hard lines. They're buried too deep. We still have time!"

More gunfire. More screams above.

"Not much!" cried Rideout. "You two, you're done, right? So get your asses over here! Move those cabinets to the door—quickly!"

The NSA programmers shoved the two waist-high cabinets, computer paraphernalia spilling out of the poorly closed doors, to block the entry. Rideout overturned a long table, spilling workstations and monitors to the floor.

Lightfoote tossed him a holstered firearm. "Mine. Give it to them." She returned to the code.

"Spread this out!" said Rideout, waving his arms across the room. He frowned. "Either of you ever fired a weapon?"

Both shook their heads.

"Either of you ever *want* to fire a weapon?"

One put out his hand. Rideout gave him the black pistol.

"Safety's in the trigger, so don't point unless you mean to kill. Got it? Pull the trigger with follow-through, you'll feel the safety release and then the shot. Slow, steady, pull. No panic. Aim and pull slowly, even if Godzilla comes through." The NSA coder nodded frantically. "You," he yelled at the unarmed coder, "grab that large wrench over there. Hide behind the server wall. If the guns fail, beat the shit out of the first person who comes in range."

Simon braced himself on the wall beside the door, gun pointed at the entrance. "I'll have the first. They won't know what hit them."

Rideout crouched behind the overturned table and motioned the NSA man with the gun over. "They'll have to get past us to get to Angel, then get around the server farm between the door and her desk. We need to buy her all the time we can. Even if that means our lives, you understand? Her code has to get out!"

The programmer simply stared at him.

"What about the servers?" asked Simon.

Lightfoote called back. "I just need this computer, this one connection to send it out through the NSA backdoors. It's the end game now."

The door shuddered from a heavy blow. Rideout and the NSA man concealed themselves behind the table, positioning their weapons forward. Heavy objects slammed repeatedly into the door, rattling the metal cabinets. The drumming was offset by the maniacal clacking of Lightfoote's keys, the two percussions accompanied by the ever present hum of the server farm between them.

The thudding stopped. Dust continued to drift down from the ceiling. The sounds of muted shouts outside could be heard, along with muffled shuffling and scrapes. Several seconds of silence followed. Rideout and Simon aimed their weapons.

Then the door exploded.

60

WAREHOUSE

The pouring rain clattered angrily on the metal roof, the storm winds shaking the thin walls of the warehouse. Daylight faded, dimmed further by the clouds, still just managing to illuminate the interior through the high windows. The air tasted of mildew and rot, chased by a metallic tang. A low rumble shook the long structure, momentarily interrupting conversation within. Two figures stood perched atop a large, moveable platform.

"I can't reach anyone," Cohen said, flipping her phone closed with a snap. "Looks like we've lost all cellular. We're blind here."

Savas nodded, examining the readout on a small control unit. "Not completely blind," he muttered. "As long as the power holds."

Cohen limped over to Savas and wrapped an arm over his shoulders. "Frank got the motion sensors up?"

"Yeah," Savas said, turning toward her. There was another roll of thunder. "We'll at least get some advance notice."

"Crunch time, Johnny-boy." She ran her fingers through his hair. "I'm starting to get a little tired of the world ending around us."

He kissed her, cupping his hand behind her head. Her breath was warm in the frigid air of the unheated warehouse. A cloud escaped his mouth as he pulled away. "Don't ever say I didn't show you an exciting time, girl."

"Just don't make me climb any more ladders until this damned leg is healed."

A shout from across the expanse of the building brought them back to their surroundings. Their eyes caught sight of a figure slamming shut the main door, water dripping from his muscular form. Miller jogged back toward their position, an automatic rifle in one arm.

"Motion detectors mounted and signaling," he called.

The space within was long abandoned. Decaying, discarded crates the size of trucks littered the floor. The ex-marine dodged back and forth, zig-zagging as he approached. The detritus provided the perfect cover for their needs. Fawkes and his mercenaries would need to expose themselves several times in order to get near.

Savas and Cohen looked down from a raised, metallic platform. Once used by a supervisor directing the traffic in the warehouse during better years, it now served an unintended strategic purpose. They had positioned several crates facing the entrance. Together with the advantage of height, the cover would ensure that only an elite commando force of some number would make it through. Whatever they would face, they were sure to do it much hurt.

Miller finished scaling the ladder and dropped heavily onto the platform, water scattering and dripping through the metallic mesh of the platform floor. He scanned the interior of the building and grunted.

"Of course, they could try blasting or cutting their way through any number of weak points in this flimsy structure. But I think that's giving them too much credit and time to plan. And only if they had the numbers." He pointed to the main entrance. "My money is on the front door. John and I can take positions on opposite sides of this platform—there and there. Rebecca, we could use your gun, but we can't trust that hacker. Keep it trained on her the entire time. We're vulnerable from behind."

Cohen smiled. "Good plan. I refuse to move this leg again." She turned behind them, looking down on the bound form of Poison. The hacker glared back. "Sorry about the cuffs."

"Fuck you Feds. Maybe I should help him kill you."

Savas crouched down beside her. "We don't know that you won't, Poison. Try to see it from our angle. There isn't much trust going around when it comes to Fawkes and Anonymous."

"He's not Anonymous. Not anymore."

"Who's to say? He claims he is. He's sprung several traps on us, tried to kill us. We can't assume you're on our side."

"Why would I be here?"

"Maybe the bait is to hook *us*."

She scowled at him but remained silent. At that moment, the monitor on the floor of the platform began to beep. Miller scooped it into his hands, glaring downward.

"They're here. Barely time to prepare. Ten yards in front of the door. We've got seconds."

Cohen leaned into one of the crutches, holding her firearm pointed at the platform near Poison's feet. She stared intensely at the other woman. Miller and Savas shook the platform as they rushed to the opposite corners, crouching behind wooden crates and aiming their weapons toward the door.

Miller called to Savas. "If they throw frags, look away until the blast. Then back and focus."

His anticipation proved correct. The door to the warehouse was slung open, the rusted metal screaming like something dying. Several black shapes outside hurled objects into the warehouse. Savas and Miller turned their heads as the grenades exploded, the sound rivaling the thunder outside. They recovered quickly and reoriented, training their guns on the men rushing inside. And opened fire.

61

MASK BEHIND THE MASK

The incoming soldiers were dropped quickly, their position impossible to defend. They barely had time to size up their enemy and the layout before rounds from one or both of the FBI men cut them down. Their lack of strategy made it clear they hadn't expected this sort of resistance.

Four bodies lay within a twenty-foot radius of the main door. There was no further motion from outside. The smoke of spent ammunition rose as a fog around the top of the platform. Savas started to rise, but Miller held up his hand.

"Not yet!"

"You think there are more?"

"Maybe this was a feint. Stay low."

"But Fawkes isn't there!" hissed Savas.

"We don't know that. Can't see their faces."

"He's not there," said Poison, looking down on the corpses. "He's no Johnny Rambo."

"Don't shoot!"

A cry rang across the warehouse.

"*That's* Fawkes," said Poison.

Miller peered over the crate in the failing light. He strapped on a set of night vision goggles and adjusted them.

"I don't see anything, John. He's still outside."

"Fawkes!" cried Savas. "If that's you, come in with both hands high in the air!"

There was a pause. "No way! You'll shoot me!"

"Paranoid to the end," whispered Poison.

"That's not our plan!" yelled Savas again. "You're useless dead. We need you to fix this shit!"

Another pause. "Is she there? Poison?"

Savas made to speak again but was cut off by the girl.

"Fuck yeah, you piece of shit! All this is because of you! And you *bugged* me, you fucktard? Seriously?"

A dark form ambled into the warehouse from the door, his head covered by a hood. His hands raised above him.

"Turn around," called Savas. Fawkes obeyed. "Now close the door. All the way."

Fawkes grasped the handle of the sliding door and yanked. At first it didn't move and he lost his balance. After several hard pulls and better planting his feet, he managed to scrape it across the floor to the staccato bursts of metal on cement. A fifth jerk slammed it shut.

"Now back around with your hands high." Fawkes complied and Savas stood slowly and turned to Miller. "I'm going to bring him up. He tries anything, end him."

Cohen turned to Poison as Savas descended. "Will he try something?"

The hacker shook her head. "Are you kidding? He wasn't even good at first person shooters. Your man's safe."

Miller watched tensely as Savas reached the hacker. Fawkes offered no resistance, walking slowly in front of the FBI man. Savas pushed him forward with his gun, and the pair navigated the obstacle course toward the platform. Finally, the Fawkes scaled the ladder as Miller trained his weapon downward. The pair reached the platform without incident.

Poison laughed. "You still have the fucking mask. *Seriously*."

Fawkes stood shivering in a wet trench coat, water beading and running along its contours. Contrasting the black of the fabric was a white mask—the goateed, smirking visage that had come to haunt too many of their nightmares.

"Fawkes," Savas said, stepping forward. "Miller, the extra set of cuffs?"

Miller handed Savas the restraints and he bound Fawkes' hands behind him.

Fawkes looked to Poison. His voice was heavily muffled. "Looks like they're still treating you well."

"So that's it? That's all you had left to come rescue me?" The masked man said nothing. "What a sad way to go out, Fawkes."

"It doesn't matter anymore. They can't stop things now."

Cohen kept her weapon at the ready, her eyes on Poison as she spoke. "I wouldn't count on that, Fawkes. We have a plan to stop you."

"You mean the little bald girl in the cellar?" The mask laughed. "I have a larger team taking care of her now. That's over."

"You son of a bitch," Miller said, advancing on the man.

Savas held him back with his arm. "It will be hard on you if something happens to them."

"Gonna be hard on all of us soon, Special Agent. But really it was the only way."

"Only way to what, you sick bastard!" hissed Miller, a fire in his eyes.

"Can't tell you or you'd just laugh. But really, it's for the best. The things you don't know and can't believe—well, it's like a mountain. The lies you live, the truths you hold that really hold you mockingly. Your ideals and systems. *All lies.* You are slaves to masters that count on your good intentions and low intelligence. There is a world order you don't understand and can't perceive."

Savas looked at Poison. "Is this the genius you mentioned? This nutcase?"

"Low intelligence?" Poison scoffed. "You know, they played you from the start, you dumb ass. And you bought it! You took it all in your little shark mouth and they reeled you in! All those torture videos? Interrogation scripts? They were faked!"

"I know."

"What do you mean, you know?"

"Players play the players because the play demands it."

"John—" began Cohen.

"Okay, enough of this crap," said Savas. "Let's see what you really look like."

Cohen furrowed her brows. "John, wait a minute. Something's not right."

He ignored her and grasped the bottom of the mask. Looking through the eye-slits, he stared inside. "Anonymous no more, Fawkes."

He pulled. The mask didn't move.

"What the hell?"

Reaching around, he yanked the hood back, revealing a head covered in black leather straps. The Guy Fawkes mask was fixed tightly to it, concealing a bulk beneath it.

"Gas mask!" cried Miller.

But it was too late. Fawkes squeezed his shoulder blades together and there was a click, followed by the sound of two metal canisters crashing and ringing on the platform surface.

They exploded.

62

INJECTION

Fred Simon was blown backward and slammed into a wall, dropping to the ground unconscious. Debris flew across the room, smashing into the racks of computers, pocketing the overturned table, and coating everything with a thick layer of dust. Within seconds, several armed men stormed through the hole breached in the doorway, crawling over the pile of rubble from the collapsed wall, trying to get their bearings in an enclosed space choked with smoke.

Gunshots blasted from behind the table and one of the men staggered, grabbing his chest. He fell to the ground. The second began a spray of automatic fire aimed wildly in the direction of the table, but a series of shots by two weapons behind it struck him four, five, and six times. He lurched forward, falling to his knees with a scream, and rolled over on his side moaning.

As two more men burst through the opening a chaos of weapons' discharge erupted. The NSA man beside Rideout screamed and clutched his face, blood squirting from between his fingers. He rolled on the ground, howling. Rideout slumped behind the table, blood flowing from the right side of his chest, eyes swimming. His gun dropped to the ground with a clank.

Another mercenary had fallen, but two more stepped in to take his place. The invaders advanced slowly, unimpeded. The NSA man with the wrench shook behind the server racks, his pants moist around the crotch.

Several feet from him Lightfoote worked like a woman possessed, ignoring the chaos.

The three soldiers stepped forward cautiously, converging on the table and the forms of the bodies behind it. Rideout glanced upward but didn't move his head, energy evanescing from his body. They looked down on him and the flailing NSA man. Two returned their attention to the rest of the room, hunting for targets. The other fired several shots into the screaming figure. The cries ceased. He turned toward Rideout and aimed.

A series of shots roared from behind them, bullets bursting through the man's mouth and throat. As Rideout watched him fall, the two beside him spun around, firing at the bloodied shape of Simon. The old CIA man managed to empty his weapon, wounding one in the stomach, even as the assailants killed him. Simon fell against the wall, bullet holes and blood decorating the surface behind him. He slid slowly to the ground, his chest a mass of wounds, his eyes blank. He lay still.

The other NSA man dropped the wrench and walked out, falling to his knees.

"Don't shoot! I surrender! I'm not part of this group! I'm from the NSA! Please, don't kill me!" Tears stained his face as he trembled before the soldiers.

"Where's the girl?" rasped one.

"She's here. Right behind me! At the terminal!"

The soldier fired into his head, and the programmer fell. The mercenary raced forward, his companion stumbling behind, bent nearly double with his wound soaking his clothes.

The first soldier leapt around the stacks of computers and opened fire at the terminal against the wall. The chassis exploded into fragments, the continued discharge blowing it and the monitor to pieces. He ejected the magazine and reached for another.

A pair of feet swung down from the piping above, catching him square in the face. The impact snapped his head back sharply, and his arms and legs went slack before he dropped to the ground.

Lightfoote landed like a cougar, crouched low to absorb the momentum, her arm splayed to the side along the floor. The remaining soldier staggered toward her, movements sluggish and jerky, gunshots blasting wildly from the barrel of his weapon to pock the walls harmlessly.

Bright silver flashed through the air and the soldier's head snapped to the side as the wrench slammed into his jaw with a heavy crunch of bone.

His body continued to the side and toppled over. Both soldiers now unconscious.

Lightfoote leaped beside them and bludgeoned each in the head. Satisfied, she raced beside Rideout, her gaze lingering a moment on the body of Simon across the room. "JP! You there?" She slapped his face.

His eyes struggled to open, a gasp escaping his mouth. "Oh, God, Angel. Shit, this hurts!"

Lightfoote pulled off her shirt, revealing a tight sports bra. She pressed the shirt against the wound, eliciting a scream from Rideout.

She shouted over him. "JP! Listen. Here, this arm works." She pulled one of his hands to the shirt. "Stay with me! Keep some pressure there. I'm running up to get a medkit. Slow the bleeding!"

He nodded and his arm tensed against his chest. He inhaled sharply. "Angel, wait," he gasped as she turned to leave.

"What?"

Rideout stared at the blasted computers. Every terminal was destroyed. "The worm?" he managed.

She crouched beside him and kissed him on the cheek. Sweat dripped from her shoulders and arms. His blood glimmered in streaks across her scalp.

"Launched. Gone!" She smiled. "You did good. Now shut up and don't die on me."

63

ACES IN THE HOLE

The white vapor had nearly dissipated. The faint aroma of gunpowder and ash mixed with a sickly sweetness still lingering in the air. Hulking shapes breathed resonantly from within gas masks on the platform.

The FBI team was concentrated at one end of the structure, all of them handcuffed, soldiers in masks pointing guns in their direction. The captives were still coughing badly, tears and mucus running from their eyes and noses. Their weapons were in a pile at the feet of their captors.

The mask spoke. "So easy. Don't you guys ever play chess?"

Poison stood beside Fawkes, a gas mask around her head. She looked down at the FBI team. "What are you going to do with them?"

Fawkes cocked the smirking visage to one side. "Kill them, of course."

"Please, don't," said Poison, eyes large.

"Be grateful you aren't there with them. I should kill you as well for betraying me. But I don't have the emotional fortitude. You get to live because of my weakness. But not them. Not after what they've done."

"I told you!" she cried. "It was all fake! They didn't torture me!"

"Perhaps," said Fawkes, "or perhaps this is some demented state of Stockholm Syndrome. Did they promise you amnesty? Immunity? Do you think any of that matters now?" The mask studied her coldly.

"No!"

He turned to the FBI team. "Even if it was all a ruse, it was a very painful ruse for me. Until I figured it out, before I realized that it was all *too* easy, perfectly engineered to elicit an emotional response, get me to put myself in terrible danger—before all that came into focus I really went through the agony of watching her suffer." He extended his hand and received a gun from one of the soldiers. "And that will not be forgiven."

"Stop, Fawkes!" cried Poison, moving toward him. A towering soldier grabbed her from behind and lifted her off the ground as she flailed.

Fawkes motioned to the warehouse floor. "Get her out of here. She doesn't need to see this."

Screaming, Poison was taken by two guards awkwardly down the ladder. Fawkes and the remaining guard stepped in front of the FBI team. The mask turned to Savas.

"It has been an interesting game, one still with several pieces in play. But here I have the King, and, I suppose, his Queen, even if by abilities I think the real Queen is lying in a pool of blood in a basement in New York City."

"Just a video game to you, Fawkes?" spat Savas. "Our lives. The nation. The world. Millions, billions of people who will wake up tomorrow back in the Dark Ages. Most of them to die."

There was a flash of lightning and a loud explosion. A deep rumble followed, shaking their bones.

"Fittingly dramatic. A sign from God do you think?" The masked man laughed. "*Live free or die.* I think New Hampshire's motto? One of those tiny states. But a slogan that is central to the value of our short existence."

He turned the weapon in his hands, removing the magazine, checking the chamber, and reinserting the box.

"Imagine a prison so intricately constructed that the inmates believe themselves free. The slaves cannot see their chains. When you're one of the few to see through the deceptions to the heart of this darkness, most of the time you go mad, or cynical, or do something stupid and get the forces in control to erase you. That was nearly my fate."

Cohen leaned against Savas and rested her head on his shoulder. Miller squirmed vainly in his restraints.

"But knowing what I know, it's clear that the infection *must* be sterilized. Like cancer, the treatment will be horrific. It may kill the patient. Indeed, humanity may never rise again. And that might just be for the better, you know? Anyway, it won't be for any of us to see, but for those a thousand years down the road. If any civilization rises from these ashes."

Fawkes motioned to the guard beside him, who stepped forward and raised his weapon. "Sorry for the pain, but it will all be over quickly."

He raised his weapon and aimed at Savas. "Goodbye."

There was another bright flash and deafening sound. But this wasn't the storm.

The platform swayed from the force of a blast, the entire warehouse shuddering violently. Unlike thunder the rumbling was short lived, and debris rained across the interior, pieces of wood and metal thrown as far as the platform surface. The front of the warehouse had been torn apart, crates and other discarded elements shattered and burning. Black smoke filled the room, its turbulent structure illuminated by the raging flames.

Fawkes and the soldier were hurled to the floor of the platform. The soldier's weapon discharged wildly as he fell, but his impact momentarily stunned him and he lost his grip. The gun skipped toward Miller and the back edge of the platform, plunging into darkness below.

Miller used the chaos and struck outward with a blinding kick, catching the man's face full on. There was a cracking sound and the man screamed, rolling to his side as blood streamed into his hands.

Fawkes had stumbled forward and smashed into the railing beside Cohen, his mask shattered, jagged white pieces hanging loosely from the gas mask. Cohen smashed her shoulder into his gun hand, the impact dislodging the weapon and sending it plummeting out of sight.

Fawkes leapt backward, dodging wild kicks from Savas, stumbling into the railing on the other side of the platform. The soldier beside him pulled out a handgun and wiped blood from his broken nose.

"Kill them!" Fawkes cried.

But the soldier didn't even raise his weapon. Two shots exploded from behind them, and the man's head erupted in a soup of blood and flesh. His limp body dropped like a stone, shaking the platform.

A woman's voice called from below. "Don't twitch, masked-boy, or we'll liquefy your big brain, too!"

"Houston!" Cohen cried.

Savas closed his eyes in relief.

There was a clattering from the ladder. A soot-covered woman sprang upward, a pistol in one hand trained on Fawkes' slumped form.

"Got you covered from two angles, asshole, so think before you act." Her eyes darted from the shattered mask in front of her. "You three okay?"

"Yes!" Savas said angrily. "What about the other guards?"

"Killed in the explosion."

The jigsaw face spun toward her. "And Poison?"

"She's gone," said Houston.

Fawkes screamed and lunged at her wildly, his hands a pair of claws aiming for her face. With a pivot, she sidestepped his motion and used her gun arm to bring the butt of the weapon viciously down on the back of his head. He collapsed and didn't move.

Heavy steps sounded as Lopez awkwardly climbed the ladder with his one good arm. He landed roughly and glanced down at the two bodies. He exhaled slowly and smiled at the FBI team. "Better late than never, right?"

NOVEMBER 5

64

ROME BURNS

Armed men ushered President York down a dimly lit flight of stairs. On each side, soldiers took positions with weapons aimed upward, speaking quietly into headsets. Beside her was a lanky, gray-haired man, his face flushed, a sling around his arm. The group reached the bottom, the claustrophobic stairwell opening on a dank tunnel receding into darkness. Its opening was broad, wide enough for a vehicle to pass through. Water leaked out from it to pool at their feet.

"Madam President," said one of the soldiers, "this shaft will take you to the helicopter. Sergeants Holmes and Nesic will accompany you." Two uniformed men stepped beside the president. "We're going to stay here and blow the tunnel if we have to."

"And then what?" asked York.

"We'll hide out. No one knows these emergency tunnels like we do. Everyone made fun of the upkeep. Well, who's laughing now?"

"Be safe, Captain. And thank you. It's good to know I have supporters even in the military."

She grabbed her companion by his good arm and turned to the tunnel. The two other soldiers flanked the civilians and they moved forward, the neon green of glow sticks lighting their way.

"Elaine, how far do you think this is going to go?" asked Tooze.

"The coup?" she asked, pulling out a small handgun. "General Hastings isn't a halfway kinda guy, George. Unless someone puts a stop to him—and I'm not going to dress up what that means—unless someone either arrests or kills the man, we're heading for a full-blown military takeover."

"What will that mean?"

"God only knows," said York, shaking her head. "Kind of in unknown territory there. A centralized command for sure. Suspension of the Constitution and a streamlined civilian authority headed by military personnel. Either they'll get the governors on board or they'll install puppets to run the states—state militias and law enforcement. Once they have the guns under control everything else will fall into place. They're going to marshal the entire national machinery to their power structure beyond the military—NSA, FBI, banks."

"It's really headed toward a dictatorship?"

"It's a rare military coup that ends with a vote."

They continued walking, their shoes muddied and soaked from the brown sludge coating the bottom of the tunnel. "Until this all gets cleared up—and who knows how long that will take—they'll want an iron fist to hold the nation together. I see their point. I really do. I just don't think all of them see how things can go very wrong, very quickly. You walk down some paths and you can't go back."

"Do you think Hastings knows?"

Her eyes flashed intensely toward him. "My greatest fear is that he does, indeed. *Temporary* may be something only those around him believe. He always had a run of the crazy in him."

The tunnel opened into another cramped chamber, a dull light above revealing a rusted spiral staircase. The walls and metal throbbed from a disturbance above.

"Bird's here," said one of the soldiers.

They scaled the steps, Tooze awkward and often requiring assistance as they climbed, his wounded arm useless. The light grew rapidly near the top.

They exited the emergency tunnels through a hole at the corner of a helipad. The blades of a powerful helicopter thundered overhead, kicking dust and forest foliage into their path. The green and beige camouflage of the machine rose like a wall before them.

"Damn, that's a big one," gasped Tooze.

A soldier smiled. "Sea Stallion, sir. Big mother. She's loaded with an armored transport inside for when we drop you two off the mountain. Entrance in the rear."

The president and the Homeland Security director followed the soldiers around the churning aircraft, heads bowed, hands over their faces to mask the debris. They rushed up a ramp lowered from the back. Several officers and two civilians greeted them inside.

"Ms. President," said a boyish face in a mud-splattered suit. "Let's get you strapped in and get the hell out of here."

York quickly embraced him. "Daniel. So the Secretary of Defense is still with us. With Treasury I think we might just be able to field a government in exile." She smiled toward a statuesque blond in a badly torn white dress

"Ms. President, please," said the Treasury Secretary. "We're sitting ducks."

They made their way around an eight-wheeled armored vehicle with an enormous machine gun. Foldout seats were fixed to the sides of the aircraft. Civilians and soldiers took their places, buckling the belts. The rear door slammed shut.

The Defense Secretary spoke loudly over the growing din of the engines. "We were planning for an off-shore base, but they've seized control of the important carriers. They've got a version of events painting us in a bad light and we won't get safe passage."

"NORAD?" asked York.

"That's the goal. The military and civilian leadership is resisting Hastings there. But it's a ways and we're going to have to regroup with some of the armed forces loyal to you."

"Should I call them all Loyalists, now?"

The Defense Secretary didn't smile. "It's chaos out there, Elaine. The whole system is coming unglued. We've got anarchy in the streets and a governmental split. We need numbers and weapons to make it to Colorado."

York felt the tug on her stomach as the giant bird went airborne. "No arguments from me, Daniel. This is going to be ugly and long."

One of the soldiers gazed out of a window beside him and whistled. "Goddamn. The admin building's blown! I can see fires across Mount Weather!"

The president released her belt and steadied herself beside the young man, staring grimly through the glass. "Fighting has started."

Tooze shook his head. "I can't believe it's come to this! We're turning on each other. First the riots in Washington. New York by now, I guess. And now this."

York continued to look down at the retreat site, her words cold. "Rome burns."

65

THE NASH CRITERION

How they had made it back to Intel 1 was as much by miracle as by the muscle they were forced to use. Between National Guard roadblocks and bands of rioters roaming the city streets, they'd had to rely on force on three occasions. In one engagement, they'd killing several armed gang members who'd tried to carjack them. It was a scene Savas had never imagined living through, firing weapons in the middle of the day on mobs swarming them in the heart of the city. The relative safety of the Javits building suddenly seemed like a haven in a growing storm.

The staff left at the FBI building were frazzled and leaderless. The brass had fled, either called to other duties or frightened for their own skins in the anarchy spreading across the island. Savas pulled the remaining personnel from normal functions and organized them into guards at all entrances to the building. The last thing he was going let happen was for some random group of thugs to undo all that they had accomplished.

They had Fawkes. *Alive.* And now they were going to make him stop this unfolding catastrophe, or show them how to.

"He looks like a damn kid," said Miller, glaring at the man slumped handcuffed on the couch in Savas' office.

The masks were gone. A dark-haired cipher rested calmly before them, his eyes closed behind cracked smart glasses, his voice strangely controlled given his situation.

"How's the battle out there, agents?"

Cohen stared through the large window in the office down to the streets of New York. She spoke sadly. "People are dying. Many suffering. Some accomplishments you've racked up."

"Simon's gone," Savas said. "JP's critical. Good people you're not worthy of, Fawkes."

"I meant in the matrix. Where's that Angel girl?"

Lightfoote sat clacking over a laptop. "Here, boy-genius. Look for yourself."

She turned the screen around toward him furiously as he opened his eyes. With a groan he raised his head slightly, blood still coating the back of his neck from the blow Houston had landed.

"Nice shoulders," he said. "Drop that bikini top and we're in business."

"The red lines are my immune worms. The blue yours. Fucking kicking your sorry ass."

He lay back and smirked. "Going to go twelve rounds, I think. Fuck, that's beautiful, you bitch. Never imagined anyone would be that crazy."

Houston and Lopez entered the crowded office in a rush. "Okay, we've got people at the main entry points. But it's a weak job. Some are just secretaries, for God's sake! They'll fold quickly under any real assault."

Savas nodded. "Hopefully there won't be one. In the meantime, Fawkes, or whoever the hell you really are, we need to make sure Angel's code wins. We need you to shut your worms down or tell us how to do so." He pulled a chair up and placed a foot on it, leaning toward the hacker. "No good cop, bad cop. It's all bad, today. You don't look like you'd last five minutes with Frank."

"He wouldn't make it through one," growled Miller.

"So you're going to talk to us."

Fawkes laughed. "You think I built an off switch? You *fools*. This was *it*. This was meant to go the distance. You can kick me, drown me, get me to do whatever or say whatever. I'll even pretend two plus two is five for you. I'll get on a terminal and tell you I'm fixing everything. If you hurt me enough, I might even believe it myself. But it will be for nothing. *A lie*. Because I didn't build that worm to come home. No one can call it back."

"Son of a bitch," said Miller.

Fawkes continued. "You should *thank* me. You all should thank me for finally driving a stake into the world's vampires. You—"

"Shut up!" yelled Savas. "I'm not in the mood for more of your crazy."

"But I didn't even tell you the best part," said Fawkes, grin wide. "Paranoid? The best part is that I can *show* you."

"Show us what?" asked Savas.

"The truth. The truth I discovered hacking through the financial systems. The truth that they couldn't conceal from me. I know *who* they are. I know where they're working from!"

Savas narrowed his eyes. "What are you talking about?"

"Bilderberg." Fawkes sighed.

Cohen spun around. "What did you say?"

"Bilderberg."

Savas turned to Cohen. "What's that?"

Cohen approached Fawkes, removing her glasses. "The Bilderberg Group. It's a conspiracy theorist's wet dream. The biggest economic conference in the world. Center of Europe. Centuries old. Private. Secretive. No transcripts. No records. World leaders, industry magnates, academic powerhouses, media moguls. Bipartisan support in the nutcase-community that they are the real force running the world."

"That's the *nexus*," said Fawkes, eyes alight. He pushed himself up and stood before them, postured stooped. "But it's like an octopus. And it's real. Let me show you! Take these cuffs off. The next part is what is really—"

There was a pop and tinkling of glass. Fawkes froze, the top half of his head blown apart, a crimson spray painting the wall behind him. His mouth hung ajar, his finger raised to make a point. Instead he dropped to the floor.

"Down! Everyone down!" yelled Savas.

Miller had moved alongside the wall, weapon held beside his head. He approached the window.

"Sniper round," he said, examining the hole. "Long distance shot. A professional." He lowered his gun. "He got his man."

Houston came alongside him to get her own look, keeping her body away from the window. "Now I'm feeling a bit paranoid, myself."

"He's dead." Cohen was bent down beside the body, sidestepping the blood seeping into the carpet. "You don't think—?"

Lopez cut in. "That someone from a mysterious organization running the world killed him so he wouldn't spill their secrets?"

She exhaled. "If you put it like that—"

Lightfoote stared at her laptop screen, speaking slowly. "No, you'd need enormous resources. You'd really have to be an octopus in every major corner of the civilized world. Perhaps eavesdropping on our conversations to know how close we had come. In the middle of all this chaos."

Savas turned to his cybercrimes head. "Angel?"

"But maybe if you were a truly paranoid anarchist, you might do something strange. You might know this phantom group was after you. You might build in a contingency in case they got to you. Some kind of Armageddon fail-safe."

"What are you talking about, Angel?" asked Cohen.

Lightfoote looked up from her computer. "Got an email as few seconds after the shot," she said, glancing down at the body of Fawkes. "From him."

Savas shook his head. "How could Fawkes send you an email? He's dead."

"Read it. You'll see."

Savas took the laptop and held it up to his face. He read out loud.

> "*Hi Angel baby, if you got this, well, I'm toast. Linked to my heart rate, so I must be dead. I hate it when that happens! Sorry for trying to kill you, but don't take it personally: just the business of rebooting the world, you know? You're one annoying bitch. That's why this is for you. Things are much worse than you think. Only a few of us know the truth, and if you're reading this, we're all likely dead by now. Attached is an encrypted file: you might be able to crack it. If so, you've earned a shot at glory. Good luck. You'll need it.*"

Savas looked at Lightfoote. "Where's the file?"

"Scroll down to the end of the email."

Savas swiped his fingers on the trackpad.

"The Nash Criterion. What the hell does that mean?"

The office phone rang.

"I thought phones were down," said Lopez, removing his gun.

"This is an internal line. From the front desk. I'll put it on speaker."

A loud rasping sounded from the phone. Someone on the other end wheezed and spoke with a death's rattle: "They're coming. The stairways. Get out. They've shot everyone."

Explosions sounded and the line went dead.

"Let's move!" cried Lopez. He and Houston sprang through the doorway.

They left the body of Fawkes behind, Lightfoote pulling a USB stick out of the computer but leaving the laptop on the desk. She pocketed the stick and drew a gun.

The six moved down the hallway, passing empty offices and abandoned desks, Cohen lumbering on her crutches. They reached the center of the floor just as the elevator doors opened. A group of men in combat gear stepped out.

"Behind the cubicles!" hissed Savas.

They crouched low, Miller and Savas pointing weapons forward, Cohen looking behind them with a puzzled expression on her face.

"Where—" she began but was cut off by the blaring of a bullhorn.

"FBI Intel 1 division! We are United States forces here to apprehend you and the fugitives! Come out with your hands raised or we will be forced to engage!"

A deep stillness settled over the room. Miller touched Savas on the shoulder. "We're not going to overpower these guys, John," he whispered, his expression grave. "Whoever they really are, we're outgunned and outnumbered."

Thoughts racing, Savas considered his options. He was given little time.

"Last warning, Agent Savas. We know you have the terrorist. Hand him over, come out with your hands over your head and you might live!"

"He's dead!" cried Savas. "The hacker is dead in my office. We're coming out." He placed his hands on the weapons of Cohen and Miller beside him. "Put the weapons down. We'll figure a way out of this later."

Lopez and Houston! He had to keep them calm, stop them from doing anything stupid. He spun around, but they were gone.

His eyes met Cohen's. "Where?"

"Angel, too," she whispered. "I don't know where."

"Agent Savas, come forward with your hands in the air!"

Savas placed his weapon on the ground and stood up facing a group of ten men. Miller and Cohen followed suit. The soldiers aimed weapons in their direction. One called out loudly as several approached them from the sides.

"Under the authority of Directive 51 and the Military Commissions Act, you are under arrest as unlawful combatants, subject to indefinite detention and a hearing before a tribunal. You are hereby stripped of your

Constitutional rights and all rank and privilege. Follow all instructions precisely and rapidly or risk the use of force."

They were cuffed and led into the elevators. Frantically, Savas scanned the room a last time, desperately trying to locate Lightfoote and the others. But it was empty. He saw no sign of them.

The doors closed.

BEFORE:
THE ANONYMOUS EVENT COMMISSION

DEPOSITION IN THE MATTER OF:
UNITED STATES ARMED FORCES SPECIAL TRIBUNAL, Plaintiff,
versus
JOHN SAVAS, Defendant
Case No. M120039E-007X

CONTINUED DEPOSITION OF:
John Savas

CBD: And this was the last you saw of agent Lightfoote or of the two fugitives?
MR. SAVAS: That's correct.

[REDACTED]: And so we are really intended to believe that these three simply vanished before a group of trained soldiers? That you were so caught up in the moment of your arrest that you even failed to notice their departure?
MR. SAVAS: That's how it happened.

CBD: But why would they leave?
MR. SAVAS: Lopez and Houston had some good reasons. They were framed for crimes they did not commit. I think they must have thought of a way out.

CBD: How could these two know a way out of your building?
MR. SAVAS: I assume Angel told them. Probably it was her idea in the first place. There wasn't much time for decisions. And she always had a sixth sense about outcomes.

[REDACTED]: And now the explanation is that your cybercrimes head, after releasing a rogue virus through the world's computer systems, after taking secret documents with her, documents sent by the hacker Fawkes —your claim is that her escape with the fugitives was due to her magical ability to see the future! That the reason she helped the terrorists escape is due to some kind of a *vision*. A vision, agent Savas!

MR. SAVAS: I don't know about a vision. What I do know is she makes spontaneous and intuitive choices. They are usually the right choices.

[REDACTED]: This is absurd!

MR. SAVAS: So what is the Tribunal's theory?

CBD: This isn't the time, Mr. Savas for—

[REDACTED]: Our theory is quite simple. And like Occam's Razor, is what is likely true. It doesn't involve fortune telling or wishing away the documented crimes of outlaws. It doesn't require an imaginary hacker-boogieman who single-handedly brought the world to its knees. The Tribunal believes that you and your collaborators in the NSA and CIA, along with the nation's most wanted terrorists, orchestrated an attempt to overthrow the United States government, a plan carried out under the guise of this *Anonymous* organization, but masterminded by you and your cybercrime head, Angel Lightfoote. This Fawkes was only a mask, not worn by some invented hacker, but masking your crimes, Mr. Savas. When your attempt at sedition was finally stopped by our soldiers, you allowed your fugitives and computer mastermind to escape, stalling our team while they made their getaway.

MR. SAVAS: You really can't be serious.

[REDACTED]: And now the time has come for you to confess and work to bring these traitors in, or to meet yourself the swift hand of justice.

CBD: Mr. Savas, please. Is there nothing that you can provide for this tribunal about their whereabouts? Their intentions? Their plans?

MR. SAVAS: You know as much as I do.

CBD: Anything at all?

MR. SAVAS: No.

CBD: And what about this message from the hacker, this file. What is in it? What does it mean, the *Nash Criterion*?

MR. SAVAS: I have absolutely no idea. And that is the God's honest truth.

[REDACTED]: Enough. This session is concluded. The depositions are over. We will move to the next phase of this process. And may God have mercy on your soul, Mr. Savas.

(THE DEPOSITION WAS CONCLUDED AT 2:19 P.M. SIGNATURE OF THE WITNESS WAS NOT REQUESTED BY COUNSEL FOR THE RESPECTIVE PARTIES HERETO.)

CERTIFICATE OF NOTARY
DISTRICT OF COLUMBIA

I, [REDACTED], CERTIFY THAT THIS DEPOSITION WAS TAKEN BEFORE ME ON THE DATE HEREINBEFORE SET FORTH; THAT THE FOREGOING QUESTIONS AND ANSWERS WERE RECORDED BY ME STENOGRAPHICALLY AND REDUCED TO COMPUTER TRANSCRIPTION; THAT THIS IS A TRUE, FULL AND CORRECT TRANSCRIPT OF MY STENOGRAPHIC NOTES SO TAKEN; AND THAT I AM NOT RELATED TO, NOR OF COUNSEL TO, EITHER PARTY NOR INTERESTED IN THE EVENT OF THIS CAUSE.

A penny loaf to feed ol' Pope
A farthing cheese to choke him
A pint of beer to rinse it down
A faggot of sticks to burn him

Burn him in a tub of tar
Burn him like a blazing star
Burn his body from his head
Then we'll say ol' Pope is dead.

—English Folk Verse (c.1870)

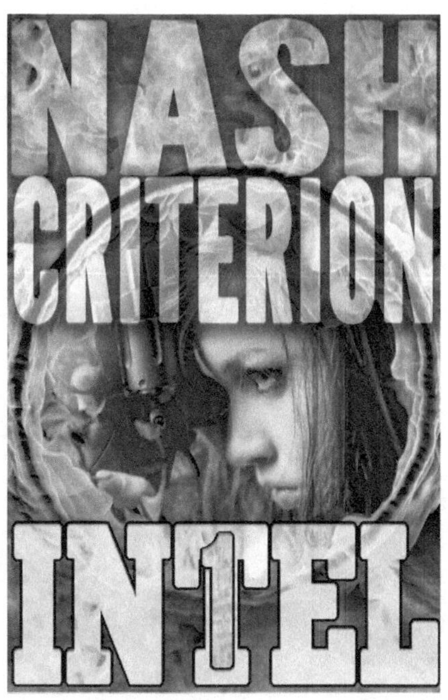

WE BELIEVED OUR GOVERNMENT WAS OF THE PEOPLE, BY THE PEOPLE, AND FOR THE PEOPLE. WE WERE WRONG.

THE NASH CRITERION
Book 4 in the INTEL 1 Series

"complex and intelligent"—Manhattan Book Review
"a chilling, fascinating, thought provoking thrill ride"
—Internet Review of Books

The Stunning Conclusion of an Armageddon Duology. A terrorist's last words lead a team of special agents to the discovery of an unimaginable global conspiracy. But time is running out. The numbers are converging. Can a group of fugitive FBI and CIA operatives prevent the coming catastrophe before the world crosses *The Nash Criterion?* LEARN MORE

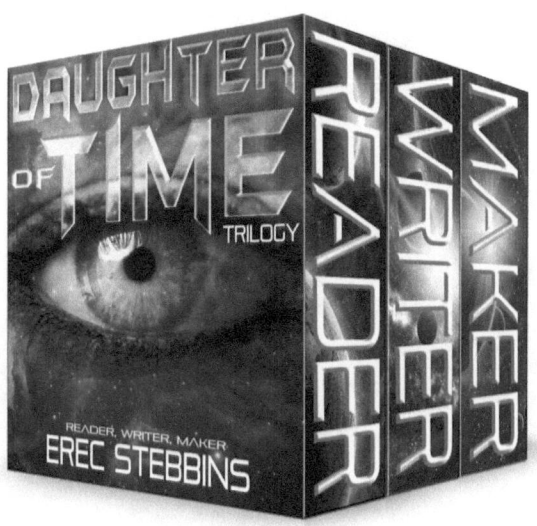

ABOUT THE AUTHOR

Erec Stebbins is a biomedical researcher who writes thrillers, science fiction, mysteries, and more.

He was born in the Midwest. His mother worked as a clinical psychologist, and his father was a professor of Romance languages at the University of Nebraska in Lincoln. In fact, his father's specialty, old Romance languages and their literature, is the source of the strange spelling of his middle name: "Erec." It is an Old French spelling, taken from an Arthurian romance by Chrétien de Troyes written around 1170: *Érec et Énide.*

He has pursued diverse interests over the course of his life, including science, music, drama, and writing. His academic path focused on science, and he received a degree in physics from Oberlin College in 1992, and a PhD in biochemistry from Cornell University in 1999. He completed postdoctoral studies at Yale University. He has worked for several decades studying the atomic structure of biological macromolecules involved in disease.

For more information:
www.erecstebbinsbooks.com
erecstebbinsbooks@gmail.com

www.ingramcontent.com/pod-product-compliance
Lightning Source LLC
Chambersburg PA
CBHW021127260626
47169CB00005B/1484

* 9 7 8 1 9 4 2 3 6 0 0 9 4 *